Dedication

To Anita Sitting Up, who is always a part of our writing.

Be sure to check out our website for the very best in romantic fiction at fantastic prices!

When you visit our webpage, you can:

* Read excerpts of currently available books

*View cover art of upcoming books and current releases

* Find out more about the talented artists who capture the magic of romance from our books on the covers

* Order books from our backlist

* Find out the latest NCP and author news—including any upcoming booksignings by your favorite NCP author

* Read author bios and reviews of our books

* Get NCP submission guidelines

* And so much more!

We also have contests and sales regularly, so be sure to visit our webpage to find the best deals in ebooks and paperbacks!

Visit our webpage at
http://www.newconceptspublishing.com

Also available from NCP by authors
Vickie Britton
and
Loretta Jackson

Path of the Jaguar
Nightmare in Morocco
The Devil's Gate by Vickie Britton
Flames of Deceit by Loretta Jackson

The Viking Crown is an original publication of NCP. This work has never before appeared in book form. This work is a novel. Any similarity to actual persons or events is purely coincidental.

New Concepts Publishing
4729 Humphreys Rd.
Lake Park, GA 31636

ISBN 1-58608-521-2
copyright (c) by Loretta Jackson and Vickie Britton
cover art by Jenny Dixon

NCP books are available at special quantity discounts for bulk purchases for sales promotions, premiums, fund raising, or educational use. For details write, email, or phone New Concepts Publishing, 4729 Humphreys Rd., Lake Park, Georgia 31636, ncp@newconceptspublishing.com. Phone: 1-229-257-0367

First NCP Electronic Printing: Sept. 1997
First NCP paperback printing: June 2002
10 9 8 7 6 5 4 3 2 1

Printed in the United States of America

the

Viking Crown

by

Vickie Britton & Loretta Jackson

Vickie Britton   Loretta Jackson

Historical Romantic Suspense
New Concepts Publishing
http://www.newconceptspublishing.com

the Viking Crown

Chapter One

The ship passage from New York to Central America had been a long and monotonous voyage. The freighter on which I had traveled carried more cargo than passengers. I had spent the better part of it in my cabin, going over my late father's notes, avoiding the companionship of the others aboard. At the dinner table, the missionary and his inquisitive wife subjected me to many prying questions befitting a young, unescorted woman traveling such a distance alone.

My father, Dr. James Swan, was an archaeologist who had spent his life studying the ancient Mayan Indians in the land I was about to visit for the first time. I felt a sense of excitement as the ship's small crew disembarked upon the Honduran shores of Puerto Lorenzo. The breezy heat of a tropical afternoon filled the air. All around me, I saw the activity of the small, busy port, men loading battered crates filled with hard, green bananas into rusty freighters bound for the States.

I stepped out upon the wharf, searching for the guide who was to meet me. A lone, shady-looking figure in a dilapidated cart watched me with idle curiosity. Something about the stubbled face beneath slouched Panama hat inspired immediate distrust. I looked away, making a silent prayer that he was not my guide.

The missionary and his wife, as well as the rest of the ship's small crew had scattered, leaving me alone upon the wharf. My eyes returned to the cart, which I now noted had been transformed into a carriage. A bench-like seat set in the front over which hung a battered top, protection from burning sun and sudden tropical rains. Two thin, bony horses waited patiently. My heart sank as the burly man in stained shirt and filthy trousers jumped down to claim me. "Swans?" he inquired in a thickly-accented voice, taking in with a look of veiled insolence my pinned hair, dark green travel dress, and lace-trimmed parasol.

"Marta Swan."

"I am Cayo," he introduced with a tip of his hat. The ocean breeze shifted hair, lank and greasy, across his round, sweaty forehead. "Your guide."

He glanced at my single trunk, which waited nearby. "Is this all of your luggage?"

"Yes," I replied, relieved that he spoke fairly good English.

Effortlessly, but with little grace, he tossed my trunk into the dirty carriage. I still clung to the small bag I carried, the one which contained the precious research for my father's book.

"You are a brave *Senorita*," he said, as he helped me up into the high carriage seat. I could see daylight through the makeshift canvas top. "Not many "*Americanos*" come to our country these days. Not with all the trouble."

"I thought the fighting had stopped."

"There's always war in Central America," he responded casually. "I was afraid you might not be here." He added with a cryptic look, "The last person I was sent to meet by the ships didn't turn up."

The thought made me uneasy. "Who were you sent for?"

"Don Orlando's son. Don Orlando is a good man, like our Morazon before him. A rich man who gives much money to the poor. The son, he was coming home from his studies in America, but he never arrived."

"What do you think happened to him?"

"He was probably kidnapped by some of Carranza's men as soon as he set foot upon shore." With a careless shrug, he added, "We'll never see him again." He grinned. "But Alan Avery will be happy to see you, yes? Maybe he will give me a big tip."

I did not know much about Central American politics. But I had heard that Justo Barrios, a strong Liberal leader in Guatemala, had been killed in battle last year. Now, in 1885, there was much political unrest in both Guatemala and neighboring Honduras. Carranza must be one of the many would-be dictators anxious to ascend to power. This Don Orlando must have opposed his dictatorship and for his efforts, lost his son.

Alan, so much like my father, would be oblivious to all the political turmoil. He would be too busy studying the Mayan ruins. "How far is the hacienda where Alan is staying?"

"Not far…but there are mountains to cross. We'll be there by nightfall…if we don't run into trouble."

"Trouble?"

"Carranza's men are all over these parts." With a boastful look, he tapped the rusted rifle which lay propped against the seat beside him. "That's why I travel with this."

We left the seaside port behind us, and began riding through lush, tropical lowlands. I felt a sense of excitement despite the exhaustion caused by the long sea voyage and now the stifling, mid-day heat. For the first time, I was seeing the country my father had spent his life studying. A primitive road had been hacked out of the dense, green jungle. Rich, dank odors of vegetation rose like steam from thick-rooted plants and low trees that threatened to encroach upon our narrow path. The wilderness around us took on a blackish hue, wide leaves blocking out the relentless, yellow sun. I imagined undiscovered ruins lost in that dark jungle, covered with tangled vines, hidden for centuries from human eyes.

My father, sponsored by the Museum of Antiquities in New York, had spent most of his lifetime working on the excavation of Mayan ruins in Copan and the surrounding area. He became intrigued by local legends, and was fascinated by the idea that a Viking ship may have visited Central America in ancient times. He had spent the latter part of his life searching for some proof to back up his theory, sometimes traveling by boat or mule or even on foot to reach distant places where Runic writing or other traces of an early Viking visitation might be discovered.

Father had never allowed me to join him in Central America. He had felt the country far too primitive for a young girl. So, despite my pleadings, he had left me at a private school in the States.

Father had died with his research uncompleted, the proof he was searching for never found. Now, Father was gone, and his understudy, Alan Avery, needed my assistance.

For a long time, Cayo and I traveled in silence. The scenery did not change; after a while the expanse of jungle greenness became familiar, even monotonous. My thoughts drifted back to the letter I had received from Alan nearly two months ago…the letter which had prompted my journey. I drew it from my bag and once more scanned its familiar contents:

"My dearest Marta:

Something incredible has taken place down here. I may be on the verge of discovering an important chain in the Viking-Mayan link! Let me tell you how it came about:

A wealthy Swede who lives down here, Ulrickson by name, invited me to look at some pieces of Mayan art in his private collection. He showed me some splendid items, including some rare Copador vases I tried to purchase for the museum.

We began to talk about the Viking Crown legend. It appears the Indians close to the village in this region have been making replicas of a phantom necklace, an ancient medallion with runic writing and the imprint of a jeweled crown…perhaps the same jeweled crown of the Viking legend! I am going to start searching for more information about the medallion. Where there are replicas, someone must have seen the original.

But there's more…. I was walking along the sea cliffs on this Ulrickson's property, when I discovered some incredible Mayan ruins, high upon the cliffs. Marta, you must see them! Mayan paintings of bearded men in boats with serpentine bows. But more important still, I came across a huge stone with strange writing upon it nearby, which might very well be a genuine rune stone! If the stone is authentic, I may have found the very proof your father spent his life searching for! I was not able to study the stone for a guard made me stop and return to the house.

There are no words to explain my excitement. I believe that this area near Quetzal could be the very spot where the Vikings first arrived by sea. You must come down and see all this for

10

yourself. Let me know when you can arrive and I will send a guide to meet you. I have temporarily taken a hacienda near the village of Quetzal, but the way is quite primitive. While I wait for your arrival, I will begin asking some questions around about the medallion.

Can you believe it has been almost two long years? I can not wait to see you again, my dearest one.

All my love,

Alan

I lingered over the endearments at the ending of the letter, imagining Alan's green eyes, lit with excitement over the grand possibilities of this find. Although I had never been down to Central America, I had been trained by my father in the skills of research and archaeology. I had provided the background for the many articles on the Mayans, which, after Father's death, had been published under Alan's name. Widely thought among our friends and acquaintance was the belief that Alan and I would someday marry; perhaps Alan and I had even grown to expect this ourselves, though neither of us had ever spoken of it. At any rate, we had the same goal, finishing Father's work. And we made a productive team; Alan with his ambition, I with the wealth of archaeological background a sonless father had bestowed upon his only daughter. Alan wanted the fame and glory, the prestige that proving my father's theory would bring him; I wanted only the recognition of my father's brilliant work.

Alan and I had corresponded regularly, but it had been two long years since we had seen each other. He must miss me as I missed him. I was anxious to see the Mayan ruins, the mysterious stone Alan had spoken of in the letter. Surely, under the circumstances, Father would have approved of my traveling down here to help carry on his research. There was no one else but Alan and I to carry on his goal. And Alan needed me!

The stifling heat was cooled by a gentle breeze as the carriage began to wind around sloping mountainsides. I could smell a steamy dampness in the air. The narrow road was knife-marked with ruts and gullies from recent wash-outs that made the carriage bounce and jog. I held on to the wooden seat, concerned that Cayo was driving the horses too fast. In places, the body of the carriage scraped against rocks and high piles of wet earth from a recent rain.

As we climbed higher into the mountains, feathery clouds descended, blocking out the burning sun. Almost without warning, drops began to pound steadily upon the carriage top.

"The rainy season," Cayo explained. "Always rains in the afternoon. It'll soon be over." Water drizzled in through holes in the canvas, dampening my hair and clothing. "I've been meaning to get that top fixed," Cayo said, rain dripping from the brim of his hat. I opened my parasol. He pointed to a nearby clearing. "We're almost there."

By the time we reached the clearing, true to his word, the rain had stopped. A short time later, Cayo slowed the carriage in front of an ugly, sprawling adobe building with pink, faded walls, which rested against the gentle slope of a hill. "The *hacienda*." I tried not to let the disappointment I felt register in my expression. I had expected the accommodations to be primitive. But something else besides the crudeness of the lodgings made me feel increasingly wary. Then I knew what it was. Not only was there not a soul in sight, but I saw no sign of a horse or carriage. The place seemed totally deserted!

I stepped toward the entrance, noticing with uneasiness that the glassless windows reflected empty rooms. "Alan?" I called, approaching the doorway, though I could tell that no one was inside. A field rodent scuttled across the threshold. It didn't look as if anyone had been living here for a very long time.

I had set out on my journey with such high hopes. How wonderful, the thought of seeing Alan again and being able to examine the evidence he had discovered that would give my Father's life work an ending full of meaning and impact. I had left New York with happy resolve which melted slowly and horribly as I stared at our vacant meeting place.

Why wasn't Alan here? Or if he had to be away, why hadn't he left word with my guide? Visions of disaster for him rose in my mind. I told myself emphatically, to control my shaking, that Alan had simply found a better place to live, no doubt in the nearby village. Of course he had written to me of his move, but with the mail being so slow, I had left before the news reached me. I clung to this hope, but in the back of my mind fears began to form. I thought of the political unrest, of Don Orlando's son who had disappeared, probably kidnapped and murdered, the moment he stepped from his boat. But who would want to harm Alan, an archaeologist?

I turned back to Cayo. "When did you last see Alan?"

He moved his fingers as if counting the days or weeks. "Over a month ago." His gaze roved over the deserted building with narrowed eyes, disappointed, as if missing the anticipated tip.

"You haven't seen him since?"

Cayo shrugged. "I don't come down this way unless I have to." Cayo began to unload my trunk.

"What are you doing?" I demanded.

"You're here." he said simply.

"But Alan's not. The place is deserted. You can't just leave me out here alone like this!"

His look said that he could, but my insistence stopped him. "You must take me to the nearest village." Surely, I would find someone who knew Alan's whereabouts there. "I'll pay you well." Even this promise did not bring the cheerful agreement I expected. Something, despite the offer of money, was making him hesitate. I saw a trace of fear in his eyes. "I don't like to go this close to the border."

"You know I can't stay alone here." I reached into my bag and drew out some bills, a generous amount of them. I felt a great sense of relief as a greedy smile spread across his rough features.

"I'll take you to the village," he said, settling the matter.

A light sprinkling began once more. We began to travel a path that followed a narrow river, made sluggish and muddy by the rain. The way was pitted with rocks and pot-holes, difficult to see in the waning afternoon light. Cayo began driving faster than ever, urging the poor, tired horses almost beyond their endurance.

13

The carriage bounced over a rain-washed gully trickling with water. Up ahead loomed a dark, empty expanse…another wide, deep place where the road had been washed out. "Watch out!" I cried, but my warning came too late. The ditch was too wide for the cart's heavy frame. I heard the frightened whinny of the horses as the carriage lurched into the air, pivoted wildly, and landed, wheels spinning, in a deep ditch to the side of the trail.

Shaken, but not injured, I stepped from the trapped carriage. I inspected the mud-embedded wheels, which at least were not loose or broken. We might be able to push the carriage out of the ditch. I would offer what help I could to get us back on the road.

The rain had stopped, but dampness loosened the neat top-knot I had made of my long, blonde hair, making wet strands of it fall around my face. Mud rose to the tops of my new laced-topped shoes.

I looked out at the green, wet expanse of jungle forest that surrounded us. An eerie twilight stained the sky, bathing the low peaks of the distant mountains in a dusky glow. Alan had written of how darkness fell all of a sudden between the mountains.

The air had grown chilly with the rain and increasing altitude. I tried not to think about the possibility of our being stranded out here, only hours away from nightfall.

Cayo was busy working with the two horses, finally freeing them. "We'll go on from here on horseback," he said, still kneeling, studying the mud-embedded wheels with a shake of his head. "I will come back for the carriage."

The uncanny stillness was broken by the snapping of twigs as some animal or human disturbed the underbrush nearby. Cayo heard it, too. He turned, a startled, half-sick look upon his face.

Wet leaves parted just a few steps away from us. The tramping of feet, the sound of voices speaking in Spanish made my heart pound rapidly in my chest. A form emerged from the bushes, then another.

"Who are they? I turned to whisper to Cayo. I saw him bring a finger to his chest, forming the sign of the cross. He rose, stumbling awkwardly, and began to run. I stood watching his grimy

14

shirttail disappear into thick foliage. The startled whinny of a horse, the thunder of hooves running away followed. The rusty rifle that had been propped against the carriage had also disappeared, undeniable proof that my guide had abandoned me.

Before I could hide myself in the underbrush, six men...soldiers?...dressed in black boots and ragged bits and pieces of military clothing moved in a rough semi-circle to surround me and the stranded carriage.

A small, wiry man, long brown hair tied back with a leather thong, stepped toward me. An unconcealed gun hung from his belt, and strapped across his chest against his sweat-stained, brown shirt was a round of ammunition. "Papers," the man demanded in English. He waited. His eyes were small and hard like dark beads. The jagged edges of a thin scar marked his forehead, disappearing into the scalp.

My mouth felt dry. Surely, these must be Carranza's men, the men Cayo feared we might encounter. "You want to see my papers?" I had never felt more fear. I pressed my lips together to stop their trembling.

He nodded. He held his hand outstretched as if to emphasize his demand.

"In here." Dutifully, I handed him my small bag. "Who are you?" I asked, struggling to keep my voice calm. I glanced behind him, my eyes scanning the surly, ragged men that encircled me. A huge machete glinted from the belt of the nearest one. Across the shoulder of another, a man with cruel eyes and pock-marked face, dangled a battered rifle. Revolutionaries! Scenes of rape, torture, death by firing squad flashed through my mind. My only hope was to feign ignorance. "Are you lawmen?"

No answer. I saw him pass my bag without even a glance at its contents, to one of the men behind him. Laughter followed, words in rapid Spanish that I did not understand. I did under-stand that these men were not likely to be interested in my father's research papers. Looks of disappointment registered on many faces as the bag passed from man to man until it reappeared in the hands of the leader.

He returned it to me. The smile on his face revealed a small space between his front teeth, a leering smile that defined some corrupt intention. Instinctively, I backed away.

My only hope was to try to bluff them. Out of the corner of my eye, I searched for some sign of the second horse, which had also run away. "As you can see, our carriage has broken down. My guide has gone for help. He will be back shortly." To stop the shaking in my voice, I paused. "I believe I will go to meet him."

Head held high, I lifted my muddy skirts and began to walk slowly away, praying silently that they would let me go. If I could get some distance away from them, maybe I could find the missing horse and catch up with Cayo, who might still be hiding nearby.

What if they began shooting at me? The muscles in my chest tightened at the thought, making it difficult to breathe. I would have to take that chance. I shuddered to think about my situation, about what being alone at the mercy of six armed men in this isolated place could mean.

Gusts of laughter followed after me as I walked proudly away. I realized what a bedraggled sight I must seem with my loose, tangled hair and muddy skirts.

"Where are you going, pretty *Americano*?" A rough hand clamped my wrist and forced me to turn to face the leader. "I think the coward guide has deserted you."

I watched the slow broadening of his ugly smile. "He has left you here for us."

The grip of his fingers momentarily paralyzed me. When I did attempt to break loose, he regarded me with the easy confidence of a cat bent upon torturing a helpless mouse, a cat that knows it has all the time in the world to make its kill. The others, grinning, ragged, moved forward, surrounding us, blocking off any avenue of escape.

Trembling, I at last managed to jerk my arm away from him. I clutched my bag against my breast, as if it could somehow offer magic protection against the assault of hands or bullets. I could see my fate in his eyes. He surely intended to rape me, then let one of his men cut my throat! I closed my eyes, steeling myself for the

16

worst.

The sudden rustle of brush close by was followed by angry splashes of hooves into mud and water. Relief rushed over me. Cayo had come back for me. Or Alan!

The tall form I stared up at was neither my guide nor my friend and co-worker. I met the flashing dark eyes of a stranger, aristocratic, proud. He uttered one word as if it were a curse, "Sanchez!"

I saw the small eyes widen and constrict in Sanchez's dark face as the man on horseback reigned between me and my tormentors, forcing the men to scatter.

As Sanchez stepped back, his hand strayed toward the gun at his belt, but a sharp command from the newcomer made him think better of drawing the weapon. Words of terse, angry Spanish flowed between them. I thought I heard the name Ulrickson intermingled with words I could not understand. Ulrickson...wasn't that the name of the private collector Alan had written about in his letter?

Whoever this Ulrickson was, the name seemed to inspire a sense of obedience, respect, even a flash of fear among Sanchez and his men. No one made a move to stop the stranger as he swept me up beside him on the black horse.

I thought about my trunk lying in the carriage, but I was glad that I still held my bag containing Father's papers, which even now seemed as important to me as my own life. My free hand held tightly to his sturdy frame. As we galloped away, neither Sanchez nor any of his men made a move to follow. But where was he taking me?

I might have been afraid of him if not for the eyes, large, thick-lashed, somehow discerning as glanced back at me, as if to reassure me that everything was all right.

The rough fabric of his brown jacket seemed like some sort of uniform. My gaze fell to the gun strapped to his belt. Not knowing if he could even speak English, I asked, "Does everyone around here carry a gun?"

The hint of a smile that crossed his lips in profile gave him away. "There are times when a gun is quite...necessary," he replied in perfect, unaccented English.

"Thank you. For rescuing me. Were...were those Carranza's men?"

"When the money is on his side, so are they." He gave a derisive laugh. "Sanchez and his men are a ragged band of local mercenaries. Sanchez likes to think of himself as a spokesman for the poor. In truth, he is little more than a common thief."

I studied his profile, the dark lashes, the straight noble look of his features. Maybe it was the fact that he had come to my rescue that made me think he was one of the most handsome men I had ever seen. Thick, black hair, not long, but stubborn, unruly, fell across his forehead in dark waves. Once again I noticed that the coarse jacket, casually unbuttoned at the throat, looked like a sort of uniform. "Are you a soldier?"

The shadow of a mustache made his teeth seem even whiter as he turned back to smile at me. "No. I am Ramon Santiago...a guard. For a man they call the Viking. I will take you to his villa. He will put you up for the night."

"The...Viking?"

"Thane Ulrickson. But he's called the Viking around here."

The jogging gait caused me to cling more tightly to him. The road twisted upward until a dark, towering castle came into view. As we drew closer, I saw that it was constructed of black, volcanic rock.

Ramon drew to a stop at the thick, wooden gate, which two men immediately swung open. My eyes strayed to the immense wall, also made of lava, to the barbed wire and jagged bits of broken glass along the top. The villa he had spoken of looked much more like a fortress.

A fortress that it was Ramon's job to guard. He looked so very different from the two guards who greeted us, shoddy-looking men, comparable to those who accompanied Sanchez. Ramon spoke to them in Spanish, laughed at something one of them said, and continued on. A servant waiting at the stables took charge of the black stallion.

"I am Marta Swan," I said after we had dismounted and began

walking toward the mansion, which rose two stories, with a tower room straight above the front entrance. Balconies framed by twisted iron posts ending in high sharp points made the rooms behind them seem ugly and formidable.

"I am from New York," I told him. "I'm down here looking for a friend, Alan Avery. He was staying at a *hacienda* near Quetzal, but I found the place deserted this afternoon." Again, worry over Alan, delayed over fears for my own safety, resurfaced. It's been two months since I last heard from him. I was on my way to see if I could locate him in the village when Sanchez and his men appeared and my guide deserted me."

I thought I saw a flash of recognition cross Ramon's face at the mention of Alan's name. "Do you know Alan? He mentioned something in his letter about stopping by to see Mr. Ulrickson about some pieces of Mayan art."

Ramon hesitated. "There are so many people that come and go at the Viking's house. He's a man that must be surrounded by company." With a look of disapproval, he added, "He even entertains Sanchez."

The thought brought fearful memories of Sanchez's leering face, his thin fingers locked on my wrist. As if reading my thoughts, Ramon quickly reassured me, "Sanchez will not bother you with the Viking around. You will be perfectly safe here."

"What's going to happen to my luggage? Everything I value except for my father's work is in that trunk."

"Don't worry," he said with a confident shrug of broad shoulders. "I'll send someone back for it."

"And the horse…."

"Do not worry about the horse. It will find its way back to its owner." His lips curled into a rueful smile. "And if it does not, perhaps it will have a better life. Most local villagers would welcome the sight of a horse to share his burdens." Ramon stopped walking, as if to delay our entrance into the house. I followed his gaze up the sharp slope of a nearby hill. I could make out distant heaps of volcanic rock. I had never seen anything like the barrenness the dark mounds of porous lava created.

"Honduras is volcano land," he said. "Not many use the lava rock for building, but you'll find the Viking is a bit...eccentric."

"Eccentric?" I felt a little shiver of apprehension. The way Ramon said the word made me wonder if it wasn't just a charitable synonym for 'mad.'

"Don't worry. He's perfectly harmless, even though some of the natives are afraid of him. He's just a little... obsessed, caught up with the local legends that the Vikings once visited here, in Central America. That's why the locals call him the Viking. Or some call him *Quetzalcoatl*."

I felt a little catch of excitement. The Indian god, half-bird, half serpent, was mentioned often in my father's notes. I thought of Alan's letter. The ruins with the unique drawings and the rune stone must be somewhere on these very grounds.

"Legends are found in all corners of Latin America about a light-skinned, reddish-bearded man, venerated as a god, who the Indians called *Quetzalcoatl*," he ventured to explain for my benefit.

"Yes, I've heard of him. The original *Quetzalcoatl* was said to have brought a new culture to the Indians, ideas for a new way of life."

As surprised by my knowledge of the subject as I was of his, he added with arched brow, "Some of the legends say *Quetzalcoatl* appeared by sea long before the arrival of the Spaniards, which is where the idea that he may have been a Viking came from. Some of the local natives believe that Ulrickson is a descendant of the original *Quetzalcoatl* because of his Norse ancestry, his reddish-gold beard. Mr. Ulrickson is pleased by the comparison. The illusion of being a living legend delights him."

Confused by Ramon's royal bearing, by his wide knowledge, I began wondering how he could possibly be only a hired guard for the eccentric man of which he spoke. Curiosity about my host was mingled with apprehension. What if this Thane Ulrickson turned out to be stark-raving mad? Before we reached the door, courage quickly drained from me and I turned to Ramon for reassurance. His eyes were shadowed, his expression unfathomable. "Now you must come in and meet the Viking," he said.

Chapter Two

We walked down a long, dimly-lit hallway until we reached a large, cavern-like room. Rough, blackened walls of volcanic rock gave natural insulation that held the heat from the roaring fireplace and enclosed odors of smoke, pine, and the aroma of strong coffee. I followed Ramon past a great, wooden table, the kind one would expect to find in some medieval castle, and toward the primitive fireplace.

A big man with a reddish-gold beard rose from his chair close to the fire and came toward us. I felt awed by the bright beard, his broad stature, the look of recognition in his keen blue eyes. He stared at me as if he already knew me, even though we had not yet been introduced. I felt his gaze taking in every aspect of me…my tall form, my large, gray eyes, the cascade of damp, cornsilk blonde hair half-fallen from the confines of its pins.

"This is Marta Swan," Ramon explained. "Her carriage broke down just outside of Quetzal. Her guide abandoned her. I told her she would be welcome here." He made no mention of Sanchez and his men, or the way he had bravely rescued me from them.

"Most welcome." The bearded man extended a large, warm hand. Almost as if he had been expecting a guest, he said, "We have the best room waiting for you."

"I…that's very nice. But please…I wouldn't want you to go to any trouble…."

"Trouble?" His laughter was deep, booming. "Nothing would be too much trouble for you, my Princess." I might have taken offense at the term "princess", but I immediately saw that the Viking meant it as a sincere compliment, not careless flattery. He

21

seemed of an indiscernible age, but I guessed from the deep, rough-hewn lines of his face that he must be in his early fifties, yet his eyes were bright and blue, as inquisitive as the eyes of a child. That look again, one of delighted recognition crossed his face, disturbing me slightly. I turned to Ramon.

Ramon's eyes remained as remote and expressionless as they had become the minute we entered the house. He could have been carved out of wood. What caused the change in him?

Ramon began telling the Viking about my trunk and saying he would send someone after it at once. Again I was puzzled. The two men seemed to meet on the level of peers, not as wealthy land-owner and hired man.

Ramon left abruptly. I felt a sense of uneasiness, almost fear, at being alone with Thane Ulrickson. Ramon's presence in the room with us had given me a sense of security in this totally foreign atmosphere. As the Viking took my arm, guiding me toward the warm hearth, I glanced back to see Ramon's form, tall and proud, disappear down the long hallway.

The air inside the big house, like the mountain air outside, had grown chilly from the rain. The warmth of the fireplace upon my damp hair and clothing made me shiver.

"You're chilled," the Viking said with great concern. "Come closer to the fire." He offered me the woven blanket draped over one of the heavy chairs. "Here, put this around your shoulders." He poured me a mug of coffee from a huge metal pot hanging in the open fireplace. I took a small sip. The strong, earthy flavor revived me.

"I am looking for a friend of mine. Alan Avery. Maybe you can help me."

"Oh, yes. Avery." A look of recognition crossed his face. "He is staying at a hacienda not far from here."

For the first time, I began to feel real worry about Alan. "The guide took me there. The place was deserted. I assumed he had found a better place in the village."

"Oh, I wouldn't worry about your Mr. Avery. He comes and goes."

22

"I heard that he stopped here to see you a couple of months ago."

"Oh, yes. A nice young man. He contacted me about buying from my private collection for some museum. I showed him some of these items, which are not for sale." He took a vase from the mantel and handed it to me. "Alan begged to see some of the rest, but, of course, I told him no. Some of the pieces in the collection don't belong to me. I'm only keeping them, though they've been in the Ulrickson family for years. Passed down from generation to generation."

The vase Thane Ulrickson had handed me was a unique buff-orange color, decorated with black, lineal, almost harsh designs. The Copador style, I recognized without doubt...one of the vases Alan had mentioned to me in the letter. "Alan said the vases are authentic," I remarked as I handed it back to him.

The Viking's laugh was hearty. "Of course they are authentic. Everything I own is authentic." He leaned closer to me, his blue eyes catching the brightness of the firelight. "But what I showed Avery is of little importance. The real treasures are not for the common eye. Many items in my collection date back to the ninth century and before."

I felt a little stirring of excitement. Objects that old, if authentic, would be virtually priceless.

"I even have some things the Vikings left behind."

"I didn't know the Vikings had ever been here." The excitement rapidly left me. At first, I had thought that the eccentric, red-bearded man might actually be in possession of relics so priceless that he had not even risked showing them to Alan. But now I realized that the Copador vases he had shown Alan were probably the best items in his collection. The rest of his treasures were no doubt all in his mind.

Such a sad, disappointed look crossed my host's face that I quickly added, "I mean, if the Vikings ever were here, it's never been scientifically proven."

"Don't you know that around 967 A.D. a Viking ship on the way to Iceland was blown off course and was driven by strong ocean currents to our coast? Local legends tell of the arrival of large, fair-skinned men who came in boats from the sea. The leader of the Vikings was hailed by the natives as a god, who they called **Quetzalcoatl.** His likeness appears on many of the stone carvings in Copan and other places nearby."

"Yes, I've seen pictures of him in textbooks and his likeness carved in stone." The bearded man that I had seen had borne an uncanny resemblance to Thane Ulrickson. A myth, according to Ramon, that the Viking did little to discourage. "But, still, there's no proof of who the red-bearded man was, or where he came from. The idea that he might have been a Norseman is only a legend."

The notion of the Vikings visiting Mexico and Central America had not been given much credibility in the modern world of archaeology. My father had received much ridicule from the academic world for his belief that such a link between the Vikings and the ancient civilizations of Latin America might have existed. I thought of his fascination with the Viking legends, which had triggered my own interest, and Alan's.

"There would be proof if Alan found the Viking Crown medallion," Thane Ulrickson said, as if reading my mind. "He won't, though, he added with an air of mysticism. "It's not meant for him to find."

Of course...the medallion! Alan had mentioned in his letter that he was going in search of information about it. Perhaps his research had led him to some remote spot which had delayed his return. "Alan said that the Indians around Quetzal have been wearing replicas of the necklace with its Norse inscription on the back. He thinks the original may be nearby."

"Many have searched for the original medallion. But it will never be found. Not until the Sun Maiden returns to claim it."

"The Sun Maiden?"

"That part of the legend only I and a few others know. The medallion actually belonged to a woman, the Norse king's intended bride. She was along with him on the voyage when the ship was blown off course. The crown-inscribed necklace was part of her dowry, as was the jeweled crown itself. The Indians called her the

24

Sun Maiden because she had long, fair hair, the color of the sun."
As he spoke, the red-bearded man's eyes fell upon my own hair,
escaped from its pins, long and shimmering in the firelight.

"What happened to her?"

"An Indian priest was fascinated by her fair hair and skin, her
exotic beauty. He tried to capture her from the Vikings. There was
a bloody battle. The Vikings were driven back to their boats by the
Indians. They all left, except for the Viking king and his maiden."
The way he spoke gave me an eerie feeling. How could he knew
the exact details of something that had happened centuries ago?
Of course, he must be making it all up. And yet, something in his
voice made it sound like he had actually been there and experienced the story he told.

"What happened to the maiden?" I asked with sudden interest. "Was she captured? Murdered, made a slave? Or did the
Viking king find her?"

A sadness came into Thane Ulrickson's voice, as if he truly
believed and felt the sadness of the legend. "No one knows. She
was never seen again. Lost."

"And the Viking?"

Thane Ulrickson raised one thick, dark brow. "The Viking?"
Firelight made the reddish-gold beard and brilliant blue eyes glow.
"He's still here."

***

The Viking, as if we were king and queen of a palace, person-
ally escorted me up the wide stairway to my room. "Thank you," I
said, relieved to have the heavy door closed between me and
those shining eyes, eyes a little too adoring, a little too bright.

Was he mad? Could he actually believe...?

No, I firmly told myself, much more likely the source of my
disturbance came from my own mind. The long day had been too
much for me. I shrank at the memory of the hoard of bandits. My
head spun from the rapid changes in my well-put-together plans.
Dramatic rescue, Viking Crown medallion, Sun Maiden...who would
believe it?

I stepped woodenly to the vast window, gripping the protective bars that could be opened only from the inside. The thick iron felt cold against my hands as I gazed down into the courtyard. A crude fountain made of volcanic rock set in the center of a small square, cleared, but still wild, hidden by tall trees.

My eyes wandered across the men below, hoping one of them might be Ramon. A glimpse of his handsome face, his dark, watchful eyes, might now be comforting, might arrest my growing feeling of disquiet. Ramon was not among the five men. They wore shabby clothes and leaned against the fountain or lounged on the rock benches, as if accustomed to and content with hours of idling. In spite of their dawdling manner, the thought jumped to my mind that they performed some important function. Were they all the Viking's guards?

A barred door led out onto a small balcony, but I remained motionless, not wanting to be seen. I noted the branches of a nearby tree that grew very close to the wall. I visualized my gripping the limbs and inching my way down the twenty-five feet into the patio. No one would believe that I would attempt such a climb, but I was agile and I felt certain I could make an escape in this fashion.

Alarmed at the edge of panic in my thoughts...as if I were actually being held prisoner...I turned back to the room. Again I felt a sinking of heart...such a formidable place! I had the same, uneasy feelings I had when I had first entered the great dining hall below, that I was enclosed by impenetrable layers of thick, black stone. The feeling persisted despite the fact that here the volcanic rock was concealed by panels covered with paper etched with the finest, most delicate designs. That touch of feminine grace was totally destroyed by the crude and massive furniture.

The bed's headboard rose to the ceiling. Images cut indistinctly into the dark, ancient wood and I drew closer trying to determine if the faces were human or animal. The same carvings were on the huge, oppressive chests. Everything here looked as if it had been drawn from the depths of the ocean. How would I ever be able to sleep in such a place?

Just for one night, I told myself. In the meantime I must dress for dinner, accept the hospitality that certainly wasn't lacking, even though the mind of the giver of it was in question. I must try hard to appear a gracious and grateful guest.

All of my good clothes were in my truck on the abandoned carriage. From the small case I had managed to bring, I drew my one change of clothes, a gray dress with high neck and prim, lace collar, and quickly slipped into it. For a moment I stood in front of the great mirror that partly covered the west wall. My image, indistinct and slightly distorted in the aged glass, looked deeply troubled; damp and disheveled hair added to the effect.

When I returned to the bag for a comb, I began rummaging anxiously though stacks of notes for my father's book. What had happened to the brown envelope containing my money and travel papers? I dumped the contents on the bed. Images of the leering faces of the men who had circled my carriage, who had passed this case from hand to hand, arose. One of them had stolen my money! Why had I believed there was no need to hide the stack of bills that represented the total funds of my New York account?

This money must have looked like a fortune to those bandits! How foolish! Now I would have to borrow money from someone in the States and go through the long siege of paperwork to obtain permission to reenter the country!

Until then, I was a captive...of this oppressive fortress, of a madman! Panic gripped me. I tried to calm myself by the thought that I was overreacting, by the thought of Ramon. He would surely help me! I hurried down the curving stairway, and made my way back to the big room with the fireplace and huge table.

I stopped, stunned to find that the room was now filled with people. Some extravagantly dressed, some wearing little more than rags, they milled about. The table of hewn wood, running half-way the length of the room, was heaped with food that anyone seemed to partake of whenever they desired.

I spotted Ramon standing at the entrance. He faced the door, but I recognized at once the wide shoulders, the glow of thick, black hair. Even after he gave a slight turn and saw me, he remained stolidly at his post, as if it were what he was being paid to do.

I watched his dark eyes slowly lighten. When I came within reach, Ramon's hand caught mine. Confused by the unexpected intimacy, I freed myself and stepped back, trying hard to ignore the tingling warmth his touch had left.

Doubts assailed me. For an instant I was certain Ramon was not who he represented himself to be. He could not be just one of the many guards the Viking employed, not when he had about him such an air of importance, of total authority.

Was my being here part of some plot? Once again I was afraid not only for myself but for Alan Avery, for whatever was going on first of all involved Alan. Because of Alan I was waylaid and brought here. My throat was suddenly dry. Dryness sounded in my voice. "Those bandits stole my money and my papers!"

The light quickly faded from his eyes, which seemed now to avoid me.

I continued, voice growing faster as I poured out to him details of the theft. As I spoke Ramon's manner, like his eyes, seemed to retreat.

I stopped talking abruptly, drew myself up and with what dignity I could muster, asked, "Are you going to help me?"

"The money you have lost." His deep voice that seemed to suggest a shrug, angered me. "The papers I will try to get back, but I can make no promises."

"But my money...you see, it's my entire savings. There is surely something I can do to get it back! What about the police?"

He seemed surprised even at the suggestion. "You are not in New York City, Miss Swan," he said. "Out here, we act as our on police."

"But how...."

"I will do all that can be done," he answered quietly.

It was clear he intended to do nothing. My anger flared again. "What about the carriage? Did you bring it here? I need my luggage."

"The wagon, carriage, as you call it,"...once again he avoided direct contact with my eyes..."was gone by the time I got back."

"Gone! It couldn't just disappear!" Tears now mingled with

28

the anger choking my throat. "I must leave here. At once."

"Even I wouldn't be out on these roads at night," he answered. "Why don't you just get some food and some rest. I will try to locate your trunk."

I turned away from him angrily.

"Try not to worry." His voice, so calm it sounded indifferent, followed after me.

I entered the room. Not locating the Viking, my gaze settled upon a young, black-haired woman who sat at a wooden loom. I approached her, hoping she would speak English and would be able to help.

The woman's elongated face did not suggest beauty until I noted the fine structure of high cheek bones, thin lips, and long, finely chiseled nose. Her dark eyes seemed possessed of both fire and ice. "Who do you want? Why are you here?"

The rudeness might be only a result of an imperfect grasp of English. "Do you know a man named Sanchez?"

The woman, with a curt turn back to the loom, said nothing. I waited, seeing only thick, black hair cascading across delicate shoulders. Her hands work quickly and deftly, straightening the yarn, drawing down the wooden handles. Obviously she didn't intend to answer.

"Dear Princess!"

The booming voice caused me to shrink a little closer to the woman and the loom.

"I've been waiting so we could eat together." The Viking, so very impressive with his great height and dignity, held out a strong hand to me as he spoke.

I allowed my hand to be covered by his, allowed myself to be led toward the table. I glanced over my shoulder at the woman who had stopped her work to glare at me. My gaze moved instinctively toward Ramon, who in spite of my suspicions had somehow had become established in my mind as protector. His eyes smoldered a little as he watched me. Then he seated himself close to the door, as if once again resuming his duties.

I confronted Thane with my recent losses. He listened, head

bent. "Don't worry," he said. "Ramon tells me the carriage is more like an army wagon. Who would be able to hide such a cart out here? My men will comb the area for it." Linking my arm in his, he began walking. "As for your money, I will replace it."

"No, I can send for money. But," I added, "I must get my travel papers back."

"Nothing to worry about."

The Viking had stopped at the head of the table where a rugged-looking man of late middle-age sat eating from a platter filled to overflowing. Thane Ulrickson addressed him as *the general.* "My most faithful friend, Francisco Perez. She's back," he added with a good deal of satisfaction. "The princess has come back."

The general's eyes swept over me, eyes, black, like Ramon's, and with the same perceptiveness. Permanent lines of laughter etched around them, cutting deep into great folds of flesh. He seemed at first startled, then he laughed, his ample body shaking. "Welcome home, my dear!" He took a bite of bread, chewed heartily, before saying, "We've been waiting for centuries, eh, Viking?" He laughed again.

Thane Ulrickson's rejection of the good-natured joking caused a chill to run through me.

"The next time you see her, she'll be adorned in silk and wearing *her* jewels! You do look nice," he said, in a slightly lower voice, "but cotton is not the material for a princess."

"Wait till I tell Lucia," the general chuckled. "My wife will be glad to hear you're back!"

"I've never been here," I managed to say somewhat coldly. I was beginning to feel a distortion of reality, as if I had dropped in on the Mad Hatter's tea party. I was aware of the challenge in my voice as I asked, "So how could I be back?"

"If the Viking says you're back," the general's grin revealed large, yellowish teeth, "then you're back. That's the way it is here. By the way," he addressed Thane, "What is the name of the princess?"

"Marta Swan," I quickly supplied. Ignoring the Viking, at-

30

tempting to place solid reality back into the conversation, I added, "My grandparents immigrated from Varnamo, Sweden. When they came to America, they dropped the *son* from their name."

"The name Marta is not Swedish," the general said, rubbing a gnarled hand through graying hair. "Spanish, I'd say."

"Indian," the Viking corrected.

This time I ventured a glance at him. The reddish glow from his beard seemed to reflect into his brilliant eyes. How could Alan have believed Thane's stories of ancient crowns and Viking links? Alan, so quick to see falseness, surely couldn't have been taken in by this madman! I felt a sudden dread over what might have happened to Alan.

"Have you met Alan Avery?"

The general's eyes fell to his plate. For a long time he continued to eat. "Oh, yes. He is a frequent visitor here, eh, Viking? About two months ago, I saw him in Santa Augusta. Santa Augusta is where I have my plantation. West. Toward El Salvador."

"What was he doing there?"

The general looked at Thane, and when he answered the same huge grin, slightly edged with corruption, cut deep lines into his dark, heavy face. "He is on a...wild goose chase...is that what they say in America? He is hunting for the gold necklace."

The general's words confirmed my worst fear. How much did they know or care about Alan's activities? "What gold necklace?"

"Your necklace, of course," Thane said in a clipped voice. "It isn't mine!" I protested, startled at the realization that Thane had spoken to me as if the lost Viking princess of the legend and I were the same person. Surely, he couldn't believe....

The general laughed aloud. "Didn't you know you've lost your necklace, Princess Marta?" He winked, as if we shared some private joke. Unaware of the general's mockery, Thane burst out indignantly. "All Alan Avery will find are hundreds of cheap fakes."

"The original...was there an original that has been seen?"

"Of course," the general said. "Seekers of fortunes have always chased after it. The gold medallion is something anyone would kill for!"

I felt a lurch in my heart at his words, but managed to say without emotion. "I understand it to be only a part of a legend that probably isn't even true."

"Legends are based on fact. That is why this necklace is so profitably copied."

"What does it look like?"

"Huge," said the general, holding out his hands to the shape of an orange. "On one side is a crown deeply set with rubies and emeralds. The Viking Crown! On the other side are the strange markings of the ancient Vikings."

"She was wearing the necklace when she was lost," the Viking spoke up. Before, he had addressed me as if he believed I were the princess; now he spoke of her in a faraway voice, as if she were someone he had known long ago, or only in dreams. "I have other parts of the collection."

Ignoring Thane's interruptions, I inquired of the general, "How can I locate Alan?" Alan, gone, off on some wild search for a non-existent treasure because he had actually listened to Thane's deranged assertions!

"Avery will turn up. The most likely place will be here. Right, Viking?" the general said.

"Do you think Alan is following a real lead?"

"You are asking a practical man," the general answered, "a man who has fought practical battles for over twenty years. I think he is wasting his time." I was growing accustomed to his wide smile, which I had at first found slightly offensive. "If a man wants to make a fortune here, he doesn't chase necklaces, he runs guns."

The mention of guns made me look toward Ramon, still seated near the doorway. "Is he a guard here?" I inquired.

"We are all...like good Vikings...on guard," Thane boomed. "But, no, Ramon is a friend, like the general."

"Ramon tells me the carriage that brought me from the port is missing. Whoever stole it, also stole my money and my permit to enter the country. General, what would you do if you were me?"

Thane gave the general no opportunity to answer. "I am

aware of everything that goes on. It will be taken care of. So just eat and enjoy yourself." He pushed a platter toward me. "I recommend this. *Guapotos*." The dish looked like fish prepared in thick sauce. To be polite I spooned some on to my plate.

Encouraged by my acceptance, the Viking offered another platter, boiled eggs shaped like ping-pong balls. "*Lachrymos*."

"Turtle eggs," the general's black eyes shone with humor. He went on explaining. "Great turtles lay eggs in the warm sand along the coast. Women gather them in huge baskets. They balance them on their heads." He made gestures of precarious balances, which caused Thane to laugh.

"I think I would rather have that salad."

"Excellent choice, Princess Marta."

But I possessed no appetite. At first I felt only an increased feeling of uneasiness, and attributed it to my position directly in the center of the room, the chair of honor. Later I realized the source of my growing discomfort. I looked around somewhat nervously to face dark eyes which bored into me with a frightening hatred.

The snapping eyes of the young woman locked relentlessly on me in the same motionless way that her thin, brown hands locked on the loom's wooden handles.

The general observed in his humorous, self-important way, "Evelia is in one of her moods."

Thane turned to view Evelia, who began working the loom with angry speed.

"Pay no mind to Evelia," the Viking said. "She detests all outsiders. But once you get to know her, she will like you."

"Evelia," the general grinned, "with all of those hard stares, is beginning to look like Sanchez's twin."

"Who is this Sanchez? Where can I find him?"

"You wouldn't want to find him," the general answered. "Sanchez is a *little* man who thinks he is very big. He dreams of being another Napoleon. But in the end he will only find out he has been out-maneuvered."

What did that statement mean? "Is he a general, too?"

Francisco Perez laughed loudly, though in spite of my continued questions, would say no more on the subject.

The dinner at last was over and saying I was very tired, I started toward the stairway. Still disturbed over Evelia and wanting to know what was wrong with her, I stopped once more beside the loom.

The massive hall with its walls of dark, porous stone made even the great wooden loom look small. Deciding to make some attempt to communicate with Evelia, I spoke words of admiration for the partial appearing of a woven bird, the rare quetzal bird, a brilliant, shimmering green, touched on head and wing with black.

Evelia's quick eyes darted from Ramon to Thane before settling on me. Was she a wife or girlfriend to one of them? Which one?

"Get away from me!" Evelia spat out. "Get away from this house! If I see you here tomorrow, you won't be able to leave at all!"

* * *

Early the next morning, after a long, sleepless night, I encountered the Viking waiting for me outside of my room.

"Today you can go to the villages," he said. "I must go to Santa Augusta. While I'm there, I will take care of your problems for you."

Gratitude filled me. I visualized being given charge of a carriage and having the entire day to look for Alan. But the Viking called to Ramon before we had reached the bottom step. "Here she is, delivered to you. You must do as I said, and show her the local sights. Entertain her well, for I want to see a happy glow in my princess's eyes when I return tonight!" Thane took my hand in both of his. "There is so much to see here! Just enjoy yourself."

Ramon did not speak until the Viking left. "I've had breakfast," he said, "but you should eat."

The great table was now filled with various dishes of fish reminiscent of Scandinavia. The thought of fish for breakfast made me feel queasy. I took the coffee Ramon offered and bread from the nearest platter.

"Will you take me to Puerto Lorenzo? I can stay there until I get my papers. In fact, I can look for Alan from there"

Ramon hesitated. "I think it would be better to let Thane take care of things. We will have a day of sightseeing."

Angry over his insistence on sight-seeing, I did not speak to him as he assisted me into the carriage, but I did feel great relief to be leaving, even temporarily, the Viking's volcanic-rock fortress.

As we descended from the mountainside into the lowlands, trees became thicker and the still air became pierced by the chip of birds and insects. I thought with growing dread that today would end with my returning on the same road. Everything about Thane's estate I found threatening . I leaned against the carriage seat and, remembering Evelia's shrill warning, wished I could heed it.

My eyes locked on the battered rifle between the seats, ready to be gripped by Ramon's quick hand, and my voice rose in challenge, "What if I refuse to come back with you?"

I had expected a harsh reply and was surprised by the sympathetic light that illuminated Ramon's dark eyes and by his soft answer. "Until I can put you on a boat back to New York, you are far better off with me. Now, what do you want to see?"

"I want to search for Alan."

"The ocean is not far from here," he suggested. "Would you like to take a ride along the beach?"

Ignoring his words, I insisted with determination, " I would expect to find Alan in the nearest town. Quetzal."

"I will take you there." His eyes changed, became teasing, "We will find the gold medallion that belongs to you before Avery does!"

"The necklace doesn't belong to me. I've never even seen a copy of it." Ramon's response was a smile.

Ramon, skillfully guiding the carriage, pulled off the main road on to a scarcely visible trail. Trees and vegetation encroached into the path, in places almost obscuring it totally. I became a little frightened of being completely enclosed by the vastness and wildness of the jungle.

"From mountains to jungle. Everything changes so quickly here," he said.

"Where are we now?"

"We're taking a short cut to Quetzal."

"Is the town named for the bird?"

"Of course. The quetzal, as you know, is regarded as a deity by the Mayans. But I'm sorry to tell you, it is rarely seen."

Out of the corner of my eye, I watched him. In the shadows, for little sunlight penetrated the area, he looked deeply mysterious, like some Spanish lord, overseeing his vast estate.

But he was not. Nor was he a companion in sightseeing, I assured myself with increasing anger. He was *my* guard! How could I escape from him? Besides the fact that the very carriage was armed for battle, I suspected that he carried a weapon underneath his jacket. But even if I could manage to get away, where would I go? Being a woman alone in a strange country, unable, even, to speak the language, I would be in far worse shape than I was in now.

After a long, silent drive, we came to a clearing of adobe buildings and make-shift huts. "This can't be Quetzal!" I cried. "What did you expect? You're very far from New York here...and civilization." Ramon's teeth gleamed white against his black mustache.

"Who might know about Alan here?"

"Ordinarily I would say a friend. But I doubt that anyone like Alan Avery could find a friend."

"What do you mean by that? He is very prominent in New York. He will no doubt manage the Intercultural Museum some day."

"That means nothing to us down here. Perhaps we judge a man by different standards."

I felt a resurgence of anger.

"Don't take offense, Marta. The Viking was quite charmed by him." Ramon added with another smile, "Not as charmed as he is with you, however."

Once through the tiny, run-down village, the carriage made a sharp turn.

"I want to stop in the village and inquire about Alan."

"I have already done that. I assure you there is no one in

Quetzal that knows where he is."

Disappointed over my ruined plans and suspecting that he was lying to me, I remained silent. Ramon soon stopped the carriage in front of a very neat home with a small patio of terra cotta earth. Behind it I could glimpse the tiles of a steeply slanted roof.

"I'm going to introduce you to a very fine craftsman. Estos markets his goods throughout Honduras."

The small-framed man who appeared wore a pajama-like suit of white. I tried to speak to him, to ask about Alan, but he shook his head and addressed Ramon in rapid Spanish as he led us around the house to a small workshop.

Inside was a waist-high kiln and tables cluttered with sculptures. I roamed around. A man of many talents, I thought, lifting a wood carving from one of the tables.

"Driftwood," Ramon explained. "From the east beaches."

The man lifted a statue and spoke in Spanish.

"Swamp wood from the rain forest," Ramon interpreted.

Masks, Mayan faces with bright, enamel eyes met my gaze. When I bypassed them, Estos indicated another table of pounded tin.

Ramon spoke to him again in Spanish. The craftsman smiled, went into an adjoining room and returned with a large box. Ramon sorted through the gold filigree jewelry, through the brightly colored beads, and lifted a medallion.

I felt the weight of the large necklace against my chest as Ramon placed it around my neck. I looked down at the crown, very tastefully and delicately raised from the pale gold surface, set with jewels gleaming red and green. "It's lovely. But I haven't enough money...."

"It is my gift to you. A replica of the necklace worn by the Sun Maiden." I felt the warmth of his fingers against my skin as he turned the medallion around to show me the inscription on the back. His deep laughter sounded close to my ear. "Don't ask me what it says."

"You mean you can't read runic markings?"

Ramon studied the inscription for a moment. "Oh, yes, I've made it out now." He stared deeply into my eyes. "To the most beautiful woman I have ever seen!"

Chapter Three

Ramon's gift of the necklace caused me, in spite of my better judgment, to like him. On the way back to the Viking's estate, I found myself confiding in him, telling him about Evelia's threat.

"It means nothing," he said. "She is only jealous."

Inwardly I rebelled at the injustice of Evelia's menacing words. "Who is she jealous of?"

"She is very temperamental," he said evasively. "Who knows?"

"I feel like I am a prisoner. I am afraid to leave and afraid to stay."

"The Viking will not let anything happen to you."

Becoming irritated at his teasing references to Thane and me, I demanded, "Why do you work for him? It's obvious he's insane."

Ramon did not comment for a long time. "I'd prefer not saying insane. Obsessed." He paused. His voice had deepened, lost all air of banter. "Your Mr. Avery is looking for the medallion; the Viking is looking for the princess. One is as foolish as the other."

Surrounded once more by trees which obliterated the sunlight, I again felt worried and threatened.

"The Viking can be a kind and generous friend, but he can also be very dangerous." Ramon's eyes shaded now by shadows of trees, held to the rutted trail. "He's studied the legend far too much; he can no longer tell what's real from what is not."

"He's not going to let me go, is he?"

Ramon still did not look toward me. "The Viking won't harm you. He has infinite patience and makes no demands on anyone."

"But he won't allow me to leave! I won't be able to get away

38

from him without help!"

"I intend to help you, Marta, but you do not begin to see all the problems. We must go very, very slowly."

* * *

Having been unable to sleep, I welcomed the morning, and at the first light of dawn ventured down the wide stairway. Surprised to find no guard stationed at the door, I wandered outside, through wild vegetation, and into the patio area just below my room. The crisp air was filled with the tinkling songs of small birds. The evasive little birds...I had never seen any like them before...were everywhere, their sounds reverberating up and down the mountainside.

I felt the roughness of volcanic rock through my thin cotton dress as I leaned back against the building and through the shield of trees watched the three men meandering around the gate. Slow-spoken words of Spanish, broken by laughter, drifted to me.

The sight of the gate brought with it a sinking of heart...the great height of solid rock topped with jagged glass set in adobe forbidding entrance...or exit. This morning the gate was flung wide open, but this by no means meant access to the outside. Each of the three men wore heavy belts laden with bullets and guns.

Trapped inside, I yielded to waves of panic. Were the Viking's delusions real or a mere pretense? Even if he did genuinely believe me to be the Sun Maiden, this might not be the actual reason I was being held here. Thane Ulrickson might be afraid of what my search for Alan would uncover. Was Alan even alive? I closed my eyes and saw Alan's lean face, the sandy hair and determined mouth, the flash of cleverness in his clear, green eyes. I longed for the safety of the past, the old days, filled with Alan's 'nothing can beat me' sureness. Alan's life could depend on what I did now, yet being a captive myself, how could I help him?

Once more I regarded the immense wall that must surely enclose the entire estate, then with half-sickened resignation turned to go back inside. Just as I did Ramon pulled up to the open gate and jumped from the small carriage. He called sharply to the three men, who followed him into the building, which set like a watch -

tower beside the entrance.

I drew a deep breath and stared toward the abandoned carriage. If I acted with enough haste, I would be able to drive through the gate to freedom!

I did not give myself time for second thoughts. Without even a glance left or right, I raced to the carriage. My hands trembled as they gripped the reins. I had never driven a carriage before, but the horse, feeling my anxiety, trotted off with unexpected speed that hurled me back against the seat.

The carriage wheels hit ruts in the road head-on, at times jolting me with such force I thought I would be thrown against the waiting rocks. Ramon would waste no time pursuing me. He would be certain to overtake me on either of the main roads. The smartest thing to do would be to hide...but where and how?

Despite the reckless speed, thoughts came calmly. Ramon, if he did expect me to turn off the road, would not believe I would take the opposite direction, straight up the mountain, back toward the Viking's land.

The spaces between scrub oaks and pines looked passable, a hilly area scattered with boulders of heavy rock. I was able to get the horse to stop, but had to climb out and lead him into the rugged terrain. After the ground leveled, I returned to the carriage seat. The further I got from the road, the more frightened I became. It would be so easy to lose all sense of direction.

After a long and slow assent, I came to a vast clearing where a volcanic eruption had left porous, charred rocks piled as far ahead as I could see.. a landscape of barren black. I would proceed no further in this direction. I decided to remain here for an hour or so, then turn east and work my way down the mountain and eventually connect with the road.

The stopping of the carriage left profound quietness. Once again I slipped to the ground. Everything seemed suddenly eerie, as if I had left the planet and had become an inhabitant of some barren, hostile world.

In the intense silence I fearfully acknowledged the truth...stealing Ramon's carriage had been a desperate and foolish act. Now I was all alone. I must travel through strange, deserted country where I had so recently encountered armed bandits. I wasn't even sure I would be able to find Santa Augusta, where General Perez said he had last seen Alan. Even if I could escape my followers and find the village, I had very little chance of locating Alan.

The thought of Alan comforted me, his assured, buoyant manner. I had worked around Alan long enough to know what he would do if faced with this situation; I had studied his careful logic, his steady and determined responses.

Thane, a very wealthy, hospitable host; Ramon, an enigmatic and handsome guard...probably Alan would not even consider my circumstance dangerous. I wished Alan could see for himself the weird glow that came into the Viking's eyes whenever he looked at me. Alan would then realize as I did, that I must get away from him!

I began aimlessly picking my way over blackened heaps of rock. In one of Alan's letters he had mentioned a friend from Santa Augusta. I recalled clearly that Alan had referred to someone named Arnold, but Alan, careless with names, had no doubt Americanized *Arnoldo*. If I could only remember his last name!

I approached a gigantic upheaval of stone. From the top of it, a deep crack opened into what looked like an immense cave. Gazing around, I thought that many such caves must exist here in these volcanic mountains.

Mountains! When I had first read his friend's name, I had thought of Spain and mountains. I suddenly remembered a city in Spain, Seville! In my mind, I made the connection...Seville with an *A*,. Saville. I would head to Santa Augusta and hope I had the right name...Arnoldo Saville. Surely he could lead me to Alan!

Tired of walking, I lingered for over an hour, sometimes sitting on the rocks beside the horse and carriage. The horse, brown and long of legs, was unable to be slowed as we started straight down the slope. I was grateful when at last the land leveled and I was able to see the winding trail I had traveled on before.

The carriage bounced across the gully to follow a weedy path. On either side of me green slopes rose sharply. I urged the horse forward and for a long time kept a fast and steady gait. Just rounding a corner on the heavily wooded road, straight ahead I encountered two men. They moved forward to stand in my path, the taller of them waving a warning to stop.

My heart pounded. Was this some kind of roadblock set up by the soldiers of the revolution I knew so little about...or by the Viking? I did not think they were bandits. The two men did not look shoddy, like the men who had robbed me, still I noted their ragged clothes with apprehension. I was too close to them to turn around, and they made no attempt to get out of my way. The only choice I had was to stop.

The tall man stepped forward and held out his hand to me. I looked around at the empty seat beside me, made gestures to explain the absence of bags or papers. My voice, sounding far away and fearful, explained in English I knew he would not understand. "I am staying at Thane Ulrickson's. I am just going into the village."

At the mention of the Viking's name, the two men exchanged glances. The tall man, with a great air of importance, walked around the carriage, returned, and waved me on.

My eyes left him and settled on the fork in the road. "Which way is Santa Augusta?"

He said a sentence or two in Spanish and pointed several times straight ahead.

I breathed deeply when the two men were out of sight. The heat increased as I descended into lowlands, from mountains to jungle. I became surrounded with a magnificent wildness, a place overflowing with tropical plants and creatures. The trees had become coated with tangles of fern and vines. The broad leaf of the heliconia I had seen only in textbooks thrust upward from vegetation so dense it would demand a machete and a strong arm to enter it.

I had never seen a place less civilized. Fear stole over me and caused me to long for a moment for Ramon. I thought of the stability his presence gave me time and again during the long drive through complete isolation.

At last I spotted land that had been cleared. Soon I passed a hut built of bamboo cane with reed roof, where a woman sat outside overseeing children. The huts became frequent. I knew I was approaching a fairly large village and hoped it would be Santa Augusta.

The village faced an unpaved square and consisted of an erratic line of buildings, some with open stalls where I glimpsed fruit, vegetables, and tinware. At the end of the buildings stood a church; the best place, I decided, to try to find someone who might speak English.

A woman in bright dress, tugging a crying youngster, an old man lazing in the shade, and another near the church, were all the people I saw. Did they have siestas in Honduras as they did in Mexico?

The man near the church worked slowly feeding a fire that burned in a stone fireplace very near the entrance. He looked more ragged as I approached him, and his rapt gaze did not leave his task. I wondered if this fireplace represented some sacrificial altar and if he were preserving some ancient Mayan ritual. With a shiver I moved into the shade of the church.

My eyes first fell to a large tray covered with candles, moved to a makeshift altar, and on to a lone Christ on the cross that adorned a cracked, dingy wall.

A man appeared from a side doorway. He looked like a priest, his thin face gentle and glowing, but he did not wear priest's clothing. He appeared young, except that his short, smooth hair was gray. His voice had a dreamy, far-away quality, rising and falling like poetry as he addressed me.

"I do not understand Spanish," I answered.

"You are from America?" he asked in perfect English.

I introduced myself and told him I was looking for Arnoldo Saville.

"I do not know anyone in Santa Augusta by that name."

"Do you know any Americans?"

"No."

He listened respectfully as I explained to him about Alan and

43

why I believed he would be here.

"Are you alone?"

"Yes."

"Women do not travel alone here," he said, speaking only a statement without condemnation.

"It's very important or I wouldn't." I liked his responsible manner, the concern he showed over me. Feeling that he was a man I could trust prompted me to ask, "Is there any way you can help me locate Alan Avery?"

"Probably no one can help you."

Another clear and simple statement, earnest, yet pitying. I hesitated a moment, but he did not speak or make any attempt to continue the conversation, so I went back outside. To avoid the merciless sun, I moved into the square, overhung with branches. Complete exhaustion from the long drive, from the layers of heat, momentarily overcame me, and I sank into a bench beneath the huge rock statue of a soldier.

When I at last opened my eyes, I saw that the man had followed me. As if he had been aware of my tiredness, my desperate thirst, he extended a tin cup filled with thick juice. I accepted it gratefully. The warm liquid tasted tart, some tropical fruit I could not identify.

He stood above me, looking at the statue. "General Francisco Morazan," his soft voice said. "He was hated for his liberalism and was shot." He sat beside me on the bench. "Still they erect a statue to him. Will I ever understand what goes on?" During his long pause we seemed to share the same sense of weariness and frustration. "What are you going to do now? Where are you staying?"

"If I can't find Alan, I will drive to Puerto Lorenzo."

"It is many miles to Puerto Lorenzo. You will not be there before darkness falls." He remained silent for a while as if studying out a way to influence me. "The roads are not safe at any time. We are at present involved in deep, internal conflict and there is much violence."

I cast a glance at the slender priest. He was gazing across the road to the church.

"Violence is often directed against the innocent. Against the church." I felt for a moment stifled by the heat, by the warning. "What else can I do?"

"I should not do this," the man said, "but I will take you to Alan Avery. He will know what you should do."

He drove the carriage. We turned south from Santa Augusta, he silently watching both the trail of road and the deep green mat that covered the rolling hills. "We are close to El Salvador here," he said. After a while he spoke again. "There is a hut just ahead, that is where I will get out."

He had no more than spoken when I saw the bamboo hut, an armed man standing in front of it.

The priest said as he slipped to the ground. "Around the next curve in the road you will see an adobe house against the hillside. Alan will be there. Tell him we are here and watching. We will warn you if someone approaches."

"Why does Alan need protection?"

"That is a question you must ask him."

As I prompted the horse forward, I glanced back to see the priest in a wake of dust. The somberness of his dark face added to my fear. Who were they protecting Alan from? Thane Ulrickson?

The carriage jogged along quickly. In minutes I would see Alan. He would hold me and realize how much anguish I had gone through to find him and to help him.

The small structure ahead, a dirt-streaked white, glared in the sunlight. I would have thought it deserted had it not been for my instructions. Very close to the entrance I called, "Alan," then with suspended expectation, pushed opened the door. Alan jumped up from where he had been seated at a bare table. He wore a white shirt, stained and old, like the wall behind him, and his sandy hair hung in lank, damp strands across his forehead.

"Marta!" he gasped. "What are you doing here?"

I recalled the many times I had entered his office back at the museum...the confident smiles, the clever, easy banter, the meticulous neatness of his clothing. Both manly and boyish, that was always my first thought of him.

Today, he seemed neither.

He stepped closer. His eyes, a murky green, like jungle water, stirred with a stark terror that caused my heart to constrict. I attempted to explain to him. "When I didn't find you at Father's house, I knew something was wrong."

He turned away as if he could not bear the thought of my presence. "You should never have come out here!" He sounded enraged, helpless. "You are going to add to my problems!"

Alan's usually clean-shaven face, shadowed and rough with beard, made him seem like a stranger. Or was it the recently acquired thinness...making him almost gaunt? He bypassed me and at the entrance stood staring down the overgrown path I had just driven. "How did you ever find me? Was anyone following you?"

"I met a man at the church. He is waiting below."

"Arnold?"

"Gray-haired, but not old. I think he's a priest."

"Many times Arnold has risk his own life to help me! But," he added with misery, "you're not going to. You're going right back to New York!"

"You've got to tell me what kind of trouble you're in!"

The distress in my voice must have moved him. He opened his arms in a jerky, awkward movement and said huskily, "Little darling."

Gathered tightly in his arms, I felt no sense of comfort. "Please tell me what's going on," I pleaded, trying not to cry.

Long fingers linked in mine as he drew me toward the bare table. "Things have changed since I sent for you. I just can't let you get mixed up in any of this. It's far too dangerous."

"Is it the medallion? Have you found it?"

Once again fear sounded in his voice. "What makes you think that?"

I explained to him how I had been taken to the Viking's estate. "Alan, I'm afraid of him. He...he thinks I'm someone else."

Alan looked relieved. "That is just the place I want you to be! You must take a look at the rune stone. It is east of the estate,

46

in the cave area below the cliffs. You must also see the Mayan ruins...the stone drawings...on the cliffs near the sea."

"I'm afraid of him," I repeated.

"I wish you hadn't got mixed up in this, but since you're here, you are going to have to do exactly as I tell you. You must return at once to the Viking's estate. I'll assure you, he will not harm you, if you remain in good standing with him."

"I can't just blindly..." my voice died away. "You must tell me everything so I can help you." Once again he turned away. My heart softened toward him. He looked so thin, almost ill. "I can tell you only one thing. I am on the trail of something of unbelievable importance. My findings will be worth millions to the archaeological world!"

Had he actually found the original medallion...or thought he had? Another thought leapt to mind...what if he had stolen the medallion from the Viking and that's why he was hiding? Alan might be here waiting for a chance to get out of Honduras with his proof of the Viking connection. I thought of my father, whose job Alan had taken over, and wished I could again hear his solid advice. His death two years ago left me with no one to turn to. "Let's get help from the museum," I suggested.

"You must not contact the museum!" Alan said harshly. "That would be the worst thing you could do! Promise me you won't!"

He spoke with such desperation, I now felt certain he had located the medallion and was being chased by the Viking's men. Alan believed I had led his trackers to him and this accounted for his ardent turning away from me.

I studied him. Alan couldn't be a common thief! Not common, I told myself, not capable of picking anyone's pocket, or embezzling funds...but able to rob from what he would consider a madman for the good of posterity, ambitious enough to snatch credit for a find that would have a booming impact on centuries of thought and theory.

"You have found the medallion," I said.

Before Alan had time to respond, a barefooted boy raced through the front door, shouting, "Mr. Alan! He's coming!"

Alan tensed. The dampness I had noticed in his sandy hair appeared on his pale skin. "Look what you've done!" He shouted at me as he darted to the entrance.

"Alan! Where are you going? How will I find you?"

"I can't stay here anymore. You've ruined that! You go back and stay with the Viking. I'll contact you there. Soon!"

With legs shaking too much to stand, I sank back down at the bare table where I waited with growing terror, hearing the sound of hoofbeats, foreign shouts, the crash of the door against adobe wall.

I saw first high riding boots, bright and polished. My eyes rose slowly up the straight body to the rock-hard face.

Ramon clutched a pistol, which disappeared under his loose shirt after he had circled the room, searching every place possible for Alan to be concealed.

He stopped at the door. "You stay right here. I'll be back."

I heard him calling sharp words of Spanish to someone outside. I waited, feeling paralyzed, afraid that I might hear shots, afraid that Alan would be killed or dragged back to the cabin. When nothing happened, I finally rose and walked to the door. My carriage was gone; I saw only empty hills, an abandoned stretch of road.

They had left me unguarded! I could run back to the bamboo hut, to Arnoldo, but I knew in my heart he had fled at the first sight of Ramon. The shaking of my legs increased. I really had no choice but to wait here for Ramon, do as Alan ordered, and return to the Viking.

Hours seemed to have passed before Ramon returned. Even though I knew at a glance he had not captured Alan, he had about him the same unruffled bearing. I put my hand to my forehead and for a moment hated him. "How did you find me?"

"By tracking the path of the carriage you stole this morning. You left a very wide trail."

"I am not a thief. I fully intended to see that your carriage was returned."

Ramon's black eyes roamed around the room before they

settled on me again. I wondered how they could look both sympathetic and mocking.

"I'm not going back there," I spoke up with weak defiance. "I'm going to insist that you take me to Puerto Lorenzo."

Ramon did not speak for a long time. "I'm afraid you have no choice. If I lose you, Princess," he said with a trace of irony in his voice, "the Viking will have me thrown overboard."

Chapter Four

Rain, at first so fine it seemed only to exist as part of the air itself, began streaming. Thick clouds...where had they come from? Only a moment ago the sun had blazed from an azure sky with unbearable fury.

The rain felt warm, pleasantly welcome to the hand I extended from the wooden, overhead covering, not sufficient to protect us where we sat close together on the hard carriage bench.

Ramon slowed the pace, for already puddles settled deep into ruts, splashing muddy water at every turn of the wheel. Thinking I might be able to protect the only suitable dress I had left, I moved a little closer to him.

Ramon, used to the sudden rains, unmindful of wet shirt and damp, glistening hair, alertly watched the road, however my closeness, making him more aware of me, prompted him to speak. "I must make you understand how much danger exists on these roads," he said. "They are occupied by hundreds of men, exactly like Sanchez. Men who have respect for nothing!" Images of many Sanchezes rose to mind and inwardly I shuddered.

As if trying to extract some suitable verbal response, Ramon's voice grew more challenging. "I had to send out men today to look for you. You put them all in great jeopardy. Carranza is forming an army to resist the election of a new president. The hills are crawling with his butchers."

My eyes wandered toward the dense vegetation flanking each side of us. Anywhere, concealed by forest depths, enemies could lie in wait.

"I don't expect you to understand." Ramon's voice had soft-

50

ened. "Carranza's army is not like any you have ever seen. They are robbers, killers; most of them do not even know the issues involved. That is why you must be protected until you are safely on the boat to New York City."

"When will that be?"

"It will take time, but I will see to it that arrangements are made. Until then, I expect your cooperation. Your safety is my responsibility."

"Sanchez, is he one of Carranza's men?"

"Who knows? Here lines are not clearly drawn. Many use the constant state of rebellion in our country for their own ends."

For the first time I felt part of the conflict he spoke of and cared about the outcome. "Is Carranza trying to overthrow the government?"

"Since Barrios was assassinated, there is no existing government. Just a mad scramble for power."

"Who is Carranza?"

"Carranza was Barrios' second in command, not at all like Barrios. Barrios dedicated his life to helping the poor, and got shot for it. Carranza, who may have been his assassin, is totally corrupt. He must not be allowed to gain control."

"Who is opposing him for leadership?"

"A number of factions, led by soldiers, mostly. I, myself, support Don Orlando. But many people don't trust him simply because he is rich...and Spanish."

"You will probably join his force," I said. I thought to myself that he looked like one of the conquistadors of old; proud, powerful, ruthless.

"I have a job." A faint smile appeared, and the image of conquistador was replaced by that of gallant knight. "One I take most seriously. Protecting you."

I felt suddenly grateful for his presence and began to believe that Ramon really did care what happened to me. For a while I was able to put aside my own plight and Alan's and sincerely wished Carranza would be beaten and this Don Orlando would prevail.

Ramon shifted the reins, his right hand moving to close over mine. I was aware of his waving, black hair, the strong profile of nose and chin, the artful line of his lips. I recalled the hardness of them as he had addressed Sanchez, but I instinctively knew they were capable of great tenderness. I wondered what it would be like to kiss him. The thought...I had never kissed anyone but Alan...prompted me to remove my hand from the stirring warmth of his, and shrink a little toward the edge of the carriage seat.

Ramon, as I drew away from him, smiled, then the lips I had been thinking about relaxed into humorous contemplation. "There is no need to be afraid of me," he said. "I would give my life for you!"

"I know nothing about you," I answered primly. "And what I do know about you makes absolutely no sense to me. How are you able to speak such flawless English?"

"That's easy to explain," Ramon said. "My mother is American."

"And your father?"

"For many years he ran a plantation, much like General Perez's. At that time, he traveled widely and met Mother on one of his business trips, in South Carolina."

"Why aren't you working for him, instead of the Viking?"

"Times are not good here," he answered briefly, in a manner that firmly closed the door on further personal inquiries.

"What about the Viking? No matter how much he plays the mystic, he surely must have an explainable history."

"Explainable and respectable," Ramon answered. "Ulrickson is a very old, established name in Honduras."

"But you spoke of Thane as dangerous."

"Because," I could sense in his hesitation doubts about exactly what he should and should not tell me. "he acts without thought. Rashly." He paused a long while before continuing. "Thane's father lived to be very old. When he died about twelve years ago, Thane burned his father's home and personal effects, as if he were burning some huge, Viking ship. Then he moved to this mountain and built his monstrosity, his lava castle."

"I think Thane selected the site because he believes this is exactly where the Vikings first landed," I said.

"Though its never been proven, I believe the Mayan Indians had many sea-voyaging visitors," Ramon responded. "Possibly the Phoenicians, the Orientals. I'm sure each of them made some difference in their culture and art."

"But the Norsemen were first! Eric the Red discovered Greenland in 986. What if other Norse voyagers made discoveries never recorded?" I could hear the excitement growing in my voice. "What if the Vikings were the first outside contact of the Mayans?"

The sudden shrug of wide shoulders expressed his doubt.

"Is it so impossible? My father worked for years on that very theory. James Swan, have you ever heard of him?"

"Yes. He worked with Maudslay on excavations at Copan."

"I'm going to finish and publish his life's work."

"Quite ambitious, for a pretty, young girl," Ramon said. His dark eyes moved across my damp dress, to wet, stringing hair, and locked on my eyes. "But I am very attracted to ambition!"

"Then you should like Alan Avery. He is the most ambitious man I've ever met."

At the mention of Alan's name, Ramon's eyes darkened. "There is more than one kind of ambition," he said. "Sanchez is ambitious, too."

"Let's not compare them," I spoke coldly. "Alan has carried on Father's research here in Honduras in a very admirable way. If anyone can prove Father's theories correct, Alan will."

Alan...where was he now? I avoided looking at Ramon. The mere mention of Alan and our work separated us. The cloudburst had ceased with surprising suddenness, leaving sharp odors intensified by tropical rain. Fragrant scents of flowers, spicy leaves of fig trees mingled with the earthy smells of the forest.

Sounds, like scents also mingled in air...the chatter of small monkeys, the scream of parrots. I watched a toucan with a ridiculously large beak ascend in awkward flight to a higher branch.

Ramon's deep voice cut into my own thoughts. "Your Alan is chasing necklaces, not theories."

Automatically my hand rose to the necklace Ramon had given

me. Had the Viking's necklace been stolen? Had Alan taken it? That must be the reason Ramon had been trying to find Alan. I tried to make my voice sound matter-of-fact, as if I had no suspicions of what must be going on. "Does the Viking have the original medallion?"

Ramon's tone became remote, evasive. "There are rumors that Thane has an abundance of Viking jewels...even a crown. But no one has ever seen them."

"I have heard there are stone drawings on the cliffs...Mayan carvings of bearded men in boats with serpentine bows like the Norsemen sailed in. And-- I have also heard that there is a rune stone on Thane's land inscribed with markings left by the ancient Vikings.

With reluctance, Ramon acknowledged, "The Mayan ruins are high upon the cliffs near the sea...very difficult to reach without a steep climb. Only one building is still intact...an ancient temple. A remarkably well-preserved frieze is within, so protected by thick stone walls that it still bears some traces of paint."

"How fascinating!"

"The frieze covers half a wall. It depicts a sea battle between the Indians and some foreign invaders. There are other paintings, also, but so weathered they are difficult to make out."

"I would love to see them."

He glanced at me, appearing almost amused by my great enthusiasm.

"I will take you out there if you must see them," he offered. "But please don't try to make the climb alone. The way is steep and could be dangerous."

"I would also like to see the rune stone."

"I cannot take you there." Ramon's eyes darkened. "The stone is near the lava beds." He turned to me with warning in his eyes. "You must keep away from there!"

"Why?"

"The lava beds are even more treacherous than the cliffs. The ground is weakened by a network of caves below the surface. Hollow areas in the rocks often break and give away, tumbling into

54

chasms far below. But...there is also another reason."

At that moment, Ramon slowed the carriage. "Here is where I found your trail to the caves," he said. "I was quite alarmed when I found you had taken that direction. Besides the natural danger, the caves are alive with Carranza's men. You must stay completely away from this area, even on the Viking's land! You must go nowhere without me!"

I could not consent to that, no matter had adamant his request. At the first opportunity I intended to visit the ruins upon the cliffs, and also to search the area below for the rune stone. After all, finding the Viking link was why I had made this journey to Honduras.

Though I was anxious to see the Mayan ruins, I especially wanted to see the rune stone. Only the stone with its runic characters would be true evidence that the Vikings had ever been here. I felt a catch of excitement at the thought that the proof my father, and now Alan and I had searched so long and hard for might actually be here...in this very place!

Ramon seemed to be awaiting some statement of compliance. Surely, his warnings about men hiding in the caves were only an attempt to discourage me from exploring. Was he just being overly cautious in his efforts to protect me? Or was there actually some vital reason he wanted to keep me away from the lava cave area? If so, was it linked to his pursuit of Alan? "I thought the Viking's land was well-guarded."

"I'm afraid," Ramon said, "The fortress has been invaded. Even though Thane Ulrickson is not in the least aware of it!"

* * *

Once alone in my room, able to collect my racing thoughts, I felt relief mingled with undercurrents of even greater fear. Alan was safe, but for how long?

The Viking, whose wrath against Alan I felt certain was justified, would be a relentless enemy. Only one thing puzzled me. The Viking's emotions seemed to be so simple and clearly expressed, yet when he had spoken of Alan I had witnessed no signs of malice. He had been smiling, even affectionate. Unless the Viking was not what he appeared to be. Could he be some master of deceit, hiding behind false impressions of himself that he worked long and hard to establish?

That was nonsense I told myself. No one would try to appear mad. There would be no reason for it.

Seeing Alan had given me momentary peace of mind, but this gain was balanced by the knowledge that from now on I would be watched much more carefully. I opened my door a crack. Down the hallway, now dimming with evening light, a rugged, bearded man stood, a gun in a holster around his heavy waist.

I drew back into my room and feeling suddenly very weak, sank down in the nearest chair. The feel of the straight high back sickened me further, the thought that the seat I had taken seemed more like a throne. Princess Marta! I stood up quickly, confronting my image in the mirror. I had never looked so disheveled, face pale around damp hair, dropping skirt streaked with rain and mud. I was still watching my own features and saw them react with startled fear as a knock sounded loudly on the door behind me.

I shrank at the thought of the Viking standing there awaiting my answer. For a long time, scarcely breathing, I postponed an answer, but at last forced myself to asked, "Who's there?"

A feminine voice replied, "Please open the door."

Evelia faced me. She seemed a little sad, her eyes wider in her thin face. The width added a dimension of depth to her I had not earlier noticed. She carried a tray with a copper pot, and, beside it set thin cups and a basket heaped with pastries.

"I thought you would be too tired to come down for dinner. But that is all right. Thane will not be back from Santa Augusta until late."

The memory of her rankling threats ringing in my ears made me hesitate to stand aside and let her enter. She could not have had a change of heart so rapidly, even though I could detect nothing less than genuine warmth in her smile, as appealing as a small girls whose sudden temper had flared and faded.

Evelia placed the tray on the chest and flashing another smile more entreating than the last, said, "I have come to say I am sorry.

Her short laugh sounded self-condemning. "I am always saying things I do not mean. When you get to know me better you will understand. I try so hard to rid myself of this trait, but it has always had a hold on me. Please forgive me."

Even though I did not trust her apology and wondered why she had really come to my room, I accepted the cup she poured with coffee and took a flaky pastry.

"Let's sit and talk," Evelia suggested, pulling a smaller chair closer to the huge one where I had again seated myself. "It is so good to have a woman to talk to! Mostly I see only men. And, men!" she said with derogatory passion. "They only care about war and fortune!" Evelia's voice became mellow and sweet, so quickly that I could hardly bridge the change. "Wouldn't it be nice if we could be real friends?"

How could that be, when I found myself even hesitating before I decided it would be safe to partake of the food and drink? I was very hungry and the thin crust tasting of some sweet berry was delicious, the strong, hot coffee, refreshing.

Evelia watched me closely and noticing how quickly I had eaten the pastry, offered me another.

"There are so many things I want to know from you," she said. "What is New York City like? It has been my life-long dream to journey there, to mingle with the fashionable ladies, to be one of them!" With the exhilaration of a child, she inquired, "Do you go to great parties?"

I sorted through the hum-drum functions that made up my rather lonely life for something that might interest her. "Before Alan left for Honduras, we attended a grand dance very near the capital building in Washington D.C., in the most beautiful hall you could imagine. The grand affair was thrown by Alan's brother, who is a general in the U.S. Calvary, and I danced with generals and senators. I will never forget it!"

My words brought a wistful sigh. "What did you wear?"

"A gown of the palest pink. With an enormous skirt and fragile lace designed with dark pink flowers."

"How lucky you are!" she said, and with a lift of her small chin, stated, "Someday, I will see such places for myself! It's so hard being isolated out here. Being nobody." She squared her thin shoulders. "Someday, soon, I will be special, be a lady of fashion!"

Stillness followed her words. I finished my pastry and rose to place the dishes back on the tray.

Rousing from her dreamy silence, Evelia finally asked me, "Are you in love with Alan?"

I hesitated. How often I had asked myself that same question. "Everyone naturally thinks of Alan and me as a pair. We work together."

Evelia laughed, "But that is not an answer. Love," she brought up a hand, long and thin, like her face, to give a wide gesture, "is 'not what everyone expects'. Love is not so business-like!"

Something about the passion of her words caused Ramon's handsome face to appear to me.

"Now, a girl could easily fall in love with someone like Ramon!" Evelia continued, watching me closely. "He is so wonderful! Don't you think he is?"

Quickly I tried to brush his image aside and change the subject. "What about you? Do you stay here because of Thane Ulrickson?"

"I stay here...because it is nice here. Outside of these walls, I would have nothing. I would live in constant fear."

Evelia's mood had swung to one of morbid emptiness. Her long silence caused me to think about the hardships most of her people must suffer. It brought to mind the revolution that had meant so little to me I had barely thought about it...how much they must sacrifice in the hopes of establishing for themselves a better life.

Surprising me, Evelia jumped to her feet. "Look at you!" Gathering her long skirt, Evelia left the room. When she appeared again, she announced, "While the servants are drawing your bath, you must come with me. You are about my size. I will loan you some of my clothes."

Reluctantly, I followed after her. She hurried way ahead of me, back into the hallway where lights had been lit and now flickered and caused shadows. Behind me I heard a soft footfall and glancing back over my shoulder, I saw that the rugged guard was moving doggedly forward. He made no attempt to hide the fact that he would not shirk his duty as my guard. I hurried to catch up with Evelia, who stood at the open door to her room waiting for me.

Evelia's room was not heavy and oppressive like mine. Flowered paper, various shades of pale red, covered the walls, and great vases crammed with living plants that dangled to the highly polished floor, set everywhere. A beautiful, multi-colored bird, very tiny, perched in a gigantic cage. I could hear a faint chirping, a protest of disturbance.

"Do you like my room, Marta? I decorated it myself, to suit my tastes."

"It is very lovely." Why had Thane Ulrickson provided her with such luxuries? I assumed Evelia was one of the housekeepers, though I rarely saw her do any work. Was this lovely, exotic woman Thane's mistress?

"Thane has a dressmaker in Telas make all my clothing. She and her girls can design anything!" Evelia flung open wide closet doors. Within, clothing of every shape and hue hung in abundance. She tilted her head to one side, making the shiny silver hoops in her ears dance. "You only have to ask, and Thane will have her make dresses for you!"

"I don't want to take anything from him!" My mind rebelled at the idea of being obligated to him in any way. I imagined myself, dressed in luxuries, kept fed and comfortable, as much a pet as Evelia's bird in its swinging cage.

Evelia smiled at me. "You are thinking Thane and I are lovers, but that is not so. Thane gives me dresses because he knows they make me happy." With unexpected generosity, she gestured a slim hand toward the closet. "Pick out anything you like."

Tempted by the beautiful dresses, I stopped. "I can't. They are much too expensive. I could never...."

"Someday, when you get back to America and you marry a rich general, you can send me fashions from New York!" As she spoke, she gathered petticoats and undergarments from a huge chest.

I stepped along the row of dresses, finding, as I studied them, that they were shockingly bright. I had never worn such colors, or ever seen necklines that fell so low! I was able at last to find among them a simple blue dress that more suited my style. "May I borrow this one?"

"That is one I would throw away!" she scoffed. "But suit yourself."

Seeing a riding habit, I lifted it, "I would like very much to use this, too."

"Of course. I might have known you were a lover of horses. Wait till you see the Viking's stables. He has great horses, tall and white!" As she spoke, Evelia snatched a dressing gown from the rack, muslin, but dyed a brilliant yellow and trimmed with darker, deeper shades. "Take this, too. You will look lovely in it. Like you are made of pure gold!"

* * *

When I returned to my room, I first noticed a copper tub placed in front of the fireplace someone had lit. But whoever had been here had come and gone. I quickly removed my soiled, damp garments and sank into the luxuriant warmth of steamy water.

I lay with closed eyes and listened to the peaceful crackling of the fire. The long, soothing bath made the day, so filled with pain and frustration, recede and a drowsiness began to steal over me. I did not hear the servants returning for the tub, for I had slipped into the plush covers of the bed and fallen into an exhausted sleep.

I awoke before dawn, the night's sleep renewing my resolve to see for myself the Mayan ruins and to locate the rune stone Alan had spoken of. I took from my case a notebook and pen and ink so I could copy the runic writing, an exquisite addition to my father's book.

I dressed in the riding habit I had borrowed from Evelia. The brown garment fit snugly, would have even on Evelia's much thinner frame, still I was glad to have the protection of rough fabric as I began the treacherous descent from balcony to nearest branch.

I had allowed myself but a moment to scan the grounds below, to make sure no one would see me. Safely clinging to the tree limb nearest the balcony, I began having second thoughts. The ground below now seemed much more distant, the way down severely blocked by branches laden with masses of sharp pine needles.

Images arose of my being discovered, of Ramon stepping from the trees into the patio below, waiting to escort me back into my prison.

I took a deep breath and reminded myself that this might be my one and only chance to explore...to visit on my own the cliffs and to locate the rune stone. Surely, the Viking rune would turn out not to be authentic. But if it were, then I would soon see with my own eyes something my father had searched for his entire life!

Caught up by the sense of impending discovery, with new determination I continued my descent. My foot examined each limb, testing the sturdiness of it before I allowed the weight of my body to rest on it. Luckily the foothold of limbs were well-spaced and soon I found myself standing on solid ground. I paused only a moment, not aware until now of the sting caused by scrapes of bark against bare hands and the uncomfortable prick of pine needles which had been able to pierce my clothing.

The sea would have to lie directly east of the house, no more, Alan had told me, than two miles. He had mentioned that the rune stone set very near the cliffs. I would walk in the direction of the ocean until I could see the Mayan ruins.

The trail I took led deep into a forest, where great mahogany trees towered. Rough-barked sapodillas were scattered among the pines on the surrounding slopes. Even though the forest here was not like the one Ramon and I had driven through, it had the same earthy smell of plants unable to fully dry.

I walked briskly for about a half a mile, when I was stopped by the sound of approaching voices. My startled reaction was to duck into the thick trees, where lianas drooped from overhead branches meeting the tangle of undergrowth. Concealed, I waited, holding my breath.

Sharp, quick exchanges of Spanish grew clear and distinct. I heard a woman's voice, then the terse, almost hateful tone of a man. As they rounded the curve in the trail, I glimpsed a face I recognized. My heart sank. Sanchez! His thin face, tense and frowning, betrayed a deep anger as he listened to his companion. The woman, until then blotted from my view by Sanchez. I stared toward them with alarm. My own sense of shock surprised me, for I had been baffled, but never fooled by Evelia's sudden display of friendship. Still I did not know why even she would be out here with a man like Sanchez!

Evelia drew to a sudden halt. Dangling silver hoop earrings jingled with her quick movement. Her voice rose in furious opposition. Sanchez answered in a certain, unyielding tone. Whatever he told her increased her fury. For a moment I expected her to strike out at him, instead she whirled from him and ran past me out of view.

Sanchez, looking disturbed by her departure, stood immobile for what seemed to me like an eternity. Once, narrowed black eyes looked in my direction. I crouched lower into the wet shield of foliage. I could not bring myself to risk trying to see him again.

At last the slow sound of his steps passed me and grew faint. I remained where I was, too terrified to move. The noises around me, before unnoticed, intensified. The cry of birds seemed harsh, the movement of the forest inhabitants loud. I thought of the multitude of snakes and insects hidden with me in the jungle growth.

This thought gave me the courage to return to the trail. I set out at a rapid pace. Because of the humidity and the speed of my steps, I soon felt overcome with weariness. Stopping to rest, I noted that the trees had became sparse, a scrubby evergreen or two, a distant palm tree. To the right side of the trail, black beds of lava encroached upon the floor of vegetation.

I left the trail and climbed up the crusty, black rocks to a cone-shaped height where I could see the entire area. Surrounding me were lava beds, filled with hollow caverns and deep caves. Ahead of me about a forth mile, I caught a glimpse of shimmering blue water.

The land surrounding the deserted beach, directly ahead, narrowed into sharp, rising cliffs. I shaded my eyes from the glare and soon spotted among the high cliffs the tan walls of the Mayan ruins.

I paused for a moment and gazed up at the cliffs in awe. The rocks would be difficult, but not impossible, to climb. From where I stood I could just barely see the outline of the ancient temple, the crumbling stone walls of partial buildings that surrounded the main one. I tried not to think of Sanchez or the possibility that I had been followed. I ventured out into the open, making my way slowly, carefully over hilly uprisings of sharp, volcanic rock toward the cliffs. A scattering of charcoal-colored boulders dotted the area below the cliffs, heavy basalt with a weathered, ropy texture like solidified snakeskin. Centuries ago, streams of hardened lava had formed islands around existing hills, creating a mottled texture to the rocks. As I drew closer to the cliffs, the dark rock gradually became interspersed with huge sections of lighter, sand-colored stone.

I spotted the rune stone at once. I had expected it to be nearer the Mayan ruins, perhaps on the shelves of cliffs above me, not here. But there it stood, directly ahead, surrounded by giant heaps of lava. Carved of weathered, gray-black basalt, it rose three or four feet from where its base was solidly embedded in stone.

Could I really be looking at a genuine rune stone? I stared at it in breathless reverence. I had spent many hours before I left New York studying all about Viking rune stones. Usually Vikings carved them as memorials to the dead. Sometimes the inscriptions were combined with curvilinear decorations as well as writing, but this one was not.

I bent and studied the carvings in the stone. They consisted of six vertical rows of writing and two horizontal rows at the base. The inscriptions were without doubt in the runic alphabet!

Could the stone slab be a fake, copied from some monument Thane had seen on his travels? Could it have been transported here? I felt the rock-hard basalt from which it was formed...it would be virtually impossible to move such a structure, which probably weighed more than two tons. The carving, once so deep, seemed worn by time and elements, in places scarcely visible.

Was it some ancient poetry? Would it tell of a voyage of a person that could be identified in history? Later, Alan and I would return with tripod and camera, sheets of paper to make a rubbing of the entire monument. But for now, pen and ink would have to suffice.

I could not possibly copy it all. I would have to make do with a sample. Quickly, I chose the two horizontal rows near the base. My hand shook a little as I began carefully copying each inscription. I wished with all my heart I could interpret the script right now, without the many hours of labor involved, the help of books and experts.

If the writing was authentic, that meant that it would be centuries old, probably the ninth century, the same time frame as other Viking voyages reaching the American continent. Evidence of a previously unrecorded voyage!

Away from the protection of the trees, the sun beat down mercilessly upon my uncovered head. I worked rapidly, not liking the idea of being in such clear view of Sanchez and other sources of possible danger.

Quickly I checked my copy for accuracy. As I arose, I gazed upward to the cliffs where the Mayan ruins waited. Slanting rays of early sunlight made the walls seem bathed in gold. My knowledge of the Mayans had come from textbooks and from endless talks with my father. I had never seen a Mayan ruin.

What sights awaited me, just out of reach? From where I stood, I could see the bare outline of the temple. Most Mayan ruins were in flat areas, but this small settlement, fortified by the cliffs, overlooked the sea. At the cliff's edge, I saw a row of plumed serpent heads facing the sea. I longed to make the seemingly impossible climb to the top of the cliff, to enter the ancient, abandoned temple, to see the painted rock carvings which might represent a long-forgotten voyage to Central America!

I shaded my eyes against the sun, and for a long moment deliberated making the rugged, steep climb. I wondered if the ruins might be more approachable from a different direction, perhaps by circling the cliffs and trying to ascend from the shoreline. Such exploration would take time...time I did not have.

Finally, with much regret, I forced myself to turn away from the ruins, back to the trail I had before taken, that led to the house. For my future plans, I must slip back into my room unnoticed. To do so, I could not risk being gone from the Viking's castle any longer.

Chapter Five

Thane Ulrickson waited for me at the bottom of the winding stairway where he appeared to have been standing for a very long time. His massive shoulders, his upraised face topped with shaggy, red-gold hair, brought to mind the image of a huge lion keeping watchful surveillance.

He bounded up the stairs to meet me. "You're back, safe and sound!" he said with great pleasure. As he spoke he took both of my hands in a grip that seemed stronger, more possessive than before.

I had been prepared to face the Viking's anger. Now I was disarmed by his absolute joy at my return. Quickly, I disengaged myself from his welcoming embrace, and stepped away from him, answering, "Not by choice."

Before my eyes, his joy began to rapidly fade. "Aren't you happy here?" Thane asked. The great bewilderment, the immense sadness reflected in Thane's keen blue eyes melted in part my resentment.

"Is there anything you want or need? Entertainment, clothing, jewelry...whatever it is, just ask. I can provide!"

"You know what I want," I retorted, once again irritated over Thane's pathetic attempt at bribery, "I want to be able to come and go as I please."

"Where do you want to go? I'll have Ramon take you anywhere you desire."

"I don't need a bodyguard."

"Oh, but I can't let you wander about alone! It's far too dangerous! You must not take matters into your own hands like you

66

did yesterday. I told you I was taking care of things."

"Then what have you found out about the missing trunk? About my passport?"

The Viking stroked his reddish beard. "I have people in Santa Augusta working on the problem," he responded evasively. "In the meantime, I will plan some entertainment to take your mind off your worries. Yes! We need some diversion from all this trouble." The Viking's eyes brightened with an enthusiasm so great that I became frightened.

"Yes! Entertainment is the answer!"

My hand rose, nervously entwining the chain of the medallion Ramon had bought for me in the village the day before. Despite the heaviness of the necklace, I had not taken it off since Ramon had placed it around my neck. The weight of it, warm against my skin, provided me with a sense of security in this strange, unfamiliar environment.

Thane had been smiling. Now, his gaze fell to the medallion with its deep-set, glittering stones. The strange glint that came into his eyes made a chill creep up and down my spine.

"The Viking Crown medallion!"

I drew in my breath as his large fingers closed around the necklace.

"Where did you get this?"

"Ramon bought it for me. In the village."

"Ramon?" He shook the necklace lightly with his fingers. "I should have guessed. This...is unworthy of you. It is nothing ...a cheap replica!"

I wondered if it were the fake medallion that disturbed him, or the fact that Ramon, not he, had given it to me. "I like it all the same." I responded defensively, not willing to have him belittle Ramon's gift.

"Ha! It is nothing!" Thane's fingers dropped from the necklace. "I have the real Viking Crown! I can show you magnificent treasures...treasures from my collection. Riches like your beautiful eyes have never before seen!" He tilted his head to one side, watching me from the corner of his eye. "Do you want to see them?"

"I don't think so."

"Come with me, Marta." Thane gripped my arm and walking slightly ahead, moved down the stairway, not speaking until he had ushered me through the dining room toward a back door where twisted steps led into a long corridor. There he let go of me and opened a door, saying as he did, "My study."

The wooden walls of the study, raised blocks of red and blue, were reminiscent of Swedish designs. Behind the huge desk ceiling-high shelves were crammed with books and Mayan artifacts. From the only wall without shelves hung great, brownish maps. I stopped before the largest one, a pen-and ink drawing of the Copan ruins, studying the winding course of the Copan River, then settling on the great courtyard dominated by a central pyramid.

"We will go there some day," Thane said. "From the top of that large pyramid, you can see the whole world." His eyes, very large and blue, shifted from my eyes to the exit. "That door," he said, "connects with my storage shed. We must pass through a long tunnel."

I hesitated.

"Let's get started, Marta."

Part of me longed to see the collection he spoke of, invaluable to my final chapter of Father's book; another part of me wanted to refuse to go. "No one has ever set eyes on my complete collection. Only me, and now you. I am going to show you the plunders of a Viking king!"

* * *

My deep reservations centered around the idea of being alone with him, no telling where, but even beyond Ramon's help. The collection might not even exist, except in his own mind. Yet art was my life's work; how could I, in the event that such a collection did exist, pass up such an opportunity? The Viking Crown! So many, including Alan, would pay any price to have the chance to see if it really existed.

Doubt clouded my mind in spite of Thane's persuasive, earnest manner. He himself did not look authentic, but as if he had just stepped off of some theatrical stage. He wore a long, beige shirt that served to exaggerate height that needed no exaggeration. A belt looped around his waist, not given to paunch, but muscular, like his huge arms. The V-neck of the shirt exposed a mass of blonde hair, with hints of red, like his beard.

The door opened into a primitive tunnel. Thane lit dim gas-lights as we went. As if to encourage me, he said, "This collection of mine is the most fabulous one in the entire world! Many of my treasures are Mayan. Occasionally I take an item or two out to show or loan for exhibit, but the collection as a whole, has never been seen."

The damp, chilly air reminded me of some ancient mine shaft, without space enough for us to walk side by side.

"You are acquainted with the work of Maudslay," his voice sounded from behind me. "He has explored the ruins of Copan and written about his findings. Have you read anything by him?"

"Yes. Most of my knowledge of the Mayans of Copan comes directly from him. Father and he have often worked together." I paused, then added, "Maudslay thought the Mayans might have old world origins." I was beginning to feel less nervous because the subject was so familiar. "My father believed that such trans-oceanic contacts were possible."

"Maudslay and others have investigated the idea that the Mayans originated in Egypt, Greece, even the lost continent of Atlantis. With the exception of your father, they have traced connections back to many cultures, but have failed to examine the Viking contact."

During the long walk, Thane spoke non-stop about the Mayans. His detailed knowledge was impressive, and so interesting that instead of being increasingly afraid, I was sorry when we reached the end of the tunnel and he fell silent. A heavy door opened into an immense shed, filled to overflowing with ancient carriages and stacks of stored goods covered with canvas.

"We'll leave this unlocked," he said as we left the shed and moved out into an evening made darker by the thick growth of pines. We walked for a very long time in silence. The trees soon became sparse and scrubby, the ground rugged with chunks of loose stone. Mounds of lava rock appeared in the distance and Thane's steps became harder to follow as he hurried toward them.

Try as I did, I could not orient myself...could this be the same area I had been in early this morning?

Standing on a slick surface of lava, full moon making clear his face and form, Thane stopped to wait for me.

My hand caught hold of the necklace Ramon had given me. "Are you going to show me the original medallion?" I asked, trying to conceal my excitement.

"I don't have it. The Indians took it, then..." his deep voice drifted off. "But someday I will get it back for you."

"For me?"

"Yes, my Princess. For you!"

After the Viking's brilliant talk on Mayan civilization, I was jolted by his total transformation.

"I am not who you think I am." I felt foolish even speaking to him like this. "I am not the Sun Maiden. She's been dead for centuries."

Thane smiled as if I were protesting a well-known fact. "I know who you are," he said. "And I've protected your treasure for you. Tonight you'll see it again." His voice changed into almost a rumble. "The Viking Crown!"

He set off with rapid stride toward one of the nearby mountains of lava. I saw no evidence of a door cut into the black rock, but I watched him push up an attached stone and began to work a lock. He turned again to wait.

Why had I been foolish enough to follow him here? Had I really believed he possessed authentic Mayan and Viking treasures?

I stopped, gripped by a reluctance to intrude, the way I might have if entering someone's tomb. Thane lit one of the torches that waited near the entrance. Then he closed the heavy, metal-reinforced door.

The Viking had to stoop to enter. As he did he glanced back

with an encouraging smile. "Wait here while I light the lamps." he said.

I gazed at the steep passageway leading directly downward. I could see light from the chamber below, which rose in dim shafts across molten lava, hardened and ice-cold. The Viking waited for me to join him.

The cave-room we descended into was not the storage place I had expected. Carefully arranged cases and tasteful exhibits rivaled the New York City museum. Awed, my eyes roamed across gigantic statues and steles of priests, warriors, and animals.

Glass cases were filled with objects of jade, ceramic figures, and masks. My gaze swept over a huge, jade bird with a long, twisted beak, across round-bottomed cooking jars, Copador vases, and rows of human teeth inlaid with small discs of jade or pyrite. My eyes returned to one of the vases, a rare color of red containing hematite. Its black, geometric design was almost abstract. Exactly like the ones within the house, the ones he had shown Alan.

Were they real? Or were they reproductions, set up by the Viking to sell for huge profit, to purposely trick and defraud? Was Thane Ulrickson's reputation of insanity part of a ruse by which he took advantage of rich collectors and made a fortune for himself? Had he a scheme to fool, even scholars, even Alan Avery?

I turned to look at him. He stood in front of a free standing statue of a Mayan carved in stone. "Come here, Marta. Notice the prevalence of straight line and block form. You see here `cubic' character. There's also an attempt to communicate an objective truth independent of time. This statue was definitely influenced by the art of Egypt."

I bent closer to see if I could tell if it were authentic or a recent attempt at copying.

Thane did not allow the time I needed to study it, but drew me toward a stele, taller than himself, where he traced the image of a man's head. The face bore a beard, raised in high relief from the stone. I felt my breath catch. The bearded head looked so much like Thane's! Had he hired someone to carve an image of himself?

Thane stared at me, blue eyes intent, seeming to burn brighter than the torch he carried in his hand.

"Are you pleased with my collection?" he asked. "I have many objects of great value...and beauty."

"But why haven't you shared them with the world?"

"Because they are mine!" Thane's eyes left my face to roam around the great cave. "Some of my collection dates back as far as I can trace the Ulrickson family, centuries ago, back to the old country. Back to the home of the Viking Crown. A jeweled woman's crown, fit for a princess to wear!"

"Where is the crown?"

Strong fingers locked on my arm and steered me toward tall cases that lined the back wall. I held my breath, anxious to see the Viking crown for myself!

Thane suddenly released me, walked away, and returned, extending a bracelet bearing good luck inscriptions in runic character. "These jewels are yours, my dear. All of them!"

I stood holding the bracelet as Thane walked back to the hand-carved trunk where he had taken it. The wood of the trunk reminded me of the wood in my room, the same sea-marred appearance.

"I don't understand...."

"There are many things I do not understand," Thane interrupted. "But it is our lot to accept, not to know." He smiled with great patience. "People rush and try to cram all truth into a few short years. I don't know why. We have all eternity before us!"

I could see from where I stood that the trunk was filled with jewelry. Did the precious original medallion lie somewhere within?

"Your dowry!" he said, pleased with the wonderment I could not keep from expressing.

I came hesitantly forward and placed the bracelet back among the great mass of gold and stones.

"Is the crown here?" For a moment, fascinated by the atmosphere of the place, I felt a real desire to see the fabled crown for myself, to hold in my own hands the object that would prove beyond a doubt my father's life work.

Thane seemed not to hear me. "We will journey back to

Scandinavia, you and I," Thane said. "But only for a visit. Odin has transplanted us here. So we must accept it. It is his will."

Odin? What was he talking about? I sorted through knowledge read long ago in old textbooks and recalled the fact that Odin was the ancient Viking god...chief god of the Norsemen. Was he teasing? I cast a look at him and knew in my heart that he was not. His feverishly bright eyes were locked on items he now lifted. His huge hands drew up gold scabbards, weighty necklaces, ornaments marked with abstract plant and animal motifs. I glimpsed shimmers of light reflected from gold, gleams from precious gems.

"Don't you miss the old country?" he asked. His deep voice grew far-away, sad. "Someday soon we will go back to Sweden, the dark forests and lakes, to Norway, the mountains and fjords."

Images of Scandinavia created in him a sort of trance that intermingling with the firmly rooted unreality of his mind, placed him somewhere beyond reach.

He began chanting, voice rising and falling in low and eerie strains, so eerie an iciness settled over my heart.

"Odin, who put sun and moon in the sky, who endows me with life and soul, who gathers my broken body from the battlefield, God of all conquerors, subjugator of all who war against You..."

His words changed to Swedish or Norwegian, or to a strange mixture of the two. Instead of increasing in volume, they lowered. In the chant I felt the cruel isolation of Norway's peaks, the ice-cold water of the fjords, encasements of darkness and snow.

Thane had turned from me so I could see only the great width of his shoulders, the shaggy image of his raised head, the muscular arms rising toward the porous, black rock that made up the ceiling of the cave.

I edged away from him, horrified, my desire to see the crown abandoned in the face of this madness.

The Viking's voice, changing back and forth from hushed to shrill, echoed against the lava walls. My backward steps brought me to the stairway. I ran, stumbling, up the steps to the heavy doorway of the vault. I slipped outside and stopped short. My first thought was to slam the door shut, lift the rock as I had seen him do, close the lock and trap him inside! But why? He seemed so totally absent from my world!

The Viking's threat was something a closed door could not remedy. His delusions...I could not strike back at them; they loomed over me, hideous, unshakable, like some evil men.

A full moon glowed across upheavals of rock, magnifying their ghostly shapes and casting shadows. The Viking's haunting cries resounding across the volcanic mountainside prompted me to give way to both tears and the desire to run.

The uneven ground covered with jagged lava made footing precarious. I fell, caught myself, and rose, shaking my right hand, which had begun bleeding freely from the sharp impact of rock. The house would be north, through the trees. As I fled from the clearing into the forest area, the tears which had only appeared as a stinging in my eyes changed to sobs.

"Marta!" Ramon's commanding voice came from directly behind me. How could I have passed him without seeing him? I turned instinctively into his arms.

I clung to him, grateful for his saneness, his solidity. He held me tightly, not speaking, until I stopped shaking and my sobbing ceased.

Then he demanded angrily, "Did he harm you?"

I shook my head.

"What happened then? Why are you crying? Where did he take you?"

I started to tell Ramon about the cave filled with precious objects, about Thane's trance-like state, but I stopped myself. What if Ramon couldn't be trusted? What if he, like Alan, wanted possession of the Viking's jewels? I could not place Thane in such danger. I wanted in no way to add to his vulnerability. "He was trying to convince me that I am the Sun Maiden."

Ramon hesitated. "Is that all?"

"I believed at first he was only joking about that. But he isn't. Ramon, he is mad, stark, raving mad!"

Keeping his hands locked on my shoulders, Ramon drew me away from him. Moonlight illuminated his large, deep eyes, his thick, black hair, the dark line of mustache above his artfully-shaped lips. "You might drive anyone crazy," he said.

I expected him to pull me back into his arms and kiss me. For a moment, because of the dismay I felt, I actually wanted him to. His lips lowered until they almost touched mine, then, swiftly, he stepped back. "In a few days I will have papers for you and ship's passage back to New York."

The dark eyes that gazed into mine showed his reluctance to let me go. As if battling his own desires, he said, "You must leave the country. It is the only way I can guarantee your safety."

I thought of my life back in New York; the bustle of carriages and people, the three blocks I often walked to the museum to carry on my father's research. The life I had left such a short time ago no longer seemed to belong to me.

Ramon watched my expression alertly, his features tense and set, as if he were struggling between nobility and self-interest. Once again, as I did when I was certain Thane was going to show me the Viking Crown, I drew in my breath. Had Ramon fallen in love with me?

"What about Alan?" I could hear myself saying. "I can't leave the country without him."

A muscle tensed in Ramon's jaw. "He got himself into this mess. Let him get out of it. You must see to your own safety by getting out of Central America. I will help you get out of the country at the first opportunity," he promised. "Until then, you must stay close by my side."

* * *

The light of dawn, broken by barred windows, fell across the dark, ponderous furniture of my room. Restless dreams had been filled with scattered images...the Viking's glittering eyes, Alan, hunted, running from someone or something, Sanchez's leering face. The sleepless night had been filled with debating, and the same tormenting questions, upon waking, arose once more.

The Viking Crown...did such an item actually exist? Were the jewels and artifacts in the cave genuine? Thinking back over the short tour Thane had given me, I recalled how quickly he had guided me from object to object, not giving me time to study the objects or make any decisions about their authenticity.

I pictured myself back in New York City, without Father, without Alan. I made up my mind that I would not leave the country until I had spoken to Alan and convinced him to return with me. After dressing quickly, I passed through the vast emptiness of the dining room and went outside. The cold air made me less groggy. I wandered away from the door and stood listening to the birds, their sounds like fragile bells.

An old wagon with men riding on the back pulled in through the gate and clattered to a stop. The general stepped out, hurriedly up the walk, and stopped beside me.

"What are those birds?" I asked him after a period of silence.

"*Guardabarrancas*," he said. "The mountains are full of them."

"They sound very peaceful."

The general shrugged. "Life is not peaceful. Last night in Santa Augusta two men were shot. Political notes were pinned to their clothing." He paused. "Here all crimes are blamed on to politics, whether they are political or not."

"Did they catch the killers?" I asked with concern. "The police do not solve many crimes. These men were unknown to us. Trouble pours in from every direction. I must see the Viking."

After General Perez disappeared into the house, thinking I would sit for a while beside the fountain beneath my room, I started around the corner of the building. A deep voice, Ramon's voice, caused me to step back quickly, but not before I had glimpsed who Ramon was talking to. Sanchez, his leering, gap-toothed smile, the thin shoulders, the shiny, long hair knotted back with a cord...he looked exactly the way he had last night in my disturbed slumber. Why was Ramon talking to him so earnestly?

I could not understand what they were saying, but I remained motionless, listening. I heard Ramon distinctly speak the name Saville. Arnoldo...the man who had taken me to Alan...why would they be discussing him?

Their voices became louder as they approached. To avoid being seen, I ducked back through the front entrance into the

76

dining room.

The general was standing beside the dying fire pouring coffee from the huge, hanging pot. He seated himself leisurely in the big chair that was no doubt Thane's. "The Viking must be sleeping late," he said as his small, black eyes wandered me. "He is a man who does exactly what he pleases. To him," he held up his mug of coffee, "I drink many toasts."

"Why do you act as if he is sane?" I spoke bitterly. The leathery face, crisscrossed with deep lines, lost the big smile, but it appeared again after an interval of silence. "Robin Hood was not a bandit. Evelia's heart is as pretty as her face. Our leaders do not break promises. What makes the Vikings delusions of more consequence than our own?"

I sank into the chair opposite him. "Do you know Arnoldo Saville?"

Again the smile vanished.

"He is a priest in Santa Augusta," I explained.

He stared at the black liquid in his cup. "He is not a priest. Although he lives in more ways than one very close to the church."

"Is he a revolutionary?"

"Arnoldo is a champion of the oppressed!" The general's voice had a ring of the derogatory. "How did you meet him?"

"Alan spoke of him."

The general arranged mugs on the coffee table beside him as he spoke, "Arnoldo wants to get from here to there without taking all the little steps between."

"Is that wrong?"

"Is that possible?" The general settled back comfortably. His crossed legs showed boots of expensive, hand-tooled leather. "Arnoldo is young enough to be my son, but because he offers up his neck to every noose, I will outlive him." The general laughed. "Perhaps I will erect a statue for him, so we can all stand around it and say, 'Poor Arnoldo'!"

"Don't you agree with his ideas?"

He laughed again. "If I didn't agree with his ideas, why the statue?" The dying laugh left a smile that revealed something

77

unpleasant, a hint of corruption that had from the first caused me to mentally draw back.

"What I'm trying to tell you is that somewhere between the practical and the ideal is the real champion. I might suggest that I am that champion."

"Martyrs," I disagreed, "are the people who make the difference."

"Martyrs," the general said, "are people who are *dead*. The difference, my dear, is made by the rest of us."

"You mean men like Sanchez."

"You do not understand me! Sanchez is just a grubby little man who wants all he can get for himself. He would sell us both the same box of cigars!"

"I saw him outside a while ago. If he is so bad, what is he doing here?"

"The Viking is a generous man who really does fail to distinguish between good and evil. The Viking likes him. Sanchez is given the run of the place, just as if he were as good as me. The Viking probably thinks he is a valiant warrior. He does love a warrior. That is why we are such good friends. Do you want some coffee?"

"No, thank you."

The general took a long drink. "I warned him against Sanchez. Just the same way I warned the Viking to watch out for Alan Avery."

Again, the idea that Alan might have taken the medallion from Thane rose to mind, and I struggled to fight against it. "Has Alan done something to injure the Viking?"

"Sanchez and Avery are men of the same mold. They only dress and speak differently. But beneath," he tapped his chest, "They are identical. That is why I warned him."

"Alan is highly respected."

The general roared with laughter. "I wouldn't trust him with my coffee beans!"

"Archaeology is a very difficult field. Alan has taught and lectured all over the east coast."

"In Central America we don't admire lecturers." Black eyes sparkled from their crinkled surroundings. "We like medals." Gold and brass clambered as he opened his jacket. "The Viking is very impressed with these." Francisco Perez paused a long while before going on. "In Central America we admire generals. That is why everyone here who wants to be somebody calls himself a general."

Chapter Six

The Viking stepped into the room, a smile on his face, blue eyes glowing. "Marta, I have a surprise for you!"

Francisco Perez spoke with humorous slowness, "I'd be wary of the Viking's surprises."

"Oh, but Marta will like this. I've arranged for her to spend the day at Telas." He turned to me to further explain, "You will ride with Ramon. He is to meet a man at the old Spanish hotel who is interested in viewing parts of my collection. Telas is a beautiful village by the sea. The beaches there are lovely. I'm sure you will enjoy the view."

"I'm not interested in sightseeing," I said firmly.

"But our beaches are the most beautiful in the world," the general encouraged, his smile widening, deepening the crinkles about his eyes.

"I'm sure you are right. But I have obligations." I cast a hopeful glance at the general. "Perhaps I could ride out with you this morning. I must make arrangements to leave Honduras to-day."

The general shrugged his big shoulders, as if whether or not I stayed or left made no difference to him, but he made no offer of assistance.

"Leaving?" Thane responded, puzzled. "Why do you want to leave? Your destiny is to stay here!"

The general responded with a laconic laugh. The shrewd eyes beneath heavy lids displayed amusement, as if he found Thane's delusion that I was some sort of Viking princess vastly entertaining.

80

"If you insist on going back to New York, it can be arranged," Thane spoke finally, his voice slightly hurt. His eyes searched mine pleadingly. "But for now, can't you enjoy this beautiful country just for a single day?" His voice became coaxing. "Once you see Honduras's magnificent shoreline, I'm sure you will never want to leave."

"Thane is right." Ramon suddenly appeared at the doorway, black hair shining, brown guard's uniform perfectly fit, boots neatly polished. "Come with me now, Marta, and you won't regret it. The carriage is ready and waiting."

My eyes locked with Ramon's. I felt a dizzy surge of joy. Surely, this was the opportunity he had spoken about last night! He was going to help me escape!

Enthused by the prospect of leaving, I forced myself to look away from Ramon, back to the Viking. "Perhaps you are right, Thane. I will see the coast."

"You will love it!" the Viking exclaimed with delight. "Everyone is captivated by Telas!"   "Are you ready?" Ramon asked.

I glanced down at the dress I wore...the plain, blue one of Evelia's, slightly faded, flared at the waist and embroidered at the loose, round neck and full sleeves with worn, white floral designs. As if reading my thoughts, Ramon said, "You're dressed fine for a day at the village."

"I must go up to my room," I said, planning to gather my father's notes, which I did not want to leave behind.

Ramon nodded. "I'll be waiting.

I quickly gathered up my father's papers and the few things that belonged to me. I would see that Evelia's dress was returned to her later. I would also send one of New York's newest designs to her once I got back to the States.

"What are you doing with that?" Thane asked as I came down the stairs, bag in hand.

"I am bringing some art supplies. I might want to make some sketches of the seascape," I replied.

"An excellent idea!" he said, satisfied by my explanation.

"Bring us back some shells," called the general with one of his exuberant laughs.

The Viking insisted on following us outside to the carriage. He leaned closer to Ramon to speak in private, conspiratorial tone, "Ramon, you know what I want you to do," were his last words as we drove away.

The words rang ominously in my ears. What did he mean by them? Was there some other mission to Ramon's trip besides meeting the man who wanted to view Thane's collection? As the carriage moved past the oppressive gates of the solemn stone walls surrounding the Viking's huge estate, I felt light-hearted and free. Then, I chanced to look back at Thane. He stood watching us leave, and the sight of his standing there alone caused a peculiar twist in my heart, an unexpected pang of sympathy for his delusions. I was leaving now; I could afford to be generous. Impulsively, I raised my hand in farewell.

He lifted his own arm high in the air in answer. He looked a little pathetic, waiting there for some non-existent princess. For all of his madness, he had been kind to me. More than kind...he had adored me, worshipped me as the ghost or reincarnation of his Viking princess. I thought about how disappointed he would be when Ramon returned this evening without me. I was surprised to feel a little sadness at the thought that I would never see him...or Ramon...ever again.

And yet, of course, it had to be! "How long will it take us to get to Puerto Lorenzo?" Plans filled my mind, returning me to reality, quelling my moment of elusive sadness. Once Ramon left me at the port, I would contact the missionary and his wife that I had met on the ship and tell them of my plight. Surely, they would take me in and help me to locate Alan!

A muscle flickered at the corner of Ramon's mouth. His eyes turned flat and hard, as if preparing himself for the argument that was to follow. "We're not going to Puerto Lorenzo."

Ramon's words were like cold water dashed into my face. I waited, but he offered no explanation. His features might have been carved from stone. "Then where are you taking me?" "We are going to Telas, as planned."

82

"But you promised to help me leave at the first opportunity!" Crushed, I added, "Surely the opportunity is here. Today!"

He turned his face away from me, toward the reins. I studied his rock-hard profile, the firm, strong line of his nose and chin, the eyes which had become suddenly shadowed and obscure. "I will have to wait and make it look as if I am not involved in your leaving. I must be able to return."

"Do you enjoy so much being a guard for that...madman," I mocked, "that you obey his every whim like some simple, obedient servant?"

I saw a spark of temper in his eyes, a flash of pride, as if I had struck a nerve.

I tried to keep my voice from quivering. "You never intended to help me," I challenged. "It was all a lie!"

The proud lift to his head made Ramon look more than ever like some arrogant Spanish lord. In an icy voice, he responded, "If you knew me better you would know I never go back on my word."

But I didn't know him. He was a total stranger to me. In my desperation, I had read qualities in him, emotions of empathy, kindness, and understanding that simply did not exist! I turned away from him, trying to hide the tears that burned against my eyelids.

"Marta." Softly, he spoke my name. "I haven't been able to get your travel papers yet, but I will," he promised solemnly. "You must believe me. When the time is right, I will help you leave." Firmly, he added, "But I won't allow you to risk your life running around Honduras alone, searching for Alan, which is exactly what you intend to do."

"We could look for Alan today," I persisted stubbornly. "Together. You could take me to him." His impatience returned, and I felt hurt by the sharpness in his voice, "Did it ever occur to you that Alan may not be worth looking for?"

Almost against my will, my gaze returned to Ramon's profile, handsome and determined, then dropped to the gun always partially concealed beneath his jacket. Why had I ever imagined he would help me? What good was the word of a man who was being paid to be my bodyguard, whose sole function seemed to be to prevent my escape?

For a long time we rode in silence. Feeling as if my last hope were gone, I once more turned my face away from him.

"Telas isn't far," he said, ignoring my angry silence. "Only a two-hour ride. We'll follow the ocean most of the way. Soon you'll be able to catch a glimpse of the sea."

The jungle area thinned as the carriage trail edged toward outcroppings of tan rock. Like magic, the irregular edges of a jagged coastline appeared. Through partings in the trees, I felt warm sunlight, caught sight of the glimmer of the pale, blue waves of the Caribbean. The sight of crystal blue water and bone-white sand lifted my spirits. The scenery was so beautiful that, for a moment, I almost forgot my anger, turned to Ramon, and smiled.

I marveled at how quickly the scenery could change from jungle to mountains to sea. The area we traveled was isolated, but interspersed with small settlements of thatched huts.

Despite myself, I felt a stirring of interest as Ramon pointed out sights of interest along the way.

"We are on the outskirts of a banana plantation," he said. People seemed to appear out of nowhere from the jungle wilderness; men working in the groves; women tending children or washing clothes by small streams.

Down by the wharf, huge bunches of bananas were piled high upon a small, floating platform surrounded by little boats. A man in wide-brimmed hat dozed upon wooden planks in the shade of his banana cargo.

"Bananas are Honduras' gold," Ramon explained. "The bananas are shipped green. Small boats will take the cargo from this plantation to Puerto Lorenzo, where it will be transported upon huge American ships."

We still spoke little, but the lapses of silence were companionable as new sights and the brightness of the day worked to erode my anger.

"Telas is just ahead," Ramon said. "You can see the old Spanish hotel high upon the cliff." In the distance, a sleepy little village burrowed against the shelter of high peaks. I felt renewed interest at the sight of cobbled streets, and adobe houses with roofs of bright red tile. High upon the hillside I saw the bare outlines of a turreted building that looked like a stone monastery.

"In the 1600's, the Spanish Hotel was a mission. For a time in this century, it also served as a presidential palace. Now, guests from America and Europe as well as Hondurans stay there. Most of the guests who stay at the hotel, like Thane, are immeasurably wealthy."

"Who is this man we are going to see?"

"An art collector from the States by the name of Gavin Bertram. He wants to arrange a meeting with Thane to view his private collection."

"Thane refused to show the collection to Alan," I said, remembering his disappointment at being denied sight of anything more than a few pieces of pottery. "Why would he show it to Bertram?"

"He may not," Ramon replied skeptically. "This Bertram may get no further than Alan."

The village was surrounded on one side by green mountains and on the other by impenetrable sea. The road we were on was now shared by cart and burro, barefoot women carrying huge vases upon their heads, a peasant in serape balancing a huge wooden contraption of caged birds upon his shoulders.

"Telas is a very isolated village," Ramon explained. "We are lucky to be able to reach it by carriage. During heavy rains, when the few roads wash out, it can be reached only by mule or boat. Besides a few coconut plantations that survived the last hurricane, nothing lies beyond the village but miles and miles of uninhabited coastline."

"I wouldn't expect to find a grand hotel out here in the middle of nowhere. Doesn't the isolation discourage visitors?

"Many find its inaccessibility intriguing. Telas is an outpost of sorts, a stopping place for explorers anxious to penetrate the unknown world of the jungle beyond. You'll find a variety of people here, as well as goods of every kind." As we approached the village, Ramon seemed carefree, almost happy. "Telas is a very interesting place."

The village dozed in late morning sunlight. The poverty of simple thatched huts gave way to adobe houses. We moved along a wide avenue flanked on either side by sun-baked adobe buildings whose tiled roofs shone in the warm sunlight. Flowers grew along walkways, lining the main avenue with thin-petaled mountain blossoms of white, yellow and blue.

Great white stone steps rose from the edge of the main avenue to form a steep, cobbled trail up to the grand hotel. Instead of taking the way up to the hotel, Ramon slowed the carriage in front of one of the adobe buildings.

"Why are we stopping here?" Bright bolts of material, ready-made cotton shifts and skirts displayed at the window identified it as a dressmaker's shop.

"You'll see," Ramon said, turning to me with sudden good spirits. He helped me down from the carriage and took my arm. I was aware of his handsomeness, the way the darkness of his eyes contrasted with the brightness of his smile.

"We're going shopping?"

"You'll need a dress for the fiesta," Ramon said, humor dancing in his eyes.

"What are you talking about?"

"The Viking is at this very moment planning a huge party in your honor, Princess Marta. He's had this seamstress and her girls working day and night to design you a beautiful dress. He has instructed me to stop by and pick it up today."

The thought of my now inevitable return to the Viking's delusive world made my resentment toward Ramon surge back even stronger. Any lightness of mood broken, I responded, "Then the Viking is sorely mistaken. I'm not attending any party." I turned, prepared to walk past the shop.

Strong, white teeth flashed as Ramon laughed. His mustache made his smile seem mocking as he caught up with me. He reached out and tucked my arm in his. I felt the strength of his body beside me, a subtle reminder that I was in his custody, and he was not about to let me get away. Not that there would be any place to

86

escape to, in this isolated mountain village, trapped as it was between mountains and sea. The knowledge renewed my sense of defiance, and I glared hotly at him.

"I've always heard a new dress lifts a woman's spirits." Still smiling, Ramon guided me into the dressmaker's shop. "Let's see if it is true."

At the entrance to the shop, I stopped to warn Ramon. "I don't want a dress. I won't take anything from him!"

He considered me thoughtfully. "Let's just go in and take a look at it. Maybe when you see this dazzling creation you will change your mind."

"I won't," I insisted.

A plump, dark-haired woman in multi-colored skirts approached us, greeting Ramon as if she were expecting him. Ramon and she began to talk rapidly and earnestly in Spanish. Nodding and smiling, she disappeared into a small, adjoining room. She returned with both arms full of clothing.

"It seems Thane has commissioned Maria to fashion you an entire wardrobe," Ramon said, amused. "She and her daughters are very skilled. They make dresses for Evelia and for Lucia, the general's wife."

The village woman began to place gowns upon the counter. Without trying them, I knew they would be a perfect fit. Since Evelia and I were of a size, Thane must have instructed her to use one of Evelia's dresses as a pattern to fashion clothing for me!

Proudly, she displayed the frocks, one at a time, for my approval...a day dress of pale pink trimmed with beaded black fringe; a bengaline dress of light and dark blue stripes. My attention was attracted to the prettiest of the three, a lilac silk suitable for special occasions, trimmed in white ribbon, with matching hat and gloves. I glanced down at the borrowed dress of Evelia's. The idea of having something new to wear was tempting. Yet I could not bring myself to accept anything from Thane. With great power of will, I shook my head. "I don't need any clothing."

The seamstress disappeared once more into the storeroom, leaving Ramon and I alone together. "Marta," Ramon said. "If you won't accept anything from Thane, then accept these dresses as a gift from me ...to ease my conscience. I feel I owe it to you...for the trunk of yours that was lost."

Before I could answer, the dressmaker returned with a beautiful, emerald ball gown draped at the shoulder and waist with folds of shimmering gold lace. I gasped sharply at the sight of the material...it was by far the most beautifully designed garment I had ever seen! The dress of my dreams...and made especially for me! "I don't want it." I turned away, hiding a sudden, wistful pang from Ramon's dark, observant eyes.

I stood stiffly as Ramon took the gown from the dressmaker and, ignoring my protests, held it up to me. "I tell you, you're wasting your time..."

The cut was perfect, the cloth shimmered like a pool of emerald water against my skin and hair. I felt a little shiver as Ramon's hands moved my long hair, draping the material around my shoulders.

"I know this dress will please the Viking!" Ramon's smile was playful as his gaze lingered over the folds of emerald and golden lace, but his eyes had grown dark with longing. "It certainly pleases me!"

"I won't have it!" Angrily I slipped away from him and stood by the open doorway. As I watched, a skinny dog searching for food wandered from a narrow alley. My gaze followed his journey, shocked by the sights that suddenly filled my eyes.

What a charming place Telas had seemed at first glance, until my gaze chanced to wander beyond the red-tiled roofs and colorful flowers of the main walkway.

The sight of ramshackle huts, poorer than any of the villages we had passed, made me realize that the attractive main street of Telas was but a facade, a front no doubt maintained for the wealthy guests who frequented the hotel. A glance down that dismal side street gave views of filthy shacks, pitiful slums, rotting piles of garbage. A beggar child, shoeless and dirty, emerged to stand for a moment in my view before disappearing like a wraith into dark shadows of the alley.

Ramon spoke, drawing my attention back inside the shop. I turned away from the entrance to hear him say, "I have told her you will not accept the dress."

Out of the corner of my eye, I saw the hurt and crestfallen look of the dressmaker, who thought I was displeased with her handiwork. She and her daughters has obviously spent long hours on the dresses. The pride that had shone in her eyes told me that the exquisite green ball gown was probably her best work...her pride and joy.

"Please, Ramon. Try to explain to her."

He nodded. I listened to Ramon and the dressmaker exchange words of Spanish. Though I could not understand what he was saying, his words brought immediate results. I was relieved to see her injured expression gradually change to one of acceptance, even amusement.

"It's settled," Ramon said. "Fortunately, there is a way to compromise with no loss to anyone."

"Thank you." I said. I guessed that he had suggested she sell the dresses to another patron, probably Evelia, who would delight in new dresses and was so near my own size. The dressmaker looked over and smiled at me. Although I was glad the matter had been settled without loss to her or injury of her feelings, I felt a slight tinge of regret at the thought of how beautiful Evelia would look in the green ball gown designed for me. I could not keep my gaze from wandering to it one last time.

"There is still a chance to change your mind," Ramon said.

Firmly, I shook my head. "My mind is made up."

"Perhaps you should at least take the lilac day dress," he suggested. His hand lifted the pale lilac dress with matching hat and gloves. "Formal attire is expected in the hotel dining room. I keep a change of clothing at the hotel for such meetings." His gaze swept over the simple dress of faded blue cotton that I wore, as if speculating what reaction my casual attire might bring. "I am concerned that you will suffer embarrassment. Won't you reconsider?"

"No."

Ramon released the silk dress from his grasp and let it fall back with the others. "As you wish." He added with teasing smile, "I must admit, I was hoping you would change into that beautiful dress for our dinner appointment this afternoon. What a pleasure it would be to escort you!"

I raised my chin to meet his amused black eyes. "If you insist, I will accompany you while you dine with this Mr. Bertram at his fancy hotel. And if it is your desire, you may wear a coat and tails. But I will wear just what I have on."

With a laugh, Ramon conceded, "As you wish, my princess!"

*　*　*

The steep ride up winding, cobbled street to the hotel might have taken us into another world. Not even New York's finest inns, where Alan or my father has sometimes taken me, could match the opulence of the elegant dining room. I glanced around at the wealthy guests in their Paris creations, and actually feared that we might be refused entry.

The poverty I had glimpsed in the village made the excess within the hotel, the red velvet draperies, the gilt-edged mirrors and candle-lit chandeliers reflecting tables set with sparkling crystal and silver, seem wasteful, decadent, unnecessary extravagance in the face of such extreme need. I noticed how the headwaiter's eyes swept curiously, but without change in expression, from Ramon's uniform to my simple dress and bare hands. With a wave of his hand, he dismissed Ramon in perfect English, "You may wait in the back while Madam dines."

I felt a moment of embarrassment for Ramon, and wished that I had heeded his advice about our changing clothes. Undaunted at being mistaken for my valet, Ramon took my arm in his and stepped forward. "We'd like a table for two," he said.

"Very well." The maitre d', brow arched slightly, ushered us into the dining room. He began to look for an obscure place to seat us.

"That table...the one by the window," Ramon insisted, pointing to the best seats in the house, a highly visible spot with a lovely view of the sea.

"I'm afraid that's not possible."

"Why isn't it possible?" Ramon demanded. "It looks empty to me."

"That table is reserved," the maitre d' responded with a haughty, superior look. "It is Thane Ulrickson's table."

"And we are his guests," Ramon told him. The headwaiter's shocked expression caused the sparkle in Ramon's dark eyes to intensify. "A party of three. Gavin Bertram will be joining us."

The Viking's name, as on other occasions, caused immediate attention. With new respect, as if we were dripping in diamonds and jewels, the maitre d' promptly escorted us to the table of Ramon's choice, smoothing the bright linen himself and pulling out the heavy wooden chairs.

"Come with me, Princess Marta." Turning back to me with a charming smile, Ramon said, "Our table awaits us."

I glanced around the room, seeing women in fancy gowns, men wearing formal black attire, or decorative uniforms, and felt immediately ill at ease. The patrons, American, European, as well as native Hondurans, were obviously all people of wealth and status. "Where is this Bertram?" I asked Ramon.

"Don't worry. He will join us shortly. "No wealthy collector would pass up an opportunity to view the Viking's mysterious treasures."

"This place...I've never seen such wealth. It makes me uncomfortable."

"You get used to it," Ramon replied. A dark look momentarily crossed his face. "The contrast between the rich and poor is a fact of life in our country."

The waiter brought a sweet wine. As we sipped our drinks, Ramon's good spirits returned, and we exchanged light banter. But I remained uneasy. At the next table sat a party of four. An elegant woman dressed in high-collared black silk and pearls kept sneaking surreptitious glances at us.

Like the haughty maitre d', she raised a censorious brow as if wondering what right we had to be at Thane's exclusive table. She sniffed at Ramon as if he were a penniless beggar who had wandered in from the village. Then her glance fell upon me, condemning with a look my windblown hair, the borrowed dress with the low-cut bodice that all Evelia's dresses seemed to favor. Why, she was looking at me as if I were a common woman of the streets! With a flush, I turned my face away from her to stare down at the spotless white table linen.

"What is wrong, Marta?"

"I'm afraid I'm not dressed for the occasion," I confided miserably. Lines of humor appeared around Ramon's mouth and eyes, but to his credit, he made no mention of the lilac silk I had so stubbornly refused to wear.

My gaze slipped back to the nearby table. The woman had leaned forward to titter to her companions, who now also regarded us with the same condescending air, as if we had no right to be among them.

"My father always taught me to hate snobbery of any kind," I said. "But I don't think I've ever hated it as much as I do at this moment."

"Pay them no mind." Sensitive to my feelings of discomfort, his hand suddenly reached across the table to cover mine. "They are only jealous...because I am with the most beautiful woman in this room."

I gazed into Ramon's dark eyes rimmed with thick lashes and felt a sense of closeness to him. It must be the atmosphere of the moment, I thought, that made Ramon, in his humble guard's uniform, seem the most desirable escort in the hotel. For a moment, he seemed not my guard at all, not a man I was forced to be with, but a chosen companion, a friend.

"Whatever Thane's shortcomings, you cannot accuse him of snobbery," Ramon said. "He treats all people as equals...the rich the poor, the good and the evil." A pensive look momentarily flickered across his face. "In the end, I fear his generosity of spirit will cost him dearly."

"What do you mean?"

"His association with...men like this Gavin Bertram...is not wise." He spoke of the man we were soon to meet with the same distaste that he had spoken of Alan, a certain hatred for self-seeking greed which he expected to find in Bertram. Yet Alan's desire to see Thane's collection was purely for unselfish reasons...to find evidence to support my father's theory. Surely, he did not place Alan in the same category as that of some opportunistic private collector.

Still, Alan must have sought Thane out in much the same manner as this Bertram. His search for Viking relics must have eventually brought him here to Telas and this hotel. "Were you the one who met Alan here?"

"Yes." Ramon's response was brief, almost curt, as if unwilling to discuss Alan.

Remembering Alan's desperate flight from Ramon, I wondered once more if Alan had removed something...the medallion-- from Thane's collection. Did Ramon feel responsible for a theft that had occurred as a result of his bringing Alan to Thane's estate? Once more, I was tempted to believe that Alan might have stolen some relic from the Viking, yet my heart rebelled against the idea of Alan becoming a thief in the name of my father's goal. Surely, it could not be true. "Are you certain Alan did not see any of Thane's collection?"

"To my knowledge, no one has ever seen the Viking's collection," Ramon responded.

I wondered what Ramon's reaction would be if he knew that Thane had taken me out to the caves. I remembered the cavernous, black-walled room filled with statues and art objects, the shimmering jewels that Thane insisted were part of the lost princess's dowry. If I had not fled in fear, frightened by Thane's delusions, by the glittering madness in his eyes, would he have shown me the Viking Crown?

Curiosity made me press on, wanting to find out more about Ramon, and his relationship to the Viking. "Do you think the treasures Thane always speaks of are real?"

"No one has ever seen the Viking Crown yet!" His response

was light, but Ramon's expression had become suddenly thoughtful, solemn. "But, yes, the treasures are very real...real to him, at least."

"If they are real only to him, then he must be crazy." How much could one trust the words of Thane Ulrickson, a man with so little contact with the real world? The thought slipped back into my mind that the items I had seen in the cave could all have been clever forgeries, created or commissioned by Thane himself, an attempt to add substance to his fantasies.

"Don't be fooled. Thane Ulrickson is both crazy and clever."

"How long have you worked for him?"

"Not long." He hesitated. "I had been living in La Ceiba."

"Did you grow up there?" I asked, genuinely wanting to know more about him. "Is your family from there?"

A shadow fell across Ramon's face. The mention of his past caused a resistance, as firm as a door closing.

"I still don't understand why you work for Thane."

"I suppose I am attracted to his idealism. He reminds me of someone...a man who had a great influence in my life when I was just a boy.

"Who was this man?"

For a silent moment his eyes held mine. I did not know whether he would have answered or not because we were interrupted at that moment by the sound of a voice announcing with a sharp impatience that demanded immediate attention, "I'm Gavin Bertram."

The look he gave Ramon was superior; his clipped voice condescending. As I studied the thin face and narrow, long-bridged nose, the prominent Adam's apple visible through fine silk cravat, I wished that I could have sent Bertram to join the snobbish party at the next table. His imperious manner caused my first impression of him to be one of instant dislike, though my judgment of him was hasty and perhaps unfair.

"Isn't this Mr. Ulrickson's table? I was supposed to meet him here."

Ramon stood to greet him. "I'm afraid Mr. Ulrickson couldn't get away. He sent me. I'm Ramon Santiago." He turned to intro duce me. "And this is Miss Swan."

Bertram looked annoyed. A waiter rushed over, anxious to attend him. Bertram finally accepted a chair and sat down. The waiter continued to hover nearby.

Bertram glanced at Ramon. "Why don't you order for all of us?" he suggested, as if Ramon were a mere servant. The wave of his hand made the heavy ring on his finger, diamonds set in pale silver the exact shade of his thinning hair, glitter. "I have trouble getting these people to understand me."

Ramon ordered for us, and the waiter promptly disappeared.

Mr. Bertram, evidently not a man given to small talk, cut right to the point. "I've heard this Ulrickson has quite a collection." His words told me the rumors of Thane's treasures had spread through important circles. "I'm anxious to make some purchases. Mayan artifacts have become all the rage in the States, you know. I own one of the more exclusive antique shops in New York."

"I'm from New York, also," I said. Bertram glanced at me as if noticing me for the first time. "My father was Dr. James Swan."

A parade of silver-domed dishes arrived at our table...steamy soup followed by fresh bread and tortillas and plates of fresh fruit and cheese.

"I've heard of Dr. Swan," Bertram said, spreading butter upon his bread. Bringing the topic back to what interested him, he added, "The work of your father and other archaeologists has created a wave of interest in Mayan art. Everyone who is some-body wants a piece of the Mayan culture to display in their parlor. Statues from Copan and other sites are bringing top dollar...I'm getting prices comparable to mummified hands and other Egyptian artifacts people are so mad about these days."

"Like Egypt, Central America is slowly being plundered," Ramon said tersely.

Bertram's boastful words had caused an inward shudder, and I felt inclined to agree with Ramon. How Father would have hated the idea of exploitation being an end product of his work. He would have been saddened by the thought of objects from the sites he had uncovered, items that should be in museums, disappearing into wealthy drawing rooms and private collections.

Ignoring Ramon's remark, Bertram directed his next question to me. "Have you seen Ulrickson's collection?"

"My friend Alan has seen parts of it," I said. "Some Copador vases he believes are authentic."

A look I recognized...greed, like I had read in Sanchez's face...lit his gray-flecked eyes as he said directly to Ramon, "I was told Mr. Ulrickson could show me something...rare."

Ramon met his gaze with sudden coldness. "Mr. Ulrickson has agreed to let you come to the estate. Beyond that, I can't make any promises."

Chapter Seven

The main course arrived, a huge fish baked in banana leaves. "The local specialty," Ramon said.

"It looks delicious!" Bertram exclaimed, unexpectedly appreciative.

As we dined, my attention was suddenly diverted by the appearance of three well-dressed gentlemen at the entrance to the dining room. Dark jackets of fine velvet decorated with medals and braided epaulets proved them to be high officials of some kind.

"Don Orlando's men," Bertram explained, noticing my interest, as I watched the three men be seated at a table near the doorway.

"Orlando is in town?" I noticed a sense of alarm in Ramon's carefully-controlled expression, an element of being taken by surprise that he could not quite conceal.

"He's staying here at the hotel. He arrived rather unexpectedly last night. This afternoon, he's planning to give a speech in the village square before traveling back to Santa Augusta. The election is coming up soon, you know."

"It should be interesting," Bertram continued as he speared at his portion of fish. "Some of Carranza's men arrived this morning, so both sides are represented. And that means trouble."

Bertram indicated another table in the opposite corner of the room, where a man, obese and ostentatiously dressed, with round, florid face and large nose, sat surrounded by several companions. "That's Martinez, one of Carranza's "finger generals." Look at him! Corrupt as he is fat! See how he loves to eat?"

"What's a finger general?"

"Being a Yankee, I don't claim to know much about Central

American politics, but I can tell you that, " Bertram said with a shrewd laugh. "When a new man gets into power, he points to his friends and he says, 'you're a general, you're a general and you're a general....'" He spread out the fingers of his hand. "And there you have...five new generals."

His explanation made me think of Thane's friend, General Perez. Was he a real general? If so, whose general was he...or did his allegiance belong solely to Thane Ulrickson and his imaginary kingdom?

For a long time Ramon had remained silent. I turned to find him watching the area near the entrance where Don Orlando's men sat. At first I thought it was dislike of Bertram that made Ramon speak so little, then I realized that his tense watchfulness instead was associated with the entrance of the three newcomers and the knowledge that Don Orlando was in town.

"Since Barrios died, things have gone to hell down here," Bertram said. "I was here a few months ago, and you could almost feel the tension in the air. They say Orlando is almost certain to win the election." Though I could not bring myself to like Bertram, I was beginning to admire his shrewd interest in every subject, from antiquities to politics.

"From what I've heard, he would make a good president," I said.

"If he ever gets to *be* president. The elections here aren't like the ones back home," Bertram explained. "There is no real democracy. Votes are freely rigged. The word is that Carranza doesn't intend to be ousted. If he can't get rid of Orlando before the election, or win the election by legal or illegal means, he plans to take over by force."

"What is his opponent, Carranza, like?" I asked Bertram. "Have you ever seen him?"

"A fighter. Lean...dour looking. Battle-scarred." His description put me in mind of Sanchez, causing an involuntary shiver course up and down my spine. I glanced over at the corpulent "finger general" stuffing himself in the corner. The men who surrounded him, despite their fine clothing, looked shady and sinister, reminded me in some way of Sanchez's band of ruffians.

"Why do people support him instead of Orlando?"

"Orlando is a rich man," Bertram hastened to explain. "They say he does not know what it is like to be poor." Addressing Ramon as if he were a lowly servant, he added, "Isn't that right, Santiago?"

"Carranza was born a poor man." Ramon responded in an evenly-spaced tone that belied the proud anger in his eyes. "Yet sudden wealth has corrupted him. Orlando promises for my people realistic changes: better wages, roads, and education."

"Yes," Bertram conceded with arched brow, "but Carranza promises them the only thing peasants can understand...gold."

"The only one that will see wealth is Carranza himself." Ramon said.

"Word is, Orlando will have the presidency," Bertram said. "That is, if Carranza doesn't put a bullet in his back before he has a chance to take office." Bertram laughed wryly at his own cynical observation.

Bertram's talk made me think of the rag-tag army building in the hills around Thane's estate, evidence that an uprising was brewing. The thought that Carranza intended to take power, one way or another, made me feel frightened and uneasy.

The country stood balanced at the edge of internal war, yet inside the hotel, Carranza's men and Orlando's dined in the same room, and the sense of everyday life and normalcy made the prospect of revolution seem remote and far away. Bertram was going to go on, but the waiter appeared to clear away the plates and bring steaming coffee in demitasse cups and a platter of dessert pastries.

The waiter soon returned. He leaned close to Ramon and spoke in Spanish. Whatever he said caused Ramon's expression to become serious and intent. Ramon rose with the sudden scrape of his chair against the tiled floor. "You must excuse me. A problem has come up. Something urgent."

"What? Where are you going, Santiago? We're not finished making arrangements..."

"This matter must take care of at once." He addressed Bertram with an air of command that caught the other man off guard. "You two must stay right here until I get back. Don't leave Miss Swan for a single minute! I want your word on that!"

Unable to recover from his surprise, Bertram gave a cold nod of assent.

"I will return for you as soon as possible, Marta." Ramon's eyes, dark and shadowed, had filled with a frightening sense of purpose that alarmed me.

My gaze held to Ramon's tall, straight form as he moved away.

"What kind of urgent mission could Ulrickson's man have?" Unaccustomed to taking orders, Bertram added in a tone that belied his resentment, "Rather overbearing for someone of his position. If I were this Ulrickson, I'd have him dismissed."

I barely listened to Bertram's words, for I was noting how Ramon deliberately bypassed the table where Don Orlando's men sat. Almost, I thought, as if he did not want to be recognized. I watched until he disappeared through the huge doorway that led out into the lobby.

"I believe we have a mutual friend," Bertram said, turning to me. He seemed more relaxed now that Ramon was gone and business taken care of, more amiable. "Alan Avery. He's spoken of you to me...and of your father."

"You know Alan?" I said, brightening at the thought. "Yes, I met him right here at the hotel. On my last trip. A few months ago. Alan was very enthused about seeing Mr. Ulrickson's collection. I haven't been able to contact him, so I decided to get in touch with Ulrickson instead, since I'll be returning to the States soon. I'm anxious to see his artifacts." Bertram sipped coffee from the tiny, china cup. "You're a guest of Ulrickson's, aren't you?"

I hesitated. "I've been staying at the estate."

With eagerness he questioned, "Have you seen the Mayan ruins upon the cliffs? Avery told me he'd heard of interesting drawings within the ruins, carved ships that he thought might be some ancient recording of a Viking voyage to this area."

"The ruins overlook the ocean. The climb is very steep. I've never been close enough to them to get a good look. Thane probably told Alan about them and added his own interpretation."

"I'd like to see them when I come to the estate tomorrow afternoon. Then, I'm ready to go back home to my wife." While Bertram had been curt with Ramon, he spoke to me in the manner of a peer, someone from his own country and background. Now, he smiled fondly at the thought of the wife he had left at home. "She wanted to come with me, but she's very delicate, just can't bear to travel. You must meet her when you're back in New York. You'll have to visit our shop."

Bertram's unexpected friendliness made me wonder if I should confide in him. I wanted so much to ask for his help! Surely Bertram would agree to assist me in getting away from Ramon! But where could I go in this isolated village where Ramon wouldn't immediately find me?

Bertram leaned closer to me, lowering his voice in the manner of one about ready to make a confession. "It's not Mayan artifacts I'm really interested in. There are plenty of those around for the buying. Because you are Dr. Swan's daughter, you will know what I am talking about." His pale eyes glittering and intent, he said, "I've been told Ulrickson might have some genuine Viking relics."

I thought about the treasures I had seen in the Thane's cave and wondered again if they were real. "It could be only local rumor I said hesitantly.

"Alan Avery thinks they are real," he insisted. "Have you seen Alan?"

"Yes, but we didn't have a chance to talk."

"He's probably on his way back to the States. I'll be sailing back to New York myself in a few days. When do you plan to return?"

Taking a deep breath, I responded, "I may need your help getting back there."

Bertram arched his brow, as if not certain that he had heard me correctly. "What did you say?"

I glanced nervously around the room to make sure Ramon had not returned. "I'm being held at Thane Ulrickson's estate against my will."

Bertram looked uneasy, then skeptical. "How could Ulrickson possibly be holding you against your will?"

I explained briefly how I had been left stranded by my guide, and how I was taken by Ramon to the Viking's house. "And now I am without money and travel papers," I finished. "And Thane refuses to let me leave."

"You are here today..."

"But not unescorted." My voice lowered to a whisper. I looked quickly around, half-expecting Ramon to return at any moment. "Everywhere I go, Thane sends a guard with me. He says that it is for my protection, because of the political unrest. But it is really to prevent me from getting away."

"You could leave now."

"But where could I go in this small, isolated village? Ramon would find me without the least trouble."

"It's hard to believe a man like Thane Ulrickson is keeping you prisoner."

Realizing how preposterous my story sounded, I tried to further explain, "Thane Ulrickson isn't like other people. He is convinced I am someone else, someone that is not even real!"

Bringing up the hint of the supernatural was a mistake. The glint of doubt in Bertram's eyes glowed brighter, became coldly cynical, as if it were my own sanity he questioned.

"I know how unbelievable this all sounds, but it is true." I could feel tears rise to the surface of my eyes. I quickly brushed them away. "I don't expect you to understand. You don't have to. Just help me! I will never get away from him if you don't!"

"This meeting with Ulrickson means a lot to me. I must not do anything to jeopardize my chance of viewing his collection." Bertram considered me with a long, skeptical look. I noticed a sudden change in expression, as if he read into my words some advantage to himself. "I must admit, I can't begin to comprehend your situation," he said finally. "But there's no reason why, when my business with Ulrickson is done, you couldn't leave with me."

"It won't be that easy. He won't just let me leave."

"We'll think of some way."

"You could take me to Puerto Lorenzo. That is all I ask. I know a couple there who would help me."

"Don't worry. I won't just leave a fellow American stranded down here. As soon as I've spoken to Ulrickson, I'll take you away in my hired carriage. We'll go straight to Puerto Lorenzo."

I leaned back in my chair. "I don't know how to thank you."

His rejoinder suggested a way and revealed to me how seldom he missed an opportunity. "When we get back to the States, you can stop by my shop. I have some items I'd like the daughter of Dr. James Swan to authenticate."

Almost half an hour had passed, and still Ramon did not return. Watching the entrance for sight of him, I saw Don Orlando's three finely-dressed men leave the room.

"Orlando must be getting ready to make his speech. What the devil do you suppose is keeping Santiago?"

"I don't know." What *was* keeping Ramon? His long absence was making me increasingly uneasy.

Bertram looks at his watch. "I don't want to miss Orlando's talk. I'm tempted to walk down to the plaza. Do you speak Spanish?"

"No."

"I know a little, enough to interpret for us. Let's walk down to the village."

"But you promised Ramon we would stay at the hotel."

"He'll easily find us in the square, I'll wager. That's probably where he's gone himself. You can stay here if you prefer. I'm going."

His word to Ramon about staying by me every minute had meant very little.

I accompanied Bertram down the winding, stone walk-way that led into the heart of the village. Beyond polished blue and white tiles and bordering flowers, painstakingly groomed to impress the prominent guests of the hotel, I could sense the encroachment of another world, a hard world filled with misery and burden. I resented the carefully planned concealment of such great poverty. I glanced at Gavin Bertram and it flitted though my mind that Thane Ulrickson had no doubt set up his own false front, more convincing, even, than this one.

We soon approached the plaza, and I heard cheers arising from the large group of people. Caught up in the excitement, I strained to catch a glimpse of Don Orlando. Surrounded by guards and dignitaries, he ascended the stone pavilion and began to address the crowd.

"Good. We're not too late," Bertram commented above the noise of the gathering. "Let's work our way to the front."

When we stopped walking, I looked up at Don Orlando. His black eyes, piercing beneath wings of dark brows, swept the onlookers and settled directly on me. His deep voice gained in tempo, and although I did not understand a word he said, I felt my own growing support for his message.

His mane of thick, black hair, touched slightly at the temples with gray, revealed him to be a man of around fifty. He had about him the air of the seasoned aristocrat, but his face seemed magnificently noble and kind.

Each time Don Orlando's voice rose theatrically; thunderous applause followed. Don Orlando raised a hand to silence the cheering throng. When his talk resumed, his voice was as full of fire as his snapping, dark eyes. His aura of strength, the confident set of his shoulders, drew my undivided attention and forced my gaze to remain focused upon him.

The gathering, mostly men in battered hats and ragged clothing, listened just as intently as I to this powerful-looking man. They, too, must be drawn by the conviction evident in his voice. I wondered what promises he was making to these people, who, no doubt, had heard their share of them. Were they promises of hope, offering shelter to their burdened lives? Whatever he said, they believed him, and without knowing why, I wanted to cheer, too.

"What is he saying?" I asked finally.

Bertram was too engrossed in Don Orlando's speech for any rapid reply. "Orlando is reminding them of the good work he has done in this area, the hospital, the school. He intends to help the laborers, their oppression by the wealthy plantation owners. They believe him. Orlando is a man known to keep his word."

Bertram's attention was again lost to me. I searched the crowd for some sight of Ramon. At last I located him near the entrance to a run-down building across the street from the plaza. Or was it Ramon? I felt a sense of alarm at the change that had come over him. He seemed tense, wary. I noticed how his eyes moved across the crowd, alert, watchful, as if trying to identify some source of danger.

I nudged Bertram. "Isn't that Ramon?"

"Where?" Bertram, caught up in Orlando's speech, seemed annoyed by my interruption.

"Across the street."

I gestured toward where Ramon had been standing, but he had disappeared.

"I don't see him." Bertram, entranced by the speaker's charisma, turned back toward the podium. He did not notice as I stepped away, slipping through small groups of ill-clad people to the spot where Ramon had been standing.

At the edge of the plaza, I hesitated. Ramon was nowhere in sight. I crossed the street to pause at the entrance of the building he must have entered. The building looked worse upon close range. Huge chunks of adobe had fallen, leaving great black gaps. Although I could not read the battered sign, the stale smell of alcohol and the blaring music told me it was a cantina.

The darkness within was blinding after the brightness of the sun. Most everyone had come out for the speech. Only a few men sat drinking at a dingy bar, which seemed at the moment unattended. Bleary eyes stared at me, boldly moved across my body, making me aware that this was not a place for a woman to come unescorted.

To the west of the bar across a sloping floor, tables and chairs cluttered. Two men were seated in the semi-darkness of a far corner. I quickly identified Ramon, by his wide, straight shoulders, the way he leaned slightly forward as he listened intently to his companion. The man who faced me, I recognized. The graying hair, the kindly face that, even in the setting of the dark cantina, put me in mind of a priest. Arnoldo Saville!

The unexpected sight of Arnoldo made me slow my approach, made me stop before either man had seen me. Why was Ramon meeting here with one of Carranza's loyal supporter? What were they discussing so covertly?

Then it occurred to me that Arnoldo himself must have sent a message to Ramon at the hotel. Ramon had purposefully come here to meet him! As Arnoldo continued to speak, I stepped back into the shadows and listened. Their voices possessed the secretive tones of conspirators.

"We must act quickly," I heard Arnoldo say as I stood, frozen, one hand braced against the edge of the long, wooden bar. "Before Don Orlando ends his speech. What I'm asking you to do is very dangerous."

Ramon's response was prompt. "I am willing to take the risk."

Arnoldo sounded sad. "I will do all I can to support you."

Ramon turned slightly and I could see his firm and solid profile. Not a muscle moved along his neck or jaw line. I could not see his eyes, but I imagined that they would be cold and unfathomable, the eyes of a mercenary, a stranger. A twist of irony filled his voice as he said, "I am the only man for this job."

My instincts told me to leave the cantina before either of the men saw me. But before I could start toward the door, Ramon's sharp voice called, "Marta!" The look of shock drained color from his face, making his black eyes seem to smolder. "What are you doing here? I told you to stay with Bertram at the hotel!"

"Bertram wanted to hear Orlando's speech, so we walked down to the plaza. I saw you come in here..."

Ramon had risen. Now with a firm grip on my arm, he led me out into the sun-baked plaza.

"What is Arnoldo Saville doing here? "

He did not answer. The anger had vanished from Ramon's face, replaced by concern. "We are expecting a good deal of trouble. That is why you must find Bertram and return immediately to the hotel."

"Is that what you were discussing with Arnoldo? Trouble? I

thought he was one of Carranza's men."

"There are noble men on both sides of every issue." His words made me think of General Grant and Lee, both good men, forced by loyalty and conviction to take opposite sides of our own Civil War. "Barrios was his close friend. Arnoldo remains loyal to Carranza and the cause Barrios once believed in. I cannot condemn him for his loyalty, nor convince him of his blindness. Today, Arnoldo is here to help me."

"What are you going to do?"

"We must find Bertram." His hand, tight over mine, reinforced the sense of urgency and warned of impending danger.

"He's over there near the platform."

Ramon guided me straight to Bertram. "Hurry!" Ramon urged before he disappeared into the crowd.

"Where have you been?" Bertram inquired in a preoccupied manner.

"I found Ramon. He said there might be trouble. He wants us to return to the hotel."

"What kind of trouble?"

"He didn't say. But I believe we should follow his advice."

Bertram, resentful of taking orders, dismissed my words with an impatient wave. A stubborn look crossed his face as his gaze moved back to the stone pavilion and Don Orlando. "This is just getting interesting. A few minutes more, and then I'll be ready to leave."

Unable to force Bertram to heed Ramon's words, I waited nervously. A sudden hiss from a group of men standing close to us near the pavilion interrupted Don Orlando's speech. The ten or twelve ruffians looked hostile and dangerous. They reminded me of Sanchez, and half-expecting to see him and his shoddy followers among them, I skimmed their faces. I caught no sight of Sanchez, but to my dismay I noticed that several other such clusters of Carranza's men had infiltrated the crowd.

On every side of us stirred sounds of discontent. A scowling man with heavy, black beard shook his fist in the air and shouted, "Viva Carranza!" Other voices joined his, until Orlando's words were drowned in the outcry.

Frantically I looked for Ramon, but could not see him. I pulled on Bertram's arm. "We've got to leave!"

Bertram's pale eyes filled with alarm as he appeared to notice for the first time the pack of angry men surrounding us.

He started to speak, but the swift crack of gunfire cut off his words.

Cries of startled fear spread through the mass of people. Several shots whizzed by us toward the pavilion where Don Orlando stood. The bullets ripped into stone, sending a scattering of chips.

Orlando, his features calm, whirled to face several men, the bearded one among them, who were bounding up the steps.

Before they could reach Orlando, the three men who had been in the hotel dining room, reacted. They hastened forward, formed a shield around Don Orlando, protecting him with their own bodies.

I could no longer see Orlando or be sure of what followed. Mad yelling broke out and the confusion of a hand-to-hand clash. All around us was the noise of frightened bystanders, of running feet.

"Orlando's trying to reach his carriage!" Bertram said.

Orlando was barely visible through the circle of men impelling him forward. Other of his supporters had succeeded in separating the menacing opposition.

Another shot exploded nearby. Ramon, gun drawn, pushed his way through the crowd toward me. "Get down!" he shouted. He half-dragged me to the base of the pavilion, where we crouched, breathlessly.

Bertram, looking bewildered, stood stupidly, like a frightened sheep, directly in the line of fire. Ramon rushed forward and forced Bertram to join us.

The three of us, Ramon ready with his gun, waited. No more shots sounded.

To my relief Don Orlando had been delivered to the waiting coach. The carriage, wheels skidding, throwing dirt and sand, tore away from the plaza. To my surprise, all the opposition seemed to have scattered. I watched the lone carriage that no one pursued.

"It's over." Ramon said, rising. "The danger has passed." His gun had disappeared and his empty hand reached out to assist me. "Are you all right?"

Still shaken, I nodded.

"What is going on, Santiago?" Bertram demanded, looking weak and pale.

"Someone tried to assassinate Don Orlando."

"I mean what is actually going on. Who tried to kill him? I could not even tell where the shots were coming from."

"From one assassin," Ramon said. "But many were involved in the plot."

"How can you be sure it's over then?" I asked.

"Because Don Orlando has already reached a place of safety."

As he spoke, his eyes swept over the square. I followed his gaze across the now empty and strangely silent plaza. "My carriage is over there. I'll take you back to the hotel, Bertram. Marta and I are going to leave."

"Will the roads be safe?" Bertram asked.

"They are never safe," Ramon answered. He turned the carriage up the sloping, cobbled path and stopped outside the high fence that separated the luxurious hotel from the poverty of the village.

"There is no danger now. Still I'd advise you to stay inside until morning. If you would rather not make the trip out to Thane Ulrickson's estate, I will explain to him."

Bertram, seeming to have lost some of his arrogance, said, "What happened today does give a man second thoughts, but, no, I do not intend to change my plans."

"My instructions were to look you over and if I approve, to give you this." Ramon took an envelope from his pocket. "You will find a list of all the items Thane will be willing to sell. You will also find a map directing you to his villa."

"We will see you tomorrow," I said, my spirits brightening with hope over Bertram's promise to help me escape.

Bertram got out of the carriage. "I'll be there by late afternoon."

The carriage made a wide circle and rolled back past the deserted plaza. As quickly as a tropical storm, the danger had flared and then faded as if it had never been. "What happened today is not unusual. Assassination attempts are a way of life, almost a part of the system," Ramon said. "Our politicians learn to live with this danger."

"The politicians here must be very brave men." I thought of the noble-looking Don Orlando upon the stone podium, and was grateful that none of the bullets had met their intended mark.

"Don Orlando is a brave man. And a very lucky one."

The sudden edge to his voice, the darkening of his eyes, puzzled me. I remembered that Ramon had looked the same way a short time ago when he had held the gun in his hand. Doubts bombarded me. Ramon's disappearance at the hotel, his urgent message from Arnoldo Saville, Carranza's major supporter...had the two of them been plotting Orlando's death?

Was Ramon concealing the fact that he, like Arnoldo, was a follower of Carranza? Or could he be, instead, a hired assassin? The thought made me shiver.

I stole a glance at Ramon's rugged profile, remembering how quickly he had appeared to save us. But where had he been when the major attempt on Orlando's life had been made? My eyes slipped down to the handle of his gun visible beneath his loose shirt. Had Ramon himself fired those shots?

Quickly, I pushed the dark thoughts to the back of my mind. What had happened today, I did not fully understand, but how could I doubt Ramon when he had practically saved my life? And Bertram's.

Ramon urged the horses on and, as if they had sprouted wings, they took us with great speed away from the village.

Chapter Eight

As the carriage moved swiftly along the coast trail, the area grew more wild, more desolate until the line of dense trees was broken only by the sea. "This part of the coast is virtually uninhabited," Ramon said. I shivered, thinking that the tangled groves of trees would be a perfect hiding place for Carranza's men, for pirates, thieves, or fugitives hiding from the law. Ramon seemed to know the area well, and that increased my apprehension. Ramon slowed the carriage and stopped without warning on a deserted stretch of beach.

"What are you doing?"

"I promised you that we would stop and look for shells."

How could he possibly believe I still wanted to sight-see after the frightening events of the day? They had left me more suspicious of him than I had ever been before and half-afraid to be alone with him.

Our trail close to the ocean was overrun with tangled vines that extended from the jungle, already a mass of shadows. The huge yellow sun hung low in the sky and added to my fear. "I would rather not stop here. We should travel as much as we can in daylight."

"I'm sorry you had to be involved in what happened today. But, Marta, there is no need for you to be frightened now. As I told you before, the ordeal has passed." Ramon tapped the handle of the gun, obscure but at the same time prominent. "You are perfectly safe!"

The gesture, meant to put my mind at ease, only increased my wariness. "I have no desire to find shells."

"A bit of rest will do you good." He guided the horses from the path across a wide stretch of sand toward the water. The animals strained to keep the wheels moving as the sand grew deeper. Once he had stopped, as if I weren't even along, he stepped down from the carriage and stood looking out across the sea.

Sunset tinged the sky with pink over bleached white sand and pale, almost translucent blue water. Macaws screeched from the nearby palms. This place, so deserted, reminded me of a desert island or some hidden, tropical paradise. Ramon and I could be the only two people in the world.

Realizing he did not plan to leave, I left the carriage and walked along the water's edge. The beach had a calming effect on me. The cooling air, the vast empty space, invigorated me, gave me a sense of freedom I had not felt for a very long time. As I wandered down the beach, stopping occasionally to inspect or save a shell, the fear and pressure I had felt began to ease.

The day, filled with such tension, made me long for simple pleasures. Suddenly, I wanted to laugh, to run through sand and water as I had done as a child. Impulsively, I slipped off my shoes, lifted my skirts, and began to wade into the water.

Ramon stood by the carriage, waiting for me. As I circled back toward him, he looked down at my bare feet and smiled. I noticed how the tense lines had vanished from his face, how the wind tousled his dark hair, making him appear relaxed and carefree.

"Aren't you going to hunt for shells?" I called to him.

He took off his jacket, removed the gun beneath it, and left them on the carriage seat. Quickly reaching me, falling into step beside me, he caught my hand and examined the brown, fan-shaped shells I had found.

"Nothing special here," he said. His hand, lean and warm, remained around mine as we strolled past a grove of *corozo* palms, which grew close to the shoreline. Suddenly, a flutter of brilliant green plumes rose high above us before disappearing into tangled leaves. I caught my breath, recognizing the form and color of the bird upon Evelia's tapestry.

"The Quetzal bird!" Ramon said. "A sight very few people

ever see! When one is spotted, it is said to be a sign of good fortune."

I gazed up at Ramon's handsome face and fell for a moment under the spell of the bird's omen.

As the sunlight glinted across the waves, it glowed with rainbow iridescence. The sea near us was transparent. The water was so clear I could see bright flashes of silver fish darting around chunks of coral. Soon, unmindful of the deep water soaking his boots and clothing, Ramon ventured away to lift a shell, which he gave to me. "I'm looking for one of the blue ones. Star-shaped. There's plenty of them around, but they are hard to find, the exact color of the sea."

Ramon's search for the perfect shell sent him deeper and deeper and deeper into the ocean. Finally, waist-deep, he called to me. "Success!"

Forgetting to protect my skirts, now damp along the edges, I hurried into the gently lapping waves toward him.

"Here it is! The perfect star!"

"It's beautiful!"

"You're beautiful!" As Ramon spoke his arms encircled me, and he pulled me close.

"Ramon...." Doubts of him returned, dark thoughts and fears closing in on my happiness. He looked deeply into my eyes as if reading my troubled thoughts.

"This moment belongs to us." He twined my damp hair in his hands, drew me against him, and silenced whatever words I might have spoken with his kiss.

The meeting of his lips with mine seemed as fiery as the sunset, as restless as the waves that swirled around us. We seemed to sink further into the water as I returned his kiss with a passion I had never before felt.

An unexpected wave washed over us, left us drenched and clinging to each other. I felt Ramon's arms pulling me even closer against his solid body. "I don't ever want to let you go," Ramon said.

I looked into Ramon's sparkling eyes and smiled. For a second time his lips captured mine, and I believed at that moment I would never distrust him again. For a while my world seemed beautiful, as crystal clear as the surrounding water.

***

A swift change of mood...I couldn't tell whether it was sadness or anger...settled over Ramon, arising as quickly as a storm across tropical waters. As the carriage drew closer to Thane's estate, Ramon's coolness became more pronounced. Didn't he want to take me back? Or was there some other reason for the distance that grew between us?

The chill of Ramon's mood transferred itself to me. Far ahead, in the fast-falling darkness, I made out the crude, massive blackness of Thane's mansion, surrounded by its thick, high walls. My recent joy seemed only a brief dream. Once again I felt hopeless defeat, as if I were an escapee being led back to total confinement.

The carriage passed the thick iron gates and slowed at the entrance to the house. We lingered for a moment in the darkness. As he handed me the bag I had packed so hastily this morning, a deep depression filled me. The sight of it brought home the finality of my return. "Do you want to take the shells?"

Ramon's hand lingered upon mine as he handed them to me. For a moment, his brief touch brought back memories of the beach, of his lips.

"Let's not mention to Thane what happened at the village today," Ramon cautioned. "It would only serve to upset him." The memory of the shots fired in the crowd, the attempt on Don Orlando's life, dissolved the last lingering traces of my new-found happiness, made the heavy mantle of doubt return. As if sensing my thoughts, with a brooding kind of silence, Ramon ushered me into the house.

I wondered how long Thane must have been sitting alone in his big chair by the fireplace, waiting for me. I had not expected to see him again. His blue eyes lit as he rose. He looked so strangely vulnerable despite his powerful build. His shaggy beard glowed with red lights as the flickering fire played across his face.

He did not mention the fact that we were very late. He merely continued in his adoring way to gaze at me. His expression caused me to feel again the sense of pity that had made me turn back to him this morning as the carriage had moved away.

At last he looked from me to Ramon as if envying the sea-dampness of our clothing, the lingering glow that our brief stop at the shore had given us. "Did you enjoy yourselves?"

"Yes. The beaches were lovely. We found such pretty shells." Ramon, with no word to Thane or me, abruptly left the room.

Slightly embarrassed by our being suddenly alone, I extended the star shell to the Viking. "Ramon found this one for me. I've never seen such a beautiful shade of blue."

Thane glanced down at the shell. "It's only a common variety," he said. As his eyes returned to mine, I saw a trace of hurt in them, recognized that wistful look touched with envy. I had seen the same look in his eyes when he had first noticed me wearing the medallion Ramon had bought for me in the village.

"I have shells," he said finally. "Exquisite shells from our most distant beaches." His voice grew anxious. "You must see them!"

"Tomorrow," I promised. "Tonight I'm very tired."

Thane stood at the foot of the stairs and watched me go up to my room. The dreary room with its weighty furnishings was so familiar to me now I almost thought of it as my own.

I was surprised to see that packages waited for me upon the bed. While I had been downstairs talking to Thane, Ramon must have had them delivered to my room. Sure of what I would find, I tugged open the nearest one. Inside was one of the dresses I had refused at the dressmaker's shop, the dress of pale pink trimmed with black.

At first I felt a sense of anger that Ramon had gone against my wishes. Then I saw the note pinned to the top of the first package.

You must accept these dresses as payment for the trunk I promised to recover for you. Otherwise, I will be forever in your debt.

Ramon

I remembered the talk I could not understand between Ramon and the dressmaker, the way she had responded with a pleased smile. I recalled Ramon's assertion that they had come to a satis-factory agreement.

What could I do but keep the dresses? As I looked down at the packages, I felt my anger slowly subsiding. It had been thought-ful of Ramon to discover a way for me to have them without being obligated to Thane. Since the dresses were here, I would keep them, I decided. But I would be certain to pay Ramon back as soon as I was able.

I returned to the packages and drew out the serviceable ben-galine day dress. Carefully, I hung the two dresses in the near-empty closet, and turned to the remaining package, which must contain the lilac silk.

I undid the outer wrappings and looked inside. My breath caught as I drew out...not the lilac silk...but the beautiful emerald ball gown!

Impulsively, I held it up to my body in front of the hazy mirror. My reflection seemed to swim before my eyes, all in shimmering green satin and soft-spun gold lace.

I remembered the look in Ramon's eyes as he had held the dress up to me, how his fingers had lingered upon my hair. Almost as if caught in a trance, I imagined Ramon and I dancing, Ramon holding me close, his kiss.... A knock sounded upon my door and startled me from my daydream.

I placed the dress carefully across the bed and moved reluctantly toward the door. "Who's there?"

"I've brought up your shells," responded the deep, booming voice, which could only belong to the Viking. I felt a moment's hesitation as I stood, fingers upon the heavy bolt of the door that separated us.

His adoration of me seemed so platonic, so unfounded in reality, that I knew I had nothing to fear from him. He would not come up to my room for any other reason than to deliver his precious shells.

I opened the door a crack.

The shells in the small wooden chest he held gleamed like rare jewels. He watched me eagerly, his eyes as bright as the sheen from the rich, pearl-like clusters shining from folds of velvet.

Once in the room he placed the chest on the bed. "This one reminds me of you."

He held up to me the largest abalone shell I had ever seen, at least fourteen inches in length and tinted with deep iridescent tones.

"It's very beautiful."

"But does not compare with your own beauty!" His worshipful voice added to my discomfort. I wished I had not opened the door for him. But, beyond transferring the shell from his hand to mine, he made no move to touch me.

"I've brought you a variety: a scorpion shell, an apple star, and this," he lifted a perfect white shell with segments marked off in black, "is a marbled cone." He pointed to another shell with spiny fingers. "A Venus comb, fit for a princess! And the little shells are limpets, related to the abalone. I will have a necklace of them made for you."

"You shouldn't go to all this trouble."

"No trouble." As he spoke, his gaze left the shells and rested on the ball gown still lying across the bed. A look of sheer pleasure filled his eyes. "The gown will be perfect for our dance. The hall will be ready three days from now. Saturday." Without another word, he turned and left, closing the door soundly behind him.

After he left, I found myself looking forward to the dance. Suddenly, I wanted to wear the beautiful emerald gown...not for the Viking...but for Ramon!

Chapter Nine

The next morning I slipped on the bright yellow dressing gown Evelia had given me. True to Evelia's words, my hair caught the brilliant sheen of the color, making my reflection in the shadowed mirror seem pale and ethereal, like some ghostly apparition bathed in sunlight.

The Sun Maiden! The thought made me pause my brush in mid-air and lean closer to the glass to study my image with horrified awareness. My long, blonde hair I blamed in particular for setting off the Viking's illusions about me.

I had always liked my hair long and had never cut it. For a moment, desperation made me think of grabbing a pair of shears and cropping the waist-length tresses close to my head. Instead, I plaited it into a long, loose braid.

The "Sun Maiden" remained gazing back at me with complacency.

Flinging open the door to the big, wooden armoire, I exchanged the dressing gown for the practical bengaline day dress with its dark blue stripes. Turning back to the mirror, I wound the braid around my hand and pinned it at the nape of my neck in the style of a prim schoolmarm. Then, satisfied that any resemblance to a long-lost Viking princess had been destroyed, I turned from the vanity and went downstairs.

Neither Thane nor Ramon were in the dining room. After a solitary breakfast, I wandered out to the open courtyard to see if there was any sign of Gavin Bertram. Guards by the nearby gate laughed and argued among themselves, engrossed in a some game. The sight of armed guards reminded me of my plight. My spirits,

118

lifted by the day away from this place, made my sense of imprisonment at having returned even stronger. I combated hopelessness by reminding myself that Bertram would soon arrive.

A rattling sound caught my attention. Could Bertram be arriving already? An old wagon, five or six shabby-appearing men balanced on the back, moved through the gate and came to a rumbling stop. The driver jumped out. Sanchez!

He addressed the guards with an arrogant good-humor. They laughed at whatever he said and went back to their game as he hopped back into the bench seat. Shading my eyes against the sun, I watched the wagon jog off across the hilly terrain. I wondered where he was going with a wagon load of men so early in the morning. I detested Sanchez and the fact that the Viking had given him free rein of his estate.

Sanchez and his wagon load of ruffians disappeared from my view. I began following the route they had taken, climbing one of the stony hills behind the house to see if I could once more spot the wagon. I caught a glimpse of it just before it disappeared behind an outcropping of rock. Sanchez and his men were headed in the direction of the lava beds.

Losing sight of them, I hurried by Thane's castle taking the familiar trail, thick with scrubby trees and dense underbrush. Eventually, I found myself at the entrance to Thane's storage shed. The doorway gapped open. I stopped to peer into the entrance, but saw no one inside. In the surrounding stillness I recalled how Thane and I had emerged here by way of the underground tunnel the day he had taken me out to his vault-cave. The Viking's hidden treasures lay in exactly the same direction that Sanchez had taken!

Passing the shed, I walked to the edge of the hill where I had a bird's eye view of the area. Far in the distance, I could see the tan cliffs where the Mayan ruins set against the sea, though from this far the ruins were invisible; the cliffs on which they sat were but a bare outline on the horizon.

I looked down at ridges of lava nearby, trying to see if I could, from this angle, spot the rune stone which lay below the cliffs, directly behind the cave.

Stony outcroppings of rock, in shades of charcoal and black, blocked my view, making the rune, if it could be seen from this angle, impossible to identify. Still, I recognized the flat top of the highest, darkest lava mound. Thane's cave lay concealed somewhere in the heart of that black mountain. I wondered if, without Thane's help, I would be able to find again that door cut into solid rock, the hidden entrance into Thane's cavernous rooms filled with treasure.

The thought of Sanchez, the wagon loaded with men, once more intruded into my mind. My eyes swept the area to see if I could spot Sanchez, but all traces of the wagon had disappeared from sight.

Did Sanchez know about the riches buried deep in the mountainside? Could he and the load of men at this very moment be searching for a way to steal Thane's treasures?

I was certain that only Thane...and I could find it again by searching...knew the exact location of the cave. Unless someone had been watching us the evening Thane had taken me out to where his treasures were hidden. I thought about encountering Ramon on the way back that night, so near the cave's location. Distrust of Ramon, I had thought gone forever, rose again. He could be a spy and a thief. If Ramon worked with Arnoldo, why not with Sanchez? Together they could be plotting to find a way to rob the Viking.

I started down the incline to search for some sign of Sanchez. After a while, my skin grew damp and hot, my arm weary from shading my eyes from the sun. From a distance I could view the approximate location of the entrance to the Viking's cave. Layers of hazy heat hung over the vast, empty space, which was totally undisturbed.

If Sanchez and his men were searching the area for Thane's cave, it was obvious they did not know its exact location. Thane's artifacts and jewels, for the time being, were safe.

I turned back toward the house. For all the good it would do, I felt compelled to warn the Viking about Sanchez and tell him of my suspicions. Despite Sanchez's shadiness, I sincerely doubted that

Thane would listen to me.

I retraced my steps back to the large storage shed. A grave-yard of old carriages and wagons surrounded the open doorway. Thane, or someone, must have been out here recently, or else the door was often left unlocked. Brushing damp hair away from my face, I stepped into the coolness of the shed. If the passage door was not bolted, I could enter the house by way of the long tunnel which connected to Thane's study.

Inside the shed set more old carriages, one of them covered carefully with a large piece of canvas. It must be an ancient carriage, I thought. Bare wooden spokes jutted out from behind canvas, where the carriage wheels had once been.

My gaze slid from the covered carriage to a stack of wooden crates piled high along the south wall. The crates stirred my curiosity. What would these wooden boxes contain? Were they artifacts from Thane's collection, packed and ready to sell to Bertram? If so, were the crates filled with authentic items or replicas?

I attempted to lift the lid from one of the crates, but it was nailed firmly shut. I glanced around, searching for some tool to use to pry open the top. A rod-shaped piece of metal lay on the floor beneath the covered carriage. As I reached for it, from my kneeling position, I caught a glimpse something familiar, something that made me drop the metal rod, crates and their contents forgotten.

A cry of absolute horror escaped my lips as I pulled back the covering from the hidden carriage. My hand flew up to my mouth. I felt almost as shocked and frightened as if I had discovered a corpse. Beneath the canvas was the missing Army wagon that belonged to my cowardly guide, Cayo.

What had happened to Cayo? Fear for him filled me as my eyes moved across the gutted skeleton of the carriage, riddled with the holes of a thousand bullets. My trunk, the object I had first recognized, lay beneath the carriage, empty, top thrown back, pitted with bullet scars.

Fear made my heart thunder in my chest. Why had Ramon told me that the carriage had been missing when he had gone back for my trunk? Why had Thane insisted that they were continuing to search for the carriage? All lies! I had been tricked and deceived by both of them. The carriage had been hidden here on the estate the whole time. Either Thane or Ramon had purposefully crippled the carriage to prevent my leaving!

And what of Cayo? Had Ramon murdered poor, shabby Cayo when he had returned for the carriage? Even though Cayo had deserted me, left me in the hands of bandits, I pitied him, understood his cringing fear. Visions of his body lying somewhere in the jungle, riddled with bullets, filled me with outrage and horror.

Throat tight with fear, I pushed at the doorway to the underground passage leading to the house. Whoever had gone through it last had left it unlocked. Intent upon confronting Thane with my discovery, I walked rapidly through the long tunnel. The dark, narrow passage increased my apprehension, my anger. By the time I reached Thane's study, my breath was coming in short gasps.

I paused by the cluttered desk, feeling faint, struggling to catch my breath. Light from the small, high windows behind Thane's desk fell across the sea of maps and charts that covered every bare space on the walls. My fear made the contents of the room look ominous...the old books, the Mayan artifacts, the giant Conch, big as a turtle's shell, that rested in the shadows behind the huge desk. Beside the shell sat an empty crate similar to the sealed ones I had seen in the shed.

I heard footsteps coming down the hallway toward the study. A glimpse of the Viking through the open doorway rekindled my rage. I stepped quickly from the study into the hallway to confront him. "Why did you lie to me about the carriage?" Not caring that my voice had risen, that I might even sound a little bit hysterical, I continued. "And what did you do with Cayo? Did you have Ramon shoot him?"

"You found Cayo's carriage?" A thick, reddish-gold brow arched in surprise. Unruffled by my accusations, he said, "Don't be upset, Marta. I can explain."

His absolute calmness increased my anger, but before I could fling another accusation at him, he placed a finger to his lips to silence me. "I'm bringing a guest into my study."

I looked beyond him, and, with some embarrassment saw that Bertram had arrived at the house while I had been outside, tracking Sanchez's movements.

Gavin Bertram, lagging far behind, slowly approached us. The sound of my raised voice caused him to slow, his sharp, interested gaze shifting curiously to me, then back at Thane.

"Please, go on inside and wait," the Viking said, ushering Bertram into his study with a sweep of the hand. "We'll be right with you."

When Bertram had disappeared inside the room, Thane said to me, "Listen, Marta. The explanation is quite simple. One of my men found the carriage a few days ago, abandoned in the jungle and brought it here. I'm sorry to say, the contents of your trunk were missing." He paused, stroking his red beard. "One of the bands roaming the hills must have used the empty carriage for target practice and stolen the contents of your trunk. I didn't want to upset you by having you see the condition it was in, so I simply had it removed to the shed."

"Then what about Cayo?" I demanded, unconvinced. "Did you bury his body somewhere so I wouldn't see that, too?"

The Viking responded with an indulgent laugh. "I assure you, nothing has happened to Cayo. Why would you even think such a thing?"

"The carriage...."

"I paid him well for the damaged carriage. I ran across him in Santa Augusta. He is probably still there. Do you want to see Cayo? I will bring him here!"

Was he bluffing? I studied Thane's steady gaze and found my suspicions concerning him melting. I really did not think he was a killer. The shock of discovering the bullet-ridden carriage had made me over-react.

What Thane told me certainly must be true. After all, what real reason would he or Ramon have had to track Cayo down and murder him?

"Shall I send a messenger for him?"

123

"That won't be necessary," I said, feeling suddenly exhausted, defeated, even a little foolish.

"Then it's all settled," he announced with great relief. "Are you happy?" As if my happiness was all that mattered to him, he smiled and took my arm, "Now, Marta, let's go into the study and greet our guest."

I lingered a moment. "While I was outside, I saw Sanchez and a group of his men. They were headed toward the caves."

Just as I feared, the Viking brushed away my concerns with a hearty laugh. "Don't worry. Sanchez is free to enter and leave my villa as he pleases."

"That is your mistake. You should stop him. I think he may be trying to find a way to steal from you."

"Do not worry." The Viking bent closer, adding in a lower tone, "Our hiding place has never been disturbed. Sanchez would not even begin to know where to look." He continued to gaze at me with a secret smile. "No one has ever been out there but...." you and me. Your treasure is safe, my princess, as it has been for centuries."

As Thane guided me into his study, I was aware of Bertram's pale, watchful eyes. Bertram, dressed fashionably in a light gray frock coat and matching trousers, moved politely forward to meet us. As his eyes settled on me, they became more alert, more skeptical, as if he believed that it might be I, not Thane who was mad. Self-consciously, I brushed a hand through my tangled hair, realizing how distraught and disheveled I must appear. My braid had escaped from its pins to fall in a long, loose plait down to the small of my back.

"I was just going to show Mr. Bertram some items from my collection," Thane said. He turned to Bertram. "Marta's father was the great archaeologist, James Swan," Thane explained. I had feared he would introduce me as his long-lost Viking princess, and was relieved by his unexpected rationality. "She can authenticate my Copador vases."

I felt an odd flutter of excitement as I took the dusty-red vase Thane offered from the cluttered shelf behind his desk. The faint pattern of dark, linear designs identified the vase for me as a genuine Copador.

Alan had believed the Copador vases Thane had shown him to be authentic. He would have made a purchase if Thane had been willing to part with them.

"What is your opinion, Marta?"

I handed the vase back to Thane. "I really can't say," I answered, though my knowledge of color and design told me that the vase was no doubt authentic. "I'm not an expert on what is real and what is a reproduction."

"It doesn't matter." Bertram waved away my reluctance to authenticate the items. His shrewd, gray eyes met Thane's "What do you want for this one, Ulrickson?"

"Oh, I couldn't bear part with it! That vase has been in the family for centuries."

"Don't get sentimental on me, Thane. After hiring a carriage and making all of this special effort to get here, I won't like it if I end up with a wasted trip."

"Remember the list Ramon gave you? That is all I promised to offer you. The bulk of my collection is decidedly not available. Although I do have smatterings of pottery and other items that I would sell." Thane now sounded somewhat uncertain. "But I must get what they are worth."

"Money is no object if it is something I want," Bertram said definitely.

Thane lifted a buff-orange vase from the shelf, a twin, except in color, to the red one. Thane held it out to the art collector. "This one is invaluable, my friend."

Bertram studied the vase, frowning. "It's not worth half as much as the red. But...how much do you want?"

"I'm not sure I want to sell it." Thane appeared to be stalling again. He rubbed thoughtfully at his reddish-gold beard, then turned clear, blue eyes upon me. "What do you think, Marta?"

"It's really not for me to say," I answered coldly.

"Copador pottery is so rare. Marta, do you want to keep it?"

"It's not mine." If Thane were only pretending to be mad, if instead he was a fraud, a con artist who made his money by deceiving wealthy collectors, I would not be drawn into his schemes.

"I believe I could part with it," Thane said reluctantly.
"If you must have a Copador vase."

"You know I won't turn one down. Though my main interest is in statues rather than pottery. Mayan heads and the like."

I suspected Thane might be purposely baiting the art collector, setting a trap for him. The doubtful way the Viking looked must be a part of his deception. He wasn't crazy. He was deliberately setting the wealthy Bertram up. I felt my anger increasing. I would stop him if I could. "The vase might be a reproduction," I warned.

"I thought you said you couldn't tell," Bertram said, eyeing me with a pronounced increase in skepticism.

"Forget the vases," Thane said with sudden good humor. I've decided I can't part with either one of them. Now, here is something you might like." He lifted a statuette from his cluttered desk. "This came from the ruins at Copan."

Thane offered a stone likeness of a priest in full ceremonial dress to the collector.

"Incredible!" It must be pure jade." Bertram's eyes gleamed. They reminded me, despite the great difference in color, of Sanchez's eyes. "I do want this!"

Bertram's eyes continued to glitter as he turned back to Thane, the diminutive priest with his crossed arms, jutting nose and intricate plumed headdress still in hand. "Let's talk price, Ulrickson. And don't change your mind on me."

"I said I'd sell you this one. I won't go back on my word, even though I hate to part with it."

"I bought one similar to this in the States for $5,000."

"The head alone is worth that!" Thane boasted with a great laugh. "Maybe I should break him into pieces and sell you half." I noted impatience in Bertram's voice and manner. "I want a price, Ulrickson."

"Why don't you take Mr. Bertram back up to the dining room?" Thane suggested to me, as if suddenly anxious to be rid of both of us. "Evelia will fix you some coffee and pastries. I want to be alone to think about prices, what I can and can't bear to part with."

"You had better make up your mind, Ulrickson." Bertram replied sharply. "You know I must leave today."

As if to appease him, Thane said, "After you've had some refreshment, Ramon will take you on horseback to see the Mayan ruins you've been asking me about. Would you like that?"

"I would be interested in seeing the ruins," Bertram responded, the acid in his voice beginning to neutralize.

Thane turned to me. "Marta, you may ride along, if you wish. I know you'd be interested in seeing the stone carvings of Viking ships and men. I've been meaning to take you up there myself, but:..he gestured to the books that cluttered his desk...my research keeps me so busy, you understand." The titles of nearby books caught my eye...volumes like the ones that had graced my own father's study...books about Copan and the Mayans, the works of Maudslay, Stephens and Catherwood.

I walked with Bertram down the long hallway.

"You know he won't sell you anything," I confided to Bertram as soon as we were out of Thane's range of hearing. "He showed Alan the same vases he showed you. And doesn't plan to part with any of them."

"Incredible!" Bertram raised one finely-arched brow. "Now that I've met him, I'm beginning to believe this Ulrickson is as mad as you say he is."

"We should leave now," I suggested, feeling a sense of anxiousness. "While he is down in his study."

Bertram hesitated. "That Mayan priest looked genuine to me. And not a nick on it! Do you know what kind of price something like that statuette would bring in the States?"

"He'll never part with anything of value."

"Still, it might be worthwhile for me to wait and see what kind of offer he makes me," he insisted stubbornly. I did not like the intent look in Bertram's eyes or the smile that spread thinly across bloodless lips. "Let's play along with him. We'll ride out to see those Mayan ruins. By the time we return, Ulrickson will be ready to deal with me. We will plan to leave at dusk."

Memories of the assassination attempt on Don Orlando's life, the bullets whizzing past our heads that could have gotten us both killed, prompted me to ask, "Aren't you afraid to travel at night?"

"I didn't have any trouble on the way here," he responded with unfailing confidence. "And I don't expect any now. The secret is to mind your own business, and let others mind theirs."

Still, a man who displayed his wealth as noticeably as he did, with jewelry and fine clothing, might be an easy target for bandits. I remembered the way he had looked in the plaza, stripped of his arrogance, like a frightened rabbit paralyzed by the sudden hail of gunfire. Bertram was a gentleman, not accustomed to defending himself. I doubted that he even carried a gun. "We could wait until early morning."

"Don't worry," he said in a clipped tone. "I've traveled in isolated areas all my life. Just have your bags packed when evening falls. I assure you, my dear, we will leave then regardless of whether or not I succeed in buying anything from Thane Ulrickson."

* * *

The thought that we would soon be far away from here eased my mind, so that I began to look forward to riding out to the ruins. The delay in our departure might even be for the best, I told myself, for surely it would be a shame to leave without looking at the Mayan drawings which Alan had insisted I see. The ancient carvings might turn out to be an important link in our search to trace a Viking voyage to this area. And my very reason for being here in Honduras was to help Alan prove my father's theory.

The great dining room bustled with activity. Maids, supervised by Evelia, were cleaning the crystal and polishing silver. Bertram and I entered and seated ourselves at the end of the long wooden table.

Evelia, as if expecting us, paused in her work to bring coffee, fresh fruit, and pastries covered with honey. With a flashing smile, she introduced herself to Bertram. She looked striking today, in a dress of bright scarlet that drew attention to her dark, exotic beauty.

"Forgive all the clutter. We are getting ready for the dance," she explained to Bertram. Slanting her eyes at him, she asked, "Will you be staying for the fiesta? It is Saturday, only three days from now!" As she spoke, I noticed how her gaze moved over his fine clothing, lingered with interest upon the gray silk lining of his vest, upon the big ring studded with diamonds he wore on his long, thin hand.

"I'm afraid I cannot stay. I must return to the States. My ship leaves tomorrow evening."

"Do you have to go so soon?" Evelia's full lips pouted and her eyes met his in a flirtatious manner, which Bertram pointedly ignored. I remembered Evelia's comment about wanting to go to America and be a fine lady. Her speculating glance made me wonder if she were now weighing possibilities.

"Yes, I must." As if her flirtation annoyed rather than flattered him, he added, "My wife grows tired of waiting for me."

At the mention of a wife, Evelia's interest immediately waned. "I must get back to my work," she sighed, moving away with a sway of scarlet-clad hips. Languidly, still watching us from the corner of her eyes, she lifted a cloth and wiped at the crystal dishes.

We were finishing our coffee and pastries when Ramon entered the dining room. Today, instead of his usual uniform, he wore a white shirt, black pants, and riding boots. I could not help noticing how the white shirt contrasted with his flashing black eyes and made the dark waves of hair gleam.

I was aware of the appreciative glance Evelia tossed Ramon as he walked passed her toward our table. I could hardly miss the way she hurried over with coffee. The interest that had died for Bertram had rekindled, flashing brightly in her dark, heavily-lashed eyes.

"Ulrickson says you'll guide us out to the ruins," Bertram immediately addressed him.

"Yes. I've already spoken to him," Ramon replied, making no move to be seated. Declining the coffee Evelia offered, he said, "I just came by here to tell you it's all arranged."

"May I come, too?" Evelia, standing near him, tugged on his arm. "I've never been out to the ruins. And I simply must get away from this house for a while."

Ramon nodded courteously. "You may come along with us if you wish. I will get the horses ready. We will all plan to meet at the stables in half an hour."

Chapter Ten

"I can not wait to see the ruins," Evelia said brightly as we walked toward the stables. She smiled with one of those rare displays of friendliness toward me that was becoming increasingly harder to trust.

Evelia had changed from scarlet dress into a black, velvet-trimmed riding habit. The small, matching hat, hair pulled back from her thin face, emphasized high cheekbones, the animated glow of wide, dark eyes. Although she was looking forward to the outing with great pleasure, up until now, Evelia had expressed little enthusiasm for the ancient Mayans. I doubted that a sudden desire to see the ruins had compelled her to join us. Bertram's presence must have sparked her sudden interest...or Ramon's.

Bertram and Ramon waited at the stables. Ramon directed each of us to one of Thane's beautiful, Arabian horses. The horse he had selected for me was my immediate favorite, small, in comparison to the others, and wonderfully gentle, his coat a shining mixture of white and silver. Evelia took the reins to the dappled mare with dark mane and tail, and Bertram mounted a giddy, pure black stallion. That left Ramon with a wild, spirited horse of pure white, with sculptured face and flowing mane.

The horse, I thought, looked as if it should belong to him.

"We will follow the high trail through the pines, and avoid the rough lava beds," Ramon explained. "Marta, since you are not used to riding, stay close to me."

My horse seemed content to follow the lead of Ramon's spirited, white Arabian, that expressed dislike of our slow pace. After a while the slow jogging gait lulled me into a sense of well-being. I began to enjoy the feel of the warm sun and cooling wind upon my face, the clip-clop of the horse's sturdy hooves beneath me. Behind us on the trail, I could hear Bertram and Evelia's voices in pleasant exchanges of talk. Ahead Ramon waited for me so we could ride side by side.

The horses picked their way around the uneven edges of a high ridge that looked down upon the barren rises and depressions of the hardened lava flow. This route, slightly different from the shortcut I had taken on foot earlier, would circle Thane's cave and approach the cliffs from a different angle.

Being so near the cave area reminded me of trying to follow Sanchez this morning. Down below, I could see the rutted trail his wagon had taken before reaching the lava beds. Since Thane had brushed off my warning, I decided to caution Ramon, "I saw Sanchez enter the estate this morning with a wagon load of men."

"Thane allows Sanchez to come and go as he pleases," Ramon responded, seeming unconcerned, yet I noticed a flicker of interest in his eyes as he asked, "Did you see which way they went?"

"Somewhere in that general direction," I said, carefully pointing out for him the trail Sanchez had taken. Ramon traced the ruts to the desolate area where the lava formations rose in spiny ridges, forming bare, black mountains and deep caverns...the area Ramon had warned me to stay away from. "The wagon disappeared in those upheavals before I could tell exactly where they were going," I went on, "But I believe they were headed in the direction of the lava caves."

For a while, we rode in silence, still paralleling the outer reaches of the lava beds. In places, the dark scars of lava formations cut like jagged black rivers across our trail, and we were forced to guide the horses around them.

As we worked our way past the lava flow, the dark, igneous rocks became less prominent until they dwindled into a few porous, scattered boulders at the base of tan, limestone cliffs.

At the foot of the cliffs, we waited for Bertram and Evelia. "We'll leave the horses here and walk the rest of the way," Ramon said, as, side by side, they rode in together behind us. It appeared that Bertram was prepared to tolerate, if not possibly enjoy, Evelia's attentions. We dismounted and tethered the horses in the shade beneath the cliffs.

Ramon, leading the way, scaled the first ledge. "Be careful," he cautioned. He paused to take my arm and help me climb up beside him, then turned back to give Evelia a hand. She scrambled agilely up the sloping rocks to join us.

A shower of pebbles rained down the cliff as Bertram struggled up beside us. Ramon quickly reached out to steady his arm.

"Thank you," Bertram said stiffly, a little embarrassed at needing assistance. "These city boots weren't made for climbing."

"It's not far to the top," Ramon encouraged, as we reached the flat shelf of rock just below the ruins.

"Why would the Mayans build a city up here?" Bertram asked, when we paused to catch our breath. The sunlight was warm; I could see a thin layer of dampness upon his pale forehead. I, myself, felt unaffected by the heat, but since my skin was inclined to tan, wished that I had thought, as Evelia had, to wear a hat.

"No doubt the location made a natural fortress against enemies as well as a lookout point," Ramon explained. His open shirt revealed a bronzed, muscular chest, curling, dark hair that glistened with sweat.

"Is this dreadful climb the only way up to the ruins?" Bertram asked curiously.

"No, there are several ways to get to the top of the cliffs," Ramon replied. He pointed out the way I had taken earlier to the base of the cliffs. "There is a trail through the lava beds, but it leads to a place where the cliffs are sheer and even more difficult to climb. The ruins can also be reached by climbing up from the beach when the tide is out. But that route can be also be very dangerous, especially for one not familiar with the tides."

Once more, Ramon reached down to give me his hand as I climbed up over the last of the rocks. I waited, surveying the view from the top of the cliffs, as Ramon guided Evelia and Bertram to the final level.

We stood upon a flat plateau, a center courtyard lined with

crumbling stone walls, which overlooked the startling blue ocean. Only a few palms grew up here, but vines clung to ruined remains of what had once been great buildings. Weeds and orange flowers poked through the cracks of old stone steps which led to the only solid, remaining structure. I studied the arched, shadowed doorway of the ancient temple, marveling that its thick stone walls had remained intact while the lesser buildings surrounding it had fallen prey to the elements.

Bertram slipped away to explore on his own. I could see him looking around the fallen walls, interested in everything he saw. Evelia rested in the shade, fanning herself with her hat. I moved toward Ramon, who had walked over to get a view of the sea.

The wind made wisps of dark hair curl around Ramon's face, made his white shirt billow in the breeze. The cliff's edge behind him dropped off sharply toward the sea, a sheer plunge broken only by a sharp outcropping of limestone.

Near the edge of the cliff, piles of stone which had once been the entranceway to a vanished temple broke through the earth. A row of serpent heads that had once served as a border remained, forming the top of a low stone wall.

I paused to observe the serpent heads. Once the carved statues had been magnificent, now many of them were so badly damaged that they were virtually unrecognizable. I counted five of them, evenly spaced, the small, square heads upon jutting necks forming an unbroken line facing the sea.

"*Quetzalcoatl*," Ramon said, moving to stand beside me, "is often represented by the Mayans as a feathered serpent. This entire complex was built as a shrine to him...the god who came from the sea."

Traces of black paint clung like shadows to depressions in the weathered stone, emphasizing the eroded feathered plumes, making dark-ringed eyes seem deep and hollow. The eyes, I thought, seemed to stare out to sea as if watching for a distant sail.

The air felt warm, despite the ocean breeze. Bertram approached, carrying his lightweight gray frock coat in the crook of his arm. Seeing us gathered together, Evelia rose lazily from her stone perch and wandered over.

Bertram's attention focused immediately upon the serpent heads. "I'd like to have one of those snakes to display in my shop window," Bertram said. "A curiosity like that would be sure to draw in customers." Turning to Evelia, he asked, "Do you think you could talk Ulrickson into selling me one?"

"Cut one of those stones away?" Her response was a scornful laugh, as if he should know better than to even ask. "Thane would never let you do that."

"They are just old stones." Bertram insisted, "And badly damaged, at that. They wouldn't even bring a good price. Worthless, except as a curiosity piece." He shrugged. "Who ever sees them up here? One might as well be in my store window."

"This place is special to the Viking," Ramon said.

"Yes, he comes up here all the time," Evelia agreed, fanning herself with the hat. "I think it is his favorite place in the whole world."

Ramon, as if anxious to draw Bertram away from the serpent heads, suggested, "Let's walk toward the main temple. You'll want to see the stone murals, the carvings of the Viking ships." With a last longing glance at the serpent heads, Bertram went amiably along.

On the way I paused to inspect the random carvings on one of the crumbling rock walls we passed. I found them fascinating because I had never seen anything like them before.

Images, once deeply etched into stone, now worn smooth and in places obliterated, leaped out to catch my eye and imagination. Mayan gods and warriors, plumed serpents and rows of priests in feathered headdress, all frozen in time, made me want to stop and study each one of them, to ponder what stories they were meant to tell.

My attention focused upon one of the carved figures along the battered wall which looked different from the rest. It was clearly not the form of a Mayan priest or warrior. I leaned closer to get a better look. The figure was so badly eroded that it was difficult to make out the details, yet something about the loose clothing, the barest hint of a face covered by headdress or long hair, gave me a strange, eerie feeling.

"The carvings inside are clearer," Ramon said, slowing to wait for me. I turned from the wall to look into his eyes, noticing the crinkles about his them as he smiled. "You should see them first. Then, if you want, you can come back and look at these."

Reluctantly, I moved away from the wall and followed Ramon through the high arch of the main temple, which the others had already entered. The air inside was damp and cool after the heat of the sun. The change in atmosphere made me feel slightly dizzy, and my legs shook a little from the strenuous climbing.

As I stood at the entranceway, a sense of awe came over me. Nothing could have prepared me for the wonder of what lay within. Muted light from the doorway fell upon carvings which covered every bare inch of the stone walls. Chips of yellow, red, and ochre still clung stubbornly in places to the crude, rough-hewn figures etched in stone.

"The ships are here," Ramon said, directing our attention to the closest wall. Figures of Mayan Indians in plumed headdress looked out to sea, watching the approach of three long boats with serpentine bows. I heard my own sharp intake of breath as Ramon reached out to trace with his fingers the form of a ship...almost the perfect replication of a Viking ship!

"Uncanny!" I heard Bertram murmur beside me as he moved closer to study the carved ships with a look of pure intrigue. Evelia, barely glancing at the magnificent murals, waited, her indifference matching Bertram's intense interest.

"Over here, you can clearly make out a battle scene," Ramon said. He pointed out a section of the next wall where the crew of the foreign ships appeared to be disembarking upon the land. Distinct figures of helmeted and bearded men fought fierce battle with Indians in headdress, lances drawn. I drew in my breath. I had not expected the murals to be so well-preserved, the scenes of ceremony and battle so vividly depicted.

I stared at the scenes before me, entranced, almost becoming a part of them. All of the stone murals seemed to merge together into one long, unfolding story. Could it be the story of the Vikings first arrival in Central America?

I could hear, as if from a long distance, Bertram reflecting my thoughts aloud. "All this is fascinating! It convinces me that the Vikings actually landed here at this very spot."

"Still, real evidence is lacking," Ramon commented. "This could only be a depiction of some entirely mythological event."

"But maybe not," Bertram responded.

"Or, the murals could signify a historical account of a foreign invasion by the Phoenicians or some ancient people other than the Vikings," Ramon said. "They also wore beards and dressed in armor."

"Quite true," Bertram agreed. "Despite our speculations, only some relic that could be specifically traced back to the Norsemen would be actual scientific proof."

As they spoke, one of the bearded figures from the battle scene caught my eye. He stood his ground, weapon raised, fighting bravely even as his men began to flee. I could not help noticing that he bore an uncanny resemblance to Thane Ulrickson.

"I'm convinced that someday evidence will be found," Bertram said. I remembered our talk in the hotel, his admission that his real interest was in finding out if Thane had some relic in his collection that could be traced back to the Norseland.

"You are talking about the Viking Crown medallion," Evelia said, suddenly coming to life, as if seeking for fortune was something she understood. "The one that Alan Avery wants to find."

"These murals are very convincing," Bertram said. "It makes me believe such a relic might exist."

"I believe the medallion does exist," Evelia said. "And someday Alan or someone like him will find it."

At the mention of Viking relics, Ramon's tone changed, his words became suddenly guarded. "For centuries men have searched for Viking relics around this area, but none have ever been discovered."

Something in his voice made my glance fall upon Ramon for a moment, noticing the high cheekbones, fine features, the thick-lashed eyes that cast shadows upon olive skin...eyes that seemed as mysterious as the Mayan ruins themselves, as full of secrets as the carvings upon ancient walls that surrounded us.

His veiled look made me wonder if he really believed what he was saying. Or was he purposefully discouraging talk about Viking relics to protect Thane? Did he, too, know, or at least suspect, that the medallion or even the fabled jeweled crown was part of Thane's collection?

"I've heard there's a stone on Ulrickson's land that may have runic writing on it," Bertram persisted. His thin lips compressed and drew attention to the sweat that had formed above his mouth.

Ramon's eyes flicked over to me before he asked Bertram, "Who told you that?"

"I believe it may have been Alan who mentioned it to me," Bertram answer was evasively prompt, as if he were trying to leave the impression that naming the informer was unimportant. "Will you take us to see the stone?"

"It is in the lava cave area. I'm afraid Thane will allow no one to enter that part of his estate," Ramon said, repeating to Bertram the same warning he had given me. "The area is filled with caverns, and the ground is unstable and dangerous."

"I'd still like to see it," Bertram insisted, sounding intensely disappointed.

"I'm afraid that's not possible."

Their voices seemed to fade as I turned my attention toward the mural upon the third and final wall. Here, the pictorial battle raged on, while the foreign invaders hurried back to their waiting ships. Once more, I noticed the slim lines of the boats, the curved bows reminiscent of Viking ships. One was already out to sea, the others preparing to launch.

A lone, bearded figure remained behind, standing tall and brave against the Indian attack, even as his men deserted him, sailing away from danger.

I leaned closer to study the likeness of a bearded man in strange, armored clothing. The stylized figures of Mayan gods, priests, and warriors with almond-shaped eyes, jutting noses and slanting features bore an almost monotonous similarity to each other. Yet this was clearly not the face of an Indian. The features were definitely that of another race...Phoenician, Asian, Viking....

I felt a little catch of excitement. Could the original *Quetzalcoatl* have been, as Father had believed, a brave Viking warrior left behind and captured by the Mayans? A stranger who had gradually earned the respect of the Indians, and eventually became venerated in their legends as a god. *Quetzalcoatl*, the god who came from the sea....

I moved closer, studying the mural. At the very edge of the battle scene I saw an obscure figure, similar to the one I had noticed on the crumbling stone outside the temple, a ghost upon the wall. Time blurred the features, making the details indistinct. The figure was virtually formless, faceless, only a bare sketch in the background, a hint of a person with headdress or very long hair crouched as if in hiding, watching the battle.

At first I thought the long-haired figure was one of the Mayan warriors who had fled from the scene of bloodshed. But a second glance made me wonder if the elusive figure with the long hair was meant to represent a woman. Was it the lost Viking princess? Had she been frightened away by the battle, taken cover, only to be left behind by the sailing ships? If so, then the legend of the Sun Maiden might be true!

"Ramon, look at this..." I said, but my breathless words echoed hollowly into an empty room. I tore my eyes away from the captivating scene upon ancient stone to find that I was alone in the temple. I had not even heard the others leave. How long had I stood there, hypnotized by the tale told by these ancient murals?

I looked back down at the obscure stone figure, but all resemblance to a woman seemed to have vanished. I could see now that the figure was most likely a young Mayan warrior in headdress, as I had first believed. All of Thane's talk about the Sun Maiden was making me lose my logic, causing my imagination to run away from me! Feeling slightly dazed, as if I had traveled back in time, I stepped from the ancient stone temple into the sunlight.

Bertram, once more on his own, was exploring the crumbling

walls near the big stone temple. Shading his eyes, he looked downward toward the horses, then across the lava beds. Ramon, beneath the shade of a palm tree, stood talking to Evelia, but I did not join them. I felt a sudden need to be alone with my thoughts.

I climbed up to where the remaining stones of ruined walls looked out over the sea like a weathered fortress. I stared out at the ocean, imagining the Indians spotting the long boats upon the horizon. The men who sailed upon them must have seemed like aliens from another world.

The sight of the stone carvings had filled me with inspiration, an understanding of my father's life goal that I had before this moment never quite captured. I felt a sense of wonder that I could be standing in the exact spot where the Norsemen had landed centuries ago! It drew me even closer to my beloved father and his great, lifelong quest.

My musings were interrupted by Ramon, who appeared suddenly by my side. His voice was deep, a little teasing, "Do you see a Viking sail on the horizon?"

The wind whipped long tendrils of hair about my face. "Up here...looking out at the ocean...it doesn't seem so impossible. The sea is timeless, a sort of vast eternity...."

"You're talking like the Viking now. Could it be that you are beginning to fall for his delusions?"

I found myself responding to the nearness of Ramon, smiling into his dark eyes. "No, but I've always shared his obsession for the past."

Black eyes, sparkling, but sincere, looked deeply into my own. "And I share his obsession for you!"

***

Hand in hand, Ramon and I walked down the sloping rocks toward where Evelia rested on a stone outside one of the ruins. "We should be starting back now," Ramon said as we approached. He glanced around. "Where is Bertram?" His gaze scanned the ancient courtyard, "I thought I saw him here, near the temple."

"He was here." Evelia shrugged, idly slapping at a buzzing insect. "But he left."

Ramon frowned. "Did he go back inside the temple?"

"No." Evelia pouted, as if his leaving had disappointed her, left her abandoned. "He said he'd seen enough. He went down to wait by the horses."

"When?" Ramon asked.

"Only a few minutes ago."

I saw a muscle in Ramon's jaw tense. I knew he was thinking about the steep, dangerous rocks, Bertram's fancy leather boots not made for climbing. I knew he considered Bertram's safety his responsibility. Bertram should have waited, or at least told Ramon that he was starting down.

The way down was much quicker than the laborious climb up had been. As we reached the lower shelf of rock, I caught sight of Gavin Bertram near the horses. He was busy freeing his black stallion, when he glanced furtively over his shoulder and saw us.

Nervously he awaited our approach.

"Why didn't you wait for us?" Ramon demanded, his voice cold and reprimanding. The silence between them stretched tautly as the two, strong-willed men regarded each other.

"I guess I got in a hurry to leave," Bertram said finally, with an arrogant shrug of his shoulders. His smile was thin, assured, but his hands, still holding the reins to the black stallion, trembled slightly. "The heat, the height...too much for a New Yorker."

"We will return to the house now." Ramon said with grim authority. "You will please stay with the rest of us."

As we rode, Ramon once more took the lead. I noticed how he kept turning back to check on Bertram, who seemed to keep lagging further and further behind. Once more, we took the trail that circled the barren, crater filled landscape of volcanic rises and depressions. When we reached a point in the trail which twisted and curved around trees and high piles of rock, Bertram disappeared completely from view.

Only Evelia's horse emerged through the trees. She slowed beside us. We paused upon the trail, waiting for Bertram, but horse and rider did not appear.

"He must have taken a wrong turn," Evelia said finally, watching the wooded path behind us.

140

I remembered Bertram's eagerness to see the rune stone, the way he had hurried down before us to the horses. I wondered if he had really gotten lost upon the trail, or if he had all along purposefully planned to slip away toward the lava beds in search of the stone with the runic writing.

The thunderous look upon Ramon's face told me that he shared my suspicions. "Evelia, you and Marta go on back to the house," he commanded. "I'll ride back and find him."

I watched Ramon gallop off angrily down the trail in search of Bertram.

"Stupid man," Evelia said scornfully. "How could anyone get lost as easily as that?"

Evelia became sullen and silent as we rode back to the house. The thin veneer of friendliness was fast wearing away, becoming sharp and brittle around the edges. I was glad when we finally reached the stables.

"I will see to the horses," she said curtly, brushing aside my offer of help. "You will only be in the way. Go back inside the house."

I went up to my room to change from the riding habit into the pale pink day dress. I paused to splash cool water upon my face and to comb and pin my windblown hair. Then I went back downstairs.

I immediately encountered Bertram just entering the house alone. He looked ruffled and annoyed, his fine clothing dusty from the ride.

"So you've been found," I said, relieved to see him again.

"Ramon caught up with me," he corrected, "And made me come back."

"Where did you go?"

"I started down by the caves. I wanted to get a look at that rune stone."

"Did you see it?"

"No. But I'm going to find that stone before I leave. Do you know where it is?"

"It's very close to the cave area. But I think you should heed

141

Ramon's advice. Lava caves are very dangerous." I heard myself repeating Ramon's words, "Often the crust looks solid but it is actually thin and breaks away at the lightest pressure."

"I'm not going anywhere until I get a look at that stone."

"What about our plans for tonight?"

"We'll leave right after the evening meal, as soon as it is dark. I'm going down to talk to Thane now. After I meet with him, I'm going back to do a little...exploring."

"I wish you wouldn't." I knew nothing I could say would have any effect on him, so I added, "Please be careful, Mr. Bertram."

He laughed carelessly. "Don't worry about me. Just have your things ready. We'll leave at dusk, as planned.

"Where shall we meet?"

"Just be near the front door. You'll hear my carriage pull up."

"I'll be ready."

As Bertram headed toward Thane's study, I thought of telling Ramon of Bertram's plans to go back and view the runic writing, but decided against it. What harm would it do for Bertram to see the rune stone? I, myself, had been out there and returned safely.

I went up to my room to gather my belongings for my escape. Time passed slowly. Somehow, I had not been able to bring myself to go down for a last evening meal. Instead, I waited, staring down at the courtyard beneath my window, watching for the first hazy signs of darkness. Every minute now brought me closer to freedom.

Instead of relief I felt increasingly shaken by the knowledge that I would so soon be free of Thane Ulrickson's estate, of my imprisonment in his hideous, volcanic castle...free of Ramon!

I felt shocked by sudden feelings of confusion, even of sadness. I told myself sternly that this opportunity to leave with Bertram was the answer to a prayer. It could not be passed up, not if I was going to be of any assistance to Alan, who was in deeper trouble than even I fully realized. My allegiance must be to Alan, the man who my father had trusted and taken as partner in the work that had meant everything to him. Why did I have to think now of Ramon and already begin to miss him!

Perhaps it was only a manifestation of my fear of what tonight might bring, and Ramon as a figure I looked to as able to protect me. Although I trusted Bertram's desire to help me, I failed to trust his ability. He seemed too much an opportunist, preoccupied with his own interests. The imminent dangers of war would be the furthermost from his thoughts. Even if we did make our escape through dark, rebel-infested roads, what was I going to do then?

I attempted to blot out each looming fear telling myself that I would take only one step at a time. A glance outside the window told me that it was time to go downstairs and wait for Bertram. The thought of immediate goals prodded me to action. Nervously I stuffed a change of clothes into the case bearing my father's precious manuscript.

Before leaving, I took a last look around the room I had hated so much. The image of ancient wooden chests and the gigantic bed where I had so often lay awake would remain in my thoughts long after I had left here.

I had heard tales of prisoners not wanting to leave their cells after long years of confinement. Could this explain my sudden reluctance to leave?

I took one more look around the room. Had I left anything behind? Nothing but memories...memories of fear and helplessness and...unexpected joy.

Something made me cross the room, open the huge armoire, and gaze one last time at the emerald satin gown that I would never wear. By the time of the dance I would be far, far away. For a moment, a feeling of overwhelming sadness stole over me.

I closed the door to the armoire and turned away from dreams of dancing with Ramon and other foolish fantasy. Instead, I forced myself to channel my thoughts toward what lay ahead. When I returned to New York, I would concentrate on completing the new research for Father's book. I thought about my future, which must surely include Alan. I paused for a moment at the doorway before descending the stairs, wondering if I would truly ever forget Ramon's dark eyes.

Chapter Eleven

The great room below that I had wished to be vacant was not. The general and a pleasant-looking woman were seated in front of the fireplace, talking amiably and looking very comfortable. As I moved forward, I hurriedly deposited my case behind the draping folds of woven blanket which was spread across Evelia's loom. Neither of them appeared to notice.

Francisco Perez got slowly to his feet in chivalrous acknowledgment. "My wife," he said, gesturing toward the short, stout woman, who had risen also. "Lucia, this is Thane's friend, Marta Swan."

Because of their air of familiarity, the closeness in their ages, I should have known she would be the general's wife. Lucia wore her black hair clipped short around her heavy face. Her features were blunt, but radiated a kind and warming light, a great dignity that was sweet and calming.

"I'm so glad to meet you, Marta," she said graciously. "Francisco has told me all about you. I don't often get to talk to such an educated person as you are."

"We don't want to talk," Francisco Perez interrupted. "I want to eat. Why don't we move over to the table?"

"He thinks Thane's food is his own," she sighed in pretentious rebuke, as she glanced toward the huge table which I had never seen without food. "And this man is always hungry."

All I could do is bide my time, hoping they would leave before Bertram arrived. I should even try to eat something before my long, hectic journey.

A huge, empty space beyond the big walnut table made the

144

dining room seem strange to me, unfamiliar though I had been in it many times. Furniture had been pushed aside and the polished floor gleamed ready for the dance a few days away.

As I accepted the chair at the head of the table between them, I regarded more closely the general's wife. Despite the gentleness, she had an alert face, a subtle way about her that seemed to match the general's in wit and insight. She looked Indian; I detected the slightest hint of an accent that did not seem Spanish when she spoke, "Francisco tells me you are from New York City. So very far away."

"And she just can't wait to get back," the general interceded. "Which is something I really don't understand." His dark eyes were sharp and piercing. "Most young women would, if you don't mind my saying so, dream of being in your circumstance. There is nothing the Viking wouldn't do for you."

"Everyone in the world isn't out to get what they can," Lucia reminded him. "Marta looks to me like a very nice girl."

The general laughed and passed me a platter filled with rolls baked a golden brown.

I accepted the bread, studying the general as I did. How much did he really understand of my plight? Whose side would he be on if he did know? Lucia, I knew at a glance, would sympathize with me. Lucia was smiling at me now, very compassionately, as my own mother, who I had never known, might have smiled.

"How long have you known Thane Ulrickson?"

"For many years," Lucia said. "Francisco loves him like a brother."

I glanced around to make sure the Viking was nowhere present before saying, "Don't you feel...pity for him?"

"Pity?" Once again the general laughed. "He sees Ramon as a gallant knight, me as a neighboring king. He lives in constant expectation for the return of his Sun Goddess. What's there to pity? He should pity me!"

The general ate quickly, hungrily, before he spoke again. Eyes, half-hidden by drooping folds of skin, twinkled. "What I see around me are the indolent, the decadent, the cruel. I don't wait for happiness to return in any form."

"That is because you have happiness with you," Lucia reminded him, indicating herself.

"My princess," he said, pointing a fork at Lucia, "snores and nags."

"Not as loudly as you do!"

They were accustomed to joking with one another. I joined their laughter and for a moment felt at ease.

"In everyone's life there is much fantasy," Lucia added. "This is the man who used to sing songs outside my window!"

"In truth, I would still," the general said. Then to me, "I love the Viking for his pure brilliance. I've looked high and low for such a being...for a seeker of truth."

"Truth? He seems the antithesis of truth."

Francisco shrugged. "Thane is the nearest I have found. I'll admit, there is a point where reality and Thane part company, but as Lucia so poignantly reminds us, that is the way it is with us all."

A clever man, I thought...a clever woman. My eyes left them and strayed toward the door. Surely Bertram would be driving up in his carriage soon. How long would they detain me? I realized suddenly they were both watching me, waiting for me to comment. "Couldn't Thane be helped?" I inquired.

"You mean could one of your big-time Yankee doctors talk him out of his illusions?" He gave a deep chuckle. "I don't think so. He is convinced that everything is...not as it is...much better than it is."

"What kind of insanity is that?"

The general, amused by my question, laughed again. "The best kind!"

"Francisco," Lucia said. "Thane is your friend. I wish you wouldn't laugh at him."

The general chewed thoughtfully. "Lucia so seldom criticizes me. So I must be wrong. Can we laugh about something else?"

"Francisco tells me you are associated with the Alan Avery and his work. Now, if he will keep quiet, I want to learn from you. What do you make of the legend of *Quetzalcoatl*?"

The general answered promptly. "A white man." Heavy folds of skin obscured his eyes. "Tall of stature. With reddish beard and strange dress. Sounds to me like Thane Ulrickson!"

"Now, you quit! It's Marta I'm asking."

"Of course *Quetzalcoatl* existed, or at least the myth was based on some true person."

I was going to go on, but the general cut in again.

"The *Quetzalcoatl* legend is known throughout Mexico and Central America, although he is called by many different names. Some legends refer to him as a god, others a stranger from a distant land who sailed here upon a magic raft of serpents."

I thought of the ruins upon the cliffs that I had just visited, the murals showing men with beards and flowing hair, the slim boats with serpentine bows that looked so much like Viking ships.

"Some legends tell that he died on the coast of the Gulf and his followers burned his body and his treasure. I myself don't believe that for a minute. I think he settled very near here."

"I told you to stop!" Lucia admonished. "Marta, why do you believe this legend?"

"Who could doubt that the man existed? References are made to him in so many places in history. Montezuma mistook Cortes for *Quetzalcoatl* returning. That's why a few Spaniards could conquer a mighty nation."

"The Mayans…" Lucia said, "I am a Quiche Indian…spoke of two heroes that bear a similarity to *Quetzalcoatl*. *Itzamna* and *Kukulcan*, both portrayed as bearded men, led their ancestors into the Yucatan. *Itazmana* was an enlightened leader. He invented letters used for the first Mayan books."

"It is too bad the Spanish destroyed those books," I said.

"The other god, *Kukulcan*, was a great architect, a builder of pyramids."

"Whatever name they are called, they are all one," I said, "And based on one real person. But where do you think this foreigner came from, Lucia?"

"Where else?" the general answered. "He was a Viking! Remember it was Eric the Red and Leif Erickson who reached the new world 500 years before Columbus."

"Have you seen the stone near the lava caves with the runic writing?"

The general's glance darkened by his wife's question. His laughter this time sounded dry and forced. "So it is set down," he said quickly, "and seconded by me, that Thane is, if not *Quetzalcoatl* himself, his direct descendant." He rose wiping his mouth with a napkin. "But now, my dear, we are late getting started back."

"You are a remarkable girl! So much knowledge! I could spend days taking to you," Lucia said with great sincerity. "You must visit us soon!"

I cast a glance at the sky's fast-sinking light as I stepped outside and I determined the general and Lucia would not reach their estate before darkness fell. But Francisco, a cautious man, had provided for their safe journey. Four heavily armed men on horseback immediately rode toward them as they started away and followed the general's carriage as it passed through the gate.

Lucia looked back to wave fondly before they disappeared from view. Under different circumstances I would have enjoyed meeting Lucia and would have looked forward to seeing her again. I admired and had responded to her great interest in all subjects. And even the general's bantering remarks had offered distraction. Without their company the time spent waiting for Bertram would have dragged heavily.

I looked down the wide trail that passed in front of the mansion, east into the trees, listening, even though I knew it was far too early, for the sound of Bertram's carriage. Except for three men near the gate, all looked deserted.

Where was Ramon? I had expected him to be my major challenge, the one formidable opponent standing between me and tonight's escape. Generally when he departed, he left some substitute, usually the old man. But perhaps he was around, watching from some unseen point.

Inside Thane had just come up from his study. Someone had lighted the lights and flames reflected into the depths of his glowing eyes. "I had a wonderful visit with Francisco and Lucia. He is always better company when Lucia is around! Where are they? They surely haven't left without saying goodbye!"

"They did not want to disturb you. The general said you were busy with your research."

"So I am! And to my study I must return. But, first, I will take the time for a cup of coffee. He looked around the empty room. "Has our guest Bertram left, too?"

"I don't know." The thought that he might have already left made me uneasy. What if he decided to break his promise and just ride off, leaving me stranded? Yet, Bertram had seemed sincere enough in his offer to help me. It was only the long wait that was making me increasingly anxious.

"Will you join me, Marta?"

Relieved that he planned to leave so soon, I complied to his request. I seated myself on the chaise lounge nearest the fire and accepted the coffee.

"We haven't really had much of a chance to talk since you returned from the village," Thane said. "Bertram tells me you attended a speech. I didn't know politics would be of any interest to you. You continue to surprise me. To please me."

"An attempt was made on Don Orlando's life, I suppose Mr. Bertram told you?"

"We spoke in length of nothing but artifacts. I did like the man at first sight! He shares my...our...passion for the past. The Mayans, the Vikings...he was so interested in the Vikings. That is why I insisted he see the ruins."

I hesitated, then wanting to turn the subject back to Don Orlando, said, "The speech you mentioned was in Spanish, but Orlando's manner of delivery was very convincing. How well do you know Orlando?"

"I have run across Don Orlando several times. He is such a gentleman. He inspires my confidence much more than Carranza, who I fear loves only himself."

"Did you ever meet Don Orlando's son? The one who disappeared?"

"No," the Viking said. "He had been away, in the States, I

think."

"It is sad about his disappearance." I took a sip of the strong coffee. "Carranza has probably killed him."

Thane leaned forward, his manner confiding. "There are rumors," he said, "that Orlando's son disappeared by choice. That he is a scoundrel, who has turned against his own father to help the cause of his father's enemy."

"You surely don't believe that?"

Thane leaned back again. In his manner and the words he selected he seemed to be imitating the general. "I would prefer to believe that all men are honorable."

The Viking's voice, so realistic, so normal, began to fade. The lower pitch reminded me of the time I had gone with him to the cave, and I felt gripped by the same fear.

"I would prefer to believe that young men do not betray their fathers. That Orlando lost his only son in death, to Odin!"

Thane drank the rest of his coffee, placed aside his empty mug and stood. This activity seemed to have restored him. "I must get back to work. But what about you, my dear? Shall I send for Evelia to entertain you?"

"No, I would much rather be alone for a while."

As I looked up at him, I held my breath. Thane paid no attention to the sound that drifted to my own ears with alarming clarity, the distant rumble of hooves and carriage wheels, becoming more audible as they drew closer to the door. Bertram and my escape were fast approaching!

"I will stay with you if you like?"

"No, your work must come first."

Thane smiled and at the doorway paused again before he left.

I lost no time. I grabbed my case concealed by the blanket draped across the loom and raced to the door. Giving my eyes time to adjust to the blackness, I drew to a sudden stop, then making out Bertram's carriage and the tall form of a man holding reins, I hurried forward. "Are you ready to leave?"

"Marta, is that you?"

Once again I halted. The voice, deep and demanding, was

familiar to me. And it was not the voice of Gavin Bertram!

Ramon jumped from the carriage seat. As the dim light from the entrance mingled with his features I noticed the hard, pressed line of his mouth, the dark brows drawn together. A sense of fear, a premonition, made my heart begin to pound.

"Why are you...driving Mr. Bertram's carriage?"

He answered with a question of his own. "Where is he? Did he loan this carriage to someone today? Is he here?"

"No. I haven't seen him all afternoon."

Ramon hesitated. "I found his carriage out near the ruins, in the draw where we tied the horses. I've searched everywhere, but I can't find Bertram."

My voice was hollow as I answered. "He wouldn't have come back here without his carriage."

"I'm afraid something may have happened to him."

I stepped back, feeling the strength draining from my body, feeling overcome by guilt. His being missing, did it have some connection with my plans to leave here with him? Had I been a part of whatever fate had befallen him?

"He must have gone out on his own back to the ruins. I'm afraid he might have met with some accident upon the cliffs." Ramon attempted to comfort me by adding, "Or he may only be lost. Whatever has happened, we must find him. I'm going to get a search party and go back to where he left the carriage."

"May I go with you?"

"No!" Ramon's voice grew softer as he added, "It would be better for all of us if you stay here. The cliffs are much too danger-ous, even in daylight." I was aware that dusk was already giving way to darkness.

I turned to go back in the house. "I'll get Thane."

"I do not want Thane on the cliffs either. I will find Bertram myself."

"Bertram is Thane's guest. Why shouldn't Thane..."

"You know how he is," Ramon cut me short. "I don't want him getting stirred up. No telling what would happen then. Promise me you won't tell him!"

I returned to the dining room, replaced the case where it had been hidden, and sank down in the lounge where I had sat while talking to Thane. I had been surprised then by the Viking's talk of current events, his awareness of the political scene. Temporarily, I believed he was capable of rational action.

Even if he wasn't, I felt he should be told of Bertram's disappearance. I questioned Ramon's insistence upon protecting Thane as if he were a mere child, too simple to understand the life that went on around him. Or was Ramon shielding information from Thane for his own purposes?

During the endlessly long hours before dawn I waited with fear and dread for Ramon to return with some news of the man who had promised to help me escape.

* * *

The communication between the general's plantation and Thane's estate was fast and constant. Having been unable to bring myself to go up to my room at any time during the dreadful night, I had toward morning fallen asleep on the lounge near the fireplace. I awakened to the sound of Francisco Perez's voice, strange because it was sharp and decisive as he addressed Ramon. "As long as Thane is busy with his research, he will not concern himself with us."

Whatever had passed between them that I had not heard had brought to Ramon's features a tense agitation. My stirring caused him to face me. "We are going to search the area near the ocean," he said.

"I want to go with you!"

Ramon glanced at the general again. Francisco's voice had become his own, lazy and patronizing. "What we may find might not be a sight for your pretty eyes."

"We're certain now Bertram has met with an accident. He must have fallen from the cliffs." Ramon's dark eyes dropped away from mine.

I stood up, straightening my ruffled hair, my dress. "Let me go. Oh, please! I just can't bear to stay here any longer!"

My expression of agony must have convinced him, for Ramon

told the general, "Marta can ride with me."

Francisco shrugged. "A poor decision, but yours, not mine."

"It is what Marta wants. We'll met you at the ruins."

As the general left, Ramon stood motionless for a moment, then took a step toward me as if he intended to embrace me. I would have welcomed the comfort of his arms for already I felt the horror of what we might find.

"Bertram told Thane he was leaving yesterday before nightfall, but he never passed through the gate," Ramon told me. By-passing the trees that grew thick along the low area, Ramon urged the horses up the rocky incline. The carriage tilted and I slid against him.

"When Thane told me he hadn't seen Bertram at all after the deal they made in the study, I began to worry. I went out looking for him and found his empty carriage."

"But you found nothing during your search last night?"

"No, but in daylight we might uncover some clue."

The jolting ride over rocks turned my full attention to bracing myself to keep from falling.

"I think he must have gone back for a final look at the ruins," Ramon said. Those rock ledges are so treacherous! I warned him about climbing those cliffs alone!"

The general's men, fanned out along the base of the cliffs, combed the area inch by inch. Ramon looked at the ground around us as he drew the horses to a sudden stop. "Here is where I found his carriage. I traced his trail east, toward where we had climbed the cliffs yesterday."

I followed Ramon's gaze up the sheer, towering rocks and saw the general, alone, swiftly and agilely progressing upward. As I watched, he waved for us to join him.

"You are not dressed for climbing. You must wait down here."

"I'm going with you."

Ramon did nothing to oppose my insistence. The climb up was rigorous. Because of lack of sleep and food, I soon felt an unaccustomed weakness. I began to doubt whether my legs would carry me safely to the top. "Why don't you go on ahead?"

"I will wait for you." Ramon led me to a flat rock and insisted that I rest, while he, standing alertly beside me, watched the men so far below. They had now scattered, like trackers, each seeming to work alone.

At the top the general was investigating the vast center court-yard of the ruins. He stopped to touch a loose rock with his toe, then moved on without acknowledging our arrival.

Ramon went directly to the cliff's edge, which I remembered dropped precariously into the ocean. He walked the entire length of it once, then twice. I observed him a while, then stepped back to where the row of serpent heads faced the sea.

My gaze moved down the line, then returned to a gap where some of the heads were missing! I frowned, moving closer. I vividly recalled that the serpent heads, though badly worn, had all been intact when Ramon had taken us up to see the ruins.

On closer inspection, I saw that two of the heads were gone. I stepped forward and bent to examine the chunks of stone spread about on the ground beneath a third head, which was half-chopped away. Close investigation assured me that the chips in the stone had been freshly made.

It was obvious why Bertram had made one last visit here before leaving Thane's estate! I remembered his expressing his desire for one of the heads to place in his shop window. Even though the serpent heads were far from being a collector's dream, what better artifacts than those taken with his own hand from actual Mayan ruins?

The half-severed serpent head was badly worn. Had Bertram started chipping it away, then decided to take ones that were less damaged? Or had he intended to take this one, too, and been stopped or frightened away before he finished the job? I searched the ground, but whatever he had used to break the stones away was gone. Could Thane have found him here? Surely not even the Viking in his deluded state would consider Bertram's crime worthy of death! Unless Bertram had other crimes, too.

I remembered Bertram's interest in the rune stone and Viking relics. I found myself wondering if Bertram had come to Thane's estate of his own accord, or if Alan had sent him.

"What have you found?"

Ramon's question caused me to straighten up from my kneeling position. The shadows from the surrounding walls seemed to deepen his grim appearance. He seemed an opponent who stood between me and some dark truth.

"This is the reason Bertram came here again," I said breathlessly, gesturing toward the mutilated stones. "To take back with him samples from actual ruins."

Ramon turned away. I did not know whether from disgust or from the thought that I would read some guilty knowledge into his expression.

"Do you think Bertram removed several of these serpent heads to take back with him? We should be able to find them."

Ramon grimly assessed the wall before he spoke again. "I doubt it. If he fell, they will be with his body."

We walked back into the brilliant sunlight toward where the general stood so close to the edge of the cliff. "We've found something, too."

I recognized Bertram's jacket, the thin garment he always wore or carried to protect his light skin against the burning sun.

"It's Bertram's coat," the general announced, "We found it very close to the place where he must have fallen."

I drew in my breath at his words, but managed woodenly to continue walking. Ramon caught my arm as I approached and leaned over to peer straight down into the deep ocean. With desolation I watched the water hit the rocks, rise and fall, rise and fall.

"See that recess before the drop," Francisco spoke. "The cliffs look as if they have blood on them."

The outcropping of rock he indicated, several feet below us, was spattered with a darkish color like old rust. Layers of heat below me seemed to rise and encircle me. The cliffs bearing what I knew in my heart was Bertram's blood started to whirl. I stepped back closer to Ramon and felt his arms tighten around me.

"No sign of a body," the general said. "He must have struck

the rocks as he fell."

"There's something down there, though," Ramon said.

"Where?"

"On the ledge."

I forced myself to peer over the edge of the cliff once more. About half way down the ledge, I saw what Ramon was looking at. A stone, about the same size as one of the missing serpent heads, was trapped in a slight crevice of the tan outcropping of rock. The shadows upon the cliffs made it appear dark, almost gray in color. Mottled designs, like the carvings upon the serpent heads, were just barely visible.

"It must be one of the heads. He must have dropped it when he fell." Images of Bertram trying to scale the sheer cliffs, greedily holding on to his stolen prize, sickened me.

"Bertram wasn't much of a climber. Why would he take the ocean way down? It's much steeper than the way we climbed."

"Maybe he didn't want to risk anyone seeing him."

"But he left the carriage in plain sight."

An eerie feeling began to creep over me. Something was wrong. Images arose, of Bertram being hit on the back of the head by one of the stones he was trying to steal, of his being dragged to the cliff's edge and hurled downward into the water.

"We should bring up the stone," Ramon said, as if in response to my terrifying visions. "I'll have to come back with ropes to climb down after it."

"It doesn't matter," the general said, "we all know what has happened to Bertram."

The general's eyes, narrowed against the glare, skimmed the horizon. "His body may wash up eventually. Or it may never be found." He sighed heavily before he turned away. "As good a grave as any. I would as soon be covered with water as dirt."

Ramon waited as I wiped away tears and tried to steady myself for the long climb down. The general, despite his great weight and the extreme heat that now beat oppressively against the rocks, led the way, gaining great distance from us. He reached the level ground a long time before we did, and waited, wiping his face with a handkerchief, beside Ramon's carriage.

Ramon assisted me to the carriage seat where once again I battled the urge to sob.

The two men, as if of one mind, gazed at each other for some time before Francisco spoke. "Let me take care of everything," he said, once again seeming with his solemn assurance to be quite another person.

His black eyes shifted to me, then back to Ramon. "I will take his carriage back to Telas. I will say he was on his way to visit Thane and never showed up. When I went looking for him, I found his empty carriage on the road."

Ramon nodded his consent. "They will assume he was taken by rebels."

"But that's a lie!" I cried.

A period of quiet followed my accusation. "A lie is not actually a lie unless it is for an evil purpose," Francisco said.

"I think in this case it is necessary," Ramon supported him.

"Nothing can be accomplished by our saying otherwise. In the state our country is in now, we have no reliable police to investigate, not that this needs investigation. All we would do is open the gate to admit men we do not want here."

"His wife must be notified." I thought of the delicate woman waiting at home for a husband who would never return and once more I felt half-choked with tears.

"I'll take care of that," the general said. "It's better this way."

"But Thane... He may feel differently. And this is his business."

Once again Ramon and the general looked at each other. Once again I felt the closeness of their unspoken communication.

"No use worrying Thane with any of this," Ramon said. "It would accomplish nothing."

"We will simply tell the Viking," Francisco added, "that Bertram left yesterday as planned."

Chapter Twelve

Sunlight slanted across the front entrance of Thane's estate where Ramon and the general stood close together. Their secretive voices did not reach me, but I could see Ramon's taut shoulders and his dark head bowed in absorbed concentration. Ramon had assumed the same tense pose in the dim cantina at Telas when he had talked with Arnoldo Saville. Plotters, I thought, as I watched them.

Ramon had been a part of the attempt to kill Don Orlando, and now he was conspiring in a like manner concerning Bertram's death.

As soon as I could, I would return to the ruins and search for clues that would prove that Bertram's death was not an accident!

Feeling ill, I turned back to the dining room. I was faintly aware of Evelia's calling out directions in Spanish to several girls who were stacking brightly colored linens on the huge, wooden table for the fiesta. Surely when word reached Thane that Bertram was "missing," the dance would be canceled!

"Marta, why don't you help us? You could sort candles."

"I can't," I said, bypassing her and fleeing up the stairs to my room. Exhausted I gave way to the tears I had up until now so rigidly controlled.

In the silence after my sobbing had ended, my thoughts drifted back to my last conversation with Bertram. He had spoken of his intent to go to the lava beds to take a look at the rune stone near the caves. Why, then, had he gone back up to the cliffs?

Had he returned to the Mayan ruins with the intention of stealing the serpent heads, or simply gone up for another look around and had given in to a moment of greed? The fact that he must have had with him the necessary tools to cut loose the stones made me suspect the worst...that he had gone up there purposefully to steal.

But why the serpent heads? Why would Gavin Bertram, an experienced collector, bother with those eroded, weathered stones, which he himself believed would not even bring a good price? Yet, I remembered his comment about wanting one of the heads to display in the window of his shop. It was possible that a personal desire to own one or two of the unusual stones had compelled him to go back and remove them.

Bertram's jacket also puzzled me. It would have been much easier for wrap the heavy stones in the jacket than to try to hold them in his hands as he attempted to descend the treacherous cliffs.

That presented another question. Why would he have taken the steepest way? He was not a good climber and Ramon had warned him about the tides.

The entire scenario looked like a definite a set-up. I thought of the way the general had so quickly spotted the jacket. It seemed almost as if the fine coat, so easily recognized, had been left in plain sight upon the rocks on purpose, as a clue to direct our attention to the missing serpent heads and the spot upon the cliffs where Bertram had supposedly fallen.

Too much about his "accident" didn't make sense. But if Bertram's death was not an accident, who had killed him?

With sinking heart, I thought first of Ramon.

Bertram's death could be tied in with the plot to assassinate Don Orlando. But how could the two incidents be connected? Recalling Bertram's interest in politics, I considered the fact that he was not who he claimed to be. It would be easy enough to pose as a collector of antiques. In truth, Bertram might have been some important American diplomat, someone politically involved in the revolution.

Again I thought of the private meeting between Ramon and Arnoldo Saville just before the assassination attempt on Don

Orlando's life. What if they were all in this together? Ramon, the general and Sanchez, a group of Carranza's revolutionaries headed by Arnoldo Saville, attempting to assassinate Don Orlando. What if revolutionaries had slowly and gradually infiltrated the unsuspecting Viking's estate and were using this place as a kind of protected military base?

But, of course, the idea was ridiculous! I trusted Ramon, and could not believe the kindly, soft-spoken Arnoldo Saville to be a brutal murderer. And I was growing truly fond of the sharp-witted general. Sanchez was the only one I did not trust or like. But as much as I wanted to blame everything that had taken place on him, I knew if he were involved, so were the others.

Bertram's interest in Mayan artifacts and Viking relics seemed genuine, almost obsessive. And his Spanish was so poor he had difficulty ordering in the hotel, or even understanding Don Orlando's speech! I had no real reason to doubt his established identity. An image of his frightened face, the sight of him frozen with fear as bullets whizzed past his head in the plaza convinced me that he had not been involved in any kind of political espionage. If the fall to his death was in any way connected to the political unrest here, then he was only a victim caught in the crossfire.

Of course the revolution did not have to play any role in his death. Thane, himself, was the most likely suspect, since it was his property Bertram had been defacing. I had not seen Thane leave the study, but he could have left through the tunnel. Thane could have wandered up to the ruins and unexpectedly come across Bertram stealing the serpent heads. In a fit of rage he might have murdered Bertram and tossed his body down the cliffs into the ocean.

Although that seemed to be the logical thing to have happened, I could not quite bring myself to believe it. Thane mistook everyone he met for some perfect being; he acted upon his failure to see the people around him as they really were by treating them with generosity and with abundant affection. Unless...there was another side to Thane Ulrickson, a darker side to his madness I had never seen.

Troubled thoughts made me rise from the bed and restlessly pace the length of the room until I stood staring down at the small courtyard below. Through the grated bars of the window I saw sunlight bright upon the pine tree, whose sturdy limbs I had once before climbed down in order to leave the house unnoticed. I could do the same thing now!

The only way I would find out about Bertram's death and put my mind at ease was to return to the ruins. But should I? My thoughts might just be running wild, I told myself sternly. I could be reading an evil event into a pure accident!

As I stood debating the wisdom of my desire to investigate, I thought about the stone caught upon the ledge halfway down the cliffs. The stone was the only object that might provide answers to my questions, a clue to the circumstances surrounding Bertram's death.

The shape and mottled grayness of the stone against the tan rocks of the cliffs had led both Ramon and I to believe that it must be one of the serpent heads.

I remembered how one of the heads had been half cut away, then abandoned. Of the two that were missing, one must have fallen into the sea with Bertram when he plunged to his death. But the other had become trapped by the rocks on the way down, and remained there, caught in a deep crevice about ten feet below.

Visions I had experienced upon the cliffs, visions of the stone, about the size of both my fists doubled together, being used as a murder weapon, made me shrink away from the window. Had Thane or someone caught Bertram at his task and struck him from behind with one of the very objects he was trying to steal? Had the killer tossed Bertram's body over the cliff, then thrown the murder weapon down after him and hurried away, not even suspecting that the stone had been trapped by the ledge?

Somehow, I had to retrieve the stone from the rocky promontory and examine it for traces of blood. If there were no blood on the stone, then I would have to accept the fact that Bertram had been up there stealing, had lost his balance and fell. But if there were blood upon the rock itself, then I would know that Bertram had been assaulted with the stone, murdered! I had to go back and get the stone now. I could not afford to wait, knowing as I did that Ramon might decide to take the very same action.

***

I could either climb down the limbs of the tree beside my window as I had done once before or try to leave the house through Thane's study. If Thane wasn't researching, I might be able to slip through the tunnel and end up at the shed where I remembered seeing tools and loops of rope hanging from the wall.

To my relief the study was empty and the door into the tunnel unlocked. I walked quickly though the tunnel and paused in the huge shed to select a rope. On the floor I spotted a burlap bag, which I also carried with me.

This time I chose the shorter trail, which left the pines to cross through the rough lava beds directly in front of the cave and rune stone.

When I reached the cave area, I forced myself to sit for a while upon a big boulder and rest. My breathing came quickly and my eyes kept watching for movement from the area of thick trees nearby.

Had someone followed me? Although I was positive no one had seen me leave the house, fear made me keep glancing over my shoulder as I rose and began to walk again. Maybe it was just being in the cave area, which Ramon had warned me to stay away from, that increased my apprehension.

I passed in front of the rune stone. The ancient writing had an obscure and hidden look as if it concealed many important secrets. I forced myself to move on until I stood at last in the shadows of the cliffs and surveyed the high, sheer walls that rose above me.

The climb would be more difficult than the way Ramon had led us, but not impossible. My gaze sought out niches and jutting edges in the wall that gradually formed a path to the top. I stopped to secure the sack and wind the long strands of rope around my waist so I could have the free use of both of my hands.

Anxiousness and exhaustion made me feel a weakness in my limbs as I found a foothold in the stone and pulled myself up to a higher shelf in the rock. The roughness of the sharp surface bit into my hands as I struggled upward, the rope and burlap bag creating an extra burden. I found myself longing for Ramon's strong hand reaching out for mine, his deep voice speaking encouragement to help me over dangerous rises to safe ledges.

Gradually, inch by inch, I worked my way to the top. My whole body felt as wet as if I had climbed from out of the ocean's depth. I ran my fingers through my damp hair and paused to savor the cool breeze blowing from the sea.

Crumbling walls shaded me as I crossed the silent courtyard to the opposite edge of the cliffs and gazed down the sheer drop to the water. Combating a wave of dizziness, I searched for traces of bloodstains upon the jutting ledge.

The stone still rested in a deep crack within the solid outcropping, about ten feet below. Shadows of the overhanging cliffs fell over it, making it appear gray and mottled, an ominous dark speck against the background of sandy limestone.

I knew I would have to anchor the rope around a solid object and use it to brace myself on the way down the cliff's edge. I located a heavy boulder lodged deeply into the earth and tested its strength to make certain it would hold against pressure and weight.

I reassured myself that the climb down to the ledge where the rock lay was not far. Holding on to someone's arm, I could almost have reached it without a rope.

Preparing myself, I took a deep, calming breath and looked down. The spatters of blood upon the rocks below, the frightening drop to the sea from where the stone rested, filled me with sudden horror. I felt sick at the thought that I must lower myself to the place where Bertram's blood stained the cliffs, dangle suspended for a short while over that plunge to the sea, then reach the ledge and take hold of the rock.

Willing myself not to think about the precarious drop, the restless waves so far below, I tied the end of the rope securely around my waist and began to start down. Bracing my feet against the edge of the cliff, burlap bag to carry the stone fastened securely, I started my descent. Slowly, like a spider, I crawled my way toward the ledge.

For a moment, suspended in mid-air between the top of the cliff and the ledge, panic overcame me. What if I had been followed? I had placed myself in a very vulnerable position! If someone had tracked me here, all he would need to do now is loosen the rope and I would drop to my death.

Gavin Bertram's last moments of life flitted through my mind. I could see his pale, terror-filled eyes as he attempted in vain to save himself. I could hear his piercing scream as he fell, the slap of his body against rock and water. Then only the faint lapping of waves sounded, just as they did now so far below me.

My limbs began to shake. My fingers that clutched the rope lost power and grip.

A wave of sickness swept over me as my dangling foot just barely grazed the outcropping of rock stained with Bertram's blood. Half-afraid to let go of the rope, but anxious to get this over with, I swung my hand out quickly and grabbed at the stone, which rested in the shadows of a dark recess.

It rolled from the crevice and almost fell into the sea. Gasping, I caught and steadied the edge it, relieved that the one clue to Bertram's death had not been lost to the waves. Fumbling, I opened the burlap bag and slipped the stone into it. Clutching the heavy burden firmly against me, I pulled with all my strength on the rope and began to climb upward.

The added weight of the stone made my ascent much more difficult. Once my foot slipped against the sheer ledge, causing me to flounder in terror as I struggled to gain foothold.

When I reached the solid rock of the cliff's flat mesa, I could have kissed the ground! The frightening ordeal I had convinced myself I must go through was over! I took a moment to close my eyes and regain my strength. Then I loosened the burlap bag and drew out the stone I had risked my very life to retrieve.

My fear and anxiety had been so strong I had scooped the stone into the bag without really examining it. Now, I stared at the stone I had brought up with a sense of shock. It was not one of the serpent heads, but a dark gray stone of about the same size. A plain, basalt stone, marbled with deep, natural markings, which, from a distance, had looked like the carvings upon the weathered serpent heads. A kind of stone that was not found here, but in the lava bed area far below.

Snakeskin markings along one side of it were stained with a darkish-red substance. A chill made the skin upon my scalp prickle. I was staring down at Bertram's blood!

A renewed weakness, greater than any I had ever felt before, caused my vision to blotch and blacken. I was holding in my hands the weapon that had killed Gavin Bertram. Spatters of blood, such as was on the jutting promontory, might have been caused by Bertram's body striking the rocks on his plunge down. But there was no possible way that so much blood could have collected on one small stone unless he had been struck with it before he fell. I studied the stone I knew did not even belong here with the cliff's light tan rocks. This stone was one of the many I had seen in the cave area down below.

What if Bertram never had intended to come back up here? What if, instead, he had gone out to the lava beds to search for the rune stone? If so, then he might have been killed in the cave area and his body brought up here to make his death look like an accidental fall.

But why would anyone go to all of that trouble?

Had Thane overheard our plans to leave? Had he followed Bertram out to the caves and killed him to prevent my escape? The thought made me feel a sense of fear greater than any I had ever known.

It seemed perfectly clear to me now that no matter why Bertram was killed, Thane himself was the killer. Possibly Bertram, in his inquisitive snooping around the lava beds, had wandered too close to Thane's cave. Thane, so protective of his jewels, might have believed Bertram was trying to find an entrance into the cave to steal his treasures.

I felt a sense of guilt that I had done nothing to prevent Bertram from going to view the rune stone, which had placed him so very near Thane's cave. Even though I had tried to warn him, I was still somehow responsible!

Yet another thought struck me: What if Gavin Bertram had actually been trying to find a way into Thane's vault? I remembered Bertram's nervous actions, his disappearing on the way back from the ruins, his obsessive interest in Viking relics. Thane might have caught him looking for treasure... not worn stone heads, but gold and jewels of immense value!

Accidentally or on purpose, Bertram had gotten too close to Thane's cave. But was he working alone, or had someone sent him? Could Alan have persuaded Bertram to try to gain entrance to the estate in order to search for the rumored treasure-vault? I quickly put the thought from my mind. I could not start suspecting Alan, the only person I had left to trust!

My accusations returned to Thane. How easily it could have all taken place. Thane would think of himself as gallant lord, Bertram some evil dragon come to steal the treasures of his cave. Thane, drifting in and out of fantasy, madness throwing a blinding cloak over his sense of reality, would without doubt be able to justify to himself what he had done.

Had Thane brought Bertram's body up here and tossed it over the cliffs to make his death look like an accident to Ramon, the general, and me? The logic of it made panic rise once again. Thane would not kill for a few stone serpent heads, but if he found someone near the caves, his instinct to protect what he thought was his duty to keep safe might have taken over his senses. He might have made Bertram's death seem like an accident to keep me from being upset over what he had truly believed he must do!

I pictured Thane's massive arms and sturdy build. It would have taken a very powerful man or two men working together to have carried Bertram's body up to the top of the cliff and toss it over into the sea. It seemed to me that only a madman would have carried out such a plan. Thane Ulrickson!

Suddenly, I could imagine Thane coming across Bertram near his precious cave...lifting the rock, bashing him in the head. The horror of the image lodged in my mind and struck terror into my very soul.

What should I do with the rock? For now, I had to find some place to hide it. Later, at some distant day after I had gotten away, I would need proof that Bertram was murdered. My eyes fell to a wall with a crumbling foundation. I dug deeply into the center of it, placed my evidence inside, and carefully rebuilt the front. I stepped away, satisfied that the gray stone was safely hidden and that the partial wall looked totally undisturbed.

Reoccurring images plagued me as I started back to Thane's estate. I could see Thane, madman and a murderer, striking poor, unsuspecting Bertram again and again. I had visions of his dragging Bertram's body up the cliffs and hefting it over as easily as if it were a sack of grain. In my horrified mind I watched Thane hurl the murder weapon down after him with the belief that it, too, had plunged into the sea!

Thane was more dangerous and deluded than I had ever imagined! I had to find some way to get away from here before Thane tried to kill me too, before the idea occurred to him that a dead princess would never try to escape!

* * *

"Marta, my dear. Where have you been? I've been looking all over for you!" The sight of Thane advancing from the front door toward me with broad steps made the blood drain from my face and caused me to tremble. For the first time, I felt fear of him, fear of his huge, towering form, his dynamic energy, the madness that set him so much apart from other people.

Trying to conceal my fear, I responded, "I've been out walking."

"A walk? Yes. A beautiful day for one, I suppose. I should have gone with you." With a look of regret, he added, "My research has kept me locked up in that dungeon of a study for days. I've been reading the complete works of Stephens. I became so involved in his volumes, I lost all track of time. Why, I haven't seen the sun for several days!" With a worried look, he interjected, "I apologize, dear princess. I hope you've found happy ways to pass the time."

"I've...managed to keep busy,"

167

"Good!" He responded enthusiastically. "Soon, we will have the big dance and then you won't want for entertainment!" With an air of disarming innocence that made goose-flesh rise upon my arms he added, "A pity Bertram couldn't stay for the dance. He's probably on a ship back to the States this very minute."

I swallowed hard and managed to nod faintly.

"An interesting fellow." Shaggy, reddish-gold brows knitted together to form an arc above startling blue eyes. "I regret I didn't have a chance to bid him goodbye, but then I expected him to come back down to my study before he left."

I forced my voice to sound natural. "He didn't come back, then?"

"No...I found it very odd. I had set aside some inexpensive Viking items he had expressed interest in for him to buy." With a shrug of wide shoulders, Thane added, "He must have changed his mind. Americans are more likely to do that than any other people, aren't they?"

"I suppose so," I responded faintly.

"Truthfully, I'm a little glad. I wasn't sure whether I should sell him anything that even touches upon our heritage." I saw in his eyes a distant look. His voice began to grow eerily strange as he continued, "These things have been left in our care by Odin. Perhaps it is our destiny to keep *all* of them, even those we con-sider of no significance."

More than ever I felt shaken by his sudden transition from reality to fantasy.

"Yes, I'm sure Odin has left them in my care. I was given your jewels to protect, to keep safe for you. For all eternity! A duty that I honor above my very life. I would never fail you, dear princess!"

My vision returned. I saw him striking Bertram on the head with the rock. His eyes must have looked just as they did this moment, glassy, irrational. I felt unable to move, unable to speak.

When I regained control of myself, I shrank away from him. After taking several steps backward, I ran around the house to-ward where the fountain set beneath my window.

"What's wrong, Marta?" Ramon caught my arms and held me close to him.

"Thane, he..." I started, breathless. I turned to look back, but Thane had not followed me.

Ramon's strong grasp guided me to the wrought-iron bench beside the fountain. He seated himself beside me and took my hand. "Now, tell me what is wrong."

"I'm afraid of him!" I said between gasping sobs. "I believe Thane has murdered Gavin Bertram!"

His dark eyes widened as if my words startled him. "Marta, Thane wouldn't harm anyone. He's as innocent as a child."

"I don't believe Bertram's fall was an accident."

Ramon's gaze seemed to reflect full acceptance of my own conclusion.

"I am going to find out what happened to him," he said reassuringly. "I am going to take a look at that stone we saw."

Ramon's observant gaze drifted to my hands. He lifted the one he still held and examined the cuts I had gotten during the rough climb. I lowered my lashes to avoid meeting his gaze.

"Marta, look at me." Ramon tilted my chin so I was forced to look straight into his eyes. "I don't know what you think you know about this, but Thane had nothing to do with Bertram's death."

"You must know much more about this than you're telling me."

"I have suspicions, but nothing else. But I do know one thing beyond doubt: Thane is perfectly innocent."

"How can you be so sure?"

"Can't you trust me?" I saw tenderness in his eyes, compassion that revealed a softer side to him. I wanted him to pull me again into his arms and hold me tightly.

I turned from him and covered my face with my hands. "There is nowhere I can turn! No one I can trust."

"Oh, Marta," he said, as if he, too, were in pain. "I wish there was some way I could let you know the truth."

What did he mean? If he thought he knew what had happened

to Bertram, why couldn't he tell me? "Please tell me who killed him. I don't understand why...."

"I wasn't referring to Bertram's fate. I was speaking to you of the truth of my feelings for you." As he spoke, he drew me closer. The feel of his body close to mine gave me an unexpected sense of comfort. Miserably I pressed my head against his shoulder and cried.

I wept for Bertram, a man I hardly knew, but was beginning to like. "Bertram told me about his wife waiting for him at home. She'll never even know what happened to him or why he died."

"Someday the truth about his death will be known," Ramon assured me. "I will do all I can to make it known. I make that promise to you, Marta."

Another promise, he added to the vow to help me escape, another empty promise.

I told myself I had turned to Ramon simply because I had no one else to turn to. At the same time I wondered how could I doubt him and still take such comfort in the haven of his arms?

* * *

The next two days dragged by with an agonizing slowness. The horror of Bertram's death cast a constant pall upon my thoughts. Long hours spent up in my room made me restless for some activity, anything to break the spell of hopelessness and despair.

The morning before the dance I wandered down to the cleaned and polished room where maids were busy with last-minute chores...setting out crystal, filling sweet dishes with nuts and dried fruits, adding tall tapers to wall sconces and candelabras to supplement the dim lighting of the room.

Evelia was busy arranging flowers into huge vases. "May I help?" I asked.

As we worked with thin-petaled stalks of orchids, Ramon and Thane entered from outside. The somber looks on their faces made me realize that word of Bertram's death must have reached Thane.

Awkwardly, as if unaccustomed to being the bearer of bad

tidings, Thane spoke, "Ramon tells me our friend Bertram never made it back to his ship, Marta. The general found his carriage on the road to Telas, not far from here."

At his words, Evelia looked up from her work, her eyes wide and anxious.

The sadness that darkened Thane's blue eyes, the remorse in his voice, seemed genuine as he said, "I wish he had let me known he was leaving. I would have provided him with an escort."

After a long silence, Evelia asked, "We will still have the dance, won't we?"

"The dance?" Thane glanced around the huge room as if noticing for the first time the polished floors, the candles, the stalks of freshly-cut flowers. The absence of the air of joviality that was such a part of him made him seem suddenly very human, very vulnerable. "Of course, we will have to have the dance. I have sent invitations far and wide! We wouldn't cancel it now."

The great suffering in the Viking's eyes made me want to offer words of consolation, as I would have to a very young child.

Before I could speak, as if the news of Bertram's fate had been a great loss to him, Thane said, "I think I will have to go down to my study a while to recover from this unhappy news."

I followed Ramon out into the hallway and we both watched the Viking move away toward his study, the hunch of his broad shoulders adding an air of dejection to his sturdy frame. Ramon's eyes, dark and pensive, moved from his friend's receding form back to me. "Do you still think Thane is a murderer?"

"No," I responded faintly. Except for a moment of pure panic, I had really never believed Thane to be capable of such cruel violence. My voice, barely more than a whisper, asked, "But if not Thane, then who did murder Bertram?"

"What makes you so certain he was murdered?" Ramon's dark eyes seemed to search mine, as if he knew that I were withholding vital facts from him. "I went back for the stone we saw upon the cliffs, but it was gone. So now we have no clue that his death was anything more than an unfortunate mishap."

I glanced away, avoiding his penetrating gaze, as he added, "I think someone must have taken the stone."

"Maybe it fell into the sea."

"I believe someone purposefully removed it," he said.

I considered confessing that I had taken the stone from the cliff's ledge myself. I debated whether or not I should lead Ramon to the place where the weapon lay concealed and show him that it was stained with Bertram's blood.

I began to speak, but a warning inside my mind silenced me. I would have spoken if Ramon and the general had not acted so suspiciously that day we had found Bertram's body, if they had not lied to Thane about the circumstances of Bertram's death with the ease of men who often conspire together. As much as I wanted to share the burden of my secret with someone, I dared not trust Ramon.

I would leave the rock right where I had hidden it until I could contact Alan. Together Alan and I would go to the authorities and ask them to investigate Bertram's death.

"What do you think happened to the stone?"

"Maybe," I answered, "whoever killed him, removed it."

"I intend to find out exactly what happened," Ramon spoke with grave determination.

Ramon knew I was keeping important information from him. I could tell this by the sudden way he turned and with very straight shoulders walked away from me.

I went back into the dining hall. The Viking's assurance that the unpleasant news concerning Gavin Bertram would not interfere with plans for the dance had renewed Evelia's cheerfulness. "These pink orchids will go well with the white," she said, handing me another fragrant, fresh-cut stalk.

Silently, we worked side by side. I found the simple task of arranging bouquets of orchids into tall ceramic vases a welcome diversion to my dark and troubled thoughts.

Chapter Thirteen

The person who stared back at me through the ancient glass of the mirror seemed transformed into someone else. I had never considered myself possessed of great beauty; my looks were certainly not in keeping with society's model of the perfect woman. A time or two I had tried to conform to the image of the curly-haired, plump, slightly pallid woman of the fashion plates, but to no avail. I was destined to be tall, my skin had a naturally healthy glow, and my hair, disinclined to curl, remained thick and straight as a horse's mane.

But tonight...I caught my breath at my own wavering reflection. The deep emerald color of the exquisite gown brought out sparkling blue highlights in my light eyes. Delicate lace, exactly the color of my hair, spread like fine net across the ever-so-slightly plunging neckline and draped in graceful folds around the full skirt. Wearing the shimmering gown, aware of golden strands of hair escaping its loose knot to cascade around my shoulders, I felt for a moment exactly like the princess Thane believed me to be.

The Viking, I knew, would be waiting. If I delayed much longer, he would come looking for me. With this thought in mind, entered the grand hall from the winding staircase that descended directly into the room.

The immense hall, filled with the flickering light of a multitude of candles, seemed unfathomable. The blackened walls of rough lava, the heavy furnishings, the wooden table laden with food, made the huge dining room remind me more than ever of some medieval castle. Not Thane, but Ramon I sorted out from the crowd that had gathered. From across the room, he stopped talking to the man beside him to watch my sudden entrance. The sight of him caused me to pause and grip the railing tightly before continuing downward.

Ramon straightened when our eyes met and seemed to draw in his breath. I felt myself reacting in exactly the same way, my throat tight, breathing suddenly difficult. He looked so very handsome, so perfect in every detail...the thin mustache, the gleaming hair, the white shirt and tight-fitting suit. Designs of red embroidery across the shoulders of his bolero jacket increased the width of his shoulders; the black of the suit added to his proud bearing a dimension of great height.

Ramon's dark eyes, glowing like the surrounding candles, traveled over me, taking in the details of the dress I had worn especially for him. I flushed at their burning approval. I threaded my way through the throng of people, gradually working my way toward him.

But before Ramon reached me, Thane cut in front of him. I shrank from the sound of his deep, roaring voice. "Marta! You look beautiful tonight! Absolutely splendid!"

Thane's strong fingers entwined themselves around my arm as he steered me away from Ramon into the mass of guests. I glanced back over my shoulder. Ramon's dark face had become impassive and hard, as it had been when he had caught up with me in Santa Augusta after Alan had fled.

"So many people I want you to meet," Thane was saying as he led me through the crowd, pausing occasionally with a great air of joviality to introduce me to one guest or another. He had to shout to be heard above the noise. Some of the Viking's guests were dressed in glamorous ball gowns like my own...others wore simple, even shabby clothing of homespun cotton.

I could not even hear the names of most of the people he introduced me to. I smiled and nodded as Thane presented me to several men, obviously of high military rank, wearing elaborate braided epaulets upon their jackets, and high, black boots. Thane stopped to speak to couples I had seen at the Spanish hotel, men and women dressed in the highest fashion. Just as proudly, he introduced me to villagers, some in simple sandals, in ragged shirts and trousers. I had never before seen such a wide range of people mixed together...old, young, rich, poor, ignorant, learned...intermingling, if not with cordial, at least with an open acceptance.

Seeming solitary, a little apart despite the big gathering, Thane searched the room as if seeking a familiar face. His eyes lit up as he caught sight of the general and his wife and began immediately to move toward them.

He strode to where the two of them sat near the head of the table. As was Thane's custom, there was no formal seating; people filled their plates and carried them off to all areas of the hall. Though platters of food were carried about by servants, just as many guests were helping themselves to the huge assortment of meat, fruit, and wine upon the table. The aroma of roast chicken and baked fish mingled with sweet tropical fruit, and the acrid odors of smoke and pine from the roaring fireplace nearby.

"Are you finding enough to eat, general?" Thane jested, as we approached.

Francisco Perez laughed and raised a plate heaping with food. "Not quite, but I'll try to get by."

"Dear Lucia!" Thane turned with delight to the general's wife. Lucia wore a modest, high-necked gown of pale blue which complemented her short, stout form. A shawl of a deeper shade draped over her shoulders accentuated dark eyes and black hair lightly touched with gray. "You must meet my princess!"

"We've already met, Thane." Lucia leaned forward to take one of my hands in hers. "I'm so pleased to see you again, Marta," Her heavy face lit with a warm smile. "You look lovely tonight, my dear. What a gorgeous gown! The emerald color becomes you."

"Thank you," I responded somewhat self-consciously.

"Let's join them, Marta. Let's have something to eat." The throne-like seat at the head of the table Thane normally occupied, and the one beside it, remained vacant, no doubt reserved at Thane's orders, especially for us. He pulled out my chair for me, then seated himself. Like the general, Thane piled his plate high with thick

175

slabs of bread and meat, and began to eat with great appetite.

Having eaten a late noonday meal, I did not feel hungry. To please him, I took a little of the sliced meat, some boiled shrimp, and chunks of pineapple and melon.

"Everything is so delicious," Lucia said. "And the hall is magnificent! Who would have ever thought this huge, barren room could be so filled with such brightness?"

"You brighten any room you enter, Lucia," Thane said. "I'm so glad you are here tonight. I was afraid you would stay home with your books. The general said he purchased several new ones for you when he was at Telas."

"When was that?" I asked, aware of the edge of suspicion in my voice.

Francisco swept my question away. "I'm always buying books for her. When she's reading, she's not nagging!"

Lucia's sweet glance moved from her husband back to Thane. "He would be nothing and do nothing without my constant prodding."

I noticed between Thane and this gentle woman their seemed an easy rapport, a special friendship, which the general appeared to encourage.

"Lucia hates big crowds," he now told Thane. "She came here tonight simply to please you."

"She wouldn't dare miss my fiesta! She is my very best friend, besides you, Francisco. Before tonight is over," he addressed Lucia, "we will show them all how to dance!"

"I'd rather not exhibit my dancing skills, Thane."

"Of course she will!" the general interceded. "Lucia loves to dance, and I don't. Not with these two left feet."

Thane's boisterousness caused a blush to spread across Lucia's face, yet she managed to smile, as if accustomed to his ways. "Only one dance, a slow one."

A very old man with a long, tranquil face approached the table. "Ah, here comes the first of our entertainment!" Thane said, delighted. The old man seemed to speak neither English or Spanish, never-the-less Thane and he communicated easily, as if they had spoken together long and often. Thane lifted the large shell of a river turtle, which hung by a worn leather strap around the man's neck.

"Very few people can make music with such an instrument. A *bigu*, it is called. Pre-Spanish." He laughed. "And so are you, eh, Juan Carlos? Play a tune for Marta and me."

The old man raised drum sticks made of antlers. This slight gesture called forth another Indian, this one carrying a flute.

The virtuoso of the flute player imitated the songs of birds; the resounding of antler against shell, refrains from the jungle. The music made me hear the faint stirring of branches, the hum of insects, the clattering of Macaws. Strains of music, a little sad, were at the same time filled with the reality of life in the rain forest.

"You are experiencing the true Indian culture," General Perez told me. "My Lucia told you she is a Quiche Indian."

Thane's bright gaze moved to the player of the *bigu*. "You are the very best, Juan Carlos!" he praised the aging Indian, who nodded as if readily interpreting the meaning, if not of the language.

When the song had ended, the Viking raised his hand for them to play another one. The music continued, as if there existed no such thing as time and rush, in song after song.

Beginning to feel more relaxed, I once again scanned the crowd for Ramon. He stood near the door, watching the scene before him with cool detachment, as if he were there, not to enjoy, but for some singular, solemn purpose. He moved to speak to a gray-haired man who had just entered. I saw, when the man turned, a face I quickly recognized, one that brought back memories of the cantina in Telas, the clandestine meeting between Ramon and him. "Isn't that Arnoldo Saville?"

"Arnoldo always attends the Viking's celebrations," the general responded. As if the subject of Arnoldo Saville was of little interest to him, he patted his stomach, his heavy-lidded eyes reflecting drowsy pleasure. "I don't think I could eat another bite!"

"We all know better than that," Lucia said.

Thane, hearing them, lifted one of the crystal goblets of wine from a nearby tray and pressed it into Francisco's hand. "Then, my good friend, you must drink!" The heavy folds of skin around cynical eyes creased as the general smiled. Accepting the glass, he raised it to Thane in mock salute. "Drink...now that's another story, Viking!"

Noting that the elderly Indian was tiring, Thane allowed him to stop playing by also offering him and the flute player a drink. Lucia and Juan Carlos began to converse in the dialect of the Quiche Indians. Excusing herself, she left us to usher the elderly Indian and his companion to seats near the fireplace.

"Lucia and Juan Carlos are from the same village," Francisco explained. "A remote place, so far away she seldom gets a chance to visit and hear news of her family."

While Juan Carlos had been playing, a band of five musicians had began busily setting up instruments along the side wall. The heavy-set band leader now moved his marimba, and another arranged huge drums behind him. The other three, I decided, must play brass. "This band is from Guatemala," the general leaned forward to explain. "Their music, like the Viking, has great vitality."

With a gesture to the leader, Thane ordered, "Now, we will hear your music!" Immediately, strains of cheerful music, brisk and lively after the languid, primitive sound of shell and flute, filled the air. Thane's eyes glittered with sheer pleasure as, listening to the musicians play for us, he finished his glass and took another from the silver tray.

Although there was nothing arrogant in Thane's manner, I realized how much he enjoyed playing the great lord. His immense wealth made him, despite his delusions, a man of great power in this poor, remote, area of Honduras. His extravagance and generosity made hundreds of people eager to jump at his beck and call.

I glanced once more toward Ramon and Arnoldo Saville, who now seemed deep in serious conversation. Tonight in dark trousers and puffy, cotton shirt, Arnoldo did not look like a priest. I wondered who he really was, and why both Alan and Ramon trusted him. What was he doing here? Were they talking about Gavin Bertram?

Or was he speaking to Ramon about Alan? The thought that he might have word from Alan lifted my spirits. Hoping to get some information from the general about him, I asked, "Who is Arnoldo Saville? What does he do?"

"He would be rich, but he gives too much away," the general responded evasively. "Still he does not need to work. Although he does, for me, sometimes...."

"Is he a revolutionary?"

The general, a little taken back by my question, deliberated for a minute before responding, as if the answer was more complex than the question. "He is one of Carranza's men, though not corrupt, like Sanchez, like so many of his Carranza's soldiers. But he is," Francisco shrugged, "a good man himself. Always in issues of war one finds noble men on both sides."

Almost, I thought, the same words Ramon had spoken that day in Telas when I had found him in secret meeting with Arnoldo.

Shrill sounds of brass-players increased in volume so that more conversation became impossible. Light and springy, at first, the music gained momentum. "Dance with me Marta!" Thane insisted, pushing back his chair. Before I could even protest, he took my arm, drawing me with him out into the center of the room. For an instant, before we began to dance, I caught sight of Ramon. He no longer seemed distant and detached, but watched us from across the room. I threw him a pleading look, sincerely wishing he would step forward and rescue me.

Everyone watched and clapped as Thane and I danced the first dance alone together. For such a big man, he was light on his feet and possessed a natural sense of rhythm. Still, I felt awkward in his arms, aware of so many eyes upon us. As if sensing my self-consciousness, Thane reached down and gently rested my head against his broad shoulder.

I was glad when other couples began to join us, until the open area of the hall swirled with ball gowns and motion. For a moment, I closed my eyes and tried to make the best of the awkward situation by concentrating upon the music and the dance.

When the music slowed, I looked around to find Ramon's gaze

still locked upon us. He stood alone by the door now; Arnoldo Saville had gone. He watched Thane and I dance, arms folded across his chest, face unsmiling. His eyes, as they caught mine, sparked with sudden fire. With surprise I realized that he had all the appearance of a very jealous man!

The dance ended. The musicians stopped playing and began furiously discussing their music. I took the opportunity of the brief pause to move out of Thane's arms.

"Don't you want to dance again?" he asked.

"Please. Let's rest."

The general had joined his wife and Juan Carlos around the fireplace. We moved from the dance area to join them.

"Come back with those drinks!" Thane ordered, stopping one of the servants, who was winding through the crowd with trays of crystal goblets.

"Lucia will say you are drunk enough already," the general observed. Still, he stepped forward to take one of the drinks from the tray himself.

"Are you busy counting our drinks, Lucia?" Thane laughed, beaming at the stout, pleasant-looking woman, who had moved to the general's side.

"I think both of you have had your share of drink," she remarked with a warning directness. To me, she added, "Too much drink makes Thane reckless and my husband boastful."

"Here, another toast, General." Thane said, raising his glass. "We will just have to celebrate in spite of her!"

The musicians, resolving their dispute, began to play again, their music even faster and more lively than before. "Shall we dance again?" Thane asked eagerly.

Remembering the look in Ramon's eyes as he watched me in Thane's arms, I sought an excuse. "I just can't dance to that music. It's much too fast."

Not in the least disappointed, Thane stood very close to me, saying confidentially, "I should have gotten music from our own country."

I looked into his eyes and could see myself and the great hall beginning to fade from him. I thought of the change that had come over him in the vault-room, and became uneasy. What if he began, once more, to lose complete touch with reality? I sought desperately for some way to prevent this from happening.

Thane's voice became even lower as if it had taken distance from the activities of the room. "The haunting strains of Scandinavia, sad and happy simultaneously. Protesting the vast, solitary darkness!"

"There is no darkness here tonight!" The general's gruff voice seemed to call him back. "Tonight we are happy! Right, Viking? Right now everyone is happy."

"But I want to dance again," Thane insisted.

As if sensing my plight, Lucia said, "Thane, didn't I hear you promise me a dance?"

"Can't you see Lucia is dying to dance with you?" the general encouraged. "You can't disappoint Lucia. You would live to regret it!"

I threw Lucia a grateful look, which she returned with a compassionate smile and said agreeably, "We will make good your promise, Thane."

"You must stay right here until I get back," Thane directed me before taking Lucia's hand.

Thane lifted high the drink he still held in hand, finished it with one quick gulp, and tossed the glass into the fireplace.
Was it madness or the spirits that made him laugh so loudly as the fragile glass hit rock and sent splinters flying into the blazing fire?

Thane and Lucia glided gracefully to a waltz-like tune. Her smooth, sure steps proved her to be an expert dancer. I glanced toward the doorway, hoping to use this opportunity to speak with Ramon.

"Lucia secretly loves to dance," the general commented, delaying me "a curse for a woman whose husband has no sense of rhythm!"

"Lucia seems to understand Thane."

"Sometimes I believe they are of one mind," the general answered, affectionately following their movements across the floor.

"I love that idealism they both share! Where else in this world will you find such simple goodness?"

The music paused, then started up again with a stirring of drum and exotic beat.

"Watch this," Francisco said, sipping his drink. "It's a local dance. It combines elements of both Spanish and Indian."

As I watched, I noticed Evelia rise from where she sat alone at the huge table. Her filmy dress caught the light from the candles, and glowed across layers of material, all of different colors, like the feathers of a jungle bird. Slowly and seductively she made her way straight toward Ramon and drew him out into the circle of dancers.

The general pointed them out. "Watch this. Honduras has no better dancers than these two!"

Ramon stood, straight and tall, motionless. Evelia began to dance around Ramon, not touching him, yet the effect was extremely sensual.

Ramon began to partake of the music's beat. Black, polished boots flashed with measured steps as she continued to dance around him.

I felt my heart react almost with anger as he took her into his arms and they whirled in frantic pace around and around the floor. How often had they danced like this? Every single movement seemed in total and perfect harmony.

Ramon swung Evelia away from him, and stopped, a solitary figure, frozen in the spotlight of attention. This time Evelia's slow, languid movements changed, became wild, abandoned.

I felt my face flush. I felt choked with some unfamiliar emotion. Ramon's snapping dark eyes watched only Evelia. He probably had spoken to Evelia the exact same words of love and admiration he had spoken to me!

People had stopped their own dancing to watch them. Forming a circle around them, they began to clap in time to the wild jungle beat, and Thane's booming laughter could be heard above their cheers.

As the wild beat began to slow, Evelia, head tilted back, loose hair hanging, leaned back into Ramon's arms. The sight of Ramon holding her in such a close embrace stirred in me such an increase in emotion, that I turned away.

Close beside me, Francisco Perez, eyes growing heavy-lidded and slightly bleary, finished the last of his drink. Narrowed, black eyes darted toward the stone hearth. For a moment he stared at the empty glass in hand, as if weighing the consequence of a moment's foolish pleasure. In the end, practicality won him over. "Thane is drunk," the general finally said, "if he thinks I am going to toss a perfectly good glass into the fireplace."

I glanced back to the crowded floor where Ramon and Evelia were beginning another dance. The fire blazing beside me made my skin feel almost feverish. The general had left in search of another drink. With Ramon no longer guarding his post at the doorway, I slipped easily out into the courtyard.

Chapter Fourteen

No wind or air, only the still softness of night encircled me. My heart rebelled at the thought that just inside Ramon and Evelia danced, oblivious to everyone but themselves. The music and laughter decreased in volume as I headed in the direction of the brilliantly lit iron gate. Security would be lax tonight with everyone coming and going, yet I had resigned myself to the fact that I could not get by the guards without help.

I cut through the tall pine trees toward the patio area beneath the window of my room and sank down upon the iron bench near the stone fountain where Ramon had just a few days before hinted of his love for me.

"You don't enjoy the dance?" The mocking tone of the voice spoken in broken English caused me to jump to my feet and start back toward the dance. Sanchez blocked my way. His reaching out for me made me instinctively recoil, as if a viper had unexpectedly slithered across my path.

"Tonight, you are the envy of many women," Sanchez said, his voice growing cold. His eyes raked over me, not in admiration, but in a leering way, a mixture of insolence and lust. "The Viking's choice! Many women want to be his choice."

I tried again to sidestep him and smelled as I did the pungent stench of alcohol on his breath. Sanchez frightened me even when he was sober. I felt relief that the lights of the dance loomed so close. He surely would not dare to harm me here. "Thane is probably looking for me now," I said loudly.

"The Viking is a fool!"

The shadows across his face emphasized his high cheek bones

184

and thin, moist lips. His hair, for the first time since I had met him, was not tied back, but hung, limp and shaggy around his thin shoulders. He had not dressed for the occasion, but wore the same khaki pants and long, leather vest that seemed battered, like his skin.

"Perhaps Thane isn't as foolish as you think."

"If he wasn't a fool, he wouldn't be taken in by you, or by men like Ramon Santiago!"

"Ramon is very loyal to Thane," I said defensively. "Of course loyalty is not a concept you are likely to understand."

Light gleamed across Sanchez's narrow face and magnified the dark, empty space between his front teeth. "Fool! You are as stupid as the Viking! Santiago is loyal to no one. He works for himself alone. He is very dangerous!"

His features twisted in an ugly sneer. "Ramon Santiago is sick with the same illness you have. He caught it from your people. Greed!" His eyes slid over me again, as he said slowly. "Anyone could look good in a dress like that!"   Sanchez's long silence seemed to emit evil. I forgot for an instant that a crowd was nearby. I remembered our first encounter, when he and his men had trapped me. If not for Ramon's intervention that day.…

"I must go back to the dance."

Sanchez made a move to take hold of my arm, but with quick steps backward, I evaded him.

"You spend money on yourself while others starve!"

He advanced toward me, menacingly, his hateful voice demanding, "How much money did that dress cost?"

My lack of an answer increased his anger. He sprang forward, clutching both of my arms, shaking me. The surprise of his attack and the sharp pain searing toward my shoulders caused me to draw in my breath. "The price of your dress would feed many hungry peasants for days and days!"

"The money you spend on whiskey would do the same, Sanchez."

I recognized the quiet, priest-like voice before I glimpsed Arnoldo Saville. Sanchez released me abruptly, as if he feared

Arnoldo and the unspoken authority the man had over him.

"Go on your way," Arnoldo, without raising his voice, spoke again. He waited, not aggressively, but unrelentingly, as if he were a man who would hold to his word no matter what the odds.

I was surprised when Sanchez, hesitating only momentarily to glower, complied. He turned, staggering a little, and walked back toward the entrance of the house.

Arnoldo's gaze held to the path left empty by Sanchez's retreat. His frown added age and weariness to his kindly face.

"Thank you for helping me," I said, remembering the time in the village when Arnoldo had come to my aid by taking me to Alan.

"I am ashamed that men like Sanchez often represent us all." Edges of great sorrow cut into his placid voice. "The good people lack power and organization, but, don't forget, they are here in great numbers."

Arnoldo took my arm and guided me, not toward the lights of the doorway, but away from them. "Where are we going?"

"I came out looking for you," he said. "Alan is here."

As we drew further into the trees, only moonlight lit our way, yet I felt no fear or distrust of Arnoldo. "Why does Alan have to hide?"

"For his own safety. And, no doubt, for yours."

I wanted to question him further, but his hand tightened on my arm biding me to stop and listen. I waited while Arnoldo moved ahead until his form was only a bare outline in the trees.

Soon a shadow…I thought it was Arnoldo returning…stepped from the cluster of pines. "Arnoldo?"

"It's me. Alan."

"Oh, Alan!" My fear of Sanchez, my grief over Bertram, my feeling of Ramon's abandonment, culminated in my rushing into Alan's arms.

I was aware of Arnoldo emerging behind Alan, pausing a moment, the disappearing in to the thick forest growth.

"Baby." The light of the moon illuminated Alan's familiar face as he embraced me. I lingered quietly in his arms, glad that I was safe, that Alan was safe. I remembered the way Alan had looked last time I had seen him...ill, hunted, frightened. He looked none of these things now. Thinner, and with hair grown slightly longer, he put me in mind of some wayfaring adventurer. His eyes had regained their clearness, his voice that unfailing air of confidence.

With traces of amusement, Alan held me at arm's length, admiring the elaborate ball gown. "I've heard rumors that the Viking is quite taken with you. They must be true. He has you dressed up like a princess!" His green eyes glowed in the moonlight as he tilted his head to one side. "Should I be jealous?"

His use of the word *princess* caused my smile to fade. "I am not here of my own free will," I reminded him.

"Still, you are right where I need you to be. Have you located the drawings upon the cliffs? Have you seen the rune stone?"

"I've seen them both. I've copied all the runic writing I could make out from the stone. When we get back to New York, we can decipher it. Alan, this writing is authentic!" "Do you have any idea what this means? Darling, we have discovered the place where the Vikings first landed, where the legend of *Quetzalcoatl* originated!"

Finding this location had been my father's dream, had become the common goal for both Alan and myself. Why did the happiness and enthusiasm I should feel be driven out by fearful misgivings?

I almost wished the knowledge had remained undiscovered.

"Alan, do you have the medallion?" I asked suddenly. "Is that why you can't let the Viking see you here?"

My question seemed to take him by surprise. "Marta, why would you even think that? You are my partner. Don't you know I would share such an important discovery with you?"

His denial provided me reassurance that he had not stolen the medallion from the Viking's collection and I felt a sense of guilt for having ever doubted him. "Then you're still looking for the medallion?"

"The leads I've been following have all sent me back to Quetzal," Alan said.

"Do you still think the medallion might be part of Thane's collection?"

"At first, I thought Ulrickson was crazy, that all the talk about Viking treasure was imaginary. But now I have reason to believe that if the Viking Crown medallion or any other Norse relics do still exist, they are very likely to be a part of his private collection. Some people think that Thane Ulrickson has the medallion...and even greater items than that...hidden in a cave right here at this very estate!"

What would Alan say if he knew that I had already seen the collection? I thought of how excited he would be if he knew that the Viking might have in his possession, not the medallion, but the very crown from which it was replicated! I thought about Thane's crown, the crown he would have shown me if I hadn't become frightened and run away that night in the caverns. If original, such an object would be beyond the scope of Alan's wildest hopes and dreams. "Imagine it, Marta," Alan continued. "Solid evidence that the Vikings made contact with Central America kept hidden by Thane and his ancestors in a cave all these years! Invaluable information protected by his madness and the illusion that the treasure does not really exist!"

"They may not be authentic."

"But what if they are?" Alan looked at me intently. "It would prove beyond a doubt your father's theory."

"Wouldn't the rune stone be proof enough?"

"Proof that the Vikings were here many years ago, yes. But, remember, I also want to prove that the legend of the Sun Maiden is true. We can only do this by finding the medallion or some Viking jewel of equal significance from this ancient collection. Then think of what a fabulous work we will put together. We'll make your father's name shine like gold itself in the scientific world! Marta, we are so close to success!"

"I think we have enough with the rune stone. Let's go back to New York now. Whoever helped you get in here can help us both get out!"

"We must not let your father down!"

I saw Alan's eyes widen as he spoke the words better spoken by myself. Moonlight glinted in Alan's eyes. If I could have seen them clearly, I knew they would be alight with shades of green, like the growth of the jungle.

"You are in a position, darling, to find out if this cave exists."

I wanted very badly to tell him how Thane had taken me to the cave, about the wooden chests overflowing with jewels, about the bracelet with runic writing on it. I wanted to say to him that I could have seen the Viking Crown for myself, that I could see it yet just by making a simple request to Thane Ulrickson.

"Has he spoken to you about his hidden jewels?"

I wished desperately that I could share everything that had happened here with Alan, but Thane had trusted me with his secret. I couldn't bring myself to betray this trust, not even for Alan, not even for my dear father's goals, which were my own.

"Did he ever talk to you about the medallion?"

"Thane does not have the medallion," I said. "He claims that it was lost centuries ago."

"There is a medallion! It is somewhere in this area. That I do sincerely believe." He paused, unable to contain his excitement. "Marta, I know you could get him to reveal to you where his jewels are hidden!"

"Even if Thane has jewels," I answered, "they might be fakes."

"Why would you believe them to be fakes?"

"Because he sells so many items to rich collectors. He might profit from the rumors they hear of vast treasures."

"Just a few hours of study would give me a good idea of whether the items are original. I've come so far, searched so long! In a short time we'll be back in New York. I must see some of the items from Ulrickson's collection before we leave! Marta, you must help me! You must find out where this cave is, or you must talk to him about seeing these jewels. I do believe he would give any of them to you! You could bring one of them to me."

Alan studied me as if I or my reluctant attitude disappointed him "Please don't underestimate the importance of this, Marta. Proving the Viking connection is the chance to validate your father's and our entire life's work! If I could even get in that cave for a few hours to take sketches, it would be better than nothing. We must come back with some kind of proof to support our theory. We can't bring the rune stone back with us. And we can't go back empty-handed when we're so close!"

I felt the truth of what he was saying settle over me, but I held stubbornly to a sense of loyalty for the Viking. I didn't want my goals to be achieved by means of deceit and treachery.

Alan, I could see, was much too zealous, like a boy who was not stopping activity to think things through. I didn't like the fact that he was hiding now from the Viking. That meant either he had tried to steal from the Viking or Thane had caught him snooping around the cave area and forced him to leave. I even believed that Alan might have sent Bertram to do his searching for him.

"Have you ever met a man named Gavin Bertram?"

"I've run across him a few times. In Telas. Why do you ask?"

I found myself pouring out the story of Gavin Bertram's fated visit. I told him all about my suspicions, about the blood on the cliffs. "He might have been trying to locate the Viking's jewels himself."

Alan nodded. "That makes sense. I remember him as being a very greedy man. Certainly not above temptation."

I told him about the rock I had hidden. "Alan, I'm sure he was murdered and that stone was used as a murder weapon!"

"Murdered? By whom?"

"I'm not sure."

"You are under too much stress, Marta. No doubt Bertram did just slip and fall."

"Then why did they cover up the circumstances of his death?" I told of how Ramon and General Perez moved his carriage and left it outside the estate.

"Death is so common here. It's not like we were back in the States. They probably did it to prevent further trouble."

I had been persuasive in what I had told Alan about Bertram's death, but Alan and the others wanted to believe he had fallen, and I knew it was useless to continue trying to convince him otherwise.

Alan ran a hand through sandy hair, rumpling it and making him seem all the more the inexperienced youth. "There must be some way I can find that cave!"

"You must stay away from the lava beds! I told you what happened to Bertram! You must not take these risks. It's far too dangerous!"

"Marta, if Thane really does have Viking artifacts, they should be in a museum for the whole world to view. They should belong to science!"

"But they don't belong to the world. They belong to Thane Ulrickson. If Thane really does have Norse relics, then I have no doubt that they are part of a legitimate collection handed down to him by his ancestors. And the Viking would never part with a single item of his collection. He would not even be willing to share them with us for study."

"There must be some way you can get Ulrickson tell you where the cave is, then you could lead me to its exact location."

Alan didn't even suspect that could if I wanted to I lead him there right now. But bringing myself to actually do so was not possible. Thane had trusted me with his secret, how could I turn around and betray him?

Noting my silence, Alan reached out and touched my shoulder. "Think about what I've said. I don't want to force you into something you don't want to do, but if you think about it, you'll see I'm right."

I knew Alan would never give up when we were so close to our goal. But I was fully willing to leave now with what information we had. Alan had entered the Viking's estate tonight, probably with the Arnoldo's assistance. Surely Arnoldo could get both of us out.

"Don't look so distressed, honey," Alan said, putting his arm around me. For a moment, my head against his shoulder, Alan and I seemed safe. We were not in the jungles of Honduras any longer, but back in New York City. We were ourselves again. We were seekers of knowledge, not seekers of other people's jewels. "Take me with you, Alan. Tonight!"

"You made a long trip with lots of sacrifices to be here with me. You wanted to help me. You can, Marta. Just stay until I have what I need. Then we will leave together," Alan promised.

I pleaded with him, but his position remained firm and unyielding. In the midst of my protests, Alan's lips touched mine briefly, unexpectedly. "You must get back to the party before you are missed. I'll be contacting you soon."

"Alan, be careful," I warned. "Bertram wasn't careful, and now he's dead!"

Alan's lean form quickly disappeared from my view, lost among the dark tangles of trees.

With a sense of defeat, I returned to the house. Arnoldo and Sanchez stood near the iron gate, apart from the laughing guards. Their rapt conversation marked them, not as enemies, but as comrades, as brothers in the same insidious conspiracies! I felt my censure of Arnoldo slowly mix with sadness: I had from the first trusted Arnoldo Saville; I did not want him to be linked with the plots of men like Sanchez.

Whether Arnoldo could be trusted, I was not sure, but Sanchez's treachery was well-known to me. I stood in the courtyard, watching them, until I was certain that Alan had been given plenty of time to slip away.

* * *

As I reentered the room, Ramon strode from the crowd and drew to a stop in front of me. He stood very straight, his eyes flashing with anger. "Where have you been?" he demanded. "Can't I even let you out of my sight for one minute?"

"If you hadn't been so busy dancing with Evelia, maybe you would know where I've been," I answered, appalled by the jealousy that had crept into my voice.

"So now you want to be guarded!" Ramon's anger dissolved into sudden laughter. He caught my hand, led me out among the dancers, and drew me close.

"Where were you?"

"As you see, I didn't escape. So why does it matter to you?"

His lips brushed the corner of my mouth, moved to my hair. His touch left tingles of fire. "It matters!" he said against my ear. "Don't you know I've been waiting for this moment all evening?"

How natural to be in his embrace! As we whirled to the

192

ever-increasing rapidity of the music, I found the familiar image of Alan Avery slipping away, being replaced by Ramon.

Ramon's handsome features swirled in the soft-red glow of the candles. Flickering light filled his sparkling black eyes, made the tumbled locks of dark hair that spilled across his forehead glisten. The warmth of the room, his masculine nearness, made me feel light-headed, almost happy.

I savored the feeling of being in his arms, the solid strength of his embrace. As the tempo slowed, I leaned breathlessly against him and felt for the first time in many days a desire to laugh and be young. Ramon's gaze was no long fastened on me. I followed where he looked as he spoke, "The Viking is getting jealous."

Thane, between the general and Evelia, leaned forward in the chair he had pulled away from the table in order to obtain a better view of the dance floor.

I had not observed in the Viking before even a hint of worry. I noted with amazement the tight knit of shaggy brows, the hard set of his mouth. How long had he been watching us?

"He has a reason to be jealous," Ramon said, smiling down at me. "He knows I'm in love with you, Marta!"

My heart reacted to Ramon's words. I could almost believe that he meant them, that he had never spoken words like this to anyone else.

Dancing with Ramon now, with the Viking's eyes continually following us, drained away my joyfulness.

The music soon stopped. Ramon still held my hand. People milled around us waiting for the music to start again.

"There's Cayo!" I said excitedly, indicating to Ramon where Cayo in ragged clothes stood scooping food from the abundant dishes that filled the long table. "He was my guide," I explained, remembering that Cayo, after diving me here from my ship, had deserted me before Ramon had come to my rescue. The event seemed like ages ago, and Cayo an old friend, instead of someone who had abandoned me to fate. Seeing him, alive and well, filled me with elation. "I really thought he had been killed. Let's go over and talk to him."

I began leading Ramon toward Cayo, but the music started again and Ramon pulled me back into his arms. This time the music had the timing of a waltz, but loud and excessive with brass and drum-beat.

The pulse of the music made me forget all about the guide and about Thane.

"Latin is music of the soul," Ramon whispered. "It is meant for lovers." His warm hand pressed me even tighter against him until my curves molded to the contours of his lean body.

Time seemed to stand still as Ramon and I danced several more dances together. I felt charmed by his very nearness. When I glanced toward the table again, I saw that the Viking's seat was empty. I had not even noticed Thane's leaving. How long had he been gone?

Suddenly, I saw the Viking stride into the room. He seemed taller, broader, much larger than life as he moved forward, brushing through dancers until he reached Ramon and I, cutting into the middle of our dance.

"Excuse me, Ramon, but the time has come! The highlight of the evening is about to take place!"

Thane threw both arms high into the air and shouted orders to the band. "Stop your playing!"

Immediately the music ceased. Broken apart by Thane, Ramon and I were shocked and speechless. I forced myself to alertness, shaking the feeling of disappointment as if I had been roughly awakened from some sweet dream.

The room became so still I could hear my own startled intake of breath as Thane gripped my arm and pushed me ahead of him toward the flat platform of the make-shift stage where the five musicians stood without motion. Thane left me there and disappeared through the doorway directly behind the stage.

Every eye in the room was upon me. Ramon had followed and stood facing me. He, too, waited, the same way the musicians and I waited, in a suspended manner that prohibited all talk or movement.

The Viking quickly reentered. Oh, no! I thought as I saw that he clutched in both hands the crown he had taken from the thick glass case in his hidden vault! Why had he brought it here to-night? If the jewels were genuine, the crown was the most price-less item any of these people had ever seen! He was flaunting his immense wealth, causing the whole community to know he pos-sessed a fortune in jewels that had only before been rumored! What he was doing was foolhardy and dangerous!

The crowd pressed closer. Snatches of faces caught my atten-tion. I looked from the brilliant, golden crown with its rubies, emeralds, and diamonds directly to Sanchez. His thin, leering face gleamed more brightly than the jewels…with a stark greed that caused me to feel faint.

The general had stepped closer to me to speak, but the sight of the Viking Crown seemed to have smacked the sentence from his lips. I noticed the way he faltered, turned, and exchanged glances with Ramon.

"Tonight the Viking Crown returns to its rightful owner!" Thane's voice snapped the mass of people who gathered even closer around him back into the party atmosphere. Shouts arose, cheers and laughter.

"No, you shouldn't have..." I started, but my words died away as his big hand brushed through my hair, dropping to arrange locks around my shoulders.

He gazed at me, satisfied. Thane lifted the crown high above my head. "I've never before shown anything from my private collection! To no one, except Marta…the jewels are hers. But now, because tonight is special, all of you can see the fabulous Viking Crown for yourself!" His voice rose. "This celebration is held in honor of Marta! It can't take place without her being once again crowned!" Slowly, reverently, he placed the crown of gold and jewels on my head.

"My Princess!" he spoke in a loud, rumbling voice. Rough beard brushed against my cheek as the Viking bent to scoop me into his arms.

Evelia…I had not noticed her standing so close by…whirled and ran toward the stairway. I watched her disappear into the upstairs hallway.

At last Thane released me. The heavy weight of the crown upon my head, the burden of fear and anxiety it created, caused me to hastily remove it. I caught one last glimpse of glittering jewels and ancient gold the color of old coin as two of Thane's armed servants hurried forward to usher the crown out of the sight of curious eyes.

The crowd edged backward, widening the path for Thane and me as we crossed into the center of the room. Thane took me in his arms and began dancing. Exhilarated by the noise, by the display of the crown, by all the alcohol he had consumed, Thane became very loud. "If only we were back in Sweden!"

"Sweden!" someone shouted. Other voices took up the cry until it resounded throughout the hall.

Locked in his embrace, Thane and I danced again and again. He refused to let me go. Captive in his big arms, I glanced back at Ramon, pleading for him to intervene. Ramon's eyes glittered with helpless anger as he watched me. I felt torn from the sweet haven of Ramon's arms and trapped in the embrace of a madman!

Then quickly, as if he could bear it no longer, Ramon stepped forward and tapped Thane's shoulder. Reluctantly, though with good-nature, the Viking relinquished his grasp on me. Gratefully I went into Ramon's arms.

I had expected Ramon to smile at me or to speak some word of half-teasing consolation. Instead, he spoke coldly. "All the time I thought this collection was just a figment of his imagination!"

"All these jewels might be fakes," I said weakly.

"Whatever they are, they do really exist! And that is very bad news for me."

"Why?"

"I'll never be able to guard him and his jewels now! Not after everyone has seen this crown!"

His voice, tense and angry, brought to me a shiver of fear. As if Ramon sensed it, he drew me closer. "You are in danger, too, Marta, because you know where they are. I can't understand how you could have seen the jewels and not told me about them."

"I didn't think…."

"No, you didn't!" His dark eyes snapped as they met mine. His hands tightened on my shoulders if to shake me. "But you must think now! Marta, you must tell me where the Viking hides his collection!"

Chapter Fifteen

I stood at the window of my room watching dawn break and thinking not of last night, but of a soiree I had attended with Alan. Alan's brother, Colonel Josh Avery, filled his Washington D.C. home with ambassadors, military advisers, and important people from all over the world.

The entire evening I had spent listening, trying my best to be a lady, to say the right things and make Alan proud of me. An immense task, for Alan, amid such distinguished people, had barely noticed me. He had mingled, danced with the daughters of influential guests, and charmed them with talk of his accomplishments, while I had waited quietly on the sidelines.

I couldn't complain of being unnoticed last night! I brushed a hand across my hair, as if still feeling the delicate weight of the jewel-encrusted crown Thane had placed on my head. Thinking about that moment caused all of the dances I had attended with Alan to fade and exultation from my once-in-a-lifetime, fairy-tale evening to return. Once again, tight in Ramon's arms, I seemed to whirl to the music.

In mid-dance Ramon's handsome, smiling face suddenly changed. Destroying every vestige of my dream-like memory, he became hard and distant. Once again I could hear his sharp voice commanding me to tell him where Thane had hidden his jewels.

Last night had left no doubt in any mind that Thane's treasure existed. Ramon's features merged slowly with Sanchez's, whose black eyes greedily stared at the jeweled crown. Ramon no longer seemed a man who really loved me. My safety was of little, if any, actual importance to him. Ramon and Sanchez seemed one and

198

the same, both motivated by pure greed.

I opened the door to my room a crack. Just outside, snoring fitfully as he slept off a drunk, sat the old man Ramon often sent to guard me. His head lopped forward, his legs, covered with tattered trousers, stretched across the hallway. Stepping around him, I hurried to the stairway.

In the dining room maids were busy cleaning up after last night's party. Evelia, looking particularly sullen, was clearing wilted flowers and melted candlesticks from the tables.

After a light breakfast of bread and fruit, I stepped out into the sunny courtyard. As if she had intentionally followed me, Evelia soon appeared. She paused to glance back over her shoulder before she joined me at the stone fountain. Her eyes, black and opaque, seemed to shield her real feelings. "I have a message for you. From Alan," she said in a hushed tone. "He sent Arnoldo here early this morning."

Doubts surfaced. "Why didn't Arnoldo wait and give the message to me himself?" "Why do you think?" Evelia's scorn faded as quickly as it had flared. "Because I am the one who must help you. Alan wants you to meet him."

"When?"

"Now."

"Where is he?"

"He is waiting for us outside the gate. I will take you to Alan. Now."

Evelia's smile, a weak attempt to conceal her dislike of me, made me wary. Whatever secret grudge she bore me seemed to have increased since last night's party. I wondered if Thane's attention, his displaying of the jeweled crown in my honor had stirred greater feelings of jealousy. "Why would you want to help me?"

Evelia spoke, her curt honesty breaking through the barrier of politeness. "I'd like nothing better than for you to be gone from here! You are constant trouble for everyone!"

"How will we get through the gate?"

"Because of the dance, the guards are half drunk. We will have no problem. You stay right here."

If I were to leave, I must take with me Father's notes. I raced up to my room. The maids scarcely looked up at me and the guard at my door still slept. Grabbing my bag, I quickly returned and for what seemed an eternity, I paced by the fountain and waited for Evelia.

I was beginning to wonder if she had only been playing some cruel joke on me, when she returned with a small, two-horse carriage. "Get in! Quickly!" Evelia snapped.

Tolerant of Evelia's rude treatment, I obeyed, willing to bear her sharp tongue if she would take me to Alan. I had never imagined that help would come in the form of Evelia. But I could believe that the offer would be motivated not by a desire to help me, but by the woman's sincere wish to have me gone.

A single guard, drowsy like the old man who snored outside my door, lounged by the entrance, a hat pulled low over his eyes. At the sound of the approaching carriage, he rose and sauntered lazily toward us.

Evelia's whole appearance seemed to transform. The heavy lashes lowered, suggesting flirtation. The sultry look in her eyes brought back memories of her dancing with Ramon and my own unexpected reaction at seeing her in his arms.

Even though the guard and she spoke back and forth in Spanish, I understood that Evelia was telling him we were going to the village.

The guard, flattered by Evelia's attention, detained us as long as he could. I breathed a sigh of relief when he at last let us pass through the gate. How easy it was for Evelia to gain entrance and exit from the Viking's fortress; how impossible it would have been for me alone.

"Where did Arnoldo say Alan would meet me?"

Ignoring my question, Evelia kept her eyes on the road. The carriage jolted and jogged along the rough trail as Evelia carelessly guided the horses. The morning sun became brighter and hotter as the carriage careened down the mountain curves with reckless speed. An intense, stifling heat rose from the steamy underbrush, thick and impenetrable as a swamp, that grew on each side of us.

The way she scowled at the mention of Alan's name made me wonder if Alan, not Thane or Ramon as I had first suspected, was the reason for Evelia's intense hatred of me. Many women had become attracted to Alan, his boyish, yet manly charm. Evelia could easily fancy herself in love with Alan. Or she could have seen Alan as a way for her to gain passage to the States.

Evelia's sudden curse broke into my thoughts. I reacted to Evelia's anger, her jerky reining of the horses, by looking up at the road. Ahead, a large, dark obstruction blocked our way. As we came closer, I saw that a big, leafy limb had fallen across our path.

Evelia gestured for me to get out of the carriage. "The branch will have to be moved before we can go on."

I obediently stepped out and expecting Evelia to follow, began tugging at the heavy limb. Evelia remained seated upon the high bench and watched with scornful satisfaction as I struggled with the heavy burden alone.

Resentment of the woman's arrogant attitude filled me. Only the knowledge that Evelia could take me to Alan kept me from dragging Evelia bodily from the carriage and insisting that she help.

The heat formed beads of dampness on my forehead. My long braid of hair felt like a heavy weight against my back as I worked to drag the great limb to the side of the road. Finally succeeding, I paused for a moment to catch my breath.

As I started back toward the carriage, Evelia suddenly raised the whip high above the horses. Hatred glittered in her eyes as she mocked me. "You fool! Did your really think I would take you to Alan? If I knew where he was, I would go to him myself!" She tossed my bag out of the carriage where it landed at my feet.

Suddenly realizing what she planned, I cried out, "Evelia! You can't just leave me out here!"

"Don't come back if you know what's good for you!" Wheels skidded as she started away. She shouted back at me, "Sanchez is my brother! He likes to torture meddling foreigners! Heaven help you if he finds you out here alone!"

With a high-pitched laugh that caused my heart to pound, Evelia cracked the whip and the horses bolted away. The thunder of their hoofbeats and the wake of flying mud from the moving carriage soon vanished and I stood looking up and down the empty road.

The knowledge that Sanchez and Evelia were brother and sister stunned me. They didn't look alike, yet they did have the same arrogant attitude and the same way of expressing themselves. Anger at Evelia for tricking me, anger at myself for falling for her cruel trick, gave way to frustration at being stuck out there in the middle of nowhere. How far away was Santa Augusta? How long was I going to last in this searing heat?

Twenty minutes of rapid walking left me drenched from the stifling humidity and breathless. The road winding through thick trees and plants remained deserted. Not even a hut or clearing broke the dense wall of the jungle. Already a shaking had started in my legs, and an incredible thirst gripped my throat. How I would welcome the sight of Ramon coming to my rescue now! I continued to force one foot in front of the other, cursing myself every step for having ever trusted Evelia.

Another fifteen minutes, and I knew I must stop and rest. How easy it would be, I thought, to close my eyes, to give way to the intense drowsiness that hung oppressively over me. I slapped at small insects that buzzed around my face as I remained seated on the ground, head against the trunk of a tree for a few more minutes. Then determinedly I rose and pushed onward.

I reacted with relief and joy to the approaching sound of a hoofbeats upon the road behind me. My first thought was that Evelia had relented and come back for me. My sense of rescue turned to fear as an ancient, battered wagon slowed by my side. I peered up at the driver's bench and straight into Sanchez's small, black eyes.

"Get in," Sanchez ordered with a jerk of his head toward the empty seat beside him. The sinister looks of the two men who rode in the back of the wagon, rifles close beside them, prevented any thoughts of refusal. I hesitated, then resignedly climbed into the wagon.

Evelia's warnings about Sanchez, his enjoyment of brutality and torture, increased the weak shaking of my body. Had Evelia told her brother where to find me? From the edge of his faded brown shirt, I could see the brass handle of some weapon, either a knife or a gun.

Sanchez tossed me a canteen of water and I drank deeply, giving no thought to whether or not the water was pure. The drink and rest, however uneasy, cleared the daze of heat and exhaustion.

"Where are you taking me?" I had intended my voice to sound defiant, fearless. Sanchez was looking at me out of the corner of his eye like a thief who has unexpectedly been handed a diamond. The look of lust mingled with hatred. I felt faint and his savage features blotted with darkness.

"If you harm me, Alan will kill you! He is waiting in Santa Augusta for me now."

Sanchez must know that I was only bluffing; Evelia had no doubt informed him of how she had lied to me about a message from Alan.

"Are you sure Avery is waiting?" The gap between Sanchez's front teeth appeared, the ugly smile which forewarned evil intention. "I'm not afraid of Alan Avery!"

Outside the village of Santa Augusta, Sanchez forced me to lie down in the back of the wagon. The two guards, leering, stood over me, no sign of mercy in their faces. I recognized both of them; they had been with Sanchez the day my carriage had broken down and the guide had abandoned me.

My gaze moved from the big man, menacing because of his size, the wicked-looking machete that gleamed from his belt, to his companion. I remembered the pock-marked face, dark, greasy hair, and cruel, mercenary's eyes. I watched the spiral of smoke rising from the thick cigar between his lips as he grinned down at me, and I shuddered.

My sense of helplessness increased as the wagon turned up a rutted trail that forked off just south of the village of Santa Augusta. From where they had hidden me from view, I saw only the sight of the church steeple as the wagon climbed up the hill away from the village. I wondered if Arnoldo would be standing near the church and if it were for that reason they had taken extra precaution.

I was allowed once more to sit upon the bench with Sanchez when all traces of the village had disappeared from sight. I now got my bearings. I remembered the road well, the same road I had taken with Arnoldo Saville. I guessed we were headed to the same adobe house where Alan had been hiding.

With dread I realized the house would be empty; I would be at Sanchez's mercy! I glanced at the evil little man. His twisted, leering smile confirmed my worst fears.

I should have run into the jungle instead of getting into the wagon with him! I would rather be shot than face what lay ahead. Panic made me think of jumping out of the wagon, but common sense told me that I would only cause injury to myself and still not get away from him. Maybe when we reached the abandoned house, I would find some way to escape!

Sanchez stopped the wagon in front of the adobe house with its sun-faded, pitted walls. The two guards, speaking loudly in Spanish, scrambled from the back. They eyed me with boldness, their evil looks a reflection of Sanchez's.

"Wait outside," Sanchez barked. Then, to me, "You come inside." Grabbing me so tightly his fingers hurt my arm, he shoved me into the empty house ahead of him.

I would not even try to reason with him. Any pleas would only add to his satisfaction. I faced him as bravely as I could. Outside, I could hear the riotous laughter of the guards as they argued and probably passed back and forth a bottle of rum or tequila.

Sanchez advanced toward me slowly, watching me all the while like a wolf stalking game. As if savoring my helplessness, he placed a hand on either side of my shoulders, pinning me against the rough adobe wall. "Now we will finish what we started before Ramon so rudely interrupted," he hissed.

His face was so close to mine I could see the leering mouth, the ugly gap between his teeth. His eyes were so black the pupils had disappeared completely. The depths of them held no spark of pity or compassion. I struggled, fighting him with all of my strength! All I was able to accomplish was turning my face away from his thin, moist lips. My entire body recoiled in disgust at his touch!

What was that noise? A sudden crack of a door slammed into adobe. I couldn't see what was happening until Sanchez quickly released me. He shrank from the open door, startled.

Alan stepped angrily toward him, a pistol calmly aimed at Sanchez's heart. "Are you hurt, Marta?" Alan asked, holding out his free arm to me. I moved into its encircling protection, wanting to sob with relief.

"I warned you to leave Marta out of this." Alan's arm tightened around me as he spoke. The gun remained steady. "I swear, if you've hurt her...."

Sanchez, for all his boasting, looked frightened. His eyes darted swiftly, not meeting Alan's, as he spoke, "I found her walking along the road," Sanchez defended himself. "We came here looking for you. I was just having some fun with her. You know I wouldn't harm her!" "Scum like you should be shot!" Alan's green eyes flared. Flecks of yellow-brown fire appeared, and for a moment I was afraid he intended to pull the trigger before I could do anything to stop him.

Sanchez's face was frozen. Dark eyes seemed to protrude from their sockets. "You need me!" Sanchez cried out, breaking the tense silence.

After a long moment, Alan lowered the gun. "I'll deal with you later," he said under his breath.

Alan guided me from the cabin toward an ancient carriage angled close to the side entrance. In numerous places holes...were they bullet holes?...lined the wooden side. Alan climbed up, then pulled me in beside him. "We must hurry."

Leaning forward from the shabby carriage seat, Alan urged the horses on. The jungle trail passed by in a blur. Glancing back, seeing that we had not been followed, Alan finally eased the horses to a slower pace.

"How did you find me?" I asked, brushing at the tears in my

eyes and trying to compose myself.

"Some of Arnoldo's lookouts saw Sanchez pass by the church. He sent his nephew to warn me that he had a hostage, a woman, with him. I suspected it might be you."

I leaned back wearily. "How could you get mixed up with a man like Sanchez?"

The altercation had left a pallor upon Alan's skin. He wiped his hand across his forehead and pushed back his hair before he spoke. "I hired Sanchez to help me track down the medallion."

I should have known the necklace, Alan's stubborn pursuit of it, had caused the tie between them.

I recalled Alan's frantic escape from the same cabin the day Ramon had come looking for him. I had even thought Alan might have taken the medallion from Thane. If not, then why had he been hiding from Ramon? I still didn't know the answer to that question.

"If the medallion still exists, Sanchez is my last hope of getting it. He is my only link to it now." Alan's mouth tightened and I felt that I had failed him by my decision to leave Thane's estate.

"Sanchez is the lowest kind of scum! How I hate dealing with him! Stupid mercenary!" His bitter hatred eased a little. "Do you know I've never killed a man before. But today, I think I could have shot him!"

"Alan, you must give up this senseless search! Let's leave Honduras now. Please, Alan! Please return to New York with me!"

"I can't quit now, when I'm so close." An exultant look filled Alan's eyes. When he spoke, his voice was charged with excitement. "Sanchez may be on to something. Soon, I may have solid evidence to support my theory!"

"Has he promised you the medallion?"

A muscle quivered in Alan's cheek. "Sanchez was…very evasive. He only said he would have something I would be very interested in buying from him…soon."

I remembered Sanchez's greedy eyes riveted to the glittering gold and jewels of Thane's priceless crown. The image made me shrink away from Alan. The Viking Crown loomed as a prize even more precious and rare than the lost medallion! I knew in my heart

Alan would pay any price, do almost anything, to acquire such an item.

"Alan, last night at the dance, Thane showed a magnificent crown from his collection. Now everyone knows his collection does exist. I'm afraid someone…Sanchez…will try to rob him!"

"You over-estimate Sanchez. He wouldn't have the nerve to try anything like that."

"You under-estimate him. You just can't get mixed up with Sanchez! All I want is for us to go back to New York! Why can't we?"

Alan's thin lips turned down slightly at the corners, drawing tight, as if he were suppressing some over-powering emotion. "When I return," he said resolutely, "it will be with solid evidence which will secure my career."

I noticed how Alan had dropped any mention of my own career from his talk now. I thought of the many times Alan had taken for himself full credit for the published papers concerning my father's work that I had for the most part composed myself. Although Alan had many important connections and had carefully explained that papers penned by a man would receive much more credibility by our peers, I could not help at times feeling slighted. Even though my goal was to carry on my father's work, I could not help rankling a bit with intense hurt as I listened to words of praise for Alan, while my own long hours of toil went unrecognized.

As if sensing my thoughts, Alan added, "This discovery of the Viking-Mayan connection will make my future, our future!" One of his hands reached out to cover mine. "We are a team, Marta. We are nothing without each other!"

Instead of resenting him, I should have realized each time he gained in reputation, so did my father's theories. Alan was doing what he had to do, not just for himself, but for both of us!

"But we must have evidence," Alan went on. "Only evidence we can take back with us can be used as actual proof. This genuine item along with all the other documentation we have gathered will serve to show that the Vikings really were here!" He paused to look at me. "I'm amazed that you don't understand how important all of this is! The impact of this discovery will startle the entire world!"

"This is as important to me as it is to you," I said. "After all, it was my father's life dream to prove this theory."

"Then you must understand why I can't leave now!"

I thought of Bertram, and where his search for Thane's Viking relics had led him. "I'm afraid for you."

"I'm not in any danger," Alan replied. "But after today, I can see that you, my darling, must get out of here! I must see to it you that you are safely on your way to New York."

"I won't leave without you."

"You must." For a long time he drove in silence. "If you won't leave the country, at least go to Copan and wait for me. There is a camp of archaeologists near the ruins. Dr. Juarez and his family will put you up until I can join you. You will be safe there. But if that is your decision, you must go there at once. I could meet you there tomorrow."

"How will I get there?"

Alan hesitated. "I'll think of some way."

"Why won't you come with me?"

His green eyes held to the road. "There's something I must do."

I had always been immensely proud of Alan, his easy, sophisticated words, his urbane appearance. I studied his profile, the limp, sandy hair, now damp from the humidity and falling over his broad forehead.

Alan caught me watching him and cast me a lingering, sideways glance. His smile possessed a boyish buoyancy which denied his cosmopolitan air and even his self-assurance.

Great danger lay ahead for Alan! The knowledge made me afraid for him. His desire to secure evidence of the Viking-Mayan link for history, for the increased knowledge of all mankind, was making him reckless. I saw him as the ultimate idealist, a blind and foolish hero. He was getting in over his head by dealing with Sanchez and other unscrupulous people.

The road that we were on had become well-kept. I saw patches of cultivated land where low, dense coffee trees grew in orderly rows. An abrupt fork in the road led to a huge gate, and beyond the gate I glimpsed a towering, white house.

Alan slowed at the fork of the road and soon pulled to a stop. "This is the Francisco Perez's plantation."

The general was Thane's friend, and Ramon's. Why did Alan think he would be willing to help me? I asked him.

"I know that the general will see that you get to Copan. Just trust me. I'm going to let you out here. I'll meet you there tomorrow."

"I don't want to go without you."

"Marta, will you please just do what I say." Leaving no room for compromise, he handed me the bag with my clothing and notes that he had salvaged from Sanchez.

"You can't just let me off here! How will I explain to the general…."

Alan smiled. "You'll think of something. But, Marta, do not mention my name to him."

"Why not? Do you think it is wise to trust him?"

"Right now, we have no other choice. Marta, no one can be trusted. Tell the general as little as possible. Just get him to take you to Copan. I'll take care of everything else."

Alan reached for me. The brush of his lips against mine was welcome and familiar. I lingered for a while in his embrace.

Being in Alan's arms again made me feel as if I were just awakening from some mythical journey. The Viking, Ramon, the general, Evelia and Sanchez, seemed all part of a preposterous fantasy. Alan was my reality! Alan and I would soon return to New York. How I wished we were safely back where we belonged!

"I must go now," Alan said, his lips lightly touching mine again. "Until tomorrow."

I stood watching the rattling carriage pull out of sight, then I started walking up to the general's gate.

Chapter Sixteen

The general's estate set far back from the road, behind a fence as high as the Viking's, but, unlike Thane's, in no way crude or primitive. On this wall no chipped glass jutted out. The tall stone fortress was carefully disguised by overgrowths of vines...as disguised, I couldn't help thinking, as the general himself, his own purpose and intention.

As I thought of the general, his wise, sardonic eyes seemed to be watching me, calculating some advantage. Appealing to him for help suddenly appeared to be a very poor idea. I clutched the bag with my father's work and what few clothes I had taken with fingers that had turned icy cold. I turned from the gate, looking down the winding road that would lead back to Santa Augusta...how far, I didn't know.

If I reached Santa Augusta, would I be able to find Arnoldo?

I would be much more inclined to trust Arnoldo. Why hadn't I suggested that to Alan, or rather why hadn't Alan delivered me to the village and told me where Arnoldo lived?

I took a hesitant step toward the gate. Between thick boards I could see a wide entranceway leading to a house that from here escaped clear vision. Trees, meticulously trimmed, lined either side like perfectly groomed sentinels.

I drew a deep breath and gripped the gate. Just as I did, two fierce black dogs bounded forward. Threatening sounds, a mingling of barking and yelping, emitted from open mouths, which exposed long, sharp fangs. I shrank back just as a well-dressed guard appeared, subduing the dogs with a curt command.

"Who are you?" he asked in labored English.

"I am a friend of the Perez's."

He made no move to open the gate.

"I am Marta Swan. I would like to see General Perez."

In response, he looked up and down the road, puzzled by my lack of transportation, then he gave a helpless gesture, as if unable to form the proper English words of inquiry. With another wave of his hand that meant for me to wait, he abruptly disappeared. Several men moved into the area. They carried rifles and had about them the bearing and precision of well-trained military men. I waited anxiously for a very long time.

Finally the general himself approached in an extravagant carriage. He jumped from the seat, laughing a greeting, "A beautiful princess dropped at my doorstep!" he called. "How fortunate! Of course, Lucia won't let me keep you."

He didn't speak again until I was beside him in the carriage. "I'm very sorry that you had to be met by guards and dogs. But they are quite necessary. I am not immensely popular in some camps. That makes me susceptible to attacks of all kinds."

The great, dapple-gray horse pranced with high step causing the carriage to move along at a parade gait. The house soon escaped the shield of overhanging branches. He measured my reaction, pleased by my surprise at observing such a magnificent structure, like the southern plantations I had once toured in Virginia. Only somehow grander, every detail wonderfully cared for, the columns twice as massive.

He seemed disappointed when I, instead of exclaiming about the beauty of his estate, told him, "I need to your assistance in getting to Copan. Right away, if possible."

Francisco Perez, with a skeptical, sideways glance, brushed off my announcement. "We are just getting ready to eat. You must join us."

"But I must leave today."

For such a weighty man, his lithe springing to the ground surprised me. He turned the carriage over to a waiting guard and once again offering his hand, guided me toward his home as if I were an expected guest.

"I will pay you for your trouble." I said. "Once I get to New York, I will send money."

He stopped abruptly, a vast column now shadowing his features. He laughed deeply. "Food and money rule the world!" he said, then added, "with the help of guns! How did you get here?"

Careful to avoid his scrutinizing glance and remembering that Alan had explicitly told me not to mention his name, I said evasively, "I escaped."

Once again he laughed. "By what means?"

I made no answer.

"I would say probably Arnoldo dropped you off. Why didn't he stay and talk to me? Did you leave with him from Thane's?"

"No."

He did not ask any other questions, instead, he said, "My home is yours."

This time it was I who remained silent, fearful because he had failed to respond properly to my request. Why had Alan ever believed this man would be willing to help me escape from the Viking? The general was, after all, Thane's closest friend. Or was he anyone's friend, but his own?

We entered a huge room, pale and comfortable. The large couches and chairs arranged around a stylish, tiled fireplace were pure white. Each item seemed carefully chosen, delicate and feminine, except for the gun case and the paintings of strong, bearded faces that lined the walls.

"Here, let me take your bag."

"I will just keep it with me."

In the adjoining room a table covered with a lace cloth and heaped with food awaited us.

"Lucia, look who's here."

Lucia's dark, heavy face lighted in benevolent welcome. "I'm so glad you have come to visit us, Marta," she said. "I have been wanting so much to talk to you. As I've told you before, I don't often get to talk to such an educated person as you are."

"We don't want to talk," Francisco interrupted. "We want to eat."

Her smile enfolded us both. "Everything's ready."

Impressed by the abundance around us, I seated myself at the walnut table. Fresh vegetables, assorted trays of meat, fruit piled high on platters.

"Francisco tells me you are finishing your father's book. You are a very ambitious girl! That is so exciting."

The general scooped baked chicken on to his plate before passing it to her. His voice was light as he spoke, "Her book is going to be about how *Quetzalcoatl*, the most powerful figure in all the mythology of Mexico and Central America, was a Viking adventurer, whose ship blew him to our very coast!"

"I think that is highly possible," Lucia supported.

"But where's the proof?"

When I failed to answer Francisco's question, Lucia commented, "Many people think *Quetzalcoatl* is only fiction. Made up by our own people."

"The story gained too much scope for that," I assured her. "You notice how different tribes picture exactly the same man. *Quetzalcoatl* did exist!" I sampled the chicken, delicately seasoned with unfamiliar spice. "Whoever he was, he was a great lawgiver, an inventor, a giver of maize. He was a compassionate king scarcely able to hurt any living creature."

The general's nod was humorously significant.

I ignored the general's teasing manner and the image of Thane Ulrickson that it brought to mind as I went on. "*Quetzalcoatl*… 'quetzal', a rare bird, 'coatl', a Nahua word for snake, 'atl' water. As a god he represents water, earth, the crawling snake, and bird. But to me the bird is what's important. The quetzal bird belongs to the Mayan lands. So why isn't it likely that the legend began right here?"

Francisco leaned back in his chair. His eyes, narrowed, slits of black sparkling as they rested on me. "*Quetzalcoatl* is always pictured as tall, robust, broad of brow, with large eyes and fair beard." He paused. "You really didn't expect to find him still here, in the flesh, did you?"

"You will not laugh when Marta becomes famous for her

213

theory." Lucia said with a smile that told me she was sympathetic to my cause. Quickly, she changed the subject, "Do you like the coffee?"

"It is delicious."

"Our very best blend," the general announced with pride. "Our Santa Augusta coffee is exported to all parts of the world. Right now they are probably drinking our coffee in France, in Japan."

"Francisco, are you bragging?"

"My wife," the general chuckled, "tells me it an ancient Indian custom not to allow husbands to boast."

"But he does anyway," Lucia added. "Marta, we have so much to talk about. How long will you get to stay with us?"

"I must leave right away."

"So soon?"

"We can not leave today," the general said. "I will take you to Copan first thing tomorrow."

Thinking about Alan's promise to meet me at the Juarez home, I insisted. "I'm afraid I must insist on leaving before then. I was hoping right after we have finished eating."

The general turned away from me, profile reflecting in the huge glass of the gun case behind him. "You do not understand where you are," he said. "The border towns are filled with revolutionaries or even worse, mercenaries. Some of them, Sanchez, go all over Central America dabbling in war. In Santa Augusta," he gestured to the smart lines of rifles and pistols behind him, "guns are of more value than gold!"

"Francisco is right," Lucia said. "There is much trouble on the roads at night. You can stay until morning." She smiled reassuringly. "That will give us a great chance to talk some more. Without Francisco."

I could tell by the general's manner that he would not be persuaded. Even if I didn't fully trust his statement that he would take me to Copan tomorrow, I would have time to talk to Lucia. Lucia, I trusted. And it was obvious that he listened to her. If I confided in Lucia about my plight, she would be sure to see to it that the general aided me.

The general finished his meal first. "I have some business matters," he said to his wife. "Something very urgent that I must see to at once. Then we will show Marta the plantation."

"No guest of his escapes without a full and complete tour," Lucia told me. "Take your time with your business. Marta and I have 'girl talk'. And the rough likes of you are not included."

Francisco looked humorously up at the ceiling before pushing back his chair and departing.

As a considerate hostess, Lucia immediately showed me to a room at the top of a steep flight of stairs. "You can leave your things here," she said, her eyes dropping to my bag. "Freshen up. Rest a while if you like. Francisco's tour can wait, even though he will not think so."

"Lucia, wait."

She turned back to me with that pleasant smile, which brought a benevolent glow into her eyes. I kept my gaze fixed on her face, which had filled with patient inquiry. In the stillness I recalled staring in horror from the rocky summit of cliff into the ocean below…water that I knew covered forever Bertram's dead body. Bertram…the last person who had tried to help me.

My throat became dry and I wondered if Lucia could see my hesitancy and my fear. "I'll be down soon," I said.

I simply had to gain her backing. I had no other choice. As I watched Lucia smile again and leave, I told myself that I wasn't wrong in not talking to her now. I would have all evening and surely a better time would arise.

I drew the drapes, grateful for the brilliant light that streamed across the immaculate room. A vase of fresh cut flowers, huge, white blossoms that I didn't recognize, set on a stand near the poster bed. Everything in the house was so properly cared for, so correct.

I turned back to the window and looked down the wide path toward the gate, which trees blocked from view. An imaginary picture of Ramon riding down the path intruded into my mind. He looked so brave, so handsome! In the disturbing image, Ramon stopped beneath my window and called to me.

Feeling a little dizzy, I leaned against the window sill, eyes tightly closed. Would his image ever fade from my mind? He did care about me, and admit it or not, I did care about him. I even condemned myself for having not trusted in Ramon. I should have waited at Thane Ulrickson's estate for the help he assured me he would give.

But was that possible, when I was so confused about what was going on? I didn't even know why Bertram was killed! What right did I have to think only of myself and not at all of Alan?

But was I actually willing to leave forever the man I loved? Love! The first time the word had intruded into my thoughts linked with Ramon. If I did love him and if he did feel the same way, then maybe someday...dreams began to filter into my mind, of Ramon traveling to New York to find me, of myself, no longer alone among wandering crowds and towering buildings. I thought of Ramon and I sailing, free and happy, on the foggy waters of the Atlantic.

In spite of the reality of my situation, my spirits had risen. I washed my face with cool water from the basin, fixed my hair, and returned down the stairway, where I found Lucia in the dining room where we had eaten.

"I did not expect to see you again so soon. But, then, young people do not need rest! Francisco is still in his study. Let's wait for him in the parlor."

Lucia with her graceful, slow step lagged far behind. I stopped to inspect the paintings and pictures that hung in masses along the north wall. The general and Lucia many years ago, the general with his trees, a small photograph of six men lined in front of an important-looking white building.

Ramon! His black hair swept back as if from a sea-breeze. His eyes, even in paper, seemed to be seeking mine. An ache filled me at the knowledge that I would never see him again. Astounded at the force of my own emotion, I wondered how I could bear parting with him forever!

Lucia's hand rested lightly on my shoulder. To seek comfort, I faced her and found in her dark eyes a wisdom that far surpassed my own.

216

"Love is so very important," she said, then, smiling a little, added, "You love Ramon, don't you?"

Words came to my mind...I hardly know him...he sometimes infuriates me...but I could not speak them. I had never before concerning any man felt such ecstasy or such pain. Was Lucia right? Was I hopelessly in love with him?

Lucia continued to study me. "You have made a good choice," she said at last. "Ramon is very much like Francisco, and I can not tell you how happy he has made me!" She paused, dropping her hand and stepping back. This motion gave emphasis to her words. "To such men, a woman is an equal partner. They cherish your feelings and they will let nothing come between them and you."

I looked back at Ramon's picture. "But I know nothing about him."

"All you need to know is what I have just told you. With Ramon, you are safe. I would not give you wrong advice. Ramon is as dear to the general and me as if he were our own son."

"Where does he come from?"

"Near the east coast."

"Is that where this picture was taken?"

"No, that was in Guatemala." As Lucia spoke, she moved closer, pointing to a very broad, bearded man with a rugged, weary face. "You have heard of Guatemala's leader, Barrios. He was brutally slain only days after this photograph." Lucia's voice lowered, rebuke edged with deep sadness. "What a shame for Central America! To kill so good a leader. His ideas of peace and reform would have spread from there to...who knows?...maybe everywhere!"

Nothing in his features looked outstanding. A sag to his mouth, a sag to his shoulders. He did not look strong or noble, like Ramon, only tired, very, very tired. My gaze shifted to the man between Ramon and him. I recognized the neat, white hair, the aristocratic features, the rigid posture, Don Orlando.

"You want Orlando to take his place?"

"Of course. But that doesn't seem likely to happen. So many are fooled by Carranza's promises to help the poor. All lies of

217

course. The man is more corrupt than any I have ever known or heard of."

"Lucia, I've had the carriage brought out front," Francisco boomed.

"Your business didn't take very long," Lucia said, joining Francisco at the doorway. I walked with them through the room and across the huge porch. The air outside had cooled and I felt refreshed from the perfect meal and the personal words I had exchanged with Lucia. A momentary sense of well-being, of trust in these two people, stole over me and I found myself looking forward to seeing the estate.

"What do you know about coffee?" Francisco Perez inquired as we started on a smooth road up a gently sloping hill.

"I thought you would have a banana plantation. Isn't that supposed to be Honduras' major export?"

"The banana is the plebeian; coffee the aristocrat."

"Not so," Lucia refuted from behind us, in the small, unconvertible bench she insisted upon taking. "The voice from the back seat is to be disregarded. Look ahead."

He indicated neat rows of trees, cut short. I could see branches laden with ripening beans.

"We clip the trees periodically. Otherwise they would grow to such a height it would be hard to harvest. We pick them by hand."

"Frost is the coffee tree's biggest enemy," Lucia said.

The general slanted me a glance. "But one I understand. Unlike the stupid revolutionaries I encounter."

Stupid mercenaries…that is the way Alan had referred to Sanchez and his followers. The similar reference struck me as more than coincidence.

My thoughts were interrupted by Lucia, "Francisco labels everyone who disagrees with his political ideas a stupid revolutionary. I am afraid you will never understand his views by listening to his talk. He hangs on to every word Ramon says. He reads everything Arnoldo writes with great interest. At the same time, he denounces Sanchez as a mercenary pig. His mind is a hopeless maze."

"What makes you put Ramon in a group with those two?" Francisco asked. "Ramon is only a guard." His eyes, now shadowed by a sudden narrowing, returned to the trees. "The loss of a single tree means loss of income on that spot for the three to five years it takes to replace it. That makes time my biggest enemy. Time and constant war."

"Why is there so much trouble here?"

He shrugged and laughed simultaneously. "Who knows? The peasants in the remote villages of Central America know nothing of issues. They fight on whichever side has the best offer at the moment. They are not adverse to changing sides."

"Marta does not want to hear about your wars, Francisco. And your trees are boring, too. Take us to the zoo. I want to show Marta my little Rickey."

We pulled close to a huge square courtyard encircled with mesh wire.

"Francisco is so proud of his birds," Lucia said, moving with great dignity toward the gate.

I was delighted by the pleasant place overhung with trees and set about with pools and fountains. Parrots called from trees and a tame monkey bounded closer, chattering for attention. The general stopped to point out two macaws, scarlet, blue, and yellow, with voices loud and filled with shrill authority. I started to reach up to touch the brilliant feathers.

"Don't get too close," the general warned. "Those powerful beaks can sever a finger."

"Come over here, Marta. I want you to meet Rickey." Lucia turned, holding a furry, long-tailed creature, whose eyes remained closed.

"Is it a monkey of some kind?"

The general laughed, "A close relative to a raccoon. This is a kinkajou. He is a superb climber. Lives in the treetops. Let Marta hold him."

I hesitated.

"Don't worry. He wouldn't have the energy to bite. The kinkajou is hyperactive at night, extremely drowsy in the daytime."

The little creature, content with Lucia, sucked at the back of her hand, making a loud, squeaking noise like a baby. When I lifted him, he opened large, limpid eyes. I felt the soft, velvet coat of golden brown, then cuddled him against my chest. He buried his head to avoid the light and slept.

After all I had been through, the gentle animal captured my heart and gave me great comfort. I carried him around the square, as we journeyed on, stopping to view the fish, and a huge, ancient jaguar in a cage. When it was time to leave, I didn't want to give the kinkajou up.

Lucia and the general found great pleasure in my love for Rickey.

How relaxing it was to be around these two nice, fun-loving people. Here, in the warmth of their estate, for the first time since I had entered Honduras, I felt perfectly safe, warmed and cheered by sincere hospitality, by the laughter I could so freely join.

As we were returning to the house, I saw a carriage with two black horses stopped by the walkway, as if it had been abandoned in a hurry. As we drew closer, I recognized the hard benches, the black, overhead covering where long fringes dangled. I had ridden in this carriage with Ramon!

Ramon stepped out into the bright sunlight from where he had been standing in the shade of the great pillars. He descended the stairs rapidly, wind stirring his black hair. His eyes, at first so dark and unreadable as they held mine, lit suddenly and in spite of the ruination of my own plans, my heart responded with momentary joy.

His slight smile revealed great solace, as if seeing me alleviated his worry, then widened as if we were meeting after years of separation. I wanted to forget my days of imprisonment at the Viking's castle, forget that Alan was waiting to take me back to New York, and rush into Ramon's arms, which were now extended to me.

Lucia, as perceptive as her husband, read my thoughts at once. Her glance, fond and kind, moved from me to Ramon. "This is a nice surprise," she said.

"Isn't it?" the general remarked innocently. Something about his tone brought me back to my senses, made me realize exactly what he had done, what urgent business he had seen to while Lucia and I had waited for him to give us a tour of his estate. He had sent for Ramon!

Since I had arrived here, I had came so close to revising my earlier opinion of him, of trusting him whole-heartedly, the way I had from the first trusted Lucia. I felt my own sharp censure at having been taken in by them...conspirators...a man and a woman that worked together as one.

I avoided Ramon's touch as I slipped to the ground. Francisco had bounded out and stood slightly behind Ramon, Ramon's shadow darkening his heavy face.

The general had not changed. The deep lines around eyes and mouth suggested pleasantness. In the depths of his sharp, black eyes I saw no hint of apology, no guilt, no regret at his betrayal.

* * *

"And there's Thane!" Lucia said sweetly.

I felt physically ill as Thane strode forward. He looked even more vital, larger than life.

"Did you enjoy yourself, Marta?" he asked exuberantly, as if he had come to pick me up after a visit he himself had endorsed. "This is my favorite place, besides my own. I expect it will soon be yours, too."

"Thane, I've been wanting to see you," Lucia broke in. "I've got the most interesting book. I've just finished it and can't wait for you to read it!" She took his arm. "Let's go right to the library. Come with us, Marta."

Ramon and the general started with us up the steps and stopped in the coolness of the wide porch.

I followed Lucia and Thane into the house, then uncertainly I lagged behind. In their eager discussion of Mayan gods, they had temporarily forgotten about me. Their voices, loud and enthusiastic, decreased in volume as they gained distance from me and disappeared into an adjoining room.

It was clear that the arrival of the Viking and Ramon was no accident…the general had sent for them! But why? My frustration mounted and added to the confusion of my thoughts. In what way would it benefit the general for me to remain the prisoner of a madman?

Whatever the reason, it was one that fit somehow into his own goals, for he was not a man I took to work for anyone besides himself. Perhaps he did not want me to meet with Alan because he was implicated in some plot I did not at present understand.

These questions, for which I had no answers, brought surges of anger. I would go back now and confront the general with his cheap trickery!

As I backtracked to the porch entrance, Ramon's voice addressing the general, stopped me.

"I think it's time we take action," Ramon spoke sharply, decisively.

I drew back, remaining concealed.

"You know what haste makes," the general's voice was languorous. "We could end up with a disaster... and nothing else."

Nothing else…my anger deepened. Greed! I should have known that was behind their actions! What I was overhearing was a plot…Ramon was openly speaking of stealing of the Viking's treasure!

My heart pounded against my chest. I could believe it of the general, he could betray Thane as easily as he had betrayed me. But, Ramon? How could Ramon, who had at times been so kind, so understanding, possibly be a plotter, a grabber of other people's gold?

"It's your show, Ramon," the general went on, his voice harder now. "If you're sure the time is at hand, then let's get rid of Thane."

Ramon's show…all of this Ramon's idea! No doubt he had obtained work at Thane's estate and gained his confidence so he would be in a position to find the Viking's hidden treasure. My pounding heartbeat seemed to fall to a stop at the thought of what Ramon actually intended to do. Not only did they intend to rob the Viking, but to murder him!

"How do I get rid of him?"

The same way he got rid of Bertram! No doubt Thane would himself disappear into an ocean grave!

"That," the general's answer broke into my thoughts, "I'll leave entirely up to you."

"Let's keep Marta here," Ramon said in the same authoritative manner. "That way we'll be sure to keep her away from Avery."

"And keep her safely out of our way. I'll speak to Lucia. Lucia can lure her to stay with all that girl talk she's been missing. It should be no problem. I'll make the Viking believe we intend to drive Marta back tomorrow."

"By this time tomorrow," Ramon said. "It should be all over."

Chapter Seventeen

My stepping out on to the porch brought an uncomfortable silence, an exchange of furtive glances between Ramon and the general. The general recovered first, his blunt features brightening with amused humor. "Lucia would be delighted if you would stay with us tonight," he said. "She wants so much to have a long talk with you." He shrugged, smile broadening. "I think sometimes she finds me boorish and desires gentler companions. We could take you back tomorrow."

A slight raise of bushy eyebrows, serving to enlarge his black eyes, meant to indicate to me that quite a different meaning lay behind his words...that it was his intention to take me instead to Copan as I had previously asked him to do.

I hesitated, giving my abhorrence for him time to drain away before I spoke. "No need for that. Since Thane and Ramon have happened to stop by, I will just ride back with them now."

Ramon's eyes drifted back to Francisco's, lingering in an unyielding gaze. As if in response to the silent communication between them, Ramon added quickly, "Why don't you take Marta to Puerto Lorenzo? I have finally obtained her papers so she can board a ship to the states."

"If I did that," Francisco responded. "What would I tell the Viking?"

"That she escaped from your estate."

Francisco looked my way again. "I suppose that is what you want, safe passage back to New York."

"That's what Marta has wanted all along," Ramon answered for me, "and now is a perfect opportunity."

When the general did not speak, Ramon continued, "You know how much faith the Viking puts in you. Thane will never believe you are involved in helping her."

Once more I felt overcome with aversion for them, at how pleased both of them seemed over the general's skills of duplicity. I looked from one to the other, liars and frauds. They were no better than Sanchez, who they censured and condemned. I wouldn't even be surprised to find that he was working with them, an equal partner in their sinister plans to steal the Viking's jewels!

In the tense silence, I thought of Thane. I had once believed he might be pretending insanity in order to sell his fake artifacts, that he had possibly himself killed Bertram for finding him out or for trying to steal from him. How wrong I had been!

Now the Viking came into focus clearly…a strange, vulnerable man, living more in a world of his own creating than in the real world. He was like a child full of guileless illusions, one that must be protected. Even though staying would place my own life in danger, I knew I could not abandon him and walk away, continuing my own life knowing I had done nothing to save an innocent victim from certain death. It had been, after all, my own fault that they knew the treasures he spoke of really existed.

I must do all I could to convince Thane of their deception, to warn him. If he knew in advance, he could prepare to defend himself against them. "I've decided to remain at the Viking's estate."

Ramon responded with an edge of sharpness. "You've been wanting to leave. We are now offering you your chance!"

"I will leave it up to you two to make the correct decisions," the general said. He left abruptly to join his wife and the man he was plotting against.

I met Ramon's gaze. His stern features brought ice to my heart. I recalled how differently he had looked at me the night we had danced. I thought of how a little at a time I had grown to believe in him, and this total reversal left me crushed, on the verge of tears.

"It's for the best," he said, his voice and his eyes becoming a shade softer.

How could he betray Thane? The ice in my heart melted into total emptiness.

Ramon stepped closer. I mustn't let him touch me. Not ever again. I shrank away, but was blocked by the wall behind me.

My recoiling erased all evidence of sympathy from his features. Straightening as if for battle, he commanded. "You are not going back there! I won't let you."

Fighting for control, I answered, keeping a steady tone. "Every time I've tried to escape, you have forced me to return. You should be happy about my decision."

"Circumstances have changed!"

"For me, too," I said defiantly. With a raise of my chin, I added, "There is no need for your guarding services any longer. I am fully content to stay."

"So everything has changed all of the sudden?" The ominous opposition beneath the surface of his eyes caused me to edge sideways toward the doorway.

"Marta! Why are you acting this way? What have I done to cause you to distrust me? I would do nothing at all to harm you!"

As his dark eyes held mine, my feelings became more complex. Perhaps I could talk Ramon out of fulfilling his hideous plan. In the awful interval of indecision, I had a vision of an empty sea, waves splashing against jagged rocks of the cliff. I stared at him a moment, realizing words were of no use. Ramon was already a murderer…he and the general had killed Gavin Bertram! I remained silent. I could not risk Ramon's knowing how much I knew about him.

The hot tears formed in my eyes in spite of all efforts to stop them. If only Ramon were innocent! Even though I had always believed in the depths of my heart that we were destined to part, I had wanted Ramon to remain always in my memory, the man who had saved me from Sanchez, my personal hero, strong and noble.

I turned away from him, saying, "You came here to bring me back. And I'm going with you. Nothing could be simpler than that."

"It's not that simple. You must for your own good do exactly as I tell you!" I didn't fully face him, yet I was aware of the spark of fire that must be in his eyes. "You won't be safe there, Marta! Believe me." He grasped my shoulders as if this action would force me to comply. "You must believe this: I am only trying to protect you!"

I felt my body automatically stiffen at his touch. I pulled myself away from his grasp, saying, "I'm leaving here when you leave."

"Marta, you can't! I won't let you!"

"Then stop me!"

He was going to reply, but his answer was prevented by voices fast approaching. Thane and Lucia's words mingled together as if they were both talking at once, broken intermittently by the general's pompous comments. Francisco lingered in the doorway of the porch as the other two drew forward.

Thane carried a huge book in both hands as if it were some rare treasure. "A most magnificent book! Where did you get it?"

"I sent for it. From London."

Thane raised the thick volume. "Lucia is loaning this to me. You must read it, Marta. It will be of great interest to you."

"Lucia spends all my money on useless books," the general remarked jovially. "Could I get you to take some more of them? We have rooms full. She won't even miss them."

Lucia smiled at Francisco, then at me. "You must stay over-night with us, Marta. You'll be interested in my library. I have collected books for many years."

The invitation sounded so spontaneous and sincere, that I would have believed it was, had I not known better. Francisco had asked her to insist on my staying.

But surely the general had kept from her the reason. Lucia could not be a party to his greed. She would have to be a trusting pawn of the general's, just as the Viking was a trusting victim. Her genuine goodness was perfectly clear in her benevolent manner. I fully believed Lucia incapable of harming others, of being any part of the bloody scheme I had overheard.

Genuine disappointment showed on Lucia's face as I replied. "No, I must go back with them now."

"We will get together soon and discuss this book," the Viking said, beaming at Lucia and Francisco. His affection for them increased my compassion and assured me I was taking the right action. No matter how much I might want to, I could not leave Thane totally unaware of his danger.

"It's not fair," Ramon addressed Thane, "to keep Marta all to ourselves. She must have friends."

"The girls will both be down-hearted if you don't let Marta stay," the general supported. Then he added, as if it were unimportant to him. "We will see that she gets back first thing tomorrow." The Viking's questioning glance fell to me. "Marta, would you like to stay?"

"No, I want to go with you."

The Viking strode ahead and placed the book carefully in the back of the carriage. I started toward him, but Ramon stepped in my path. "Thane doesn't care. So you just stay here."

The Viking returned to stand beside me. Purposefully I slipped my hand through his arm. "I think we should get started. It will soon be dark."

Thane gazed at me with adoration, delighted by my decision. "You are right. Marta wants to stay with me," he explained, casting an apologetic glance over his shoulder to Lucia. "She'll visit you another time."

"Now is as good a time as any," Ramon stated flatly, still blocking our way.

My hand tightened on the Viking's massive arm. "I'm very tired tonight. I want to return to your estate."

"Whatever you wish!" Thane spoke, his voice louder. Smiling again, he started to lead the way around Ramon to the carriage.

As I stepped past Ramon, he gripped my wrist, forcing me to remain beside him. "She's not going," he stated.

"Not going...what do you mean?" Thane drew himself up until he towered above us both.

"She told me she wanted to remain with the Perez's until tomorrow."

"That is not what she told me!" Thane's voice raised in threat.

"I must insist that you let go of her!" Ramon calmly, icily, remained motionless.

"Didn't you hear me?" Thane's look of disbelief changed slowly to rage. "Take your hands off her! At once!"

A florid red had spread into the fairness of the Viking's skin. His powerful muscles flexed. Within seconds Thane had changed into a wrathful giant, useless to appeal to, impossible to restrain.

Before either Ramon or I had time to move or speak, Thane's huge hands had locked on Ramon's shoulders. With a terrifying yell, with strength increased by fury, he shoved Ramon backward.

The unexpected attack caught Ramon off guard and hurled him downward against the steps of the porch. He grimaced from the impact of the sharp stones of the steps against his back.

At almost the same instant, Thane, as if I possessed no weight, lifted me to the carriage seat, jumped up beside me, and prompted the horses to a trot.

Hanging on with both hands to keep me from falling, I managed to cast a quick look back. In spite of the jolting pain Ramon must feel, he was already on his feet. Whatever action he planned to take was stopped by the general, who placed a warning hand on his arm. Francisco cried out in Spanish as he waved to one of his guards.

What were they going to do? Did they intend to stop us at the gate? It would not be possible without harming the Viking, and I did not think they would dare to do that with Lucia watching in wide-eyed surprise.

I caught one more glimpse of Ramon before the trees shut off my vision of him. Did the hard expression on his face reveal only fury over the fact that I had been able to momentarily thwart his well-made plans to rob and murder? Or was it a forewarning of what was to follow?

I felt increased fear because I knew Ramon would not be defeated. He would follow us...and then what?

The men who had admitted me earlier watched us our rapid approaching of the gate. "Let us out!" Thane had been prepared for another fight but none came. The two men, one on each side, parted the gate and we passed through without ever pulling to a stop.

Still bracing myself from the great speed, I kept vigilant watch as Thane plunged ahead. Behind me, beyond the spray of moist earth flying from fast-turning wheels, stretched only a blur of empty road.

"Ramon is sure to follow us!" I shouted.

The Viking, intent on manipulating the carriage, called back. "Don't be frightened, Marta. Only a clash of wills! It is over now!" As if he had convinced himself, he deliberately slowed our pace. We soon made a sharp turn into the jungle-like trail that by this time was becoming so familiar to me.

"Let's take another road back," I urged.

Thane continued on his course. "This is the road we must take to my castle. There is not a choice of roads in this country."

"We could go to Santa Augusta. Do you know someone there who would put us up for the night?" "Only Arnoldo." The mention of his name silenced my protests.

"But Arnoldo is a bachelor. He would have no suitable accommodations for you, my dear."

Thane allowed the horses to jog now at what seemed to me a slow and tedious gait.

I had traveled the road many times, but it looked different in the quickly falling darkness. I felt encased by the high walls of vegetation and apprehensive over the fact that we would surely be pursued.

"We must hurry!"

The Viking, despite my prompting, seemed to immediately relax, as if his flight from the general's plantation and Ramon's resistance were already forgotten.

I tried again several times but could not persuade him to gain speed. Darkness, made more intense by the profuse growth of branches overhead unnerved me.

I spoke to him at last. "You never should have shown that crown! Everyone wants it now!"

My sudden announcement brought no reply.

Quickly I continued. "The general and Ramon are plotting to steal the Viking Crown. They will steal all of your gold and jewels!"

When Thane still made no comment, I added breathlessly, "They plan to kill you! That's why I wanted to come back with you, to warn you! You must do something to protect yourself, before it's too late!" Thane faced me. He now looked very startled, then as if I were over-tired and speaking out of my head, he said soothingly. "Marta, nothing is going to happen to me or to my jewels. Look at all the guards I have around me."

"Guards, bought and paid for, probably by Sanchez or the general!"

The look of puzzlement on his face deepened. "The general...I don't know what you're saying."

"The general is plotting against you. And Ramon, too. He no doubt wanted a job at your estate because he had heard the rumors of your great wealth. He intended all along to rob you!"

"Oh, no, Marta. Ramon and I....like a while ago, we may fight a little, but we fight like all good friends fight. We will soon make up! I trust him implicitly. And he knows this. So he will return to work for me in spite of our differences a while ago."

"You must not trust him!" I said, frustration at my being unable to convince him sounding in my voice. " You can't trust anyone! Don't you understand? I overheard their plans!"

The light in Thane's eyes seemed to recede, leaving only a glassy facade. His voice had changed to that far-away tone that filled my heart with dread. "No, you are wrong. Ramon is my friend. True and loyal. And the general loves me as if I were his own brother! Francisco and I roamed these hills together as youths. He is as dear to me as my own heart!"

"Don't be fooled!" I answered sharply. "They are common thieves! And you are in great danger!" Even as I spoke I knew I would never be able to make him believe that Francisco and Ramon were co-conspirators.

I decided on another approach. "What about Sanchez? No doubt he is involved in all this."

"Sanchez is Evelia's blood line," he responded, trying hard to

231

calm me. "And Evelia is grateful for the help I have always given her."

I leaned back against the carriage seat and said wearily. "You have no friends, Thane! You are all alone!"

He straightened up, his form tall and impressive in the waning light. "Don't worry about me, Marta! I am a Viking!" His voice rose to a thunderous rumble. "A Viking never surrenders! Many a Viking ship has been burned, crew and all! Before we face defeat, we destroy our ships, our possessions, ourselves!"

* * *

Darkness, despite a full moon, had brought me near to panic. I could barely hear the Viking's voice as he talked about Lucia's book as if we were on an ordinary carriage ride and it was his duty to supply appropriate conversation.

Anxiously I listened to night animals stirring in nearby branches, their strange, unidentifiable sounds. Would I soon detect hoofbeats from behind us?

"Do you have a weapon?" I asked him.

"A rifle on the floor behind us. But," he smiled reassuringly, "there will be no need for one."

Was there no way I could make him see his danger? I meet his gaze. Moonlight filtering from the branches overhead fell across his bearded face, intensified the reverent glow in his eyes. His large hand lay close to mine, but he made no attempt to touch me. Even though his eyes shone with admiration, I realized how content Thane was to remain with only a dream.

I was his princess. The Viking did not want a flesh and blood woman; he did not want me to be real. My thoughts strayed to Ramon, who I knew had seen the real Marta Swan more clearly than anyone else ever had, and my heart told me that Ramon loved me, no matter what terrible deeds he was involved in.

I heard the first faint pounding of hoofbeats before Thane did. But before I could tell him, I felt his eyes on me, acknowledging the fact that he had heard them, too.

"They have waited too long! We are almost to my gate!" I saw his large hands shake the reigns, heard his confident voice calling to the horses. "There is no way they can overtake us!"

As the carriage picked up speed, it shook so hard I thought it would fly to pieces. Fearfully I hung on to the bench. The rapid clack of hooves…how many I did not know…steadily became more distinct.

I strained my eyes, but as yet they had not come into view. Ramon loved me! I still could not believe he would actually kill the Viking and me. But maybe it wasn't Ramon at all! Maybe it was some of the rebels who robbed any traveler on the road. Maybe it was Sanchez himself! In panic I managed to rise, lean over my seat, and grope along the floorboards for the rifle. My fingers without the help of my eyes located the gun. I lifted it by the cold steel of the barrel.

"Be careful!" Thane called. "It's loaded. A repeater with twelve shots!"

I propped the barrel over the back of my bench, and struggling to maintain my balance from the unexpected jolts, placed my finger on the trigger. My hands felt damp and cold against the metal as I watched alertly, barely able to breath.

As I waited, an image of Ramon's face arose in my mind. If it were him and if I did not shoot to kill, he would keep following! Darkness, more profound than what surrounded me, began to swirl like water before my eyes. I could not kill Ramon! I could not kill anyone!

The horses now emerged as speeding shadows, three of them. I could not make out faces or even forms, only shades of darkness. The black images possessed steady, relentless speed.

My hand moved on the trigger. I had never shot a gun before. The exploding sound, so close to my ear, the slight kick against my loose grasp, terrified me.

Intentionally off mark, the bullet hit far south of the men who chased us. If I had really believed the shot would caution them into slowing their speed, or giving up their goal, I had been wrong. If anything, they were riding faster.

"Thane, they're catching us!"

"If they do, get the gun to me! I will die in battle…protecting you!"

The Viking now stood, a zealous pose to his broad frame. His bearded face tilted upward so the moon shone across it. His eyes, full of fervor, glistened. In his mind he was a Viking warrior!

A madman! Murderous pursuers! This couldn't be happening to me!

Eleven shots left. Even though I could not actually shoot to kill, this time I took more careful aim. The wild bullet I had fired had had no effect on them. Maybe a close one would.

It did. It caused them to answer my fire with fire of their own. The zing of a bullet passed close to my head. I knelt on the floorboards, pulling myself up, bracing the gun and once again pulling the trigger.

Answering fire, the spattering of bullets, returned.

To my horror close beside me I heard Thane gasp. He stumbled as he turned to face his opponents. His bearded face filled with fury. In an instant the rage vanished. His legs no longer held him. I dropped the gun and tried to keep him from pitching forward. I heard it clatter against the side of the carriage and fall beside the racing wheels.

I was able to pull Thane to the floor beside me. I at the same time grabbed for the reins before they, too, slipped beyond my reach. I quickly took Thane's former position, standing, a clear target, but too desperate to try to protect myself. I heard my voice, which sounded like it belonged to someone else, pleading with the horses.

They seemed to understand our plight, and gained speed. A bullet struck the bench, embedded itself in the wood.

My only hope lay in reaching the gate! I had no idea how much further, but hadn't Thane had said we were very close?

My fearful eyes darted to Thane. He was bleeding profusely. Spreading over his shirt, the circle of blood was so wide I could not tell exactly where the bullet had struck him. Was he already dead? Above the clamor of wheels, I could not hear him breathing. Nor could I see any signs of motion.

The three men on horseback were drawing closer, but I still

maintained a wide lead. Our horses, needing none of my prompting, raced on. They knew the road, the sudden turn that led us out of the heavy growth of forest.

Thane's castle loomed ahead, bright in the moonlight. The sight of it renewed my hope. I would reach it! We would be safe!

I yelled encouragement to the animals. Plunging ahead the left wheel hit a rock. I felt the carriage shake, lurch to the side in precarious balance, then bounce back on even ground.

Quickly the empty space closed. One of the guards had spotted us. "Help!" If he heard my voice, a woman's voice, he would surely hasten to assist. "Help us! Open the gate!"

Rapidly the guard responded. He cried out to another man and the barred door swung open.

I drew the horses to a stop and looked back. The three mounted followers halted, changed directions so quickly that their ever being so close behind seemed a fading nightmare. "You must get a doctor!" I sobbed, as I sprang from the carriage. "Thane Ulrickson has been shot!"

* * *

No fire blazed in the great fireplace that night. The empty grate was heaped with ashes, as if without the Viking to tend it, no one else would ever care enough to keep it burning. The dining hall, without the vitality of his presence, was profoundly empty.

The rough volcanic walls projected a cave-like coldness that settled deep into my body. The doctor, a frail, old man, had been summoned at once from a nearby estate. Since he had waved me from Thane's room, I had sat huddled in the same chair I had taken when I had first been ushered into the Viking's house. In the depths of my solitary gloom, I desperately hoped, yes, prayed, that Thane would recover!

When I had watched him driving the carriage, exhilarated by his own view of what was taking place, I had become convinced that Thane actually was unable to distinguish between the real and the unreal. Being a Viking king was his fixation, I, an extension of his deranged vision.

Thane's lack of normal discernment increased the pity I felt for him. Thane's difference from other people harmed no one. Why couldn't he be let alone to live happily his dream-life? How cruel to take advantage of such a man!

Had Sanchez fired the shot? If so, it had been accomplished with no remorse. Or had it been Ramon's own gun, the gun kept always close at hand? The thought intensified my agony!

Deep in my own thoughts, I was only distantly aware of the men who milled around the outside entrance. Occasionally the old guard, the one Ramon sometimes left to watch me, would look in, toward where I remained in immobile waiting.

Footsteps coming from the hallway in the direction of the room where the Viking lay, drew closer. Expecting to encounter the doctor, I rose. Instead, I found myself face to face with Evelia. Her slender shoulders drooped slightly, dark hair strung across her face. Her despairing appearance accentuated her thinness, made Evelia seem to be what I knew she was not, wasted, weak.

I stepped forward, my heart reacting to what must be news from the doctor. Is he...?"

Evelia brought both hands to her face and cried.

Faintness overtook me. I reached for the back of a nearby chair to steady myself. "Oh, no," I moaned.

Evelia's hands dropped limply away from her pale, elongated face. "They won't let me in." In mid-sentence, as was her way, her mood changed from hopeless grief to temper. "Why won't they? For years he has fed and clothed me! I have a right to be with him when he needs me!"

"Did the doctor tell you anything about his condition?"

"Nothing." Once more the grief. Again sobbing shook her small frame.

I made a great effort to stifle my resentment of her...of the treachery she had shown in willfully plotting to turn me over to Sanchez, fully knowing the monstrous implications of her act. I could never be taken in by her again, for no amount of tears, yet I did feel a momentary link of shared emotion, which inclined me to clemency.

"Sit here," I said. "I will bring you something to drink."

With a hand that shook I poured juice from a ceramic pitcher into a wine glass and brought it to her.

Why did she hate me so much? Evelia had from first sight of me labeled me as enemy. Certainly she was a survivor and would do anything to preserve what was hers. Yet Thane and she didn't appear to be lovers. I couldn't really understand how his affection for me in any way threatened her lifestyle. Perhaps Evelia was simply a gold-digger, another major partner in the huge conspiracy which had formed against Thane.

"How I hate fighting!" she groaned. "I was born into anarchy! I have lived with it constantly! Stupid, stupid people fighting stupid battles!" She drank again and set the glass aside. "How many rebels attacked you?" She paused, then asked what she really wanted to know. "Were any of them killed?"

She was inquiring, no doubt, about the well-being of her bestial brother. I would not give her the satisfaction of knowing that if Sanchez were among the would-be assassins, he had gotten away safely. "It was very dark. It's hard to tell."

Evelia lapsed again into brooding quietness. Suddenly she burst out, "If Thane dies, what will become of me? Where will I go? What will I do, all alone, with dictators and butchers everywhere, with no home or money!"

I saw suddenly what I should have known all along: Evelia's tears had been only for herself.

After that we did not speak to one another. From time to time Evelia would sob, loud and harsh sounds in the stillness, but I could not bring myself to comfort her.

An hour of endless misery passed before the doctor, bag in hand, entered the room. Upon seeing him, several men from outside drew forward. He did not look at them, or Evelia, but addressed only me. His speech in broken English was slow and difficult. "I've removed the bullet. The Viking, you know, is a powerful man. He is going to be all right. He will be up and about in no time."

Relief rushed over me. "Thank you," I said.

The doctor smiled. The smile made him look younger and less

stern. He repeated the words in brisk Spanish, in a brusque manner that told me that he knew I was the only one among them willing to assume any responsibility for the Viking.

For the time being I allowed myself to bask in relief and gratitude. I had little faith in my own decision to return with Thane, but I now rejoiced. Already my returning had served its intended purpose. If I hadn't been beside Thane in the carriage, he would certainly be dead!

But my joy plunged as abruptly as it had risen. Through the facade of well-being, the truth reached me: the knowledge that Thane's safety as well as my own was frighteningly temporary.

Chapter Eighteen

Red and yellow rays of dawn streaked the sky as I entered the Viking's room. Near the huge, offset window where he could see out, Thane lay propped against pillows, his chest swathed in thick, white bandages.

"How do you feel?"

"Nothing to worry about. Only a nick." Still, I saw a flash of pain cross his face as he attempted to turn toward me. "I'll be out of bed in no time!"

"You came so close to being killed," I said, stirred by a sudden rush of compassion for him. Damp reddish hair curled in his beard and on the locks that fell across his forehead. Despite his brave talk, loss of blood had drained the color from his face and made his skin as ghostly white as the layers of gauze that bound up his massive body.

"I'm fine, Marta!" His voice had a forced heartiness, but his blue eyes brightened a little as he added, "The bullet completely missed my heart!"

"Not by very far," I reminded him. "Thane, can't I make you understand? Ramon and the general, even if they weren't the ones who followed actually followed us, are still responsible!"

Thane angled his head. The action magnified his skepticism. "You just don't know what the general means to me or you wouldn't say that." Thane laughed. "You saw us at the dance! When we are together, we are still boys! Like in the old days!"

"What about Ramon? You know how angry he was when you fought with him. Whoever attacked us last night must have followed us from the general's estate. Ramon...."

As I spoke, Thane's large eyes had riveted to the doorway. At first he looked startled, then overjoyed.

The words died in my throat as I saw Ramon, hands braced on either side of the door, form rigid. How long had he been listening?

Ramon's expression was grave. How easy it would have been…if I didn't know better…to believe he had nothing at all to do with the ruthless attempt on the Viking's life.

"I came the minute I heard," Ramon spoke with great sincerity. "I'm so sorry, Thane! I should have been with you!"
His eyes flickered to me. I had drawn nearer the window when he crossed the room so I would not have to stand close beside him. "Are you all right, Marta?"

"She is indeed all right!" Thane spoke up.

Ramon's eyes remained on me as Thane, pride deepening in his voice, exclaimed, "Marta saved my life!" Then to me, "I told you he'd be back! Our little spat yesterday was only a disagreement. Men must disagree, if they are to be men! I wouldn't accept a friend who did not have his own opinions!"

As if resolving the conflict between them was more important than his near brush with death, the Viking spoke anxiously, "I sometimes act rashly. No hard feelings, Ramon?"

I slanted a quick glance at Ramon and felt dismayed by the evidence of a noble forgiveness. Deception! The extent of his duplicity sickened me. I felt a shiver of horror as Thane accepted Ramon's outstretched hand.

My eyes locked on their tight grasp, then followed Ramon as he wandered to the stand beside the bed and gaze with a grim distraction at the vase of flowers.

Thane, happy that no rift existed between them, spoke, "It turned out you were right, Ramon. Marta should have stayed with Francisco and Lucia. If Marta would have been harmed because of my own willfulness, I could never forgive myself!"

"You had no way of knowing you would be attacked," Ramon said generously.

Thane's voice dropped in volume, as if he were speaking to a trusted confidant. "I want you to find out who followed us. Can you do that?"

"I'll try. Can you tell me anything about them? Did they look like common bandits or were they soldiers?"

Reddish brows knotted above Thane's eyes. "In the darkness it's hard to tell. Everything happened so fast, hoofbeats, shooting! The men were on horseback. I didn't get a look at them. Did you, Marta?"

"There were three of them," I said. I felt an outraged frustration over the fact that Thane chose to believe Ramon instead of me! I would never be able to convince him of the fact that I had actually over-heard the general and Ramon plotting his death to be rid of him so they could freely plunder his estate!

"Do you think Sanchez is behind this?" Ramon directed the question to me.

Another hypocrisy, I thought. He was using Sanchez to avert suspicion from himself! I did not answer him.

"I hope it wasn't Sanchez," Thane said. "Evelia takes such stock in him. Don't you believe these men were just bandits? Maybe the same ones who killed my friend Bertram."

"No one is safe on the road anymore," Ramon replied.

"The real danger is not out there," I coldly informed the Viking. "It is right here within your own walls!"

As if my words had struck him, Ramon frowned. I, at least, had reached him, if not the Viking, with my bitter warning.

Thane leaned back against the pillows as if so much talk had wearied him. "We are safe now. That is all that really matters. You are so far away, Marta. Will you come closer?"

I straightened up and tried to smile as I complied with his request.

"Stand by her, Ramon, where I can see you both together."

Ramon stepped forward. I moved away so his arm would not touch mine.

Thane watched us sadly. I wondered what he was thinking to become so suddenly heavy of heart. It was almost as if he under-stood some reality about us, some knowledge about Ramon and me, that he was fighting against accepting.

With a doleful smile, he spoke again. "It is good," he said, his voice very low, "to have both of you here with me now."

"You're getting tired," I said. "I am going to let you get some rest."

Thane made no attempt to stop my leaving. I was glad to get out of the room, to be putting distance between Ramon and me. I began quickly climbing the stairs to my room when I heard Ramon's rapid footsteps following after me. "Marta, we have to talk."

"I never want to talk to you again!"

"Little chance of that," Ramon answered, black eyes flashing with an anger that matched my own. "Because of your stubbornness, your foolishness, I am going to have to watch you every minute! You will not be able to leave my sight!"

"Just stay away from me!" I warned.

* * *

I stayed in my room, seething with anger, unable to decide what to do. At late morning I caught a glimpse of Evelia from my bedroom window. I saw her look furtively over her shoulder before disappearing into the trees. I thought about all of Evelia's countless opportunities to follow Thane out to the caves. No doubt she knew exactly where the vault beneath the mountain was hidden. At this very moment she was probably sneaking out to conspire with her brother, Sanchez.

Driven by the desire to protect the Viking and the treasure he thought was mine, I crossed over to the door of my room and started downstairs. I would follow Evelia and see if she were meeting Sanchez. If so, I would warn Thane. If he caught them digging down by the caves, then he would have to believe me!

The sight of Ramon pacing the length of the dining room below the stairs made me stop in my tracks. He had made good his promise to guard me every minute. How his imposing presence angered me!

I would never be able to get past him. His pretense of guarding me, fully endorsed by the Viking, was going to prevent me from following Evelia.

Returning to my room, I pushed back the iron gratings of the narrow door leading out to the balcony and looked down. The pines growing so close to the wall of the house seemed to beckon to me. Once more I considered climbing down them as a means of escape.

The sharp drop to stone balcony and patio was broken by the overhanging branches of the trees. Choosing the limb I knew to be sturdy enough to bear my weight, I climbed from the ledge into the stinging bed of pine needles. Ignoring the sharp pin-pricks against my hands and fingers, the rough bark scraping my knees, I found a foothold on one branch after another until I had eased my way to the rough stone of the courtyard below.

I brushed loose bark and pine needles from my long skirts, now torn and perfumed with the fragrant scent of pine. Darting to the side of the house, avoiding the stairway Ramon so faithfully guarded, I dashed into the shelter of the trees.

Evelia had vanished, but believing I knew her destination, I hurried in the direction of the lava caves.

Heat radiated from the clear sky in stifling rays. Shade disappeared, trees grew dwarfed and scrubby as I neared the rough, pitted mountains of lava rock. With difficulty, I climbed over porous, charred rock, avoiding the jagged cracks and chasms made by some ancient tremor deep within the earth. I stopped to brush damp hair from my face. Even at this high elevation the day was going to be scorching!

I reached the mounds of lava, stone piled upon stone as if tossed there by some careless giant. Shades of porous light brown mingled with walls of obsidian, shining slick and glossy in the morning sun. I recognized the gaping entrance to one of the dark lava caves. I scanned the nearby outcropping of rock, searching for the wall cut in stone, which I knew was close by…the entrance that led to the Viking's underground vault.

I heard voices before I saw Evelia emerge from the wide entrance to the nearby lava cave.

"Why should I want to help *her*?" I hate her!"

The anger in Evelia's voice made me press back against the ledge of stone. For Evelia to be talking to Sanchez about me didn't make sense.

Out of sight, but still able to observe Evelia, I watched the entrance to the cave. Not Sanchez, but Alan stepped outside into the sunlight. The shock of seeing him there almost made me cry out. Why would Alan be meeting with Evelia? What were they doing out here so near the Viking's cave? I watched Alan move toward Evelia and say in a persuasive way, "Marta must get out of here. You must help her for your brother's sake."

Evelia whirled rudely away from him. What she said to Alan I could not make out, but after she had spoken, in the same spirited way, she switched away from him. Alan's presence when I had been expecting Sanchez had temporarily stunned me. I waited until Evelia had disappeared into the trees and for Alan to begin to reenter the cave before I called to him.

Alan started at the sound of his name. As if caught in enemy territory, he spun around toward me. I saw a moment of fear in his eyes, as if he had been expecting someone else and was prepared for some dangerous confrontation. The tense line of his mouth relaxed into a welcoming smile as I came toward him.

"What are you doing here, Alan?"

"When you didn't show up at the Juarez' in Copan I about went crazy! I came back here looking for you!"

Alan had come back to save me! He had placed his own life in danger!

"How did you know I was here?"

"You weren't at the generals. Where else would you be?"

"Why were you meeting Evelia out here?"

"Evelia is going to help me get you away from here." Alan's sandy hair gleamed with sweat. He wiped at his face. "It's very hot." Placing an arm around my shoulder he drew me with him back into the cave's wide, dark entrance. "It's cool in here. We can sit and talk."

I glanced around nervously. Although Ramon was in the house, one of his men might show up any minute. "We shouldn't stay out here."

"Why not?" Alan smiled a little. "I don't think this volcano is

244

going to erupt again in the next thousand years."

Dressed in clean, white shirt and brown vest and trousers, Alan had managed, in spite of the heat, to regain a vestige of his New York image. Except for vague shadows beneath his eyes, an unaccustomed thinness to his face, which was not unattractive, no traces of illness or fear remained. His eyes glowed with a bright, unusual excitement.

"Do you want some water? I have a canteen in my pack." He sat down upon a high plateau in the cave's floor, motioning for me to sit beside him. "Bread and cheese, too. We'll have a picnic." He reached into the pack, which rested behind a nearby boulder, taking out the canteen and tin cups and offering bread and cheese to me.

"All the comforts of home!" I smiled, remembering the times I had lived on bread and cheese, not wanting to pause for a proper lunch to meet the deadlines of our published research papers, papers we soon planned to compile, under Alan's name, into a book of Father's life work.

Alan had risked his life to come back for me! And he was not even aware of the immediate danger! He knew nothing of Ramon and the general's plan to murder Thane and rob him of his jewels. I thought that I should tell him, but instead broke off a piece of bread and cheese and sipped at the tepid water.

The cave where we sat was so close, almost adjacent to the one where the Viking hid his treasure. Chambers of the Viking's cave must be within yards from the very spot where we were sitting. I peered into the depths of the cave, wondering how far back it went. In the obscure darkness, I noticed an inky spot just beyond us, where a great hole gaped, an opening that might drop into a lower level.

"Evelia and you seem to be very good friends."

Alan avoided my eyes, concentrated upon closing the canteen. "Yes. When I first met her two years ago, she even..." he laughed, "imagined herself in love with me. I think she got over that."

I suspected that there was much more to their relationship

245

than this causal statement suggested. Both Alan and myself were used to woman being attracted to him, his handsomeness, his confident manner. I had never doubted his faithfulness back in New York, why was I doubting him now? I lifted the bread and cheese to my lips and wondered if he had meant to share this lunch with Evelia. The thought made the food dry and tasteless as chalk.

I could not stop the tears that had begun to sting my eyes. As if at a loss for words, Alan watched me try to hide them, to brush them quickly away.

"Marta, you surely don't think...Evelia and I are from different worlds. Circumstances threw us together."

Alan wasn't denying the fact that they had been together. "I thought you and I were something solid and permanent."

"We are, Marta! All there ever was between Evelia and me was...flirtation. Just two people caught up in the moment."

But how far had that flirtation gone? Part of me wanted to hurt him, to blame him. But images of Ramon kept filling my mind. Me, in Ramon's arms, dancing with him, kissing him. How could I blame Alan for Evelia when I had so easily fallen under Ramon's spell? Caught up in the moment...maybe that explained my feelings for Ramon, the kiss upon the deserted beach, the fire of being in his embrace.

"Things are so different here," Alan said.

Silence hung over us tensely.

"I'll be so glad when we get back to New York!" He paused. "Evelia, like it or not, is necessary to your escape."

In the stillness I thought about Evelia's trick of leaving me stranded by the side of the road, at the mercy of her evil brother, Sanchez. Anger I had attributed to jealousy over Thane's attentions had in truth been for Alan. "I am never going to trust Evelia again!

"There is simply no other way for you to get through the gate."

I thought of our return to New York, working with Alan again at the museum, looking forward to nights at the theater or opera, attending with Alan the social functions that were so much a part of his life. To flee even with Evelia's help was tempting, but something I was no longer free to do. "I can't go back now."

"What are you saying?" Alan set down his cup and rose, coming toward me.

"I can't leave the Viking in danger."

"Thane should never have displayed that crown! You're right, every cut-throat and mercenary for miles around will be after it now."

Cut-throat. Mercenary. I thought of Ramon and the general and shivered.

Alan's mouth became a thin, straight line. "Many plots are afoot already to steal the jewels from him. You were right about Sanchez planning to rob him. And others."

Others, meaning Ramon and the general.

"If stupid revolutionaries get their hands on the crown, they will melt the gold down to buy bullets! The archaeological significance of it will be lost forever."

"But what can we do? I've tried to warn the Viking, but he won't listen."

Alan looked at me with sincere sadness. "The Viking will eventually lose the crown. He can't hold on to it with so many out to steal it. Such a loss!" Alan's hand trembled slightly as he spoke, revealing to me the enormity of the emotion he was feeling. "The crown's monetary worth is nothing compared to the archaeological significance!"

"We can't stop the theft from occurring."

"The only way we can save the crown and these other precious artifacts from destruction now is by taking them from the Viking before the others get to them. I know I can manage to get the crown back to New York. There, we could run it through scientific tests. It's not the crown's value that is so important, but it's the impact it will have on history."

"It would be out and out stealing!"

"Not really, Marta. The Viking thinks the crown belongs to you, anyway. He would give it to you willingly."

"Thane showed me his jewels, but it wasn't even me he was

247

showing them to. He thinks I am the Sun Maiden. He might be willing to give the crown to me, but I am just not able to take it." I paused. "The crown may not even be authentic. You just have to forget about it. That's all you can do."

"Thane is going to lose the crown anyway. To robbers! Our taking it might even save his life."

"I will be no part of it."

"That crown will never do Thane any good! But think of what this would mean to us, Marta. If the crown is real, we would become rich just from the publicity! Our careers settled, established throughout the world. We could vacation in Paris, London...go all over the world!" Alan paused, catching my hand. "All of our dreams just within our reach. But all that is nothing compared to what this would mean to science! I want this evidence to preserve for mankind. Imagine...the link between the Mayans and the Vikings proven!" Alan's eyes glittered with an uncanny brilliance. "It would revolutionize our entire concept of history and civilization!"

I removed my hand from his and moved slowly away from him.

Persuasively, he continued, "I don't want this evidence to fall into ignorant hands, Marta. If you tell me where the crown is hidden, I can keep it safe. Those ignorant peasant revolutionaries will chip out the jewels to buy ammunition, melt that precious crown for the gold. We don't have much time. Sanchez and his men plan to act tonight! I must get to those jewels before they do or it will be too late. That crown must be protected at all cost!"

I looked away from his rapt, compelling gaze, the eyes so clear and earnest. If he had wanted the crown for selfish motives, as Ramon and Sanchez did, I could have easily told him no. But this was Alan I was talking to. I did not doubt that he wanted it for the good of the world, for all mankind. I understood his desire to protect the rare object, but wasn't honor more important than all that Alan had spoken of?

"I'm sorry, Alan. I could not betray Thane. Besides, things are more complicated than they seem. Ramon and the general have a plot of their own. They not only intend to rob Thane...but to murder him!"

Alan looked alarmed. "Are you sure?"

I remembered the words I had heard pass between Ramon and the general on the porch of the general's house. "Yes."

"Then our first step is to get you away from here." Alan said. "I'm going to the village for help."

"You must get help for Thane, not me!"

"Leave it all up to me. I must get started at once. I'll return as soon as I can."

"But Alan..."

"Let me take care of this, Marta." He suddenly gathered me into his arms. "My Marta! When I think of all you've been through for me...risking your very life, coming to this primitive, war-torn land to look for me...." He held me close, and for a moment I rested my head against his chest. "All of this has made me realize that you are the real prize, the real treasure." Alan cupped his fingers under my chin and lifted my face to receive his kiss. "My little darling. When we get back to New York, I want you to marry me"

"Do you mean that?"

"With all my heart."

I knew how important uncovering the link between the Vikings and the Mayans had been to him, how unselfish he was being to put it secondary to his love for me.

Alan followed me to the entrance of the cave. "Because of Sanchez, it is easy for me to contact Evelia. I'll send a message to you through her."

As I walked back over the rough rocks, I felt a sense of unreality. Return to New York, marriage to Alan, everything I had ever wanted up to a few short weeks ago was about to materialize for me.

Ramon's image suddenly appeared in my mind, Ramon walking upon the beach, the sea wind whipping back his hair. Memories of his kiss left me feeling confused, and very, very sad. How could I blame Alan for Evelia when I had so easily fallen under Ramon's spell?

As if my thoughts of him had somehow magically conjured up his presence, Ramon suddenly appeared before me. But not carefree, smiling, as he had been in my imagination. I knew by the quick flash in his eye, the set to his mouth, that he was even more angry than when I had last seen him. "Where have you been?" he demanded. "How did you slip away from me like that?"

When I did not answer, he grasped both of my arms. "Don't you realize this isn't some game! Every cut-throat for miles around knows that you've seen Thane's treasures. Men who would kill to have all those gems and gold!"

"Men like you, Ramon?"

Anger made the pupils of his eyes large and dark, made him seem suddenly very strong and dangerous. I glanced toward the cave, wishing that Alan would come out. Long morning shadows fell over the entrance to the cave. Nothing stirred from within.

"You will not get away from me again if I have to lock you in your room!" Holding me firmly by the elbow, Ramon began to lead me back to the house.

"You're hurting me!"

His grip upon my arm immediately loosened. He looked at me, and I was almost taken in by the softness in his eyes. "Marta, when all of this is over..."

When Alan returned with help, Thane Ulrickson and his treasures would be saved, and Ramon and the others would be thrown in prison...exactly where they deserved to be! Without giving him a chance to finish, I lashed out angrily, "When all of this is over, I am going back to New York and marry Alan."

Ramon stopped so abruptly I almost stumbled. I thought I would face his anger, but instead his eyes were filled with pain, as if my words had wounded him. Regret, carved in harsh lines upon his face, told me that, despite his villainous heart, our parting would be as wrenching for him as it was for me. "I can protect you from mercenaries like Sanchez. But not from the treachery of men like Avery!"

Ramon was a mercenary, a plotter of deaths! How could the thought of losing him be so painful? "Leave Alan out of this! He is twice the man you are!" I cried, thinking my angry answer would ease the anguish of our parting. I wished with all my heart that Ramon was in truth as he had first appeared to me, hero instead of villain. But that was fantasy, and I must face reality! Alan and New York were my future.

Ramon's eyes were as dark and dangerous as his voice. Deep flashes of color stirred in them as he gazed down at me. I felt a thrill of fear and excitement as he drew me tightly against his strong chest, almost forcing the breath from me with his crushing embrace. "Do you think for a moment that I will let you go back to New York with him, "*mi amor*"?" I saw the ironic twist of his lips before they moved down to claim mine. His voice made shivers course up and down my spine as he whispered with savage passion, "I *won't* let you go."

Chapter Nineteen

"Is there any message from Alan yet?" I asked anxiously.

Evelia's fingers moved across the loom with fierce intensity. Her answer, a quick shake of her head, caused her long hair to sweep across her shoulders.

"Where is Ramon?"

"He went somewhere with the general. I am supposed to be watching you." She stopped short, then added with an angry brush of her hand, "But do whatever you like."

"Did they leave the estate?"

"Women here do not pry into the business of men."

I continued walking toward Thane's room, which had been my destination.

Evelia's voice coldly followed me. "Thane has been up and about for hours. You knew he would not stay in bed as the doctor advised. A while ago, he left the house."

Her announcement made my heart sink. I would never be able to protect him! His lack of logic left me no means to stop or sway him. Despite anything I could do or say, the Viking was going to act only on his own distorted view of what was taking place!

"Did Thane leave with Ramon and the general?"

"No." An ugly bitterness, like Sanchez's, marked Evelia's smile. "Don't be so jittery. I intend to help you." Her eyes revealed hatred, hurt over the romance Alan had brushed aside so casually. "Because Alan wants me to."

I faltered, hearing my hesitate voice asking, "Are you...in love with Alan?"

"Alan is more suited to you," she spoke caustically. When I

made no response, she added, "Even if I do love him he is not one of us. My brother tried to warn me."

Evelia averted her face from me, but I heard the tears in her voice and the lost, almost childlike tone to her voice.

She really did love Alan. I felt almost sorry for her. That emotion mingled with resentment for Alan and the knowledge that their "flirtation" had meant so little. Even though Evelia deserved no better, it did not keep me from blaming him.

The blame I felt spilled over to myself. I was no better than Alan. I should have denied my attraction for Ramon, should never have kissed him, should never have wanted him.

Evelia's voice, broke into my own thoughts, "I want you both gone."

I remembered the words Evelia had first spoken to me had been in the same vein, yet this time they seemed haunted, resigned, as if by my leaving she had lost.

"The sooner you leave, the better," she went on. "I will get you through the gate."

Even if I had intended to forsake Thane and save myself, which I didn't, I could never again be persuaded to trust Evelia. Yet for an instant I actually believed Evelia meant to keep her word to Alan.

Growing increasingly more worried, I left Evelia and went outside. I felt so unsure. I needed to talk to Alan. I wondered if he might be back at the cave now. I paused uncertainly. I needed to see him, if only to reassure myself. I stopped and deliberately breathed deeply of the late morning air.

Only one guard…I could see his face, bored, sleepy, gazing from the window of the tower toward the gate. I watched him for a while before I slipped into thick pine trees, glancing back to note that he did not turn or appear to notice.

During the brisk walk, trees and undergrowth slowly gave way to a lunar-like landscape. The desolate waste I encountered seemed to seep into my thoughts, seemed to represent Thane's life…the betrayal by those he considered his friends.

As I approached the cave, I knew I had only been wishing,

seeking out the last place I had seen Alan was just an act of desperation. I was beginning to act as irrationally as Thane.

As I ducked into the wide-mouthed opening of the cave, a soundless emptiness greeted me. My eyes strayed to the rocks where Alan had held me. Then I moved toward the gaping hole I had noticed this morning that dropped into a great chamber.

Enough light filtered through the opening that I could see the floor, a great distance below me. The chamber left me greatly curious and prompted me to investigate. The dim rays that penetrated the cave below would give me enough light, although I did not know myself what I expected to see.

I resisted the thought of climbing down into such an eerie place. Ramon's warnings flashed to mind, how molten rock often formed cones that looked solid but were actually fragile and often dropped into great hollows. Would such cones exist inside of caves?

Of even greater danger was the possibility of slipping on the slick stones. If I happened to fall, I might lie injured or helpless for no telling how long. Maybe no one would ever find me here!

Looking down again, I noted stones worn smooth by climbing feet. My eye traced clear evidence of handholds and footholds. This cave was being used for some purpose! I could find out what that was only by entering it myself.

I tried to steady myself. The mere thought of caves…cold and sightless inhabitants, the awful blackness…had always frightened me. But I knew I must put aside my fears if I were ever going to know for sure what was going on at the Viking's estate.

As I started slowly to ease myself downward, sharp rocks scraped against my bare hands and even jabbed through my clothing. As I descended, I was met with a clammy coldness, an almost iciness that seemed incongruous considering the temperature above. I remembered Dad mentioning the ice-caves in Idaho and the fact that lava rock insulated like refrigeration.

Relieved when my feet finally touched solid ground, I waited for my eyes to adjust to the darkness. I could feel rather than see the immensity of the chamber I faced. Overhead in places shadowy shapes of stalactites, caused by the dripping of fiery lava so suddenly cooling, added a weird dimension.

I made my way cautiously across the flat, ropy rocks that made up the floor. My advancing movement robbed me totally of sight and continuing, I stumbled into a metal, handle-like projection in front of my path. My hand followed it to the top where I felt the wick of a torch.

A light here in the cave meant someone was working here! I knelt, fumbling around the rocks beneath the torch and finding what I expected to find, a tender box filled with matches. Nervously I tried one, then another, which I struck and lit. I held it up to the wick and light flickered uncertainly into the huge chamber.

My eyes first fell to piles of stone near a small opening chipped into the porous rock wall. I moved closer.

Very slowly it dawned on me exactly what was taking place here. When Alan and I had been seated directly above, I had believed we were very near the Viking's cave. I knew that this tunnel was being constructed to connect with the Viking's vault! I thought about Sanchez, men piled on the back of his wagon, entering the gate. All along this cave had been their destination.

Evelia must have suggested that Alan meet her at this cave because that is where her brother Sanchez met with her. No doubt Evelia had found out by spying on Thane the exact location of his hidden treasure and had revealed it to her brother. Had Sanchez yet succeeded in reaching the Viking's treasure?

I raised the light in my hand and looked around. Flames gleamed across long crates stacked haphazardly around the cave, perhaps already filled with the Viking's artifacts and jewels. I stepped closer to the small opening of the tunnel. Had they already robbed the best of Thane's treasures? The first thing the robbers would remove would be the Viking Crown.

The Viking Crown, because I had worn it seemed something personal, something that it was my duty to protect. I knew I could not leave here without knowing whether or not the Viking Crown had been stolen. The only way I could know for sure was to go to the Viking's vault myself.

The coldness of the surrounding cave had settled throughout my body, had reached the pit of my stomach. It would be impossible to carry this long-handled torch though the tiny opening, but I recalled many such lights in the Viking's vault. I propped the burning flare close to the entrance and lifted a handful of matches.

With a growing terror, I paused, sincerely doubting if I had the nerve to explore through total blackness the length of this tight, airless tunnel. I was further plagued by the knowledge that because Thane's entrance would be locked, I would have to return the same way.

Not giving myself time for second thoughts, on hands and knees, I entered the passageway. The hewn walls pressed tightly around me and continued to grow smaller, narrower. Finally I just enough room remained to allow me to inch along, flat on my stomach, hands, used as eyes, thrust ahead of me, warning me of jagged stones and loose rocks.

Turning around would be virtually impossible! It was like being in a grave. Overcome by waves of fear, I stopped, face tight against arms I could not even begin to see. Despite the tomblike coldness, dampness covered my skin. I tried hard to catch my breath, to force my body to obey its commands. In the small, airless space, my labored breathing seemed to grow louder and echo around me.

I forced myself to keep moving forward. After a tediously slow and fear-filled progress, I found myself faced with a wall of solid stone. The tunnel to Thane's vault had not yet been completed! The Viking Crown, the fortune in gold and jewels, lay no telling how close to me. But the thieves had more work to do here. With luck we could still save Thane's treasure!

With no way to proceed, I painstakingly crawled backward. This procedure, awkward and slow, took time I did not think I could spare.

After what seemed like hours, I became minutely aware of light, its penetration, ever so slight, into the narrow tunnel. My eyes felt half-blinded from the long period of total blackness. For the moment I asked for nothing more than to be able to see.

Hurrying now, anxious for the full effect of light, I was soon aware of the walls widening, of the exit. Gratefully I slipped out and stood beside the flare, stretching taunt muscles and wiping at my hair, that seemed to have been dipped in water.

If Sanchez hadn't broken into Thane's vault, then what was inside the crates, nailed so securely, and stacked in numerous rows around the cave? I suspected I would find carefully packed statues and steles...Mayan artifacts stolen from the Mayan ruins near Copan. Or else Sanchez had been working with the Viking on selling reproduced artifacts as real. Then when he found out the Viking's crown and jewels actually existed, he decided to expand his operations, double-crossed Thane and began working for himself.

A crowbar lay upon the floor. I approached the first crate, long and narrow, an ordinary shipping crate, except constructed of a heavier plywood. I struggled to loosen the top.

The nails holding the lid at last gave way. I ran my hand inside, expecting to feel stone used by the Mayans, deeply carved in high relief.

What I felt was slick and cold, steel. The Mayans didn't even have metal tools. I dug through the packing and half-lifted a rifle.

I drew in my breath. The gun, exactly like the one I had fired such a short time ago, gleamed evilly in the dim light. I dropped the rifle back into the crate and rose, astounded.

Gun-runners! Even with all the talk of unrest, even having seen the ugliness of the revolution with my own eyes, I had never given weapons a second thought. Mercenaries...Sanchez and his men were using Thane's estate as a place of security to receive, hold and deliver weapons of war...not even their war. Men like Sanchez sold to the highest bidder! I wandered stiffly from crate to crate. I tried to make out in the thin, wavering light the stamp marked on the crates. At last one became visible to me...U.S.

I had very little knowledge of firearms. I did know that the Winchester repeater I had fired was an improved version of the Civil War Henry, and that these rifles, though not exactly the latest in firearms, were still being used by our military forces in the States.

So Sanchez was buying American weapons and selling them...to whom? The answer came to me quickly...to Arnoldo. From all the general had said about Arnoldo's activities, I was sure he was supporting Carranza, thinking Carranza would keep his promises to the poor. Of course. I should have known all along. I had witnessed Arnoldo's planned meeting with Sanchez right here at Thane's estate!

At the time I had not believed that the general and Ramon were working with them, too.

My heart froze when I thought of Ramon. This link with Arnoldo meant that Ramon and he had been working together the day of the attempted assassination of Don Orlando.

All of them working here together on supplying illegal weapons to Carranza, and now each of them probably working for himself to obtain Thane's fortune.

How they had used poor Thane, used his gullible goodwill for access to his protected estate, whose hidden caves supplied such perfect concealment for their operation! Since they had found out he possessed untold wealth, they would take it with them when they left, not caring in the least that it would surely mean leaving the poor Viking dead.

Voices from just above me in the cave overhead reached me. Startled, but reacting with speed, I extinguished the torch. Not a minute too soon. Whoever stood just above the entrance lost no time in starting down. Light that to my night-accustomed eyes looked bright and hazy, fluttered across trouser clad legs, shone on black boots, high-topped, like the ones Ramon wore.

I shrank away. I could think of nowhere to hide but back inside the tunnel leading to Thane's vault. I slid backward into the opening so I would be able to face whoever descended into the bottom chamber. I edged back further as they...three of them, at least, clamored downward.

One of them lit the light. I drew my hand back from the patch of it that entered the tunnel.

Above the fierce beating of my heart, I could clearly hear Sanchez's voice, speaking in English. "We'll take as many of these

258

as we can load. I need money now, so I'll tell Arnoldo he must pay upon delivery."

My assessment had been correct. Arnoldo was the receiver of the guns.

I waited without catching a breath. Would Ramon himself answer? I did not think Sanchez would be likely to address the general in English.

"He is desperate for guns. We will raise the price." The voice, so quick to reply, was low and strained, as if he were already engaged in activity. Muffled by other noises, the speaker's identity was lost to me.

During the long interval that followed, crates scrapped against rock. I did not venture a look, but I imagined their being dragged to the entrance and hoisted by rope up to a waiting wagon.

Someone had lifted the light. A glow that seemed strong to my eyes drew closer to me. Surely they didn't intend to finish the work in the tunnel!

Although I could see nothing, Sanchez's leering became strong in my mind's eye. If he found me, I would be tortured, murdered! I shrank backward into the blackness, thinking that far behind me set only a dead-end wall of rock!

Sanchez's voice, edged with sharpness, sounded very close. "Did you open this crate?"

The answer he received was terse, in Spanish.

Once more the light seemed to grow more brilliant. I could make out faintly impressions of trouser clad legs, black boots, stepping toward me, stopping. My heart felt like it would explode. My cramped body ached, but I dared not make the slightest move or even draw a breath!

Sanchez's voice grew more agitated, more distant. He had evidently walked back toward the entrance. I could still hear his words clearly, echoing around me in the small, airless tunnel. "How did that crate get opened?"

"Don't get so edgy. It was no doubt one of our men. Who else would just open a crate and leave it?" This was the same speaker Sanchez had previously addressed. His voice was so low and muffled I could barely make out his words.

"I don't like it."

"Ever since you found Bertram snooping around here, it's been the same. You've lost your nerve."

I knew this taunt would not be well-received by Sanchez.

"I'm the one who takes the risks, not you! It wasn't easy to drag his body up to that cliff and set things up to look like he had fallen!"

Bertram's death had been no accident! I had been right. Bertram had discovered their arsenal while trying to find Mayan artifacts. He had been killed right here in the cave!

"We should do everything we have to do here today. And get out for good!"

I strained to make out the words of the other speaker, further obliterated by his turning away, probably to bend over a crate. I thought he said, "We have another half hour's digging to get to the crown."

"Let's take care of these guns first!" Sanchez barked.

Another man spoke. His exchanges, in Spanish, with Sanchez, signified disagreement. Over which Sanchez prevailed.

They continued to work with haste, Sanchez yelling out commands in Spanish.

Even though they squelched the light and I heard their leaving, I waited, too afraid to come out. When I did at last order myself to do so, I felt like some hunted animal, who stands in front of his burrow and expects to be struck down.

What if they left a guard? I looked up. After the total lack of light, the penetrating rays of sunlight seemed glaring and painful to my eyes. I listened and watched for some time and finally convinced myself that I must take a chance and flee for my life.

I climbed slowly, fitting each foot firmly into the makeshift steps, trying not to think of what I might encounter at the top. I was surprised to find no guard standing above, no rifle, like those that had been transported, aimed at me. Only empty landscape greeted me, miles and miles of black, charred lava beds.

Breathless from the climb out of the cave, I still ran across the slick, dangerous rocks toward Thane's estate. I would find Thane at once and tell him everything. Maybe this time he would believe me!

I had reached the area where trees encroached, first scrubs growing from cracks in lava, then a forest. Just beyond, in the clearing, lay Thane's estate. I allowed myself to stop, to lean against the sturdy back of a pine tree and try to regain control.

As I began to emerge from the clearing, I stopped short. The general stood at the front door, idly smoking a cigar, looking a little bored, as if he had been waiting for someone for a very long time.

I suddenly realized that the task before me was impossible. I, a prisoner here, could do nothing to catch the gun-runners in the act or to stop them from breaking into Thane's vault. Still I had to try! I might have let them get away with stealing anything they wanted to, but these men had killed Gavin Bertram. And I couldn't let them get away with murder!

I watched the general toss down his cigar, step on it, and go languidly into the house. His being inside increased my anxiety. Was his purpose today to watch Thane, or when the time came, to dispose of him?

My eyes darted around the empty dining room, rested on Evelia's now empty chair beside the loom. Where was she? Where had the general gone?

No other alternative existed for me but to find Thane and make him understand that he must protect himself. Only his life was important, not the cave filled with gold that they would so very soon be breaking into.

I headed down the stairway toward his study with such frantic pace that I almost stumbled into his arms.

"The plan made to rob you is now taking place! They are digging a tunnel to your vault! There is no possible way to stop them! You must leave here at once!"

The smile which he assumed upon seeing me faded a little, but was replaced by a kindly patience. "Do not worry. That vault was constructed in secret by my grandfather. You and I are the only living people who have ever entered it. If others do, they will meet with...fate."

"You don't understand!" A sob caught in my throat. "They are planning to kill you and to take what they know now that you possess! There is no one here you can trust! No one! And it is much too late to get outside help!"

However much the Viking tried, I saw that he could not call forth that great energy, that excess of emotion and action that characterized him. With growing concern, I noted that his skin was pale and that dark smudges had appeared, making his eyes look hollow and less bright. He should still be resting in bed, not contending with the disasters today would surely bring.

"Marta," he said, mustering what strength he could, "do not worry. No one will ever get your jewels! I will swear to that! On my honor!"

On his honor! My heart quelled at his words. In them I saw the hopelessness of my task. "Sanchez and no telling who else has been using your estate to run guns! I have found crates filled with rifles in one of the lava caves. They have started digging a tunnel from that cave to yours. Nothing you can say or do now will stop them!"

"But the general is here! He will know what to do!"

"Thane, General Perez is one of them. So is Ramon."

Thane's huge hands raised to my shoulders, tightened on them. The height of the stair I stood on caused me to look directly into his eyes. "Ramon is my friend," he said with grave sincerity. "The general is my brother! I would trust them both with my life!"

"No!" I gasped. I could already see him falling, dying! If he refused to listen, refused to leave here, then I had done for him all that I could do!

I thought a moment. "They will kill you," I said. I added, "and me too," thinking that this approach, true as it was, might serve to sway him. "No harm will come to you!" Thane guided me ahead of him back up the steps. "We must find the general and Ramon. If something illegal is going on, only Sanchez is to blame."

The general stood by the fireplace. Behind him on the mantle set neat rows of Mayan artifacts Thane had shown to Gavin Bertram. My gaze fell to the Copador vase Thane had handed to me the first night of my arrival, then back to the general.

"Marta says she stumbled into crates of guns," Thane told him. The Viking went on explaining to Francisco Perez, despite the obvious fact that the general couldn't help but have heard Thane and I talking o the stairway.

The general's hand went to his breast pocket as if a cigar were a necessary step to his answer. I watched him sink down into the leather chair, light his cigar, draw in deeply. Then he raised his gaze to us.

His eyes narrowed, making more noticeable the heavy folds of skin above them, the crinkled lines, usually suggesting humor, but now only a tense awareness. Eyes much too shadowed, much too knowledgeable.

My heart pounded like a drum in a funeral possession. What was I going to do now? Of the two of us, Thane would believe him!

When the general finally spoke, his voice did not sound threatening. He reminded me of my late father…the same edge of concern, the same hesitant intrusion of advice, "You had better stay completely out of this."

"It's too late for that," I spoke up. "Unscrupulous men will do anything for their own gain. Sanchez is full of slimy, get-rich schemes. Unfortunately with the political situation the way it is, he has taken to selling guns. But weapons…." Cold, black eyes raised to mine, "I told you before they were of more value here than gold here…are not their one and only interest." His large hand lifted and fell on the arm of the chair. "You made a grievous error, Thane, showing the whole world your immense wealth. The consequences might be more than we can handle."

"The best thing for Thane to do is leave here," I said, hearing the trembling in my voice. "Let them have the treasure. He must save his life!"

The general's watchful eyes held to my face. "I'm afraid it is too late for that. The roads will be filled with Sanchez's men. The only thing you can do is stay under cover." He rose quickly.

"Thane, you must do nothing. I will handle this for you. I will run Sanchez and his dirty crew off your land for good!"

Thane regarded the general, his wide, blue eyes revealing great trust…the trust of Caesar for Brutus! "I will do what-ever you think is best!"

"Thane, you can not trust him!"

A frown appeared between the general's eyes. His glared at me reproachfully before he addressed the Viking. "Thane, you know better than that!"

Thane, seeming not to hear me, continued to look at the general. Francisco Perez's face, void of the large smile, eyes coal-black, was now edged with force. He could really be a general, determined to achieve a goal no mater what the cost. "Don't leave the house for any reason!" he said. "Make *this* promise to me!"

Thane's large hand rose to his forehead. For a moment he looked severely wounded, weak, like a staggering lion. "This is all happening so fast. I must sort things out." He turned without a glance toward either of us and started down the stairway to his study.

I remained to face the general alone.

He spoke slowly, "Why did you say that to him?"

"I think you might be able to figure that out!"

"On the contrary, I can not. I have been nothing but loyal to him."

"Did Thane know about this illegal gun-dealing before I told him?"

"Thane lives in his own world, my dear, not in ours. They are only using him, using Thane and his security system to protect their operation."

"How long has this been going on?"

"For a very long time," The general answered over his shoulder. I listened to the heavy stomp of his boots across the wooden floor.

At the instant General Perez reached the doorway, Evelia rushed into the house. She pushed past him, and he stopped, turned a little to watch her run upstairs and disappear from sight.

"There's the one not to trust," he said. Before he left he spoke again to me, "Stay with the Viking. Don't leave him for a minute!"

Through the front entrance, gaping open, I could see the general talking to Ramon. To overhear details of their plans, I drew closer to the door. To my dismay they addressed each other in rapid Spanish. As the quick words passed between them, I watched Ramon's face and form grow tense. Although I did not understand his words, they sounded clipped, alarmed.

The general waved his hand in a gesture of hurry and striding toward his carriage, he called back in English, "There's no more waiting. We've got to act at once!"

Taking a deep breath, I stepped outside. Ramon turned to face me. Upon seeing me his eyes darkened, his lips became hard. He began walking up the path toward me.

At first I did not know what was happening. The sound...the rapid spitting of bullets...cracked against the lava rocks of the building behind me, smashed into the windows so close to me, spattering glass.

I glimpsed Ramon's running form. I felt the weight of his body as he dived toward me. We both fell backward through the doorway. Bullets zinged above us. Mayan figures of ceramic and jade on the mantle of the fireplace broke and clattered like clay targets on a firing range.

Ramon, instantly regaining his footing, lifted me to my feet, protecting me with his body until I was safe behind the thick, black walls.

The steady firing of the bullets ceased as unexpectedly as they had begun. Trembling, I clung to Ramon. He spoke no word, just held me tightly.

Chapter Twenty

Thane charged over the rubble and broken glass toward us. "What's happened? Are you hurt?"

Still slightly dazed, and trembling so much I could barely stand, I resisted leaving the safe haven of Ramon's embrace.

Ramon drew me away from him, speaking gently, "Marta, I must go. You are to stay here with Thane." A warning flashed in his eyes as they met the Viking's. "And be very careful, both of you! Stay in the house. You will be safe here, but only here!"

Ramon reached for the gun tucked in his belt and cautiously approached the door, saying as he walked, "I am counting on you, Thane, to look after her. I will take care of Sanchez!"

Beginning to recover a little from the shock of the unexpected attack, I saw that Ramon really wanted to save the Viking's life. He wouldn't kill him if he did not interfere. I understood one other fact: Ramon had saved my life, and now he was in danger of losing his own.

"You don't have to play any part in what happens," I heard myself pleading. "Just let Sanchez take whatever he wants and leave! Please, Ramon, just stay here with us!"

"You know I can't do that."

I could not let Ramon leave. In the greedy battle over the Viking's treasure, Ramon might be killed. And no matter what evil plots he had been involved in, no matter what he had done, I wanted him safe!

"Ramon!" I started to run after him, but Thane's strong hand reached out to stop me. I struggled to free myself but in the end was forced to remain, hearing from outside the clatter of fast moving carriage wheels and Ramon's voice calling to the horses.

"He'll be all right," Thane said, trying his best to comfort me.

"What's going on?" Evelia's shrill voice called from the top of the stairs. She crept slowly, woodenly down the bullet-ridden stairway. Her eyes, enormous in her pale face, stared in the direction Ramon had left.

"We are being attacked by thieves!" the Viking told her. "They are everywhere. You must hide, Evelia, and hope for the best!"

Without looking at either of us, she spurted forward. Before we could stop her, she had ran by us out the front door.

"I had better go after her," Thane said. "She might be killed."

"There is no need," I answered. "Evelia is one of them. She is fleeing now to join her brother."

"Is there no one on our side?" Thane's loud voice demanded an answer.

"All of your guards have been bought by Sanchez, or he would not have been able to deliver guns in and out so easily."

The huge man gazed down at me a moment, eyes glittering. "Ramon and the general will be helpless then against so great a force! This means that I must take some action myself!"

Thane's huge hand slid down my arm, fingers locked in mine. He strode ahead of me, leading me. I tried to break his hold on me, but it was impossible and I found myself being half-dragged down the stairway toward his study.

"We are supposed to stay in here! We must do what Ramon said! Your life depends upon it!"

"I can not do that, my princess. I can not stand by and let them steal your jewels!"

The study seemed filled with sea-darkened relics and as unreal as the Viking himself, who was gazing down at me earnestly. In terrified silence I watched his light eyes lose their sparkle and become distant, glassy. His voice dropped in volume, became haunting and far-away as he spoke, "Remember what I told you about the Vikings? We are from a long line of brave people!"

"Even brave people meet with defeat," I told him. "And now we must meet this fate as we should."

Again his voice raised in volume, resounding in my ears. "We will not be defeated! Never! I am a Viking king!"

"Thane, you must listen to me," I said in agony. "I know more about what is going on than you do."

"Don't be frightened, Princess. I will not be robbed! Even if I have to destroy my own ship!"

"Ships! Kings! What are you talking about? Why can't you listen to logic?"

"I am perfectly logical, my dear Marta. That's why I have my own security system. I have set dynamite inside my hidden cave. It is waiting, ready to be ignited! Before they ever set foot inside my vault, I will destroy it all! Everything! I will blow my treasures up so no evil hands will ever touch them! I will do it for you!"

"You will be killed! Let go of me, Thane!"

His hand was like a trap from which I could not free myself. Did he mean to take me along; did he mean to kill me, too? He threw open the door at the end of the study and dragged me with him into the tunnel which led toward the shed and his hidden cave. In his deluded mind, he must surely see the cave as a Viking ship, both himself and me as Vikings who must now die instead of face defeat!

My heart turned to ice. Thane had begun to chant. I could barely make out his words. "Odin, preserve us in our time of need! Be with us and keep us from those you rise up against us! We are small, but you, Odin, are mighty! We accept what now lies ahead of us! In your name!"

The real chill of the long, secluded tunnel enclosed me. His insane chanting penetrated my heart. My whole life was just getting started. How could I die now? Was there nothing I could do to stop him? At the doorway to the shed, he suddenly released me.

"Our lives are more important than the treasures, Thane," I said, surprised that my voice was steady. "Let them take what is in the cave. You can gather forces and avenge them later!"

He stood, a hand resting upon the doorway that led into the shed. "Have no fear. I will let no harm come to you. I will leave you here!"

"No, Thane! You mustn't do this!"

My words were not going to sway him! His massive form straightened, his sea-blue eyes widened as they gazed at me, and I could feel my own eyes brimming with tears.

"No hands but yours and mine will ever touch those jewels!"

Before going through the door, he turned back once again to look at me. He seemed more than ever half real, half apparition. Immediately he was gone.

I stared at the door he had slammed shut, which still seemed to hold Thane's image…red-gold beard, the thick belt looped over loose, white tunic, the pants tucked into long boots. The image of a brave and true Viking warrior.

I could not let him lay down his life to protect his imaginary world, to save the jewels he thought belonged to me! "Thane!"

Thane slid the board into its slot, locking the door securely. "I must go now." His voice was muffled slightly because of the thickness of the wood that separated us. "I must go the cave. You can not go with me."

My fists pounded on the door. "Thane, unlock this! You can't be willing to die...for gold!"

"Not for gold, for honor! For you! Goodbye, my princess!" I made many attempts to push open the door, but it held fast. I beat upon it in rage, then fell against it, sounds and vibrations echoing into the quietness.

Sobbing, I turned and fled back through the dark, narrow tunnel, not stopping for breath until I reached Thane's study.

Grabbing the nearest heavy object, a stone statue from his desk, I stood on his desk and quickly broke out the high, narrow window above it and crawled through.

In several minutes, I was behind the house, and back at the shed. Passing the huge building, I scanned the rough, black mounds of lava just ahead of me, searching for Thane.

Ahead I spotted the rune stone and then close by I caught sight of Thane. I hadn't realized how near the rune stone set to the opening of the Viking's secret vault.

"Thane, wait!" He turned a little at the sound of my voice. I scampered down a steep, slick slope in the lava bed toward him, but I could not reach him in time to stop him or go in with him. I could only watch helplessly as the door carved into the lava opened like a gaping mouth, swallowing Thane whole as he disappeared into the heart of the mountain.

The doorway, so cleverly concealed, now blended with the total mass of black rock—invisible...as if it had never opened, as if Thane had never entered. I stopped, admitting my helplessness. I could do nothing now to stop him! Thane was entirely free to act out the final episode in his deluded life! He would die and this mountain would be his grave! A moan escaped my lips as I whirled and ran toward the direction of Sanchez's arsenal. Would they have already completed digging the tunnel connecting to the Viking's cave? Could I somehow reach Thane before it was too late?

I knew this hope I grasped at was vain, a madness as great as Thane's own. As I neared the dark, gapping entrance, I wavered and grew cautious. I slipped toward the protection of high, surrounding rocks and waited uncertainly.

My alertness magnified. I could hear clearly the voices from just inside the inner chamber. Sanchez was saying, "We've got to hurry!"

I looked, then drew back to press flat against the rocks. Sanchez had stepped out into the brilliant sunlight. The gleam of it across his features magnified what was cruel and hateful. Who was he talking to? I hadn't seen the other man, though he was speaking. I thought I heard the name Arnoldo.

Sanchez had stated when I had been hidden in the cave that the guns were destined for Arnoldo...to be used by Carranza's bloody followers against Orlando. The thought of the gentle, priest-like man purchasing contraband guns in the name of peace made me sad. I remembered what the general had told me about Arnoldo wanting to get from here to there without taking the little steps in between. He would regret his part in this revolution if Carranza won!

But whose side was Ramon and the general on? They had

talked as if they favored Orlando, but did they? Were they, too, working with Arnoldo? Did they believe enough to justify the stealing and melting down of Thane's priceless relics to buy more ammunition for Arnoldo and Carranza's cause? Or were they, like Sanchez, working for themselves?

Was Sanchez talking to Ramon or the general now? I could hear the heavy sound of boots scraping against the sharp rocks.

Then the sound stopped. The person he had addressed had no doubt came out of the cave to join him. Sanchez spoke to him sharply, "How long will it take those fools to dig through to the other side?"

"Patience, Sanchez," the second voice replied. This voice was so low I could barely make out the words. "In a few minute's time our men will break through the tunnel. Then we can get what we want and get out of here."

Any minute the whole area would explode! I had to step out in their view, to warn them, then to save myself! But I could not bring myself to move.

The voice of the second man grew louder, as if in warning. "Remember the crown is mine! Nobody touches it but me. I don't want to run the risk of having it damaged."

My heart sank. Alan himself was the speaker!

"Don't you trust me, Avery? As many dealings as we've had." I heard Sanchez's ugly laugh. "It is agreed. You get the crown, I get the everything else!"

The shock of discovery, of who was speaking and what was being said, hit me full force. I felt stunned.

"You're a hard man," Alan was saying. "This is no better bargain than I got on the last load of guns!" Alan supplied illegal weapons for Sanchez to sell to revolutionary soldiers.! I should have known that the minute I saw the crates stamped U.S.! The rifles had been stolen from our government. Alan had the perfect connection with his brother a high ranking officer in Washington D.C.! How simple it had been for him to get the guns into Honduras. Alan's presence in and out of the country, his loads to and from the museum, had aroused no suspicion.

"That crown will keep me in luxury for the rest of my life!" Alan said.

How could Alan have fooled me so completely? I had sincerely believed he had wanted possession of the crown to ensure its safety, for the impact its exposure would have on history and the study of mankind! He intended to claim the crown as his own, and if he did use it for proof of the Viking connection, it would be for his own self-advancement!

Alan wanted money from the guns but his greed went farther than that! He had become obsessed with finding the Viking Crown! He had never planned to leave the country without it. Not trusting Sanchez, Alan had tried to get me to bring him the crown before Sanchez got to it. But in case he did not succeed, he was willing to work with Sanchez to get what he wanted so badly.

Father and I had both been taken in by him. How could I have been so wrong about his desires and motives? Like Sanchez, Alan had been after money…big money made from stealing jewels and running guns! He was no better than Sanchez.

Sanchez's next words made my breath catch in my throat. "I tried to kill Santiago and that girl a while ago!"

"No need to kill her," Alan said. What he added caused my breath to catch in my throat. "Ramon, yes! And the general! If we don't, they will only be after us."

"I will do Arnoldo and his idol, Carranza, a final favor," Sanchez said. "I will kill two of his major opponents!" He laughed shortly. "I will enjoy it. Just as I enjoyed killing that snoop, Bertram!"

What had I heard? That Ramon and the general were innocent? That they were who they claimed to be, loyal supporters of Orlando and of Thane! Then what had I overheard at the Francisco's estate? Had they been preparing for the movement of illegal weapons and intended to catch Sanchez and Alan in the act? By "getting rid" of Thane, had they meant keeping him safely out of the way during the operation!

For a moment, even if I were to die, I felt a surge of happiness. Ramon had only been trying to protect me! I should have listened to my heart and trusted him!

Now I would never be able to tell Ramon that I had loved him all along, even though I had sincerely believed he was involved!

I had failed to save the Viking! I had lost Ramon without a word spoken of my love for him! All my plans and dreams were culminating in total disaster!

Too much time had passed! I had to do something immediately before it was too late. I must warn Alan and save the men working inside before Thane set off the explosives! "Alan!" As I called his name, I stepped out into plain view. Sanchez raised the rifle he had to my heart. For a moment I thought he would fire it without letting me say a word, but Alan moved forward as if to prevent this.

"You must clear the cave! The Viking has dynamite in his vault! It is going to blow up at any minute!"

Alan's face paled, became ashen. His eyes widened in horror as my words…the truth of them…sank into his mind. He looked from me to Sanchez. "You'll have to get your men out!" Alan said to Sanchez. "They don't speak English. I'll never be able to make them understand in time!"

"They're almost to break through!" Sanchez snapped back. "Let them! If she's telling the truth, they may stop the Viking and we'll get the treasure yet!"

"They'll be killed!" I cried.

Immediately Alan disappeared into the cave entrance.

"American fool!" Sanchez screamed after him.

I started to follow Alan, but Sanchez leveled the gun on me. "Stay where you are!"

I could feel moisture dampen my face and hands as I waited. Would he kill me now while Alan was gone?

"It was you who followed us from the general's estate and shot Thane," I said.

"Yes," Sanchez snapped. "If that idiot blows himself up, that will save me the trouble of killing him. And you…I will kill for my own pleasure!"

Alan appeared from the mouth of the cave. Three men, ragged and sweaty, followed close behind him.

"We must all take cover!" I shouted to him.

Alan gripped my arm as we raced away from the cave. "I never meant things to go this far!" he said. "I started out searching for the medallion. The rest just happened. I should never have gotten mixed up with Sanchez!" His voice dropped in a tone of self-rebuke that after all I now knew about him, I did not trust. "The jewels, the guns, so many opportunities."

Alan's voice died away, lost to me by the sound of a carriage bouncing over the rough terrain. Ramon, gun drawn, leaped from it. I got an image of the general, frantically pulling at the horses, reaching for his rifle at the same time.

Alan let go of my arm and began running. Standing alone, I stared at Sanchez, who had whirled around, the barrel of his gun aimed at Ramon. Before he had a chance to pull the trigger, a low rumble started from the cave. The rocks beneath them began to shift and move, as if with the first tremors of an earthquake.

Everyone scattered, fleeing down the sloping lava covering the hillside. I stumbled and fell. Ramon dived toward me, his body protecting me from the angry spew of rocks.

The entire top of the mountain appeared to rise in explosive rage, hurling cold chunks of lava skyward. Rocks fell and shifted and soon left a ruined heap where the Viking and his treasure were buried.

* * *

Instantly Ramon regained his footing. I watched as he surged down the hill, caught and struggled with Sanchez over the rifle. Behind him I could see the general threatening the other unarmed men, including Alan, to remain motionless. Ramon dragged Sanchez over to the general. At that moment Evelia darted from the cover of trees. How long she had been hidden there I could only guess. She had no doubt been waiting when Sanchez had the rifle on me, hoping he would fire it. She ran directly to Alan, embracing him, as she sobbed against his chest.

I watched Alan's face, impassive, cold.

"Leave him alone!" Sanchez snarled to his sister. "You weren't good enough for him! He used you and threw you away! I was going to kill him for you!"

A wagon filled with the general's men pulled up and Alan, Sanchez, and the three other men were being forced aboard. Evelia went with them, still clinging to Alan.

"Looks like we failed again to get Arnoldo," the general called to Ramon. "He's not here, so there's no way to tie him in to any of this." He smiled a wide smile, as if this idea did not disappoint him. The old wagon drove off, leaving a great, empty silence.

I stared in horror at the rocks, loose piles which still seemed to be moving, settling. I could no longer tell where the entrance to the vault had been, covered now with tons of stone. The whole side of the mountain had been blown apart. Only a gigantic upheaval remained...a tomb.

The disaster seeped slowly over me. Thane had set off the dynamite and remained inside with his buried treasure...the Viking now lay entombed beneath the rocks!

My hands rose to my face, but did not prevent hot tears that of their own will streamed from my eyes. I cried for the poor, pathetic man who I had somehow come to think fondly of, I cried for Gavin Bertram, and for myself. But most of all, for Thane Ulrickson, who had died so tragically, for nothing! Ramon would have saved him had I not interfered!

Ramon stepped closer to me. I told him, between racking sobs, that the Viking was underneath the rocks, dead.

Ramon seemed as shaken and grieved as I. He said nothing to me. Only his arms tight around me offered comfort.
Would his arms, his love, ever make me forget?

Thane Ulrickson...so caught up in his unreal world, so timeless...how could he really be dead? Hadn't I, too, caught some of the spirit of his world, enough even, to believe him invincible, free to wander across centuries!

"His death," Ramon's words sounded choked, "is my fault. I should have protected him instead of leaving to chase Sanchez and Avery! Their supplying weapons has flared the revolution! The general and I have known what has been going on here for a long time. But we had to wait. We finally pin-pointed a time we could catch them moving the guns! We delayed too long."

Ramon and the general's plot had never been to murder Thane, but to get him off the estate so that he would be safe when the confrontation with Sanchez started. I, by not cooperating with Ramon, had forced Sanchez's action before Ramon could get Thane to safety. "I should have never doubted you."

"Oh, Marta," Ramon said with anguish. "If you only knew the times I wanted to take you away from here, how hard it was for me to see you stay. But I knew you'd go directly to Alan and I couldn't let you do that because I knew he was selling guns for Carranza's war. Many people were hunting for Alan to kill him. I couldn't risk your being with him in that danger."

I tried to tell Ramon that I was more to blame than he for Thane's death, but he would not hear it. "It was I who failed to protect him," he said and the pain in his voice brought new tears to my eyes. For the first time since we had met, Ramon needed me. I made an effort to block my tears and be strong for him. "You did what you had to do. And, Thane...did what he wanted to do."

"I guess we had better catch up with the general and tell him. He and Thane were so close. He's going to take this very hard."

Ramon's arms dropped from me. Both of us turned, staring at the Viking's grave. No one would ever recover his body, nor would they ever find his buried treasure. The runic stone, so near the cave was gone, too, blown to bits and buried forever. All that was left of it was the few sketches I had with my father's notes. And they would prove nothing. No further investigation would be made, except by me, to determine whether or not the Vikings had actually landed here to leave their mark on the Mayan culture.

"He will always be here," I said. "Alive."
I had just finished the words, when a booming voice from behind us spoke. "I've kept them from getting your jewels!"

Thane, clothes and hair disheveled, breathing heavily, stepped a little closer to us. Still the distance or my own thoughts made him seem an apparition.

Suddenly realizing that he really had survived, I gasped. "How did you...."

"Get out?" Thane finished my words. "Through the door, the way I got in."

Thane smiled at me, a glint of satisfaction appearing in his eyes. "I've secured your jewels," he said. "They are safe now!" His blue eyes glistened. "Safe for another ten thousand years!"

Chapter Twenty One

"What will happen to Alan?" I asked Ramon later that evening.

"He will probably be handed over to American authorities and be tried for smuggling stolen weapons." Then to quell my worry, he added in a softer tone. "Even if he is detained here, the general will see to it that Avery is dealt with in a fair and just way."

"Did Alan have anything to do with Bertram's death?" I had to know.

"No, that was entirely Sanchez's doing. Bertram was murdered in the caves when Sanchez found him snooping around the crates of guns."

Bertram must have gone back to look at the rune stone and began exploring cave area for an entrance into the Viking's cave. He must have, as I had done, stumbled across the cave where the guns were stored, and encountered Sanchez.

"Sanchez, fearful that some nosy stranger could blow the whole operation, struck Bertram over the head with a rock. With the help of his men, he dragged his body up to the cliffs to draw attention away from the caves. He planted Bertram's coat there and chopped at the rocks to make it look like Bertram was stealing."

"Evelia went with us to the cliffs that day. She must have told him Bertram was admiring the serpent heads. Do you think she was a party to Bertram's killing?"

"She swears she only mentioned that Bertram was interested in the serpent heads to her brother in passing." Ramon hesitated, as if considering how much her word could be trusted. "I do not know whether she is lying or not, but since there is no proof of her involvement, she will not be arrested. Sanchez, however, will not get off so easy. The rock you saved will be used as evidence against him. He will be tried for murder."

"And what about Arnoldo?" As I spoke his name, the image of his kindly face arose in my mind. He had helped me several times and I wished the best for him.

"Arnoldo is Carranza's strongest supporter. I could never understand how such an intelligent and compassionate man could have believed all of Carranza's lies, but I think now Arnoldo is beginning to see the light. Basically he is a good man, not a cold-blooded killer, like the rest of them. When he heard of the assassination plans when we were in Telas, he came to me. And we worked together to prevent them."

Ramon reached across the table for my hand. As he did, the sparkle that lit his dark eyes caused a stir in my heart.

"I will never do anything to harm Arnoldo!" he said. "He is responsible for saving my father's life."

"Your father?" I exclaimed with surprise.

"Yes. I am Don Orlando's son."

I stared at him with surprise, all at once aware of evident traces of Don Orlando's handsome features, of the noble bearing duplicated in his son.

"When I was called back from the states because of the revolution, I decided to work in secret, right in the very heart of the opposition. The general knew that Sanchez was supplying weapons to Carranza and I believed that he and I could stop this operation." He smiled again. "We have been successful, so we are well on our way to having a safe and fair election!"

"So you disappeared from the ship and got a job here at Thane's estate."

Ramon released my hand and rose. "Yes. And this ordeal is finally over for you! I do intend to keep my promise to you, Marta. First thing tomorrow I will take you to Puerto Lorenzo and put you safely on a ship back to New York."

***

I carried my father's notes and my few belongings down the wide stairway and paused for a final look at the fireplace, where a gentle fire burned. My gaze moved across the rustic table piled with fruits and bread and across the walls of black, volcanic rock. Ramon, who had been waiting for me at the door, stepped forward to take my bag. "I have talked long and hard to Thane. I have explained that he must let you go with me today. It was very difficult, but he has resigned himself to your leaving."

Thane joined us at the waiting carriage. Although he listened to Ramon, Thane's eyes never left me. His expression was sober, as if he must bear the burden of my departure with fortitude or as if he understood my feelings for Ramon. "I know you must go with him," he said.

"It can be no other way," Ramon assured him.

"I know I can depend on you, Ramon, to watch out for her," Thane spoke, deeply saddened, but making no protest over my leaving.

I glimpsed the straightness of his massive shoulders, the bright glow of his eyes that rebelled against defeat. Thane's sudden stepping away from us seemed to separate him from every human tie, and caused me to for an instant feel a pang of compassion or sorrow which prompted me to say, "I will be back some day to visit you."

"I know," Thane answered. "I know you will be back."

* * *

Through the rain I gazed at the road, which wound its way through the fertile valley of the Copan River. We soon turned east though sloping hills covered with pines that bordered the ocean.

I would liked to have had a day to spend in the small port by the sea. Ramon had told me of some Mayan ruins a mile or so from Puerto Lorenzo. I imagined Ramon and I exploring grand Mayan structures, laughing together, and talking excitedly about our finds.

As we drew closer to the village, we passed a rickety wagon crammed with local people, dark faces, looking dismal from the back of the rain-spattered cart. An old man gazed at us without interest or curiosity.

I cast a glance at Ramon, strangely silent, as he had been when he had first rescued me and delivered me to Thane's estate. Noticing my glance, he spoke a little wistfully, as if he had been tuned in to my secret thoughts. "If it weren't for the rain, we would go to the ruins."

"It would have been nice to have seen them. I still plan to gather as much information as I can to include in my father's book. A book that would no longer bear Alan's name, but Father's and my own.

I would finish my father's book. His careful notes I had managed to keep safe during the entire ordeal. But with only my word that the rune stone and the Viking Crown had actually existed, I knew the believers of my father's theory would be few and scattered. But maybe someone, somewhere...maybe even I, myself, would keep searching and someday uncover new evidence of the Viking-Mayan connection.

Ramon was silent again until we reached the small, busy port where I had disembarked such a short time ago. Men milled about waiting to load their carts laden with goods on the huge, nearby ship launched close to the pier. The American flag flying above it stirred in the slight wind. Abruptly leaving, Ramon entered a port building, and returning as quickly, he said, "We have a two-hour wait before you can board. How about some breakfast?"

I thought of food and coffee, of the long wait ahead, of leaving. "I'm not hungry."

Nevertheless Ramon drew the carriage to a stop outside a cantina and cut around to assist me. Inside, leaving me seated at a small table beside a window, he ordered for us at the counter and returned, tray filled with coffee and rolls, fresh baked and carefully wrapped.

Ramon toyed with the wrapper, the crinkle of stiff, white paper loud in the almost empty room. As he did, he gazed at the rain making puddles in the unkempt street.

I thought of New York City. Soon I would be back in my small apartment. From my window there I often watched the great throngs of people, which moved day and night. The thought of them now made me feel alone and afraid. My feelings would change once I was back, I told myself. Soon Ramon, Thane, and my fantastic adventure would fade, would seem no more real to me than the dramas played out in the nearby Broadway theaters.

Ramon's dark, somber eyes locked on mine from across the table.

Dad would not be in New York City, anxiously waiting for me at the wharf, nor would Alan. I should be glad I had found out what Alan was really like before I had drifted into marrying him.

"You have my ticket and the papers I need?"

Ramon's hand went automatically to his breast pocket.

"I'll wire you money when I get to New York."

Ramon gazed down at the documents, then once again into my eyes. I watched strong hands shuffle through the papers, arrange them, and with a quick, decisive motion rip them apart.

I started. "What are you doing?"

Ramon's black eyes lit with a smile. "You're right back where you started," he announced, dropping the torn papers on the table and rising. "A prisoner."

In the next instant I found myself gathered close in his arms, his lips warm and gentle against mine. I clung to him, never wanting to let him go, feeling waves of joy bounding over me.

"Only this time we're both prisoners," Ramon's laugh sounded happy, breathless. "Prisoners of love!"